Clio Rising

Paula Martinac

Bywater
BOOKS

Ann Arbor
2019

Bywater Books

Copyright © 2019 Paula Martinac

Print ISBN: 978-1-61294-147-9

Bywater Books First Edition: April 2019

Printed in the United States of America on acid-free paper.

Cover designer: Ann McMan, TreeHouse Studio

Bywater Books
PO Box 3671
Ann Arbor MI 48106-3671
www.bywaterbooks.com

This novel is a work of fiction.

"Things don't fall apart. Things hold. Lines connect
in thin ways that last and last. Lines become
generations made out of pictures
and words just kept."
—Lucille Clifton, *Generations*

"—May God protect us! I wonder what you'll write /
When I am dead and gone."
—Djuna Barnes, *The Antiphon*

Clio Hartt proved a difficult subject for a biography. She famously protected her privacy, giving only one interview in the years from the publication of her masterpiece, *The Dismantled*, in 1936 to the time of her death in her Greenwich Village apartment in 1984.

The occasion was in 1966, on the publication of a thirtieth-anniversary scholarly edition of her novel, when she granted *The New York Review of Books* an hour-long interview. The *NYRB* piece provides insight into her beliefs about her work and her privacy. When asked if she would consider penning a memoir, like so many of her counterparts among the Paris expatriates, she said, "Why would I? I have said everything I wanted to say about my life in my fiction."

—From the introduction to *Dismantling Clio Hartt: Her Life and Work*, by Ingrid Coppersmith

A Very Private Writer

April 2014

The thirtieth anniversary of Clio's death came and went without fanfare. A few notices ran in academic forums about her complete archive opening to scholars for the first time, but that was it.

A couple of months later, I got the call I'd anticipated for three decades. While I was in a staff meeting to review our 2015 and 2016 lists, a buttery voice left a message: "Ms. Bliss, this is Ingrid Coppersmith. I'm a professor at Syracuse, and I'm working on a literary biography I'd like to talk to you about. You may have seen my piece in the latest *Inside Higher Ed* about the perils of doing research on a very private writer like Clio Hartt?"

I let Ingrid Coppersmith's message run its course and then I replayed it. "Ramona Costa at the Bea Winston Agency told me Ms. Winston passed away last year, and you were the best person to talk to about Clio's final months. She said you were Clio's assistant or companion? She wasn't sure exactly what to call you."

Ramona. She didn't know the secret I was still keeping.

"I've written chunks of the book, but there are these . . . gaps, especially about her final years. I've had a look at the new material. What the New York Public Library just released? I thought you might shed some light. Clio certainly was an enigma, wasn't she?" Ingrid's laugh tottered on the brink of insecurity. "Long story short, I'm anxious to talk to you. Here's my cell."

When I listened a third time, I flinched when she used the familiar "Clio." For the six months I knew her, the great writer was "Miss Hartt," and I was "Miss Bliss" or "young lady." Except for that one day when she looked at me in a peculiar way and said, "I would like to hear you call me 'Birdie.'" I did, but just once.

Now no one has called me "young lady" in a long time, except for my seventy-something dentist. But the last days of Clio's life have replayed in my head as sharp and resounding as a DJ's loop: the box under the daybed, the manuscript wrapped in twine, the sirens wailing, the cat on the fire escape, the box under the daybed . . .

Chapter 1

New York City
August 1983

Back then, room and board at the Parkside Evangeline Residence for Young Women ran me eighty-five dollars a week. Aunt Sass, who had fronted me the cash until I could find a job in publishing, insisted on a Christian women's place, the exact one where she'd stayed a generation earlier when she tried "big-city life." But the hotel fit me as poorly as my waitress uniform, and I couldn't tell anyone why. When the Parkside girls asked if I had a boyfriend back in North Carolina, I dodged the question by poking fun at my height and lanky build: "Now what guy would date me?" That made them trip over each other, offering to take me clothes shopping, teach me how to accent my cheekbones with blusher and widen my eyes with liner.

The Parkside felt as limiting as my old life in Weaverville, and I escaped whenever I could. The Friday night I met Gerri, I skipped dinner, even though it came with the rent, and ducked past Sergeant Sal as she was reciting the "no men above the lobby" rule to a prospective resident. From the chaste world of the Parkside and Gramercy Park, it was just a few long crosstown blocks to Ariel's.

Weeks earlier, I had stumbled on the bar while trekking across Manhattan to save bus fare. Black shades and a security grille obscured the front window, but the name "Ariel's" on the awning hinted at magic. I could hear and feel the pulse of disco music through the door, where a gruff woman with a pack of cigarettes tucked into her T-shirt pocket stood guard. She dipped her head at me in recognition. With a fluttering in my stomach that could have been exhilaration—or terror, I had abandoned my plans to listen to the radio in my room and stepped into my first-ever lesbian bar.

With feverish speed, I transformed into a semi-regular, and Ariel's bore most of the blame for my shrinking bank account. Honestly, I drank too much those first months in New York— not just a beer or two after work to unwind, but enough so that I struggled to navigate the streets back to the Parkside. That particular night, I couldn't afford to blow the twenty in the pocket of my khakis, but I had convinced myself it was an investment. The bouncer, when she said anything at all, had let it slip a few days back that she worked multiple jobs, and I wanted to chat her up for ideas about getting a second job.

When I arrived, the bouncer wasn't on duty yet. Beer in hand, I found a table but no chairs and asked a woman sitting alone if I could use the empty one next to her. "Why don't you join me?" she suggested, shoving her granny glasses up her nose. She was a little too heavyset to be my type, with a shadow of a mustache, but I admired her concert T-shirt—the Allman Brothers and Bonnie Raitt at U Mass—so I accepted her offer.

"I love Bonnie Raitt," I said, nodding toward her chest as I plopped down.

"My sister lives in Amherst." She took a draw on her Bud. "You're from the South."

"It shows."

"When you said 'love' it was about three syllables."

I braced myself for teasing or crude imitation. My fellow waitresses at the Village Diner, struggling actresses who had rid themselves of whatever regional accents they'd once had, poked fun at my North Carolina twang in the kitchen and locker room. "Well, land's sakes, sugar!" one of them had said on my first day when I greeted everyone on my shift as "y'all."

6

But instead of making a piss-poor joke at my expense, the woman in Ariel's said, "My first roommate in college was from Georgia, and I loved her drawl. You don't hear that kind of thing too much in New York." The chair felt comfier then, and I took a long pull on my beer, forgetting that I needed to make it last.

Her name was Gerri Burr, and she didn't want to date me. She was waiting for her girlfriend to show up so they could go to dinner. "She's late a lot," Gerri said, more as a fact than a complaint. "I've made a lot of friends because of her."

And, in fact, while we sipped our Buds, Gerri and I talked like school friends who effortlessly pick up again years after graduation. The process of finding my tribe in New York had gone slowly, and not just because I was the odd girl out at work and at the Parkside; many of the gay women I'd met were hard to connect to. There'd been women I'd danced with under Ariel's disco ball, but we had very little in common except our sexual orientation, or "preference" as we said back then. After my first-ever Lesbian Pride dance, I went home with a curvy redhead to her Brooklyn apartment—a casualness that was so foreign to me, it was like I'd become a character in a pulp novel. In the morning light, I spotted a holster and NYPD badge on a chair and questioned what it felt like to be in such a male-identified job. She must have found my line of inquiry offensive, because later she barely stifled a laugh about my desired career: "So, publishing. Really? Is there any money in that?" Neither of us called for a rerun.

So a conversation that flowed naturally made my heart lighter in my chest. Gerri had the life I wanted. She had moved to the city with Renee, her girlfriend, right after college and now worked as an assistant editor at Random House. She said her job sounded more impressive than it was, but she was meeting the "right" people and "putting in the time." One of her regular activities, when she wasn't at a bar, was attending readings by feminist authors at Womanbooks. Renee's family had money and supported her while she studied at Hunter for her MSW. The couple had adopted a dachshund named Alice B. (as in Toklas), and in their

Sheridan Square apartment they hosted a monthly lesbian salon and book discussion group called the "Women's Academy."

"Like Natalie Barney's?" I asked.

Gerri had a wide, gap-toothed smile that the girls at the Parkside would have advised her to have fixed but that she offered to me with confidence. "Somebody knows her lesbian history."

"I did an independent study on the women writers of the Left Bank. And another on the Modernists." I hadn't drunk enough beer yet to spill the whole truth: The Modernist writers were Hallie's area of expertise and I'd chosen to study them mostly so I could spend three hours a week alone with Professor Shepherd in her office.

"The group reads a lot of classics, but we tackle new work, too. Bertha Harris, Audre Lorde. This month it's *The Color Purple*."

The notion of belonging to a group of book-loving lesbians was so enticing I almost jumped in and invited myself to join. But my mother's voice was in my head, warning me to wait to be asked, so I simply dropped a few hints about being a voracious reader who was keen to work in publishing and before I knew it I had wrangled an invitation to their next meeting.

And a tip on a job. "Well, it's not a publishing house, but it's the next best thing," Gerri said, and I pressed her for details. She eyed me closely. "You know, on second thought, I really shouldn't recommend it. I like you."

As lights darted off the disco ball and across our faces, we sat watching the women on the dance floor, whose hands ran up and down each other while Boy George crooned, "Do you really want to hurt me?" My thoughts weren't on relationships, though, but on the hint Gerri had tossed out: How bad could the job be and what was "the next best thing" to publishing? Whatever the position, it had to be better than waiting tables for chump change.

"I'll do anything," I said, breaking the silence between us. "I know entry-level jobs are just grunt work, but I'm at the end of my financial rope. I mean, it's either get a real job or head back to North Carolina."

"Oh, don't do that! I'd like to hang out with you. We could go to readings together. You could meet Thea." She didn't explain who that was, instead jumping up to get us two more Buds.

"I don't mean to be cagey about the job. It's just I've heard not great things about it," Gerri continued. "You know who Bea Winston is?"

I didn't, but that didn't mean anything. I was a drooling infant when it came to the New York literary scene.

"She's a powerhouse agent," Gerri explained. "A legend. A big ol' feminist champion, started the first woman-run agency in the city. Not gay, but not a homophobe either, from what I hear. She represents some huge writers, and she's brought a lot of women novelists back into print, including lesbians like Rosalyn Clare and Clio Hartt."

I'd read Clio Hartt's *The Dismantled* in the Modernist independent study I did with Hallie, and the memory of Hallie's hand on my back as I asked her about a tricky, long-winded passage sent a wave of heat up my neck. The experimental structure and prose had been tough sledding for a college senior, but Hallie helped me unpack it—both in her office and later at a motel where we backed our cars into their parking spaces so no one could read the license plates from the road.

"Wow," I said to Gerri, trying to dispel the image of Hallie's lips from my mind. "And she has a job opening?"

"It's the office assistant. She goes through them fast. Either you do everything wrong and she cans you, or she likes you and you move up to junior agent. In the meantime, you make a lot of coffee and count pencils."

"How hard could that be? I make coffee at the diner, and I used to help my dad take inventory at his store."

Gerri nibbled on her thumb. The nails on her right hand were angry-looking, bitten to the quick. "Well, here's the thing. I knew someone who knew someone who had the job for two months and said Bea Winston was a bitch. Her words, not mine. I don't like the B-word."

"I have a pretty strong constitution," I insisted.

9

Gerri had stashed her backpack under the table as if she'd come to Ariel's right from the office. She rifled through it and pulled out a business card that confused me because it had the name Sarah Marcus embossed on it.

"My boss," she explained. "That's how I heard about the Bea Winston job. Tell Bea you found out about the opening from Sarah Marcus's 'office.' Don't pretend you know Sarah, though. That'll come back to bite you."

As I was inspecting the card, holding it in my hand like a winning lottery ticket, a willowy brunette appeared at our table. She looked a little like the photo of Rita Mae Brown on the cover of *Rubyfruit Jungle*, casually messy hair and expressive dark eyes. She leaned over and French-kissed Gerri, right there in front of me, before introducing herself. Renee didn't sit down, and they didn't invite me to dinner. And now there was even more to envy about Gerri's life.

Chapter 2

On the phone, Bea Winston had a smoky voice, and before I met her I pictured someone who sipped martinis in a sleek black cocktail dress, her hair impeccably coiffed—Marlene Dietrich, maybe. In person, Bea resembled someone's middle-aged mom, a leftover hippie-type, with shoulder-length salt-and-pepper hair falling loose over a slightly wrinkled plum silk tunic. She came only to my shoulder, but when we shook hands, her grip belonged to a much taller woman.

Bea ran her finger down the single page of my accomplishments as if she were interested. Nothing really translated to this job, aside from a BA in English from UNC Asheville and an internship at the local newspaper, where I'd basically been a gofer. She peered at me over her wire-frame aviator glasses and across the vast expanse of her oak desk. "'Oh, lost!'" she quoted, out of nowhere.

Another applicant might have been puzzled by the line from *Look Homeward, Angel*, but I jumped at the bait. "Yes, ma'am, Asheville's claim to fame." Native son Thomas Wolfe had immortalized Asheville and its environs in his first novel.

"And you've read his work."

"In my twentieth-century lit class, yes." I was hedging, nervous that she'd ask me specifics I couldn't dredge up. The two years between that class and the interview in Bea's office were a gaping hole of vanished knowledge.

"An overrated writer, if you ask me," she said, setting my resume aside in a way that suggested our interview was over and I'd failed the test. But then she added, "I'm from Georgia myself, home to the great Flannery O'Connor. You wouldn't know it because I divested myself of my accent in 1950. I stood in front of a mirror every evening and forced myself to form words differently."

Bea leaned back in her chair, farther than seemed possible without toppling over. But she knew the limits of that chair—and just about everything else. "What are you doing here?" she asked.

I stammered for a few minutes about what a giant she was in publishing, how I admired her for founding the first-ever woman-run agency—facts that Gerri had fed to me.

"No, what are you doing in New York? Good girls from Asheville get married and stay put. Especially girls named Olive Bliss."

Her question seemed vaguely illegal, but I very much wanted to be myself everywhere. In particular, I wanted my first real job to let me be me, and Gerri had said she didn't think Bea was homophobic.

"I'm gay," I blurted out. "My family actually lives in Weaverville, which is even more small-town than Asheville. My folks don't know about me." I omitted the part about leaving because I was heartbroken, too.

"Did you dress that way back home?"

I glanced down at my outfit: khaki pants, navy blazer, and light-blue button-down shirt were my idea of business attire.

"Because if you did, they all know," she observed.

My mother didn't like the way I dressed, but she'd given up objecting to it when I went to college. My sisters didn't try to set me up with men anymore. If they knew what to call me, none of them would ever use the word.

"Maybe," I allowed with a shrug. "But New York seemed like the best place for me. And no, ma'am, I can't change my name. But just so you know, everybody calls me Livvie."

Bea moistened her lips, and I waited for a curt "Thank you,

we'll let you know" that didn't come. As it turned out, I was just what she needed, in ways she didn't divulge at the time.

"Well, I can see why you'd want to move," she said. "So, Livvie." I'd never heard my name sound so smooth or rich, like top-shelf bourbon. *Livvie on the rocks, please.* "I need you to start tomorrow. The place is in chaos. The kind you get when your last two assistants have been incompetent. So, if you can start tomorrow and handle enormous stress, the job is yours." She said it paid twelve thousand a year, a princely sum when many advertised publishing jobs started at ten-five.

From a public phone on the corner I called my mother collect and told her I'd landed a good job with benefits in a nice clean office near Washington Square. Clean was very important to my mother; Washington Square meant nothing to her, but I threw it in because it sounded ritzy. I didn't expect the audible whoosh from the other end of the line, as if she'd been holding her breath since I'd moved away, waiting for the call about her youngest daughter being mugged, or homeless, or anything else bad that could happen to a girl in New York City.

Bea appointed Ramona Costa, a junior agent who had started out as her assistant five years earlier, to orient me to the compact suite of offices. As we shook hands, Ramona gave my chinos and button-down shirt a quick and wordless once-over. The girls at the Parkside would have envied Ramona's pinstripe suit with padded shoulders, but she was as thin as a strand of spaghetti and the outfit engulfed her.

With her knowledge of how everything ran, I sensed that Ramona was someone to win over. "You and Miss Winston must get teased a lot about Beezus and Ramona," I said jovially, but Ramona's face drew a blank. "You know, the Beverly Cleary novel? About the two sisters, Beatrice and Ramona? I read it about a million times when I was little."

She tugged at her jacket in what appeared to be a kind of personal tic. "No one's ever brought it up," she replied.

13

On our tour, her voice fell to a hush, as if we were in a hospital or church instead of a literary agency where the jangling of phones provided the soundtrack. "Your predecessor was unhappy," she said. "She didn't listen to me. There are tricks to getting along with Bea."

"What are they?" I whispered back.

"First, Bea hates clutter," Ramona said, pointing to mounds of manila folders toppling over each other on a long library table in the corner of Bea's expansive office. It appeared that no one had filed anything since Reagan's inauguration. Names of clients were printed in neat block letters on the tabs, a who's who of literati.

"All these files?" Ramona said, as if the contracts of luminaries were just detritus. "Get rid of them."

"Aren't these legal documents?"

"I don't mean literally get rid of them. I mean just hide the mess until you can do all the filing while she's out at lunch or something. Bea will think you're a genius. But get on top of the filing pronto, because you'll want to know where Terrence Crawley or R.J. Rose's file is when she asks. Believe me."

"Where do I stash them in the meantime?"

"There's a supply closet nobody uses except you. Right around the corner here."

"Nobody uses supplies but me?"

"Of course not. The agents request supplies from you," she corrected, as if speaking to a silly child or a very old person.

From the hallway, Ramona pointed into the individual offices of the agents. The senior-most after Bea, Therese was the only one whose space showed any personal embellishments. A vase of fresh yellow roses sat on her filing cabinet, and a poster from a Picasso retrospective at the Museum of Modern Art covered the one free wall. Framed studio portraits of two boys at different ages and casual shots of a man who reminded me of Sheriff Andy Taylor crowded the bookshelves and her desk. "Please don't order me anything but red pencils," Therese said upon our introduction. "Bea says red is a rude color, so just call me rude, I guess!"

Therese's laugh was a series of startling little booms that made Nan poke her head out of her office door. Her haircut was a perfect imitation of Princess Di's, but she had a good twenty years on the princess. "Green or purple for me, please," she said. "Since you're taking orders."

"Bea and I will only use blue. And that is Trick Number Two," Ramona said as we continued our tour. "Keep everything straight, especially, *especially* what Bea likes. And Trick Number Three is don't run out of anything."

Being someone's "assistant," I knew, entailed years of doing what people higher up the ladder didn't want to. But I couldn't help thinking about the money I'd laid out for college, the hours I'd sweated as a waitress, the money my Aunt Sass had lent me— all so I could find hiding places for files?

"Now you might think a college degree would put you above this." Was Ramona reading my mind? "But someone has to be on top of this shit and Bea doesn't see the need for an office manager with only four agents to keep track of. So you're it by default."

Tucked between Bea's spacious office and the front lobby was my cubbyhole, which itself resembled a supply closet. Thankfully, it wasn't right out in the open, like a receptionist's desk, but the trade-off was it had no windows. Gun-metal gray shelves lent it a particularly claustrophobic feel. Trick Number Four was greeting clients promptly and never letting anyone stand in the reception area for more than a minute.

"What if I'm on the phone?"

"Put the person on hold. A client in the hand is worth two in the bush . . . or something like that. Oh, and that brings me to the phone."

With ten different lines, it was a more complicated-looking instrument than required by an office with only five people.

"Everyone answers her own phone within four rings." That trick spelled relief for me; I was not going to be the telephone operator for phones that had barely stopped ringing since I'd arrived. "Never, ever answer Bea's phone unless she's on the other

15

line. Hard as it is to believe, she picks up her own phone. And sometimes yours. So keep personal calls to the barest minimum."

I attempted to memorize all the "tricks" because I thought there would be maybe seven at most, but soon we'd worked our way up to double digits and I resorted to taking notes. One of our last stops was a small kitchen area whose upkeep was also my responsibility. "Keep the coffeepot full and fresh at all times. Real milk, none of that powdered shit. No dishes in the sink—never ever *ever*! When you greet a client, ask them if they'd like coffee or tea, and how they drink it. They should have it in hand by the time they meet with Bea or else you'll have to interrupt her and you don't want to do that." Just when I thought we'd reached the end of my orientation, Ramona took in a deep breath and said, "Okay, just a couple more tricks, and you're all set."

While I was getting my bearings those first few days, I saw little of Bea. She kept her own appointment book, an oversized leather tome suitable for a doctor's office, and I managed to glance at it while attending to her filing. The crammed schedule, a confirmation of her importance, made me envy the hubbub of her life. Her hours were packed with breakfasts, lunches, drinks, and dinners—all noted in pencil for easy cancellation—most likely with editors, clients, and potential clients. A couple of times, though, she dropped names like "Ed" ("As in the mayor," Ramona explained with impatience) or "Gloria" ("Come on, you know this one. Famous feminist?") on her way out the door.

Between appointments, Bea apparently took notice of my diligent work making sense of her files. When I arrived on Thursday morning, she had already come and gone. I found a yellow sticky note tacked to my phone with the praise *LOVE what you've done!* in Bea's hand. But because her writing was more of a scrawl, I thought it read, "LOOK what you've done!" until I ran it past Ramona.

"Nice job for your first week, kiddo," Ramona said, although she was no more than twenty-seven, tops. "She *'loves'* you." There was more than a tinge of sarcasm in her tone, so I decided I should do something special for Ramona and order her own carton of blue pencils.

Friday morning, Bea was at her desk when I arrived and she waved me into her office. The smell of brewing coffee filled the air, and I could hear the Mr. Coffee drip-drip-dripping in the kitchen. I anticipated a dressing-down for coming in later than she did, forcing her to brew the first pot on her own.

But she was smiling when she pointed me into the leather chair across from her where many a famous rump had likely sat.

I missed a lot of what Bea said at the beginning of that meeting. The words "impressed" and "diligence" stood out, but I was easily distracted by my own thoughts. I was concentrating on her lack of an accent and thinking about how I might try mimicking the mirror technique to erase—or at least soften—my own.

The words "pressing problem" snapped me out of it. Despite all her "LOVE" for me, I had still managed to make some huge mistake.

"Do you know who Clio Hartt is?"

"Of course," I said. "*The Dismantled*. One of the Paris lesbians."

Bea frowned. "Do not ever call her a lesbian," she admonished, and I nodded in agreement, although I wondered just how I would come into contact with someone who was dead.

"Clio Hartt is one of the great Modernist writers, perhaps the greatest," Bea said. I noted her use of the present tense again and realized I must be mistaken about Clio's demise. "She is one of our clients, and she is in dire need of our help." Bea scribbled something onto a sticky note for me—a local telephone number and an address on a street I'd never heard of.

"I want you to call her and make an appointment to stop by," Bea continued. "Do you know where Milligan Place is? Charming little enclave. Head up Sixth and you can't miss it."

"You want me to call *the* Clio Hartt? You want me to go to her apartment?"

Bea's brow crinkled, as if she was rethinking her decision to task me with something so huge my first week on the job. "That

17

is exactly what I want you to do. Now, Clio's a challenge," she said, which sounded odd coming from someone who was her own sort of challenge. "She doesn't like people anymore. Maybe never did. She tolerates me because I sold a new edition of *The Dismantled* that's been adopted at colleges and makes handsome royalties, but I haven't seen her in person in probably eight years. She does call me several times a week, though."

Wow was all I could think to respond to the idea of never seeing a client who lived in the same neighborhood.

"You probably don't know this, but she is from your neck of the woods. Hendersonville, North Carolina. Her name was Birdie Threatt back then. No wonder she changed it, right?"

In my youthful brashness, I corrected her. I said I knew some Threatts, and the *e* was long, not short.

"However you say it, she's waxing nostalgic about her 'homeplace.'" She made air quotes, even though a native Southerner was surely familiar with that term. "I've never heard her go on quite like this. I thought she might let you help her with things like groceries and errands. Be her gal Friday."

"Oh." I pictured myself spending all my free time babysitting a closeted old lesbian—not how I envisioned my new life in New York's literary world.

"You'll do this on my dime, of course," Bea said, as if she read disappointment on my face. "I don't expect you to volunteer. It will require some juggling, though, so your work in the office doesn't suffer. If it's too much . . . well, we'll talk about extra compensation." The words "extra compensation" echoed in my ears like the promise of a cold beer at the end of a hard day. I could already see myself ditching the white crew sock where I squirreled away my cash and opening a proper bank account.

"It would be an honor to help Miss Hartt!"

"Let's just hope it works." As I stood to go, Bea assessed me in a way she hadn't before, looking me up and down like a man judging whether a woman was worth his time. "You are most definitely her type."

That stopped me again. Was Clio Hartt going to pinch my behind when I brought her milk and eggs? "Sorry?"

"Oh, don't worry, she hasn't had sex in years. She's heading for ninety, poor thing. I just mean . . . well, you look a little like Flora, that's all. Flora Haynes, the playwright? Tall, boyish, dark, that pixie haircut—"

I ran a hand through my hair. "Pixie" cuts were what my sisters and I got every summer when I was growing up, and I was horrified to think I still had one.

"I'm counting on you, Livvie," Bea said. "This is maybe the most important thing you'll do as my assistant. Being an agent is so much more than just negotiating contracts, you know. If you can get through to Clio, hold her hand, befriend her—"

I thought Bea intended to hold out a carrot like "—you'll be a junior agent before you know it." But then her phone rang and she didn't finish the thought.

I returned to my little office to stare at the sticky note, trying to pick up the phone and pimp myself out to the illustrious Clio Hartt.

Chapter 3

To my surprise, Clio Hartt had an answering machine. She also had a honeyed voice with the Carolina mountains still audible in it. Her outgoing message held no trace of the crotchety crone I'd imagined. "Caller, I cannot get to the phone. Please leave me a message, which I will treasure." Sweet as a Hendersonville apple with not even a hint of tartness.

I left the friendliest, most down-home message I could, then tackled a backlog of photocopying. Anticipating the return call, I kept poking my head out of the copy cubicle every time a phone line squawked. If I couldn't manage the first big task Bea had entrusted to me, I might get pigeonholed as the girl who didn't get things done, my career in the publishing industry derailed. I imagined Bea shaking her head as she related the tale: "The girl couldn't make a simple phone call!"

So I dialed Clio Hartt's number again, and then again, within the space of about an hour. The first time I hung up; the second time I left another message, much briefer. More anxiety set in. Bea had suggested Clio never left her apartment. Was she on the floor, in the grip of a fit or a stroke? Had she tripped getting out of the tub and bashed her skull? (Did people that old even take baths? My Meemaw was eightyish, with a distinctly unwashed smell that made me wriggle out of her hugs.)

Near lunchtime I was thinking I could either call the police or check on her in person. After a brief back-and-forth of the pros and cons, I chose option number two because, even though it might not be the New York way, that's what I'd do in Weaverville if a friend or neighbor was possibly in trouble. Maybe I could locate the super to let me in.

"Do you know where Milligan Place is?" I asked Ramona at the coffeemaker. "Bea said I should just walk up Sixth, but she didn't say how far."

Ramona gave me a thorny sideways look, as if I had inquired about something personal, maybe her bra size. "Why?"

"I'm supposed to check on Clio Hartt, and she's not picking up the phone. I thought I'd, you know, drop in."

"You do not 'you know, drop in' on Clio Hartt," Ramona said, with a thick slice of mockery. "If Bea told you to do that, she's testing your judgment. Which seems to be pretty bad." Then she grabbed her coffee and closed her office door behind her with a decisive click.

And then, just as I was reconsidering option number one, my phone line blinked and squealed, and I dove to get it before my message kicked in. A screech pierced my eardrum.

"I am about to be raped and killed!" were Clio Hartt's first words to me.

The cops were already on the scene by the time I figured out where Clio lived, on a tucked-away enclave I passed twice before a woman walking a yappy shih tzu gave me directions. Milligan Place sat behind a locked gate topped with its name in ironwork script.

Someone buzzed me through the gate without a word, but two beefy men in blue stopped me at the front door of Clio's building. "Can't go up there, son," said the older, heftier cop, raising a hand in case I tried to get through.

My haircut, along with my uniform of chinos, polo shirt, and penny loafers, had scrambled their gender signals, so I fell back on my small stash of feminine charm. "Thank you for getting here so quickly, officer! I'm Olive Bliss, the one who phoned y'all

21

about Miss Hartt? She's a client of my boss, Bea Winston. The literary agent?" The cops stared at me blankly, likely baffled to hear a woman's voice coming out of a teenage boy. "She just buzzed me in. I might be able to calm her down."

They waved me by, and I ascended to Clio's floor two steps at a time. What had seemed like a genteel building from the enclosed courtyard had jagged cracks in the hallway paint and some missing floor tiles. The air on the third floor smelled like rotting fruit.

A waif-like young man in a T-shirt and plaid shorts was looking through an open doorway I guessed must be Clio's. The unintelligible scratch of a radio dispatcher's voice traveled out into the hall. "Is she okay?" I asked the young man. He was a head shorter than I and at least twenty pounds lighter, with gray circles smudging the skin under his eyes.

"I heard her yelling at the cops from across the hall, so she's alive," he said. He nodded toward another open door, which I assumed was his apartment. "I thought she'd been murdered or something, the way she screamed. Scared the shit out of me." He held out a hand in introduction. "Eli. I buzzed you in."

"Livvie. You'll be seeing me around. I'm helping Miss Hartt."

"I would not want *that* job. I try to keep an eye out for her, but she just kind of snorts at me, and I'm positive she doesn't remember my name." His grin showed a mouthful of straight, white teeth, as if his father was an orthodontist. With my crooked bottom row, dental perfection made a big impression on me.

"I'm sure I'll be getting a few snorts of my own," I said, which made him laugh.

"I'd love to hear about it when you do." Wishing me luck, Eli retreated across the hall and I entered Clio's apartment for the first time.

The room where Clio Hartt had lived for forty-some years was fourteen by fourteen at most, with a kitchen alcove attached to a corner like a barnacle. The bathroom, visible through an open door, was barely big enough to turn around in. The space overflowed with books—not just on the long, table-like desk that straddled the two front windows and on the wooden shelves clinging to the walls, but also arranged like furniture. Next to a comfy-looking armchair, a stack of tomes with a mug and a pad of paper on top served as an end table. Towers of books also straddled either end of a narrow daybed.

Two more brawny cops faced the windows, obscuring my vision of Clio. This was my first encounter with male NYPD officers, and being oversized seemed to be a prerequisite for the job.

One of the cops turned as I entered, his hand brushing his waist holster, and I sucked in a breath. I held up two empty hands and tried to puff out my little boobs to show I was a defenseless woman. "I'm the one Miss Hartt called, officer," I said. "Livvie Bliss?"

I saw Clio then for the first time as she peeked from around the cop's massive chest. In her famous studio portraits, she was always seated, so I had no sense of how statuesque she was. When she rose to greet me, we stood at eye level. And in fact, the first thing I noticed were her eyes—her sharp cheekbones pointed directly toward them, accentuating the icy blue that looked like it belonged to some netherworld. Despite the steaminess of the room, Clio wore a calf-length, nubby-wool skirt and cardigan sweater, both in a battleship gray that matched her hair and made her eyes stand out more.

"Miss Bliss!" she said, her voice raspy but strong. "*There* you are!" The cop whose first instinct had been to shoot me let his hand travel back to his side.

"Ma'am, we'll file the report but we don't have much to go on without a physical description of the intruder," the other cop said.

Spittle flew from Clio's mouth as she said, "What more do you need? I told you, I thought I saw a *colored* man on the fire escape! How difficult could it be to find a *colored* man on a rooftop in this neighborhood? Go do whatever it is you're supposed to do and find him!"

A Northern girl might have been shocked by Clio's use of *colored* instead of *black*, but growing up under Jim Crow I'd heard it many times before from white folks, including my own family. I'd used it myself as a child.

The cops clomped out of the apartment a few moments later, and I snapped into helper mode. "Are you okay, Miss Hartt?" I offered her an arm to lean on, and we made our way to the armchair one step at a time. It was unclear if she really couldn't manage on her own or if she was putting on a good show for the help.

"I will be fine presently, Miss Bliss. In forty years, I have never had occasion to be visited by the police, and if that is what 'New York's Finest' is like, this city's in a heap of trouble." She sank onto the chair cushion with an appreciative sigh and went all good-natured on me. In fact, she was so pleasant when I offered to brew her a pot of coffee before I returned to work—"You are just as delightful as your name, Miss Bliss!"—I thought the reports of her orneriness must be overblown. Maybe, like my Meemaw, she was sweet as tea most of the time, a harpy only when her arthritis flared up.

But as I settled her in with her coffee, the other Clio trickled out. "This cup has a chip," she said, turning it around. She took a sip and frowned. "And you've put in too much sugar."

"Sorry about that. I'll get it right after a few tries."

"I am not here for you to experiment on, Miss Bliss. I like it the way I like it."

The flash of pique caught me off-guard. Bea would want me to kowtow and bring her a fresh cup, but I noticed Clio taking big, appreciative gulps.

"And yet you seem to be drinking it right down," I said.

The moment could have gone badly for me as Clio stared me down with those otherworldly eyes. But she turned back to the cup and polished off her drink with a resounding slurp.

"Bring me another before you go, would you?"

Chapter 4

Gerri and Renee's building was a prewar high-rise in Sheridan Square, the heart of gay New York. I wondered how an assistant editor and a grad student had scored such prime real estate until I remembered Gerri saying her girlfriend's folks subsidized her.

The doorman's name tag read "Jorge," and I wasn't sure how to pronounce it so I didn't. He wore a gold-trimmed burgundy coat and hat, his brown face shining with sweat.

"Good afternoon! Wow, it's cruel to make you wear that in this heat," I said.

"Apartment?" he asked, ignoring my small talk. When I gave my name, he said into the handset, "Hello, Miss Renee. Miss Libby is here." He listened, eyebrows raised. "She says she don't know no Libby."

"Livvie," I corrected. "Two *V*'s, not *B*'s. Livvie Bliss. Tell her Gerri invited me to the salon." At Gerri's name, Jorge nodded vigorously, and when Renee cleared me, he gave me a thumbs up. "Tenth floor, end of the hall."

I stepped off the elevator, glancing left and then right because Jorge hadn't specified which "end" of the hall. Renee was waiting. She was as handsome as I remembered, wearing loose cotton pants and a white V-neck tee that accentuated her dark hair and tanned arms. I handed her a box of bakery-style cookies from D'Agostino, which she accepted with a confused smile.

"Chocolate pecan chip," I said. "The soft kind."

"'*Pee*-can.' I love that. You're sweet. I can see why Gerri picked you out." It sounded like she'd found me while window shopping. Gerri, I soon discovered, had a habit of gathering up potential friends in bars, in bookstores, at concerts—anyplace where she was likely to meet people she clicked with.

"I don't think anyone has ever brought anything to a meeting," Renee said, "except beer." Gerri had told me only to bring myself, but I knew better than to go to someone's place empty-handed. I wondered about the beer comment. I would have thought a salon that took its inspiration from the Paris lesbians would be classier than that. I'd debated bringing a more upscale offering like croissants, but Bea hadn't paid me yet.

While Renee opened the cookie box and placed it on the coffee table with a stack of paper napkins, I scoped out the apartment. Gerri and Renee owned real furnishings: a comfy sofa and armchairs, a buffet adorned with a cut-glass vase of wildflowers, an oriental rug. This was not how I expected women a few years older than I to live.

"Gerri just hopped into the shower," Renee told me, running a hand through her own damp hair.

"I'm sorry I'm early." An apology seemed to be in order, even though my watch said it was almost three o'clock—when the group was scheduled to start.

"No problem. I'm always so late, it's embarrassing. It drives Gerri crazy. Everybody else will be here soon. I thought you might be Barb. She likes to be early, too."

I sat on the sofa and Renee plopped down at the other end, tucking her bare feet under her. We exchanged shy smiles, like we were on a blind date.

"This is a terrific apartment. What a location!"

"Oh, yeah, it's a great place," Renee said. "My father lived here right after the war, when he was going to NYU. He held onto the lease after they got married, and they used it as a pied-à-terre. You know, to see plays on the weekends."

Having parents who had a second residence just so they could go to plays was beyond my ken. Plus, my folks had never been to

26

any play except my high school's performance of *Oklahoma!* in which I was cast against type as the man-hungry Ado Annie.

"Too bad Gerri didn't meet you earlier. We have a party every Fourth on the roof. You'll come next year."

"That would be great."

A staccato buzz cut through the pause in our conversation. "That'll be Barb."

Renee went into the hall to greet her second guest, clicking the door closed softly behind her. When she reentered with Barb, they were laughing at some private joke. Barb sported cutoff jeans and a Joan Jett T-shirt with the neck and sleeves raggedly sliced off. Despite the homemade air-conditioning of her shirt, her moon-shaped face was shiny with sweat.

"It's a motherfucker out there," she said. "I need one of these bad boys now." At the coffee table, she plunked down the two six-packs of Heineken she'd been carrying and then cracked a bottle for herself.

"I'm Livvie," I said, standing with my hand out because I'd learned from my daddy's example how to take charge in situations where you were the odd one out. Countless times, I'd watched him step forward and say to strangers, "Roy Bliss. Real pleased to meet you."

Barb guzzled her beer, then wiped her hand on her faded denim cutoffs and accepted mine. She was stocky, not a delicate-looking girl at all, but her limp handshake belonged to a church lady.

"Libby?" She held the icy Heineken against her neck.

"Livvie, two *V's*." I flashed what I hoped was a beguiling grin.

She dropped into an armchair without offering her own name. "I've seen you somewhere before. Were you at Seneca in July?"

The local feminist newspaper had run a front-page article about a women's peace encampment near Seneca Falls, so I assumed that's what she meant. I said no, I wasn't that political.

"Huh. Hard not to be these days. Crazy fucking time." She sucked on her beer, staring at me through the slits of her eyes. "One thing you sure are is early. And I thought I was the only one who liked being on time." There was a tenseness in her voice, like I'd supplanted her status.

"It's in my genes. My family was always in the pew thirty minutes before service started."

Barb tilted her head to the right as if she was trying to decode the words *pew* and *service*.

"Livvie's from North Carolina." Gerri appeared from the far reaches of the apartment and grabbed a beer for herself. The deep timbre of her familiar voice felt like a hug. "Don't you just love her accent?"

"She brought the pee-can cookies," Renee added.

"Oooh, baby, talk Southern to me," Barb said, making Renee break into a girlish giggle. Gerri didn't share the joke, and nibbled on her thumbnail before opening her beer.

Gerri sat next to me on the sofa, heat radiating off her body from her recent shower. "You want a Heinie?"

In my book, it was a little early to drink. The Blisses did not imbibe on Sunday, but I was in a new place, setting my own rules. "Sure! We can drink to my new job."

"You got it? Right on!" We tapped our bottles together. "Bea's a total trip, right?"

The buzzer interrupted again and then a second time just a few seconds later. "I'll go." Barb went to the intercom like she owned the place.

"Get this!" I said. "I've already met Clio Hartt!" But Gerri was busy following Barb with her eyes and didn't hear me. "Bea appointed me as her 'gal Friday.' Kind of a gofer, I guess."

Renee pulled several folding chairs from a closet. "Wait, what?" she said. "You met *the* Clio Hartt?"

"Way to go!" Gerri said, diverting her attention from Barb to high-five me.

Barb returned from the door with two more women in tow: Jill, a white woman with blazing red hair and a face full of freckles, and a petite African-American woman named Thea, who wore a clingy sundress that showed off shapely arms. They each carried a six-pack, too, suggesting an afternoon of heavy drinking.

"Clio Hartt? Seriously?" Barb said. She turned away from Jill and hovered so close to me that drops of condensation from her bottle dripped onto my chinos. The drops coalesced into a circle, and I rubbed at the wetness self-consciously.

"How did you meet Clio Hartt?" Thea dragged a folding chair up to the sofa, edging Barb out of her way.

"Gerri helped me get a job with Bea Winston, the literary agent. I started last week."

"A friend of mine just signed with that agency. Where were you before?"

"The Village Diner," I said with a laugh. "For two lo-o-o-ng months. But now things are moving so fast it's unreal. I've even started looking for an apartment share."

"Liv's at the Parkside Evangeline," Gerri explained.

"That Salv Arm place?" Barb said with a derisive laugh. "Where nice girls from 1960 go to meet Mr. Right?"

"Or *Ms.* Right," Gerri said.

"No men above the first floor," I added.

"I never thought about that," Renee said. "All those women in one place! Some of them have to be dykes, right?"

The conversation bounced around me like ping-pong balls. Gerri and Renee's long-haired black-and-red dachshund, Alice B., waddled into the room and cozied up to everyone, demanding pats, and Barb scooped her up. "Alice B.! I love you s-o-o much!"

My cookies were the only food in sight, and Barb helped herself to one. After a half-moon bite, she slipped a crumb to Alice.

"Wouldn't it be so cool to have Clio come to one of our meetings? Any way you could finagle that?"

"She doesn't go out," I said. "She's a million years old."

"But we're her fan base!" Barb said. She and Gerri took turns putting themselves forward as Clio experts, trying to outdo each other. They'd both made it through *The Dismantled* multiple times and read "the" biography by someone named Montrose, but Gerri had also read other books about Clio and her work.

"The novel's autobiographical," Barb said with authority. "All about her passionate relationship with Flora Haynes."

29

Gerri snickered. "'Passionate'? From what I've read, Flora drank, fucked, and snorted too much. And wrote too little."

"Nice epitaph," I said.

Everyone laughed except Barb, who settled into her armchair again and ignored Gerri.

"Let's talk after, Carolina," Barb said, which made me assume the salon was kicking into gear.

But over the next two hours, we never got around to discussing *The Color Purple*, which I had loved. No one seemed to mind except Gerri and Thea, who inserted Walker's name several times before going quiet. It was almost as if the others in the circle had agreed in advance to talk about something else.

Barb dominated the conversation, unveiling a new art project she and Jill had dreamed up that they wanted the Women's Academy to contribute to. As she spoke, she leaned toward Jill in a way that suggested they were lovers.

Their proposal was to launch a performance piece, with salon members participating according to their interests and talents. Jill had a lead on a cheap space in the East Village. The Women's Academy boasted plenty of talent, Barb said, with an emerging poet (Jill), an emerging playwright (Barb), an emerging photographer (Thea), and a sometime modern dancer (Renee). The piece would take the Paris lesbians of the 1920s as its central theme, but everyone could interpret that loosely.

"How loose is 'loosely'?" Thea asked, twisting open another beer.

"Well, for example, I'd love to play around with their S/M sides," Barb said.

"Since when did the Paris lesbians have S/M sides?" Thea's tone oozed annoyance.

"Oh, come on, Thea! All that sexual drama? Don't tell me you never read *The Pure and the Impure*? Oh, wait, you vetoed that book."

"Colette was a straight girl who played around," Thea said. She sat back in her chair and swigged her beer, point made.

"And what part do me and Livvie play in this performance?" Gerri asked.

Barb glanced over as if she'd never given Gerri a thought.

"You're probably the most outgoing person I've ever met, so maybe you could do the publicity," Barb suggested, but Gerri didn't respond to the compliment.

Barb helped herself to a second cookie and eyed me with that head-tilt again. The gesture reminded me of my family's old collie, Maisie, staring at her humans. "And what do you do, Carolina?" she asked.

Except for singing in the Grace Baptist youth choir and being in the school musical, I'd never done much of anything creative. And those accomplishments sounded too small-town to admit, especially after my comments about the Blisses going to church.

"I sing a little." Before Barb could demand a tune, Gerri blurted out her frustration.

"Oh Jesus fucking Christ, this is ridiculous," she said, her cheeks flaming hot pink. "We're a salon! Now all of a sudden we're morphing into performance artists? I don't know about anybody else, but I'd like to get back to discussing books. We were scheduled to talk about *The Color Purple* today, but maybe that was just too vanilla for some of you. Maybe some people are still mad we didn't pick *Coming to Power*." Even more heat was radiating off Gerri now. "And would you please stop giving Alice cookie crumbs?"

At the time, I didn't know what *Coming to Power* was, or what being "vanilla" meant, but I could tell I'd landed in the middle of a long-simmering stew. After an awkward moment in which people finished their beers in silence and Barb rebuffed Alice's persistent nudges for more cookie, Renee broke the quiet with gentle teasing: "Well, gee, Ger, why don't you tell us what you *really* think?"

The salon broke up a little after five, with everyone but Barb agreeing to back-burner the performance piece and give Alice Walker her due the following month. In the hallway, I found myself waiting for the elevator with Jill, Barb, and Thea, although Thea stood a few feet off by herself, staring down at the black and white hallway tiles. As the floor numbers clicked by, Barb clued me in that she was looking for a new roommate to share her place on West Fifteenth Street.

"Jenny's the best, we've been pals on and off since Bennington, but she's moving to L.A. at the end of the month to try screenwriting. She'll be back eventually, but I can't afford to hold the room for her."

Barb described her place as a two-bedroom walk-up, and Jill rolled her eyes. "Well, it started out as a one-bedroom," Barb admitted. "I got the lease, and then Jenny carved out her own space. Not scared of heights, are you?"

"Um, no. Why?"

"Loft bed."

My mind shot to a treehouse my friends and I had built in the woods. I'd been admitted to the tight circle of boys because my dad owned a hardware store and I sweet-talked him into providing supplies. I had to share a pink bedroom with my girly sister, so I'd clambered up that treehouse ladder more times than I could count just to have a space that felt like me.

"I'm from the mountains," I joked. "I was born climbing."

I was intrigued by Barb's offer, even though I wasn't exactly sure what I thought about her as a roommate. She seemed critical and bossy, but then so were my three older sisters and I'd always stood my ground with them. As the elevator doors opened, Barb took my elbow in an unexpectedly gentle gesture and escorted me into the car.

"Those were some good cookies, Carolina," she said. "And that Southern style of yours is pretty cool. Everybody I meet's on overdrive, but you're like the definition of laid-back. I like that. I think we'd get along. If you could stand a wound-up Yankee."

I told Barb I'd consider it, and down on the street we set up a time for me to see the apartment. After Barb and Jill turned north, I noticed Thea had hung back to talk to me.

"I'd be careful with Barb," she said. "She's . . . unpredictable. She's tried to take over the salon several times. Just ask Gerri."

"I'd say Gerri knows how to manage Barb, if today's any example."

Thea grimaced. "Well, don't say I didn't warn you."

On the walk across town, I weighed the benefits of Barb's apartment. West Fifteenth Street was just a few blocks from Ariel's and an easy stroll to the Village. So many possibilities could open up for me: a circle of friends, eventually a lease on my own one-bedroom, a girlfriend, a dog or cat.

It was Sergeant Sal who really made up my mind, though. "Goodness, Livvie, you just getting back?" she said as I sauntered through the front door. "You almost missed the ice cream social!"

One of the first to congratulate Clio on the publication of *The Dismantled* was journalist Janet Flanner, with whom Clio enjoyed many an evening at Café Flore and Les Deux Magots. *You must be so pleased!* Flanner wrote on October 10, 1936. *It's a triumph, dear one. Although knowing you, you are already scribbling notes in the margins about how you should have phrased it!* She signed it, *Love, JF.*

Clio filed the note in a folder called "Ephemera," but not until she had scrawled across the top: *Typical Flanner—so cheeky.*

—from *Dismantling Clio Hartt: Her Life and Work,*
by Ingrid Coppersmith

Chapter 5

September 1983

Clio and I soon fell into a routine. I called her every Monday morning to inquire how she was doing and what she needed, and depending on her response I stopped in Tuesday and Friday afternoons, either with groceries and prescription refills or just to make coffee and listen to her. She talked to so few people, a conversational riptide greeted me when I stepped through the door. Visiting old folks wasn't new to me; my mother had dragged me and my sisters along with her while she did her Christian duty, bringing comfort to elderly people in our community.

Bea was pleased that one of her most famous clients was being so carefully attended to—and was out of her hair. It wasn't that Bea smiled at me more or even looked at me all that much. Instead, she offered juicy tidbits of approval, like allowing me to sit in on a meeting with a feminist author she was eager to sign.

And then there was the morning a royal blue box dropped with a thud onto my desk. The bright manuscript boxes in the agency's signature color were more than familiar to me: I did everything from special-ordering them from the supplier to unpacking the lids and bottoms and assembling them to laying copies of manuscripts into them and then typing and affixing the labels.

"Is anything wrong?" I asked as my eyes caught the name "Westerly, D. A." Bea still hadn't spoken, and I wondered if I had not boxed this particular manuscript neatly enough for her taste. ("Think hospital corners," had been Tip Number Something from Ramona.)

"I want you to read this," Bea said, a neatly trimmed nail pressing into the top of the box for emphasis.

My heart flapped in my chest. I had no idea what the manuscript was about, whether it was fiction or nonfiction, but I said, "I would love to!" so there was no chance she would snatch the opportunity back. Ramona had hinted that Bea would give me a manuscript someday when she thought I was "ready," but that the day would come months or years down the line, not a couple of weeks after I started my job.

"A new author," Bea went on, "with what looks like a tendency to overwrite."

"Hence the box," I said. The two-inch model, which was ample for most of our manuscripts, couldn't contain this one. It was probably close to the five hundred sheets in a ream of paper.

"Hence the box." Bea smiled. "Make notes for me, but not on the manuscript. Anywhere the story starts to ramble and you lose interest, note the page number. You know, the part of a novel when your eye starts to skip down the page."

"So-o-o, what's it about?"—a bubbly question you might shoot at your best friend in junior high when you're exchanging Judy Blume paperbacks. It wasn't something you asked a woman who represented giants of contemporary literature, and Bea winced.

"That is for you to find out," she said. The sliver of pain on her face reminded me of Hallie, who was never very adept at hiding her reaction to a student's dumb question in class. And just like a student, my chin dropped in embarrassment.

But when I looked up, Bea was smiling again. "By the way, I

spoke to Clio over the weekend. I never thought I'd say this, but she sounded happy. You must be doing something right. Just don't tell me if you're slipping something into her coffee."

The blue box was the first thing Clio noticed when she answered the door that day. Up until then we hadn't discussed my job or Bea or anything to do with literary agents. She mostly talked about herself or proffered her opinions about everything from Greenwich Village ("the only place to live, really") to the local greengrocer ("Such service! But the produce could be fresher") to her Paris literary comrades, like Gertrude Stein ("She would have been nothing without Alice"). As I listened, I noted her verbal tics, like the way she tacked "really" onto many statements as if adding to their heft. Or I watched her physical cues, like how her sapphire eyes widened jarringly when she tossed out Flora's name or closed dreamily when she recalled their apartment on the Left Bank, how the lines around her mouth resembled sideways smiles when I said something that pleased her and then became weighty pouches when she was tired of my company and needed a nap.

But she never seemed to notice anything about me. On our second meeting, she did say, "You're so charmingly . . . boyish— for a minute I thought . . ." but stopped short of completing the sentence. The apartment was devoid of photos, save for one of an androgynous young woman in a slim suit and tie, her hair cut short as a boy's, the bangs brushed into a suggestive *V.* If I'd been alive in the 1930s, I might have presented myself that way. Without asking, I understood the woman to be Flora.

So I was startled when Clio observed the manuscript box, which was too bulky to fit into my messenger bag. "For me, Miss Bliss?" Clio said, clapping her hands with delight. "What a divine color!"

"Oh . . . what? No, sorry," I said. "It's just a manuscript Bea asked me to read. Some up-and-coming writer who needs editing."

She turned away without even closing the door, and I clicked it shut behind me. By the time I put down my bag and the box, set the mail on her desk, and walked to Clio's chair, her eyes had filmed over. On the day she believed her rape and murder were imminent, she had told me she never cried, but now I understood that had been bravado.

"Are you *trying* to upset me?" she said, her voice as thin as a sheet of paper.

I knelt down beside her and put a hand on the arm of her chair because I didn't dare touch her. "Miss Hartt! I am so sorry! I'll bring you a present soon, I promise."

She wiped at her eyes roughly, as cross with herself as she was with me.

"What could you possibly bring me that I would ever need or want?"

I leaned back to deflect the verbal blow.

"I'm so sorry, Miss Hartt," I repeated, because I couldn't think of anything else. I wasn't sure if I should put the coffee on or if everything I did now was tainted and I needed to leave before she struck again. "I don't know what I did to make you so mad."

And that enraged her more. "You 'don't know'!" she mimicked, chuckling to herself. "Oh, wait, I see! Beatrice put you up to this! You're just her pawn."

My smile felt weak, insufficient, stupid even. *Put me up to what?* I wanted to ask, but that would just prove her point.

"Look around you, Miss Bliss," Clio went on. "Peruse the shelves. Haven't you done that when you thought I wasn't looking?"

I had peeked at her books, but didn't want to admit it, so I shook my head. Her questions felt like little traps set up across the room. "No, ma'am," I lied.

"Well, do it now. Tell me when you find the books by Clio Hartt."

"Should I—?" It was the time I usually fixed her coffee, and I motioned toward the kitchen nook.

"Just do it!"

The task shouldn't have taken long because there were only

two tall bookshelves and one three-shelfer. But then there were the stacks of books acting like furniture, and I had to get down on all fours to inspect those spines. I finally located her titles grouped together in a pile next to her desk: her masterpiece, *The Dismantled*, plus a slim novella-length satire called *Left Banked*, which had been downplayed by scholars but revered by lesbians, according to Gerri. There were exactly seven copies of each, like a sacred numerology.

I stood up and glanced over at her. I didn't have to announce my finding because she was already speaking.

"You have located my life's output," she said, her tone now more rueful than angry. "The novella doesn't even count, really."

"I could have sworn it was more. Must be because *The Dismantled* is worth ten of any other book. Probably twenty of the one in that box," I added, nodding toward the manuscript that had set off the uproar. My sincerity must have been palpable, because in the late afternoon light, it almost looked like Clio was blushing. "To have written a classic like *The Dismantled*, well, I can't imagine."

"Publishing is a burden," Clio said. "But *not* publishing—for a real writer—is worse."

The lightbulb went on then. I'd come to visit with the manuscript of an "up-and-coming writer" tucked under my arm, and to a blocked writer who had accomplished just one great book, it must have cut in a way she couldn't bear.

"You've been writing, though," I pointed out. "You mentioned new stories you're working on." The heaped-up papers on her desk offered proof of some sort of output, though honestly they might have been shopping lists for all I knew. I had simply assumed that papers in the home of a writer equaled writing. "Maybe you'd like to talk about the stories, help get your juices flowing?"

She looked at me like I was a peculiar object in a natural history museum whose use she had just figured out.

"I have a better idea," she said.

Clio urged me to pull a chair up to the desk. At the far right corner rested an old Olympia portable she said Bea had given her. On the other side, a collection of yellowing journals and magazines sat directly in the late afternoon sunlight spilling onto the desk. In the center, papers with loopy handwriting all over them obscured the oak surface. The arrangement of paper, I noticed, seemed to be different from the last time I visited. She didn't invite me to touch anything, and I kept my hands resting on my khakis as we sat side by side.

"You probably don't know I published a lot of stories in magazines," she began. "Before *The Dismantled*. They paid the rent while Flora and I lived in Paris. I'd get five, six hundred a story, good money then." I wanted to say it was still good money, but she continued. "I still have copies of some, but not all." She waved toward the periodicals. "An editor called me a few years ago—she was with some publisher in Boston—and wanted to make a book out of them. But I didn't know anything about her or how she got my phone number. I pay extra for unlisted, so I hung up on her."

I winced, wondering why she hadn't referred the editor to Bea. "I'm sure there would be a lot of interest in a collection like that," I said. "And if you had unpublished work to go with it? All the better." I tried to sound like the pro I wasn't as I nodded toward the papers on the desk.

"You're right. But I can't work with someone I don't know. Someone who calls me long distance. Someone named *Louise*."

Why would distance and the name *Louise* offend her? But I let the question drop out of my mind like an errant piece of paper.

"I'm sure Bea would love to hear about this," I said. "She could hook you up with a publisher, some smart editor who could put it all together for you—"

"No, no, *no!*" Her cheeks reddened. "I had to ban Beatrice from coming here because she would not leave me alone about publishing! Such pressure! You know, when I publish, *she* makes money."

It was a stereotype I'd heard everyone at the agency complain about—that literary agents were essentially parasites, feeding off the blood and sweat of real artists. "Well, Miss Hartt, here's the thing: When you publish, *you* make money, too."

A smile softened her eyes. "Well, that would be nice, wouldn't it?" Her slender fingers brushed a sheet of paper in front of her. "People still know who I am. I get letters from professors praising *The Dismantled*. They teach it at universities. Bea arranged for that new edition they all fawn over." The smile evaporated, replaced by a grimace. "But sometimes . . . well, last year, there was some dreadful little lesbian who camped by my front gate just waiting for me to go out. She actually touched my arm! She said *The Dismantled* had meant so much to her. Some horrid teacher had assigned it in a class on lesbian literature!" Derision dripped from her mouth. "She wanted me to autograph her copy. Imagine!"

Even though Bea had warned me about Clio's attitude, the phrase, "dreadful little lesbian" stung, and I tossed out a defiant comeback: "How dare she!"

Clio eyed me curiously, as if weighing my sarcasm on a scale. "I thought it was rude."

"Fans pay the bills," I said with a shrug. "Beggars can't be choosers."

Clio drew herself up straight in the chair. "I am not a beggar! I have more money than you imagine, young lady!"

"I didn't mean it literally, Miss Hartt." Although, in fact, her circumstances suggested that she might be close to beggardom. When she reimbursed me for groceries, her face was pinched in pain as she extracted the bills and coins out of a cracked leather change purse. I imagined her royalty check from the new edition of *The Dismantled* was the only thing standing between her and destitution. Could she even collect Social Security, if she'd never worked at an actual job? "I just meant fans are good for writers. You should be happy your novel resonated with readers for so many years. Even lesbians. That means it's a real classic!"

She shuffled a few papers, pretending to look at them. "It is a good book. Tom Eliot said it was among the finest American

43

novels of all time, not just of Modernism." I didn't catch the casual reference to T. S. Eliot at first, but as the weeks went on, I realized she had been on a nickname basis with the literary leviathans of the early 20th century—Joyce was "Jim" to her, Hemingway was "Hem," Sinclair Lewis, "Red."

"'American' is the key word there," she continued. "I did not write that book for lesbians!" Then her tone flipped from defiant to melancholy. "Flora and I . . . we loved each other. So very much. But that doesn't make us lesbians."

I started at the words, which echoed something Hallie had once said to me.

At the mention of Flora, Clio's hands shot up to her hair, a gauzy gray cloud tinged with streaks of white, which she wore parted in the middle and then eased back into a low, loose bun. Judging from photos, she hadn't changed the style much since the 1940s. She patted a few stray hairs back into place. The gesture touched me: *She isn't over her,* I realized, and I understood that feeling all too well. I wanted to reach over and stroke her arm, but it would have cooled the space between us, so I didn't.

"Seems like a special relationship," I said. The hollow words popped out automatically. Hallie had used that phrase, too.

"Special," Clio scoffed. "I guess you could call it that."

Gerri had told me that the playwright Flora Haynes had been a hellion. After she and Clio left Paris in the '30s and settled on West Tenth Street, her moniker was the "Village Vamp." Handsome as a matinee idol and sharp as a razor, Flora lived life a bit too fully. As "Vincent" (translation from Clio-ese: Edna St. Vincent Millay) would have said, Flora burned her candle at both ends.

There was no more talk of Flora that day. Clio excused herself and padded off to the bathroom, waving away my offer of help like I was a pesky mosquito. "I live alone!" she snapped. "I am able to get to the toilet by myself." When she returned to the desk, there were a few drops visible on her hairline as if she'd splashed her face with cold water.

"Now, let's talk about these stories," she said, taking the seat next to me again.

She kept me after my actual "quitting time," as the men in my family called it. As the fall light began to fade through Clio's window, my stomach growled audibly. Clio brought out a box of saltines on the brink of staleness, which dulled my hunger (I made a note to buy her a fresh package), and then she kept on plowing through the papers as if determined to unveil everything in one session.

Together we compiled a list of the stories she thought she had written, with vague publication dates ('32 or '33?) and their possible periodicals; but she wasn't sure of anything except the ones she had copies of. "You'll have to track them down," she said dismissively, as if that were the easiest thing in the world to do when you had no idea where to start.

And the "new" work was baffling. In one stack, which on the face of it appeared to be a story of maybe fifty pages in length (*A Clio Hartt novella!* I thought), I saw that several of the pages were in fact the first page that she kept starting over, honing and revising until it bore little resemblance to the original. Even the title suggested uncertainty about the work, devolving from "All This" to "The Less We Know."

"This one . . . it's not there yet," she said, her face lined with confusion. "It's heading somewhere, but it needs time."

"Is there, you know, a finished draft?" I asked.

"I just told you—*it's not there yet.*" She leaned back in her chair and closed her eyes. Her breathing was so shallow, I wondered for a moment if she'd fallen asleep sitting up, the way my Meemaw sometimes did. But then her lids snapped open and she pushed herself away from the desk.

"Enough," she announced. I didn't know at first if she meant the session was enough or if she'd had enough of trying to explain her work to someone as unskilled as me. "We'll pick this up again tomorrow."

"Tomorrow is Saturday," I said. "Tuesdays and Fridays are the days I stop in."

"That won't do. I'll need more of you than that. Bea will simply have to free up your time, pay you extra."

"I don't know, Miss Hartt. The agency's so busy, and I'm the only assistant."

"She will allow it." Clio handed me the near-empty sleeve of saltines, presumably to take with me as a bonus.

Chapter 6

Through the glass panel in the front door of Clio's building, I spotted her neighbor Eli struggling to negotiate his entrance. Wearing a button-down shirt and a tie, a bulging leather satchel slung over one of his shoulders, he looked like he'd come from work. He balanced two bags of groceries on his hips while trying to manage his keys at the same time. "Shit!" he said, as he dropped one of the grocery bags, and cans of Friskies Buffet careened across the courtyard.

I hadn't seen Eli since my first visit to Milligan Place, although when I passed his apartment, no matter what time of day, jazz music seeped out from under his door. "Hey, Eli!" I called out. "Let me help you there."

At first he couldn't seem to place me, but then his face registered recognition.

"Oh, hello!"

"Livvie Bliss, Miss Hartt's . . . helper?" Some people didn't understand Bea's term, "gal Friday," and I didn't know what else to call myself. From my talk with Clio that afternoon and evening, though, it looked like I might have scored a promotion.

"Of course!"

I circled the courtyard with him, retrieving the cans. "This looks like the last one," I said, plopping a can of Chicken and Tuna into the grocery bag. "Oops, no, there's another one by that bush."

"You're a lifesaver," Eli said, with a dramatic gesture toward his heart.

I had a sharp memory of my friend, Michael, one of the first friends I made during Freshman Orientation at college. He had a theatrical way of touching his heart and bowing slightly when he greeted someone. It was Michael who showed me a copy of *Rubyfruit Jungle* tucked onto a shelf at the college library: "This is what girls like you read," he'd said in a conspiratorial whisper that made me shiver. I was only beginning to understand myself in that way. Later that year, Michael's folks turned him out of the family when they found out about him and another boy, and he headed to San Francisco. "You'd love it here!" he'd written to me. "Gay people everywhere!" After a while, though, the postcards stopped coming.

The thought of Michael made me grab the bag Eli had set down in the courtyard. "Here, I'll help you get these things upstairs."

His apartment was the mirror image of Clio's, but with framed artwork and grown-up upholstered furniture, like Gerri and Renee's. Between the windows was a compact dining-room table and chairs made of sleek, dark wood. How nice to daydream while you're eating, I thought. Most often, I ate hurriedly on the street on my way somewhere or in my loft bed.

"Wow, pretty place."

"Most of this belonged to Curt," he said, without explaining who that was. Instead, he greeted a small tuxedo cat, a tiny thing about half the size of a normal feline, with paws no bigger than quarters. "How's my beautiful boy?" The cat wrapped himself around Eli's ankles, emitting a delicate purr.

"What a cutie," I remarked. "How old?"

"Probably two. I got him at the shelter, and they weren't sure."

"I thought he was just a baby!"

"He was abused, locked up in a crate, so he didn't grow properly, they said." Eli's voice thickened with emotion. "His name is Remington."

"Like the show?" I'd caught a few episodes of the detective series *Remington Steele* on Barb's TV. I had a little crush on Stephanie Zimbalist.

Eli looked confused, and I noticed then that his apartment didn't have a television, at least not out in the open. "Like the typewriter," he said. "Curt had a collection of old typewriters, but I had to sell them all."

It was another past-tense reference to Curt that dangled between us.

Eli took the bag of cans from me and removed one for Remington. "Well, I guess I should get going," I said, not wanting to disrupt their dinner. "I need to grab something to eat."

"Oh, why don't you stay? I owe you for helping me. I was going to feed Remmie and then order in. Do you like Thai? Let me treat you. I would love the company." He cocked his head toward the door. "Unless you're afraid of being called back across the hall by you-know-who."

My only plan for the evening was to pick up a couple of slices and then head to Ariel's to meet Gerri and Renee. It was too early to dance, though, and Thai food—although I'd never tried it—sounded more enticing than greasy pizza. Plus, Clio was probably working or asleep already, so I agreed to a quick meal.

Instead, it turned into a two-hour gabfest. We were both talkers, and the pace at which we spilled our lives out in front of each other over spring rolls, pad thai, larb chicken, and a spicy green curry dish was equaled only by how fast Gerri and I had become friends. Eli was from North Adams, a mill town in Massachusetts, so we had the suffocation of small-town life in common. Plus, he was as gay as me. He'd moved to New York so Curt, his lover, could take a job at a major law firm and he could try his luck as a stage designer, and they'd lived in a spacious place on the Upper East Side. "Easily five times the size of this," Eli said.

When I gingerly asked about Curt, who was obviously no longer in the picture, Eli mumbled that he had died a year earlier.

"It was quick and horrible. I can't say any more," and he shut down the topic before I even had a chance to express my condolences.

He shifted to safer subjects with what passed for lightness. It turned out he knew more about Clio than I did, having engaged her one day in conversation about her early experiences with the Provincetown Players. She'd shared some stories before clamming up: "How do I know you won't sell this to a biographer?" she'd asked him.

"That sounds like her. But, you know, I'm embarrassed I have no idea who the Provincetown Players are," I admitted.

"Really? Susan Glaspell? Eugene O'Neill?"

"Well, I guess everybody knows O'Neill," I said with swagger, although I'd never read any of his plays.

"They started a theater company in Provincetown, but they eventually moved it here, to the Village. Clio was trying to be a playwright then. That's where she met Flora. Flora designed some of their sets and had some plays produced, too." He sighed. "I saw Flora's watercolor designs in a book when I was at Yale. Absolutely stunning."

The sun had set by the time I looked at my watch. "Oh, man, I should go," I said.

"Hot date?"

"I wish. I'm supposed to meet some friends at a bar."

"Well, knock on my door any time. I mean it, Livvie," he said. His loneliness was palpable, a hand reaching toward me, and I wondered how many other people he'd lost besides Curt. I almost invited him along, but what would a gay guy do in a bar jammed full of women? Instead, I promised we'd have dinner again soon.

Leaving Milligan Place, I decided to drop the blue manuscript box off at Fifteenth Street. What happened next was all about timing: If the box hadn't weighed me down, or if I'd said no to dinner with Eli and gotten home hours earlier, I might have been spared a lot of trouble.

As I turned the corner from Fourteenth Street onto Seventh, I spied Renee on the west side of the avenue, but she didn't see me. Her head was down and she looked like she was on a mission. Or maybe she was just very, very late once again. I thought about waving and calling out to her—after all, I was supposed to meet them soon—but instinct made me watch her fly across the avenue and head uptown toward Ariel's.

She had been on Fifteenth Street, that much I was sure of. My block of Fifteenth Street. There was nothing on my block but walk-ups laced with webs of fire escapes, and a few storefronts like a Chinese laundry where I got my button-down shirts washed and pressed at the bargain rate of fifty cents each. It made no sense for Renee to be there unless she had taken it as a shortcut from somewhere farther west. I decided that must have been it and proceeded on my way home.

So far, sharing an apartment with Barb had suited me. Although I had even less space than at the Parkside Evangeline, it had been put to ingenious use. My "bedroom" consisted of a corner area that was no more than eight by nine, with plywood walls and door. A sturdy loft bed took up most of the square footage, with a desk, bookshelf, and clothes rod all squirreled away underneath. It was snug and dark, but it was mine, and I'd spruced it up with decorations from Womanbooks that I would have never dared display at the Parkside. One spare wall sported a poster-sized photograph of two naked women in a passionate embrace, while the back of the door held several prints of Georgia O'Keeffe's colorful vagina-like flower paintings.

The share suited me, too, because Barb and I rarely crossed paths. She worked the night shift as a legal proofreader in the financial district and was usually in transit when I arrived home from the agency. Because I'd left Eli's so late, I assumed she'd be long gone by the time I turned my key in the lock.

I could hear the music as I wound my way up to the fourth floor. Barb had an impressive collection of women's music albums. She told me to treat myself to a listen whenever I wanted, and I had spent quite a few late nights getting to know Holly Near, Meg Christian, Ferron, and Cris Williamson. Now the sultry sound of "Sweet Woman" drifted into the hallway.

In the dim light of the living room, I saw a sea of candles arranged on the old trunk Barb had converted to a coffee table.

A bottle of Chianti and two Looney Tunes jelly jars-turned-drinking glasses rested nearby. As my eyes became accustomed to the dim light, I saw Barb herself, naked, in the middle of the living room floor on a silky lavender sheet, a hand between her legs.

"I am so sorry!" I said, wondering if Jill was in the bathroom or if Barb simply had an elaborate masturbation ritual. "I will be out of your hair in a flash." We'd discussed staying cool and loose about each other's sex lives, with Barb requesting a heads up when I intended to bring someone home. No sock on the door kind of thing, just a casual warning. Because it was her lease, the assumption was she could entertain pretty much whenever and wherever she wanted. Since I'd lived there, Jill had been over a handful of times, and their noisy lovemaking filtered through my flimsy walls.

"Oh, hey, Carolina. I thought you were already at Ariel's for the duration," she said, removing her hand but not bothering to cover up. I'd already seen her naked plenty of times, because she seemed to prefer walking around the apartment in the altogether. "It's okay. You missed the show. My guest just left."

And then I remembered Renee's determined scramble across the avenue.

"Did you run into her downstairs?" Barb asked, standing up. My mouth had fallen open a little and I closed it with effort. I tried not to stare at a dollop of hardened wax on the fleshy mound of her breast.

I shook my head.

"You can level with me," she said. "We're adults." She flipped off the record player mid-song.

"I didn't see anybody," I said, trying to sound as blasé as I could. All I wanted was to get past her and into my cocoon of a bedroom. "And if I had, well, it wouldn't be any of my business."

She polished off the wine in a Bugs Bunny glass and smiled. "Thanks. I appreciate it. Hey, I knew this was going to work out."

I remained calm on the outside, but my blood surged. I wondered how I would ever look at Renee again. Or Gerri! As her friend, should I tell her? Or was this part of an arrangement of theirs I didn't know about? It was 1983, and on one of Barb's albums Alix Dobkin trilled, "I'm not mo-no-ga-mous any-more." I wasn't one to cast stones anyway: I'd spent as much time as I could pleasuring my married professor.

Barb picked up the wine bottle and inspected the level. "You want some, Carolina? There's a Foghorn Leghorn glass in the cupboard that would suit you just fine. Go grab it, and I'll throw on a shirt."

I ended up not going to Ariel's that night, leaving a message on Gerri and Renee's machine that I'd been held up at work. Barb and I polished off the Chianti, and then she brought out beer and a pipe. My second experience with pot wasted me right out of the gate. To get my own weed, Barb advised, I just had to go to Washington Square and listen for the guys muttering "sensi, sensi" under their breath. I could score a nickel bag on my lunch break.

"But it's not real sensimilla," she pointed out. "That shit's rare. I had it during the summer I spent in San Francisco. It doesn't have seeds. This stuff is loaded with them. Still, you can get pretty fucked up for five bucks."

It wasn't long before we were rummaging through the fridge and the cupboards for anything edible, even though I'd had ample food at Eli's. In desperation, Barb found a takeout menu and called out for Chinese. While we waited, munching from a bag of Doritos, I worked up the courage to ask questions.

"So, does the wax hurt?" Her shirt had fallen open a little in our kitchen search, and angry red blotches covered her chest.

"You never tried wax?"

I said I hadn't, but maybe she already guessed I was a sexual novice. I'd only been intimate with two women—recently the Brooklyn cop, and earlier Hallie, who had occupied my senior year. Our lovemaking had never veered toward the exotic. In what was probably our wildest time, and that was toward the end,

53

I followed her instructions and fastened her wrists loosely to the headboard with a silk scarf. But nothing we did ever hurt, and I wondered what the attraction of pain was.

"You need to get around more, Carolina," Barb said, interrupting my memory. "The wax doesn't hurt if you know what you're doing. The higher you hold the candle, the less heat. And you've got to use the right candles—none of that scented shit. I buy plain white tapers by the box at the Second Avenue Bazaar." She tugged at her shirt and glanced down at the marks on her chest. "These look bad right now, but they'll fade in a couple hours."

Barb arranged the takeout containers buffet-style on the coffee table. We sat next to each other on the futon couch, and I dug into my second dinner. Through generous bites that she hid demurely with her hand, Barb began grilling me.

"So what's your story, Carolina?" She wielded her chopsticks like a pro, while I resorted to a plastic fork.

"My story?"

"Yeah. Why don't you have a girlfriend? Seems like you'd be a catch."

My eyes got misty from all the wine and pot and beer, and I put my fork down suddenly.

"Uh oh," Barb said. "Broken heart alert."

I wiped my eyes on my paper napkin but stayed quiet, my heart rising into my throat.

"Tell Uncle Barb the whole nasty story."

I took a deep breath and let it spill out. "It's really short and not too nasty. I fell in love with a married woman, my professor, but she didn't identify as gay. The end. Now she's there—with her husband—and I'm here." There was a nasty part—the afternoon Hallie's husband, Tom, came home early and I made a dive out their bedroom window; the F-bombs flying as the two of them screamed at each other in the living room; the cruel digs Hallie and I exchanged when she ended it. I wasn't ready to share any of that.

"Straight girls," Barb said, with a knowing shake of her head. "They'll screw you every time. Literally and figuratively. I know more lesbians than you can count who've been crushed under the heels of straight chicks. You need to meet *dykes*—women who've made up their minds which fucking team they're on."

"That's one reason I'm in New York."

"And you haven't found anybody? You must be pretty picky. What's your type?"

A picture of Hallie flashed into my mind—just tall enough to nestle under my chin, a little pear-shaped. She didn't turn heads, but instead blended into the landscape like someone's aunt or sister. But she had a way of tossing her amber curls with a laugh that rippled up from her toes.

"I'm not picky," I said, knowing that wasn't true. I still wanted Hallie, but more than that, I wanted someone both to be her and to obliterate the painful memory of her. "I just want someone I can talk to. This woman I went home with on Gay Pride seemed fine at first, but then she turned out to be a freakin' cop who couldn't even understand why anyone would want to work in publishing."

Barb patted my arm in a protective, big-sister way. "We'll get you fixed up. I've been here almost six years and I swear I've met every dyke in town. Slept with a fair number of them, too. Let me think about it. I know some really smart women."

I blew my nose into my napkin and started cleaning up. I couldn't imagine why Thea had warned me against Barb, and now I realized I didn't want to.

Chapter 7

That night, I fell asleep with an empty carton of lo mein in bed beside me, although I had no memory of saying goodnight to Barb or of crawling up the ladder to my bed or of eating more food. I awoke to a grease stain on the sheets and the distant sound of a phone ringing. It took several minutes before I realized it was a real phone, my phone, not some phone in a dream or down the hall. The machine didn't pick up and Barb was making no move to answer it, so the phone whined on and on like a cranky baby.

"You don't answer your phone?"

There was no mistaking that voice, but I was unaware Bea had my new home number.

"Sorry. Somebody forgot to turn the machine on last night." The "somebody" must have been me; Barb's door was wide open and she was nowhere in sight.

"It's almost noon," Bea pointed out in a tone that suggested I was flushing my weekend—and probably my youth—down the city sewers. "Clio Hartt phoned me this morning. She says she's working on something new."

Clio had said she didn't want Bea to know about her "idea," so I was confused but played dumb. "Really?"

"She doesn't want to tell me anything about it yet. Did she mention it to you?"

I didn't know if this was entrapment or if she really was in the dark, but I continued my charade. "Not a peep."

"She wants you stopping by more often," Bea continued. "She says you calm her, and she's actually able to work after you've been there."

My cheeks felt hot at the thought that I might be facilitating Clio Hartt's artistic output.

"Now I can't spare you as much as she would like," Bea said. "She suggested five days a week, but I told her you do have a job to do for me." She paused to take a noisy sip of something, and the sound made me crave juice for my dry mouth and coffee for my fuzzy head. "Has she told you anything about her finances?"

"No!" The idea seemed distasteful, like rooting through Clio's underwear drawer.

"I was just wondering if she could afford to supplement your pay. I'll have to call her lawyer." There was another hesitation, maybe as she performed calculations in her head. "Well, never mind. If Clio is really writing a new book and somehow your presence helps that process, then I want you stopping by more often. When are you with her?"

I recited my schedule, and she added two late mornings to it. "Combine it with your lunch hour," she said. "Start bringing her lunch." She also tacked on a weekend afternoon that she'd pay an extra twenty bucks for.

"You know, Bea, she doesn't eat much. I bring her groceries, but she never wants anything but milk and bread, sometimes Cheerios or a Hershey's bar. I don't know how she does it. I'd starve."

"Well, start bringing her something tantalizing. She was talking to me about home again, so maybe some good old Southern cooking. How are your grits?"

I bragged that they were deliciously creamy, which was a lie. Not only was I a Southerner who disliked the texture of grits, but I had no idea how to prepare them.

"Eggs and grits would help her keep her energy levels up for . . . whatever it is she's doing. It's settled then. You'll start the new schedule this week."

"You mean this week as in next week, or this week as in today?"

"Today. It's high time you got up anyway." More sipping noises. "And Livvie, I will expect you to inform me about her progress. I'm paying you to babysit a legend, so part of your job is to keep me in the loop. This is as important for the agency as it is for Clio. A new Clio Hartt book would be . . . well, I can't think about that yet." There was a little shudder in her voice, like she was hearing the *ka-ching!* of bookstore registers.

"I will tell all on Monday," I finished, but I was already talking to dead air.

At D'Agostino, I located a container of "Original Instant Grits" that was closing in on its "Best By" date. The label promised you only needed to add water and cook for five minutes, which sounded like something I could handle. When we were growing up, I avoided the kitchen, except when called to dinner or taking my turn washing dishes. "You're as bad as a guy," my sister Sue complained. She, Brenda, and Gaynelle all became experts with starch and fat, and their husbands had the expanding waistlines to prove it, but my own forte had turned out to be finding the cheapest, most convenient takeout.

"Miss Bliss! What a nice surprise!" Clio said when I arrived in mid-afternoon, as if she hadn't called Bea that morning and demanded my presence. Having been there so recently, it almost felt like I'd never left. "What's in the bag?" Her face lit up like it did for the blue manuscript box, and I steeled myself for her disappointment.

"Bea said you were craving a piece of home, so—" I pulled out the grits container with a flourish. "Ta-da!"

She grabbed the cylinder from my clutches. "Oh my! I haven't had grits in years. Who knew you could buy them up here? I sincerely appreciate the thought. Would you make me some? There's margarine in the icebox."

The grits really did cook in five minutes, and I melted a plump glob of Parkay into them. Clio didn't keep salt in the apartment because of her blood pressure, so I'd brought a takeout packet

58

from a nearby deli—what were grits without the bite of salt? Clio took her first forkful of the goopy mixture and looked perplexed, as if she expected it to taste like grits.

"Well, it's not my mama's, but then it wouldn't be." She scooped up another bite and examined it before plopping it into her mouth. "Where's yours?"

"I ate already," I said, hoping she didn't hear my stomach rumble.

"You got to at least have a taste. Grits are *home*, Miss Bliss." She invited me to find a spare fork and dig in to her own helping. I would have thought that too intimate for a woman who recoiled when we brushed arms, but our shared heritage broke down her defenses.

The grits tasted like buttery sawdust, and I put my fork down after one bite. "I'm not much for grits," I said. Clio dawdled over the serving, eventually eating about a third of it.

"It was lovely of you to think of me," she said, sitting back in her chair. "It's nice to have a touch of the South. This city is a lonely place. You know what I mean by that?"

I said I did, although as a newbie I was still enamored of New York's bigness, its loudness, the helter-skelter pace. I could walk down to Christopher Street at all hours of the night and find something to eat or drink, or a store whose door was always open to shoppers. Many weekends I'd roamed on foot, taking in the city's landmarks, its colorful denizens, drinking up the atmosphere; it was nothing at all for me to stroll from the Chelsea piers to the Brooklyn Bridge. One Saturday afternoon, Gerri showed me the delights of a ride on the F train to La Papaya, a woman-owned café in Brooklyn, and I'd repeated the subway trip several times the very next day for the few grand moments when the train emerged above ground and the Statue of Liberty peeked out at me through the grimy windows.

But there were other times, too, when I lay immobilized in my loft bed or sat writing postcards home, wondering how I had ended up in such a foreign city, where many of the people I met were obsessed with the "right" things to say and do. Gerri derided the lesbians she called "The Shoe People" because they looked down at your shoes before deciding if you were worth talking to. And there were the times when I wandered to Ariel's alone, looking for companionship but finding only dancing and beer.

Clio stood up more steadily than was usual for her, and I knew the intimacy of the moment had passed. "I need to work now." It was a gruff dismissal, given how happy she'd been moments before. "I don't think I'll be wanting grits again, but I feel a rush of inspiration just the same." At the door, she tossed out a challenge: "If you happen on any pimento cheese in your travels around the city, you be sure to bring that my way."

With my weekend obligation to Clio under my belt, I knocked on Eli's door. A radio hummed from inside, so when he didn't answer, I gave it another rap.

We'd been best buddies the night before, but his manner that day was tense and testy. He hissed down toward his feet, "Get back, Remmie."

"Hey, Eli," I said, trying for casual even though his about-face was unnerving. "Want to grab something to eat? My treat this time."

"I'm in no mood to be social," he said.

"Oh, okay. That's fine. Sorry to bother you." My ears burned, but as I started backing away, his tone softened.

"Wait, Livvie. I'm sorry. There was another AIDS memorial today. Fifth fucking memorial in a month. I am so sick of hearing people read Auden poems."

"I'm so sorry," I said, although the words sounded trite even to me.

"We're all sorry," he said. "We're just one big old sorry bunch." Fat drops gathered in the corners of his eyes, and he dabbed them away with his finger. "I should go. I'd like to hang out again some time. Try me next week. With any luck, nobody else will have died." He clicked the door closed, and I heard the soft purring of Remington on the other side.

When I got back to Fifteenth Street, Barb was still not home. The answering machine's counter was blinking a bright red "2."

"Hey, Liv, it's Gerri, what're you doing, buddy? You want to grab something at Mi Chinita? Call me." Gerri's voice sounded a little too high, a little too jovial. I also noted that she didn't mention Renee, which seemed odd for a weekend night. Fridays and Saturdays, it was written somewhere in the Book of Couples, were reserved for girlfriends. I erased her first message and listened to the second, which was much less cheery.

"Hey, Liv, are you home yet? Give me a call, okay? I need advice really, really bad." There was a long pause, filled with a sigh. "It's Gerri."

"Family and friends, that's all you got," was my mother's saying. Although of course there was the glitch of what happened if family didn't understand you because you weren't a carbon copy of them, and you felt alienated from your own blood. Friends were the constant, so I picked up the receiver and dialed.

Gerri and I met at Mi Chinita, a diner on Eighth Avenue that served a combo of Chinese and Spanish food. It was the best of two worlds, where you could slurp wonton soup and munch on a side of fried plantains.

I didn't have the heart to tell Gerri I'd picked up a hot dog on the way home from Clio's and wasn't hungry. The place was empty so we nabbed a booth toward the back and ordered Cuban sandwiches. Behind her glasses, dark circles ringed Gerri's eyes.

"I don't even know where to start," she began. "I couldn't sleep last night. I almost called you, but—" She rubbed her eyes, like she was trying to stop them from leaking tears. "Have I told you I hate it that you live at Barb's?"

When I first announced that I was leaving the Parkside, that I'd found a great share, Gerri had been thrilled. But then I divulged whose apartment I was moving into, and her face clouded. "You should have asked me," she had said. "I know Barb better than you do." She'd insisted on relating one of Barb's most

61

egregious acts—how Jill, Barb's current lover, had been her roommate Jenny's girlfriend first. "I bet she told you Jenny was leaving to be a screenwriter, right?" She made the sound of a "you lose" horn on a game show. "Heartbreak city."

"Why is she still in the salon then, if you hate her so much?" I had asked.

"Thea said if we tossed her out, we'd lose Jill, too," she replied, then muttered something about Renee thinking Barb was brilliant.

Now I found myself in the awkward position of defending Barb. "Barb's not all bad," I said. "We actually hung out last night."

Gerri perked up. "You were with Barb last night?"

"Yeah, she was off from work. She had some really strong pot and we smoked it and ordered Chinese. I don't know that we'll be best friends or anything, but she acted pretty normal." The image of postcoital Barb flashed into my mind: *except for those wax burns.*

Relief washed over Gerri's face as our Cokes arrived. "Well, that's good to hear. I thought . . . well, I won't tell you what I thought." She sipped noisily. "Renee and I had this big fight, and she stayed somewhere else last night. First time since we've lived together. It freaked me out."

"Wow," I said. "Where'd she go?"

"I have no idea. She still isn't back." Our Cuban sandwiches arrived next, and Gerri just stared at hers.

"We met at Ariel's after work," she said. "She was late, as always, really out of breath and kind of flushed. And her kiss was, well, halfhearted. It missed my mouth."

Guiltily, I took a bite of my sandwich.

"So here's the thing you don't know. Renee and I aren't technically exclusive."

"I'm not sure what that means, not technically exclusive."

"It means last year we decided we could sleep with other people—with certain rules, like, no sleeping with friends. Well, Renee's the one who suggested it, and I thought it was just theoretical, you know? Like, sure, we're committed to fighting

62

the patriarchy, so wink wink, we're nonmonogamous." She sucked on her straw. "I never thought we'd actually do it. I mean, we're friends with pretty much the same people, so they'd be off-limits, and who's going to sleep with a total stranger? Besides, I thought we were happy."

The thought flashed through my mind that "technically" Gerri and Barb were far from friends, but I suppressed it.

"So she told you she slept with somebody?"

"No, I accused her of it," Gerri said. She bunched her napkin into a ball and squeezed it. "Okay, I accused her of sleeping with Barb. She screamed at me and denied there was anything going on, and then she stormed out."

"Oh, wow," I said. "Wow."

"And now you tell me Barb was home with you, so I feel like a total asshole. I need to find Renee and apologize."

I nibbled at my sandwich, not sure what else to do.

"I feel so helpless."

"Maybe she's staying with a friend. Who's that girl at Hunter she studies with?"

"Pam?"

"Yeah, Pam. You could call her."

Gerri gripped her glass. "You know, I've only met Pam a few times. I talk to her on the phone when she calls for Renee, shooting the breeze, you know, but we aren't friends." She stopped suddenly. "I wonder if 'technically'..."

"Renee wouldn't do that." The image of Renee darting out of Fifteenth Street replayed in my mind.

"She's never walked out, Liv, not even after our biggest fights. And we've had some door-slammers." Gerri hunched forward, staring at me in a disconcertingly full-on way that made me lean back in my seat. "What should I do?"

When it came to advice, I was no Dear Abby. I could listen well and express appropriate sympathy or outrage, but my only "relationship" had sputtered on and off in secret for eight months. I had no idea how real couples worked, and my crumb of guidance was a stretch.

"I'd wait it out," I said. "She'll come home. I know it's hard, but it's not like she can just leave. She'll cool down. I mean, y'all have a history."

To my surprise, Gerri nodded, taking some comfort from my tepid counsel.

I finished about a third of my sandwich, feeling full to bursting. "You should get yours to go."

"You take it." She paid ("I invited you") and excused herself to run home in case Renee called. As I waited alone for the to-go container, bile rose in my throat. I had kept vital information from Gerri, my first real friend in the city. Betrayed her, really, something I would never have dreamt of back home. Gerri had befriended me, had helped me get my job, had welcomed me to the inner circle of her salon. And why had I avoided telling her what I knew? Because I was settling in on Fifteenth Street. It was starting to feel like I could have a place there, and I didn't want to jeopardize that by giving Barb away.

On Eighth, I offered the sandwich to a homeless guy with two straggly mutts, whose homemade sign read simply, "HUNGRY."

Chapter 8

Needing to get very drunk, I fled to Ariel's like I was escaping a fire. I'd earned an extra twenty by working with Clio that afternoon, so the plan was to get so wasted I'd wobble home—maybe with a good-looking woman in tow.

The place had a dull pulse by the time I arrived. In the back room, where the dancing happened, the DJ had finished setting up, choosing "Sweet Dreams (Are Made of This)" by the Eurythmics as her opener. The steady, pounding rhythm before Annie Lennox's rich contralto burst from the speakers set my head bobbing as I waited for my shot and beer at the bar.

"Hey there," I heard, and felt a light tap on the shoulder. Thea from Gerri's salon stood behind me, although I did a double take because I didn't place her at first. When we had met at Gerri's a few weeks back, her hair was shoulder-length and braided, but now it was cropped close to her head, showing off wide-set brown eyes and high cheekbones. My heart sank a little because I didn't want to talk about the book group, or Barb, or Gerri, or lesbian literature.

"Hey, Thea. Wow, you got a haircut! Really cute." I forced some down-home friendliness that I wasn't feeling.

"I needed a change," she explained. "The extensions were looking ratty."

"Well, it suits you." I wasn't sure what to say next because I barely knew her, and I retreated into small talk. "So, fancy meeting you here."

"Yeah, imagine that, seeing a lesbian in a lesbian bar," she said in a teasing tone. "I usually go to Déjà Vu, but I was in the neighborhood and wanted to dance, so-o-o . . ."

"I guess I should get around more. I've never heard of Déjà Vu. What's it like?"

"Mostly women of color," she said. "Different music, different vibe." She flashed me a half-smile that I couldn't read.

"Well, I hope you like the music here. I just love this song." I thought that might be the end of our superficial chat, but Thea seemed to be in no hurry to move on.

"You look like you want to dance, too," she said, her smile taking over her face. "Shall we?"

I said sure, because I did want to dance and I liked her—just not in the way that I wanted to like someone. By the time she got her beer, though, the song had wound down and we stood on the dance floor facing each other. I shrugged in a goofy way, and she said, "Let's see what's up next." The DJ slid into "Walking on Sunshine" and we went with it.

I loved to dance, but once when Hallie and I danced to the radio in a motel room near Hendersonville, she had observed that I moved like a drunken penguin. Thea didn't seem to mind my stilted moves; in fact, they made her smile deepen so I exaggerated them for her benefit. She herself was more fluid as she alternated between smooth slides and quick trots. I felt more uncoordinated than usual, partly because I realized I hadn't danced with a black woman this way before. There was my friend Nikki in college, and sometimes we danced in her dorm room, but she had a boyfriend and it was all just friendly girl stuff. After a few songs, I was inwardly congratulating myself on being a broad-minded New Southerner.

The DJ started playing "Total Eclipse of the Heart," which Thea and I opted to sit out. "I'm not a very good dancer," she said, pulling a couple of chairs up to a rickety table.

"Well, you've got me beat."

"Not hard to do," she said with a laugh. I'd never known what a "twinkle in the eye" really looked like, but Thea had it. "I love the way dancing makes me feel. Kind of, I don't know, expansive."

Hallie had used to say she felt "capacious" when she moved to music. Remembering that word, which I hadn't thought about or used in months, made me miss her again, and I didn't want to, so I downed my shot, sucked on my beer, and surveyed the dance floor for her replacement. No one stood out.

"I've always been better at singing," Thea said, as my eyes scanned the room. "I sang in the choir back home."

The "home" part brought me back to the table. In my short time in New York, almost no one had talked about "back home" except Clio. It seemed like most people in the city were looking to forget they had had a "home" somewhere else. There was no trace of an accent in Thea's voice, so I asked where home was.

"Charleston. But I moved up here for college and then grad school and just didn't go back. Not yet, anyway."

"A fellow Carolinian!"

Even as I said it, I suspected we'd had different upbringings. Thea seemed so poised, so sophisticated, I pictured her with a lawyer father, a mother who'd gone to a women's college. I'd never been to Charleston, but I heard it was a ritzy town.

"I don't know about you," I said, "but it's weird for me sometimes, being the only Southern girl in the room. Like I'm some kind of zoo animal."

Thea mulled that over. "For me, it's more about being the only black girl in the room. Like at the salon."

I nodded like I understood, but I hadn't considered how being surrounded by white women might feel awkward for her, even at her friend Gerri's. The two of them had been tight since they met at a reading at Womanbooks.

"Or being the only out lesbian," Thea added. "My grad school adviser is this big ol' feminist, but she actually told me never to come out if I wanted an academic career."

"No!" I said.

"Sometimes I think, where's my place?" She stopped for a second, as if weighing how much to tell a virtual stranger, but she must have felt comfortable enough to continue. "And then here in New York, there's not just *one* place, you know? There's Barnard and the salon and Déjà Vu—" She ticked them off on her fingers. "And you got to be different people at each one, so you end up suppressing some piece of you." She'd shared something that felt big, and I held her eyes for a moment in recognition.

"I know a little bit about what you mean," I said. "Like at the salon, before you came? I laid this humongous egg when I mentioned my family going to church."

"That is such a no-no," she said, laughing.

"You know, I was in the choir, too." I lowered my voice and sang the word *Alto*.

"Nice. Methodist or Baptist?"

"Baptist."

"Me, too," she said, clinking her bottle against mine. "We are abominations together."

"You know, this is going to sound funny, but I actually do miss it some Sunday mornings."

Her eyes sparkled again at that. "Girl, you have got to be cool to sit in a lesbian bar and admit to missing Sunday service."

When the DJ played "Tainted Love," we were on our feet again and stayed there through "Rock the Casbah" and "Physical." By then, most of the women in the bar were singing along, and I could hear that Thea had a bell-like soprano that would have worked better on a stage somewhere. "Wrong key for me," she said, with an embarrassed grin.

"No, you have a great voice."

Soon I was on my second shot-and-beer combo and getting looser, singing out "Don't go around breaking young girls' hearts!" louder than anyone else in the bar. A cute blonde in strategically ripped jeans danced up next to us and purposely bumped into me. In the spirit of dance clubs, I turned toward her, mimicking her moves. When the much slower "Sexual Healing" came up in the DJ's queue, the blonde leaned over and asked me to slow-dance. But because the music was so loud, her suggestion was more of a scream than a flirtatious whisper. "Are you two together?" she asked, nodding toward Thea.

"Nah, just friends."

I looked over at Thea, whose smile now seemed more forced than before. She pointed to our table and mouthed what looked like "sit this one out."

The blonde, whose name was Wendy, was hot and needy. Within three dances, she said she was going to Miami Beach in a couple of weeks to see her grandfather and invited me along. "We could get you some really cool outfits," she said, sizing me up. "You wear men's pants? Maybe a twenty-seven?" It turned out she was an assistant buyer at Macy's with a twenty percent discount. She wasn't Hallie, or even a likely replacement, so I peeled myself away, saying I didn't get vacation days yet because I'd just started a new job. "That's it? We're done?" she asked, incredulous. Her face contorted into an unattractive frown; she hadn't planned on going home alone.

I could have gotten laid, and I was badly tempted. At the same time, I'd now compounded my guilt over Gerri with a brand-new guilt over abandoning Thea. It wasn't like me to ditch a friend like that. When I noticed Thea wasn't sitting at our table, a surge of disappointment surprised me. She'd been so easy to talk to, where Wendy had been a struggle. I circled the room, scanning for Thea's new 'do, realizing that she had been one of just a few black women in the bar.

Back at the apartment, I found Thea's phone number in Barb's address book, which sat underneath the answering machine on our kitchen counter. When she wasn't under the *T*'s, I searched every page until I found "Thea Greene" on Manhattan Avenue. I wasn't even sure where that was.

The traces of alcohol still circulating in my system made me bold enough to dial, although I was hoping for the answering machine. I thought I'd leave a friendly message apologizing for abandoning her, then asking her out for coffee. But on the fourth ring, a now-familiar voice answered. When I said, "It's Livvie," Thea was quiet for a moment.

"I thought you'd be busy," she said finally. "What happened? You strike out with the blonde?"

"She wasn't my type," I said, trying to regroup from the verbal slap.

"Oh," she said, "your *type*."

"I looked for you, but you must have left."

"Long ride uptown."

"I want to apologize. For leaving you like that. I don't do that to friends. I hope we can still be friends."

She was quiet again.

"Thea?"

"Look, I get it. The 'type' thing. Black girls are friend material, not girlfriend material. Even when they pass the paper bag test." I knew that "paper bag test" meant being light-skinned, but I had never heard anyone talk about it out in the open like that. "Believe me, that's nothing new," she continued, her tone clipped and dry. "Amazing that it still surprises me."

"Thea, I—" I had intuited her interest in me, but I hadn't let myself believe it. In the world where I grew up, a liberal-minded white girl's friendships might cross color lines at school, but those black friends wouldn't be invited home. And people of different races never dated each other unless they were looking for stares, rude remarks, or violence.

"We should hang up now," Thea said. "You'll just say something to try to make yourself feel better, and I'll get mad and try to take you down a notch, and then we never *will* be friends and someone will have to leave the salon because it'll be too uncomfortable. So let's say we'll see each other there in a few weeks, okay? Talk Alice Walker all afternoon. Keep it nice and polite, like our mamas would want it."

My hand trembled as I replaced the handset.

Chapter 9

October 1983

"Come in, come in!" Clio said, breathless. "I need to show you something." She grabbed me by the sleeve of my oxford shirt and jerked me inside her apartment, a surprisingly rough tug for an octogenarian.

"Could we open the windows?" I asked. "It feels stuffy in here, don't you think? Some air would—"

"Those old windows don't open more than a crack."

She was right. Someone had painted and repainted them so many times I could only force them up a few inches, and the exertion it took made me break out in a sweat. "This isn't good," I said. "I'll have to—"

"Forget the windows, Miss Bliss, and sit down."

I rolled up my long sleeves as Clio shoved loose papers in front of me. That morning in the office, I had reported to Bea that Clio had amassed pages of new writing, but I hadn't gotten a good look at them. I didn't want to admit yet that she seemed to be rewriting and revising more than generating new material.

Bea had got testy with me. "So get her talking!" she said, not appreciating the precarious position I was in as a lackey. "The woman likes you. Take advantage of it."

The pages in front of me were yellowed and curled at the edges, letters from various literary journals and magazines addressed to Miss Clio Hartt at an address on Rue Something.

"These will help in your search for my stories," she explained, and my heart sank a little. Bea was more interested in new work than reprints. But at least it was a better start than we'd had the week before, when Clio offered up only vague years of publication. Maybe some savvy reference librarian at the New York Public Library would locate the issues for me. "That's not all of them, unfortunately, but I'm still looking."

"Oh, great," I said.

"I thought you'd be happy. I've saved you so much work."

"I *am* happy, I am! This is great, Miss Hartt, really," I said, trying to whip up more enthusiasm than I was feeling. "How's the . . ." She looked so deflated that I hesitated to mention the new work. ". . . story you're working on? What's it called again?"

"Oh, that," she said with disdain, taking the chair next to me. "I'm working on something else now. It's called 'Madame Louise.'"

During our marathon meeting the week before, she'd derided an editor named Louise who wanted to publish her stories, and yet here she was naming a story for her.

"Is she, you know, a madam?"

Clio stared at me, open-mouthed. "Of course not! I do not write pornography! It's simply a courtesy title, like 'Miss Hartt.'" Then, after a pause: "You really should learn some French."

"So, does the story take place in Paris?" I asked, to change gears. Plus, Bea's voice was playing in my head: *Get her talking.*

"I started it in Paris, but I couldn't . . . oh my." Her voice was small as a child's who needs an afternoon nap. "I couldn't seem to see it anymore. I remember our apartment so clearly, and Sylvia's bookshop and Natalie's place in the Rue Jacob, but the city itself is fading away, Miss Bliss. I've lived here such a long time." A tingle ran up my arms as I realized she was talking about Sylvia Beach's Shakespeare and Company and Natalie Barney herself.

"Well, does it need to take place in Paris?"

She grimaced, like I'd gouged an open wound.

"Well, of course, it needs to take place in Paris! That's where we all were!"

Did the "we all" refer to just her and Flora, or someone named Louise, too, or maybe their circle of friends and colleagues? My question about Paris got her so riled I decided to hold my thoughts and make her a pot of coffee.

When I handed her a cup just the way she liked it, she regretted her earlier tone without apologizing for it. "I don't mean to be cross, but my writing goes so slowly."

"Maybe if you told me the story," I suggested. "Would that help?"

She peered at me over her cup, mulling the offer. But she finished her coffee before she replied and I sat there like an obedient servant, waiting for instructions.

"It might help," she said. "Let's see where that takes us."

Monday was supposed to be one of my "visit Clio at lunchtime" days, and I needed to get back to the office to finish typing and mailing contracts. I excused myself to use Clio's phone and dialed Bea first, but she was either on the phone or at lunch, so I tried Ramona. When I related that I would be late because Clio needed me, Ramona's anger snaked through the line.

"The typing doesn't do itself, Livvie!" she snapped. "It's stacking up. This is your job! You weren't hired to be Clio Hartt's personal assistant." Then she threw in a threat: "Bea's not going to like this one bit."

"But she's the one who gave me more hours with Clio," I said, a little snippier than I intended. "You can ask her. If she's there."

She said, "I have to go. Unlike you, I have work to do," and hung up.

When I turned back to Clio, she had fallen asleep in her chair, empty coffee cup in her lap. I got scared that she'd passed away right then and there, but when I came up right next to her and leaned in, her breath was warm against my cheek. My closeness startled her awake, and she yelped, "What on earth do you think you're doing?"

"Just . . . making sure you're OK," I said, with a sheepish grin.

"I hate to disappoint you, but I'm not dying today. Now let's get started."

It had been a year since I'd read Clio's masterpiece, *The Dismantled*, which was one of Hallie's favorite books. She and I had dedicated almost a month to it during my "Modernist Writers" independent study—a course I'd cooked up to get closer to her— as I wrestled my way through circuitous sentences, some of which went on for nearly a page. "But the language, Livvie!" Hallie had said when I balked. "These are some of the most glorious sentences you'll ever read in the English language! Forget Joyce! *This* . . . this is Modernism."

Aside from its challenging syntax, the novel's plot was a bummer. It followed the downward trajectory of an on-again, off-again relationship, in which the main character, a woman named Vivien, sank further and further into depression and alcoholism as her married lover, Marisa, had sex in turn with a man and a woman, a woman, and finally a teenaged boy. In the end, Marisa left Vivien for a mature French female aristocrat, simply known as "La Comtesse."

The sex was suggestive, not graphic; it didn't come anywhere near Henry Miller, but it was colorful enough that the novel had been banned in its day. And the prose, however tame in comparison to other books, had been hot enough to inspire me to kiss Hallie right in her office, launching our "special relationship."

Although I couldn't recall every plot twist, I remembered enough to realize with alarm that the story Clio related to me in her apartment that afternoon was virtually identical to *The Dismantled*. The only thing that seemed different were the characters' names: Vivien was now Viola, Marisa transformed into

Madeleine, and "La Comtesse" got a downgrade in status and became "Madame Louise." Hence, the proposed title.

Clio outlined the plot in detail for a full fifteen minutes until her voice rasped. I fetched her a cup of reheated coffee, which bought me time to mull over what I was going to say when she inevitably asked my opinion.

"What do you think?" Clio said, her eyes especially wide. "I know it's rough. But I think it could work. It might even be a novel. And you see now, of course, why it has to take place in Paris."

I didn't see anything of the sort, but I held that thought. "Madame Louise" sounded like high relationship drama to me—the kind of dysfunction we now sang along with at Ariel's: "Some of them want to abuse you/Some of them want to be abused." Paris served as an atmospheric backdrop, but I had no trouble imagining something similar playing out in 1980s Greenwich Village.

I wasn't sure how to answer her, but I guessed she wasn't expecting anything but praise and support. What writer wants to hear that a new story she's excited about is the same one she published fifty years earlier?

"It could work," I said, trying to keep an encouraging smile on my face.

"I'm not sure Madeleine needs to be a woman, really. She might be a transvestite. I haven't quite decided that. And I thought about making the teenage boy a dog, although I realize some people won't understand the point and I don't want it to seem gratuitous."

"What would the point be?" I said. "Of the dog?" I didn't add what I was thinking: *except to distinguish it from* The Dismantled.

"Flora's complete degradation, of course."

She sipped her coffee, oblivious that she'd said "Flora" instead of "Madeleine."

"You mean Madeleine," I corrected her gently.

Clio frowned. "That's what I said, isn't it? Really, Miss Bliss, I do wonder if you are up to this task!"

At that point, I wondered, too. And I also wondered if Bea would want me off the job, if I couldn't even tell Clio her story was soup rewarmed once too often.

But what I ended up saying was: "I'm up to it, Miss Hartt. Would you mind if I just think about your story and maybe, I don't know, offer a few suggestions?"

"What sort of suggestions? Do you write fiction?"

"No," I admitted. "But neither does Miss Winston, and she's guided plenty of authors in her day. Or look at that guy—" I fumbled to recall his name from the class in which I'd read Thomas Wolfe. "Maxwell Perkins! How he sculpted *Look Homeward, Angel.*"

The lines in her brow deepened. "You are not Beatrice Winston. Or 'that guy' Maxwell Perkins. You are a girl from the mountains of North Carolina."

"So are you," I rushed to add. "But we're both girls with a pretty good ear for a story. Why not give me a try?"

Clio nodded in a jerky way, like her head was hiccupping. "You can make suggestions, but I will probably just reject them," she said. "Remember, I'm Clio Hartt, and you aren't."

"Yes, ma'am." I grabbed my messenger bag to go. "I'll be back on Wednesday."

"Not tomorrow?"

"I need to get started looking for your stories," I said. Maybe finding some of her other work would give me ideas about what to suggest for "Madame Louise" or help steer her toward more original material.

Chapter 10

Bea appeared in the door of the photocopying room as I was stapling copies for Ramona, her hands on her square hips like a linebacker. "*Here* you are!" she said with impatience, as if we were a gigantic agency and she'd been searching for me on several floors.

My first instinct was to head off whatever offensive rush was coming my way. "I'll be back there on Wednesday," I said, "I promise!"

Her eyebrows narrowed into points. "Do you think I know what you're talking about?"

"Did Clio call you?"

"I haven't talked to her since Saturday," she said. "Should I be expecting another call? I thought you were keeping her happy, Livvie."

I explained that, instead of my usual visit to Clio's later that day, I planned to head to the Public Library to locate her stories on microfilm or in bound journals. "It might give her momentum, seeing how productive she was."

Bea nodded, her hands dropping to her sides. "Not a bad plan," she admitted. "You left me a note about some new pages she's written. Were they good? As good as *The Dismantled*?"

"Well, they're . . . similar, yes."

"What's it called? What she's working on."

Instinct told me not to divulge the "Madame Louise" title, so

I fished in my memory for the name of the other story she'd been crafting. "She only has a working title. She's toying with either 'All This' or 'The Less We Know.'"

"Not very catchy," Bea grumbled. "Well, never mind. Titles are meant to be changed. So then, just carry on as planned." It looked like she was going to leave without addressing what she'd wanted to discuss, but then her eyes flashed. "That reminds me of another bad title. Where are your comments on *Big Thunder*? They weren't in my in-box today."

It had been less than a week since the blue box with D. A. Westerly's novel in it dropped onto my desk. Either Bea thought I'd had the manuscript longer or there was another trick to keeping her happy that Ramona hadn't warned me about—do what she asks you to do immediately.

"I'm still reading it," I said. "Sorry, when do you need my comments?"

"I expected to read them today," she said. "I left my morning free for it. I'm meeting with her on Friday, so this is inconvenient. Come to my office after you finish with that copying and catch me up on what you've read so far."

"I'm so sorry, I didn't know about the deadline." Her appointment book was going to need more of my attention, since she didn't give me any clues about due dates herself. "I haven't actually read very much."

"How much is 'not very much'?"

"A chapter." I said. All I'd read were the epigraph and the first two pages. I imagined her making a mental list of my faults with "cannot adhere to schedules" at the very top.

Her lips tightened. "Get me your comments by the end of the day tomorrow," she instructed. "Don't make me regret giving you this added responsibility."

"Oh, you won't, you won't," I said, knowing I was going to have to pull an all-nighter with the manuscript, my first since college finals.

78

I hadn't seen Barb since our debauched Friday night together. She was locking the apartment door as I reached our floor after work.

"Hey, stranger," I said.

Grunting and struggling with the keys, my roommate ignored me. Her backpack was tossed in a heap on the hallway floor.

"You don't need to lock it. I'm heading in for the night."

"Fucking keys," she said under her breath as I stepped to the door. "Fucking fucked-up fucker lock."

"Yeah, it sticks," I admitted. "I'll tell Jesús, if you want." It wasn't my job to bring problems to the super because I didn't hold the lease, but helping the woman who did seemed like a good idea.

"Jesús is a useless piece of shit," she said, and I recoiled from her words. "He wouldn't know how to fix a lock if his life depended on it." The super didn't do very much around the building, it was true, but he was a sweet young guy who liked to share photos of his two chubby-cheeked babies. Now Barb gave the door a rude kick, like she wanted it to be Jesús. "I don't know how I'll get back in tonight."

"I'll be up, so just knock if you have trouble," I said. "I have to read a whole manuscript in the next—" I checked my watch. "—fourteen hours."

She retrieved her backpack with another grunt.

"You okay?" I asked. The lock seemed like one more thing that had irritated her, or maybe the final thing.

"Do I fucking *look* okay? And you . . ."

What could I have done? Against my better judgment, I had not told Gerri what I suspected about Barb and Renee.

"And me what?" I asked, because she was already trudging off down the hallway without finishing her thought. "What, Barb?"

She stopped at the head of the stairs and turned back to me with a scowl. "Did you tell Gerri anything? Did you?"

"About—?"

"About Renee. About me and Renee. About last week. Don't play so fucking coy. It annoys the shit out of me, Carolina."

"I told you that wasn't my business."

"I know what you said. But Gerri's your buddy, right? You two are tight. I knew I shouldn't trust you!"

"I don't know what you mean," I insisted, my insides twisting. "I didn't say anything to Gerri. In fact, you should thank me. I was kind of your alibi."

Her head did its collie tilt as she considered whether to believe my innocence. "What do you mean?"

"I saw Gerri the next day. She thought you and Renee had, *you* know, but I told her I'd been with you the night before. I left out the part when I wasn't with you. She seemed satisfied. So did something new happen?"

Barb sniffed and scratched her nose. "You haven't talked to her since then?" she asked slowly.

I shook my head.

"They broke up," she said. "Gerri moved out. She left you a message. Renee's a mess." Barb turned toward the stairs again and called back to me over her shoulder, her voice echoing up from the stairwell. "Don't wait up on my account. I'll stay at Jill's tonight."

Between the gulps punctuating Gerri's message, I made out that she had crashed on Thea's couch and wanted me to give her a call when I could. "I'll be hanging out at Ariel's till late tonight."

Gerri needed a friend, but the blue box beckoned. My watch read just past six, so I had some serious speed-reading ahead of me.

For the next few hours, D. A. Westerly's manuscript diverted my attention from the turmoil with my new roommate and friends. I'd had a memorable class in twentieth-century satire in college that led us through the likes of George Orwell, Evelyn Waugh, and Joseph Heller, so the style of *Big Thunder* was familiar.

The year was 2013 and the unthinkable had just occurred: Mitch Woodhead, the former star of a TV western and now the host of a popular game show, was inaugurated as U.S. president. He was Ronald Reagan II, a man who rode his horse across the

White House lawn and disappeared to his Wyoming ranch every weekend "because a fella's gotta unwind." President Woodhead's "shucks, folks" manner had won over voters, even though he'd been born and raised in Manhattan, the privileged heir of a billionaire land developer. Stupendously unprepared for office, his Cabinet included a host of equally unqualified picks, like a TV actor who had once played Thomas Jefferson for Secretary of State and a former Miss South Carolina for Secretary of Education "because she's just the prettiest little thing." Woodhead's grasp on world politics was tenuous: As one of his first moves in office, he issued an ultimatum to the country Robusta, which everyone around him knew didn't really exist but that he insisted was the United States' greatest enemy—and so assuredly that news anchors, fellow politicians, and the public soon believed him.

The novel's heroes, two freshmen members of Congress named Minnie Hanks and Bert Nowacki, were unlikely collaborators— she was a half-black, half-Korean Californian while he was a white former steelworker from Ohio. Yet together they struggled to forge a grassroots movement to eject the lunatic from office. The pages of *Big Thunder* turned quickly for me, with a plot that married the Cassandra story to "The Emperor's New Clothes."

Within a couple of feverish hours, I was more than two-thirds of the way through the manuscript. The legal pad I had poised in front of me for note-taking was almost bare. I'd scrawled, *Is the shock jock too way out there for Secretary of HUD? Not sure* and not much else. The writing hadn't tripped me up, even though Bea had seemed to think it would. In fact, I'd breezed through it, wishing the book could be in print soon enough to present to family members for Christmas. Despite ridicule, I'd sported Jimmy Carter and Ted Kennedy campaign buttons at Christmas dinner in 1980 as a protest.

"I hate to break it to you, Liv, but the election's over," one brother-in-law had said with a smirk, sending a wave of guffaws down the dinner table.

"Now, now," my father had said, pretending to tamp down the

laughter even though he could barely contain his own. "Just 'cause we have a little liberal in the family's no reason to rub it in."

I raced through more chapters of *Big Thunder*, getting closer to the climax. Although I didn't want to stop, there was the question of Gerri. Just before eleven I decided to head over to Ariel's and see if she was still there. When I got home, I reasoned, I could finish the final chapters and scrape together notes to present to Bea in the morning. With a looming deadline, I was adept at pulling off a semi-eloquent report—or at least my professors had thought so.

The smoke in Ariel's choked me the moment I walked in the door. I was used to coming home from a night out and having to toss my clothes in the laundry sack because they reeked of cigarettes, but that evening a thicker-than-usual fog permeated the front room. When I spotted Gerri and Thea at a table by themselves, an overflowing ashtray between them surrounded by empty beer bottles and shot glasses, I figured they had made a significant contribution to the haze.

"I didn't know y'all smoked," I said. "Marlboros, no less." Gerri ignored my attempted buoyancy, and Thea pretended I didn't exist.

"Where were you?" Gerri asked. "I called you hours ago."

"Sorry," I said. "Big work assignment for tomorrow. I'll be up all night, looks like."

Gerri gave the chair next to her a swift kick in my direction, almost toppling it over, and Thea excused herself to get another round.

"You deserted me," Gerri said. "Thea just got here, too. She went to hear May Sarton read."

"Wow, May Sarton—" I clipped off my words when Gerri shot me a scowl. She needed her friends, not a literary discussion. "So. What happened? You and Renee—"

"Over," she said. Her red eyes filled up. "I still can't believe it. My suspicions were right on."

After blowing her nose a few times, she outlined the events of the past few days, how Renee had come home the day after their fight and admitted that she was having sex with Barb. "Barb has 'opened her eyes' is how she put it."

I swigged my beer. "To what?"

"To sex," Gerri said. "Well, to some new kind of sex. Liv, she says she's into all kinds of stuff I had no idea she'd even thought about. Bondage. Butt plugs. Wax. I mean, she never even hinted that she wanted to try anything like that with me." She shuddered. "Not that I would. I mean, I might try a dildo . . . maybe a butt plug. But candles, for Christ's sake? That's what your mom puts on the dinner table at Christmas. What's next, dogs?" Gerri rested her head in her hands, as my mind flashed back to the proposed plot line for Clio's new story. "It's like I don't even know this person I've been with since college."

Words failed me, but luckily Thea came back with another round—for her and Gerri.

"Did you know about Barb and Renee?" she demanded, folding her arms across her chest. "I mean, you live with that woman. It would be hard not to know."

"I swear I never saw them together," I said, which was technically true. "Barb doesn't much like me. She tolerates me because she needs my rent money."

"Liv's not the bad guy, Thea," Gerri said. "She's caught in the middle." She looked at me through wet eyes. "Did you see Barb today?"

"Briefly." I related the story about the sticky lock and Barb's foul mood but left out the part where she told me about the breakup. For one queasy moment, I worried that Gerri would enlist me as a spy to tell her about Barb's comings and goings.

"Well, when you do see her, I don't want to know anything about what she's doing," she said instead. "I couldn't stand it, hearing that Renee was at your apartment, or that you saw sex toys lying around. Those two are dead to me. I have to see Renee to get all of my shit, but that's it." A little cry escaped her lips. "Oh no, how are we going to share Alice?"

"You'll make a schedule," Thea said firmly. "Joint custody, straight down the line. She can't take your dog from you, too. You can bring Alice to my place for overnighters, no problem."

It was my turn to step up to the friend plate.

"I wouldn't tell you anything painful about Renee," I assured her. "I know how that feels. Friends think they're helping you somehow but they aren't. When Hallie dumped me, people were always telling me they saw her at the mall or at some restaurant with her husband. I didn't get what they wanted me to feel."

Thea stared at me with interest. "When did it end?"

"Last April. The fifteenth, to be exact."

I suspected Thea was doing the math in her head: Six months wasn't a lot of mourning for a relationship, but in lesbian time it was an eternity not to have found someone new.

"Tax day," Gerri said with a little smile.

"It still hurts," I went on, which was true—but I also thought it might make me more sympathetic to Thea.

It seemed to work. "Mine ended ten and a half months ago," Thea admitted, as accurate a measure of time as my own. I understood why she would want to be so precise and not round up to "almost a year." "Looks like we're a single sisterhood now." We clinked our bottles. Her eyes softened toward me. Even if she couldn't forget what an asshole I'd been, maybe she'd forgive me.

But just as the mood at the table lightened, Gerri burst into a round of gulping sobs. Thea reached across the table and squeezed her hand.

"Honey, what?"

"What. Will. Happen. To. The. Salon?"

"We'll start over, just the three of us," Thea said, not missing a beat. "It'll be at my place. I have to run it by Vern. She probably won't want to join. I've never seen her read anything but comics, but we can add other people. There might be someone at school. Or maybe we keep it little."

"Little's good," I said.

84

Chapter 11

My report on *Big Thunder* was a scant double-spaced page, but well written. That wasn't much of an argument in my favor, kind of like turning in a single page for a term paper when it was supposed to be eight to ten and pointing out to the annoyed professor that at least it was grammatically flawless.

When I passed Bea's office on the way to the copy machine, I spotted her with my single sheet, her aviator glasses pushed up her nose, her head bent in thought. On my route back to my cubbyhole, I saw that Bea was, unbelievably, still reading, which didn't seem good.

"Livvie!" she called out, just as my butt hit my desk chair. "My office, please."

It was hard to read her face, which bore a strange look of neutrality. In my limited experience with her, Bea was always one way or the other.

"Sit." I waited for the announcement of my failing grade. "You read that fat manuscript in one night?"

"Into morning. I'm a fast reader when I focus. And you told me you wanted the report today." I had a sinking feeling that maybe I'd misunderstood her directive and was about to be chastised for reading too quickly and not critically enough.

"I did." She removed her glasses and set them on top of the page. "I like this report," she said, and my stomach did a happy dance. "Concise. You haven't wasted my time. Ramona and Nan repeat themselves sometimes, and Therese—" She made a fluttering motion with her hand that I knew, from photocopying Therese's letters, meant her writing rambled. "But you come directly and eloquently to the point. Very un-Wolfe-ian for an Asheville girl."

"Thanks for the assignment," I said, feeling myself color at her compliment. At the same time, I was bracing myself for a "but" with my hands clutching the arms of the chair.

"I'm not a fan of satire myself," she said. "Yet I appreciate it when artists display a talent for it. Sinclair Lewis's *It Can't Happen Here* made a big impression on me when I was young. About the rise of American fascism. Do you know it?"

I said I didn't, although I'd read *Babbitt* in college, like everyone else.

"I met his wife once," she went on. "Dorothy Thompson. A great journalist in her own right. She passed away soon after I started this agency or I would have wooed her as a client."

I smiled and nodded, wondering where her thoughts were leading.

"Now Diane is no Sinclair Lewis," Bea said, confounding me: Who was Diane? "But *Big Thunder* is, as you point out—" her glasses slid back on, "— 'a worthy addition to the genre of political satire.' And that's been the domain of male writers for too long."

"Diane," I realized, was D. A. Westerly. To me, initials hinted at a male writer—which was likely why the author had chosen that route.

"When people find out the writer's Afro-Korean-American, well, we could shake up the status quo and turn this town on its head." Bea's face glowed, like she was already planning the interviews and publicity. I'd seen a similar sparkle when she thought about a new volume from Clio Hartt, but I'd mistaken it for simply smelling book sales in the air. In fact, Bea Winston cared about the success of women writers because they were women.

"Oh, and by the way, Diane had to cancel for this Friday," Bea said as I was leaving her office. The cancellation meant I'd stayed up all night for no good reason, but at least the task was off my plate. "Put her on your calendar for two o'clock next Friday."

My calendar? "Really?"

"Yes, you'll sit in."

I didn't own a datebook, but the stationery store where I had picked up notebooks for Clio was on my walk home. My quick half-salute made Bea raise an eyebrow, but I guessed by the crinkle at the corners of her mouth that she secretly liked it.

I'd always been partial to libraries, the older and grander the better. I went into mourning when the original Pack Memorial Library in Asheville, a 1920s-era edifice built with tile and marble, was replaced in the 1970s with a shiny glass cube.

The New York Public Library's main reference library at Forty-Second Street screamed "library!" In the DeWitt Wallace Periodical Room, I was comfortably surrounded by wall murals depicting publishing giants like Scribner's and Harpers.

A helpful librarian assisted me in locating the journals and magazines that had provided Clio's meal ticket in the 1920s and '30s. It turned out that Clio had been a semi-regular in *McCall's*, a monthly magazine Aunt Sass had subscribed to one year because a telemarketer talked her into it, along with *Field & Stream*. Although *McCall's* had seemed like fluff for housewives to me, it had apparently once published serious fiction by literary lights. Clio had several dozen stories published there over the course of her years in Paris, and was also a fixture in *The Saturday Evening Post, Cosmopolitan, Redbook,* and other magazines. I spent the better part of an afternoon printing her stories from microfiche, but decided I'd need a return trip to amass them all.

Reading the stories while I was printing them out offered me a glimpse into Clio's writing. She hadn't always been the darling of Modernism, composing circuitous sentences that went on for half a page, stymieing even some scholars. There was a pre-*Dismantled* Clio whose writing was sharp, pithy, and accessible to readers of popular magazines, not a maze of words you lurched your way through. That early style had more in common with Fitzgerald than Joyce. What I found particularly interesting was that so many of the stories took the North Carolina hills as their setting. The characters weren't the jaded, oversexualized sophisticates of her novel, but down-home people like many I had known myself, facing real-world problems like poverty, lack of education, and unwanted pregnancy. What had made her switch styles? Where did the author of *The Dismantled* come from? And where had the other Clio gone, and why?

When I handed Clio the pile of microfiche copies, she grabbed me by the arms and kissed me once on each cheek. "You are my savior!" she said, and my cheeks and neck warmed with her approval. She must have noticed, because she added quickly, "That's the way we greeted each other in Paris," before returning to her hands-off policy.

"They're very good stories," I said, no matter how ridiculous it was for someone like me to praise someone like her. "I especially liked 'The Gospel According to Nelle.' I have a sister named Gaynelle, and we call her Nelle. Everybody used to call her Gay, but she got touchy about it." The look on Clio's face hardened as I wandered off-topic.

"There are more than I remembered," she said, steering the subject back to her work. "This could definitely fill a book, don't you think?"

"I do." My tone was cautious, because I knew Bea was expecting something more. "Although adding some new work would be better. You know, a cover blurb like, 'Including the first new Clio Hartt stories in fifty years!'"

She tuned me out as she fanned the printouts across her desk and scrutinized them one by one. The white print on black was hard to read, and she held them right up to her nose. As she did, her enthusiastic mood dulled to an aged patina.

"Oh, this one is downright childish," she said, tossing a story from *McCall's* onto the floor in an impromptu rejection pile.

"This one, too. I can't believe I ever wrote this way." She sat down wearily. "Maybe there won't be enough after all."

"You should have Bea give them a look, once I've collected all of them," I said. "Get another eye."

"Yes, that might be a good idea."

"Have you ever thought of . . . I don't know, writing about North Carolina again?"

She often pondered my questions before replying, but this time she said, "I couldn't possibly," immediately. "I can barely remember Paris, let alone home."

"Maybe reading these will jiggle your memory."

"I find them almost painful to read. My first inclination is to rewrite them all. And that is a daunting idea, Miss Bliss."

My immediate future flashed in front of me, sitting side by side at the desk as we both got progressively older, Clio rewriting the same page over and over. "Stuck in the Middle with You" would play as the soundtrack.

"I have so little time left," she said.

"But these were published! Editors obviously liked them enough to pay you for them. And you were in great company—wow, the table of contents on these issues! Willa Cather, Sinclair Lewis, Carl Sandburg . . ."

She picked up another microfiche copy, grimacing as she scanned it. It was the Nelle story I'd praised as my favorite.

"I don't even know what the title means anymore," she said. "'The Gospel According to Nelle.' I haven't thought about church or gospels since . . . well, I don't even know really."

"Church was a big part of my life," I added, even though she rarely responded to my personal comments. "Sang in the girls' choir for eight years. It was both a comfort and an oppression, when you come right down to it."

Clio tossed me a look that said she was listening, but barely. Maybe she was formulating her own thoughts about what church had meant to her once upon a time, before Flora, before Paris.

"I mean, a lot of these stories were so interesting to me, I could have read more," I continued, hoping that at least an echo of my words got through. "A few of them would have made great novels, if you had decided to do that."

She flipped the pages of "Nelle" until she came to the end, then returned to the beginning. "Which ones?" she asked.

"The Nelle story, for sure," I said, jumping in. "When I got to the last page, I wanted to know what happened to Nelle—whether she stayed or left."

"She left," Clio said definitively, although she'd insisted she couldn't remember the story. "There was nothing for her there."

"There was no there there," I said.

"That isn't what Gertrude meant," she said with impatience. "But it is probably one of her better lines."

Soon, she made it clear that she wanted me to go, to give her a chance to mull over the stories I'd retrieved. I told her I'd be back at the library that weekend, before stopping at her apartment, to locate the rest.

"No hurry," she said. "They'll only make me more heartsick than I already feel."

She said "heartsick," but I heard it as "homesick."

Sue was the keeper of our grandmother's recipes for Southern delicacies like pimento cheese. I'd called her only once in the five months I'd been in New York, although we'd been in almost daily touch before I left. My three older sisters, especially Sue, had taken adamant stands against the move, following my parents' lead.

"Mom, it's Aunt Liv!" my eight-year-old niece, Pokey, screamed into the receiver before she let it drop to the floor.

"What's wrong?" Sue said, her breath short and ragged.

"Well, hello to you, too," I said. "Nothing's wrong. Things couldn't be better as a matter of fact."

"Damn, Liv, you scared me. My first thought was you must have been mugged or raped or something."

"And if I had been, don't you think I'd call someone who was maybe closer than seven hundred miles away?"

Sue's tone shifted from concerned to snide. "What is it then? You taking up a collection to come home for Thanksgiving?"

Thanksgiving seemed so far away, although it was a matter of weeks. Still, I hadn't considered traveling all the way to Weaverville for turkey and dressing. Gerri had mentioned an annual "misfits" Thanksgiving dinner that she and Renee hosted, and after they broke up, she talked about moving it to Thea's— or wherever she would be living by then.

"No, I'm not calling for money either," I said, sidestepping what could be an unpleasant revelation—that I was considering spending my first big holiday away from home. "I'm calling for Meemaw's pimento cheese recipe."

Sue snorted. "A *recipe*! Livvie Bliss wants a recipe! Shit, was that a pig just flew past my window?"

I explained about Clio Hartt, whom Sue had never heard of. Clio was not part of the high school literary canon, and Sue had trained as a practical nurse instead of going to college. "She's a very big deal," I said, a bit too defensively.

She left me hanging on long distance, the minutes clicking away, while she rifled through her recipe file and scolded her children. Thinking she'd forgotten me, I was about to hang up when she came back on the line, in mid-argument with her youngest: "You better have brushed your teeth by the time I get off this call! . . . So, can you even get pimentos up there?"

"It's not Mars, Sue."

The ingredients sounded like a recipe for a heart attack, but pimento cheese was one of the great pleasures of my youth, the way it dressed up even the humblest cracker. "You have some way to grate the cheese?"

"I'll improvise."

There was stern silence from her end. "You cannot 'improvise' this, Livvie, or it won't taste right."

"I'll let you know how it turns out! Gotta go! Thanks a bunch!" She was in the middle of saying "See you—" when I hung up.

"What is this?"

I was taking advantage of Bea's lunch date to type up notes on her new Selectric. My own typewriter was an older IBM that it was getting harder and harder to find ribbons for. Bea wouldn't junk it, though, because it was among the first machines she had bought when she started her own firm.

The Selectric was positioned on a typing table in a corner of Bea's office, and I didn't hear Ramona come up behind me. I jumped, sending my chair swerving.

"It has your name on it." Ramona was holding my Tupperware container of pimento cheese.

Even though Ramona had had plenty of time to warm to me, and even though I'd gone out of my way to please her—ordering extra boxes of blue pencils, springing for the occasional egg on a roll when I knew she hadn't had time for lunch—my very existence continued to aggravate her.

"Is it dip?" she asked, holding it up to the light.

"Pimento cheese." She wrinkled her nose, so I continued, "A Southern delicacy."

"Really?"

Ramona lifted the lid and peered inside, but I couldn't afford to protest, even though she looked like she might sniff it. Bea was chummy with Ramona, often stopping in her office to swap stories, and I wanted Ramona to at least tolerate me.

"It doesn't look bad," she allowed.

Apparently, she was not going out for lunch . . . again. Unlike Bea, who was always on the move at midday, Ramona worked straight through lunch. I assumed she was building her client list so slowly that her expense account just covered breakfasts or before-dinner drinks, but not lunches or dinners.

"It's for Clio," I said with a tight smile, the "put it back, please" implied.

"I wasn't going to *eat* it," she said. She clicked the Tupperware closed again and peered down at the Selectric, straining to see my notes, like the kid in school who studies and studies but still can't figure out the test answers. Her hovering could have been annoying, but I had an unexpected stab of sympathy for her.

"I'm going out to get a sandwich pretty soon," I said. "I could bring you back some chicken salad."

She shook her head like I'd suggested a bowl of Gravy Train. Her eyes dropped to the Tupperware container again. "Do the pimentos make it spicy?"

"They give it a kick, yeah, but there's also cayenne that spices it up."

"So you actually made it yourself?" She was so interested in my cheese, I wondered if she was broke. In the past, she'd offered to pay me back for food, but when I caught a glimpse of her wallet, it was empty of anything but credit cards. All her money may have gone to her wardrobe.

"From my grandmother's recipe." As much as I hated to give in, I did, because it looked like Ramona wasn't going away. "There are some crackers in the kitchen. I can let you try a taste, if you want."

"Really? Well, maybe just a bite."

I took the container from her and she followed me to the kitchen area like a hound dog. I portioned a dollop onto a cracker from a box left over from an agency open house, handed it to her, and watched her nibble at it, eyes closing like it was caviar.

"That is amazingly good," she said, when the cracker had vanished and her eyes had opened again.

I made her a second cracker.

"Really?" The girl appeared to be starving, but I wasn't sure if it was for food or something else. "What's that tang underneath?"

"Not sure what you're tasting. It might be the mayonnaise."
The word had an immediate effect, like she was considering whether to spit it out. But instead she continued chewing and asked from behind her hand, "Did you say mayonnaise?"

"I know, it doesn't sound good, but hey, it's kind of addictive, don't you think? One time when I was in grammar school, my sister Nelle and I ate a whole bowl by ourselves. Our mother was hopping mad."

She swallowed.

"Where are you from again?"

"North Carolina. Weaverville, just outside of Asheville. A tiny speck compared to New York. How about you?"

"Pennsylvania," she said, stopping short, as if to leave the specifics to my imagination. But then she continued, not making eye contact. "Pittsburgh, actually."

I handed her a third cracker with cheese, which she nibbled while she told me about getting a scholarship to Carnegie Mellon to study acting. That career choice explained why she was paper thin. I blinked hard to dispel an image of her hunched over a toilet bowl later, forcing herself to upchuck the pimento cheese.

"So how'd you get started with Bea?"

"How everybody gets a job in New York. Or an apartment. You know somebody who knows somebody who went out with somebody," she said with a shrug.

"And do you still do any acting?"

Ramona winced. "And when do you think I'd go to auditions?"

"Well, have you asked Bea? Maybe she'd be flexible with your schedule."

"Oh, Bea doesn't care," she said. From the rapport I'd witnessed between them, I knew that wasn't true, but Ramona seemed comfortable being a grouch. "She likes you better than me anyway."

"A-a-h," I said, "Mom always liked me best."

The joke could have backfired, and Ramona took a few moments to weigh the situation before she gave me the desired response: She smiled. Directly at me. A sliver of pimento had lodged in her front teeth, and I motioned to her so she covered her mouth with her hand again.

"Thanks, Livvie," she said. My name came out silky, with none of the bite she usually gave it. I didn't know if she was thanking me for the snack or for saving her the embarrassment of walking around with a pimento smile for the rest of the afternoon.

The pimento cheese threw Clio headfirst into nostalgia.

"This is as good as my Aunt Maylene's," she said. "Hers won a prize." Pies and quilts and farm animals won awards, I knew. When I was in elementary school, my Brahma chicken picked up a Buncombe County 4-H prize for Best Show Chicken, beating out much flashier birds. But a prize for pimento cheese was news to me. I made a mental note to tell Sue. "There's a jolt to it, just like my aunt's. She was a real spark plug, my aunt. Ran a dairy farm all by herself with two sons after my uncle died. She lived to be well over a hundred."

Clio ate two crackers liberally smeared with the spread and then settled into her chair with a sigh. "You bring out the Carolina in me, Miss Bliss."

That was Bea's plan. "I thought maybe it'd help with your memories," I said.

"It does take me back. But I just . . ." Her eyes brightened suddenly, like a floodlight went on behind them. "I kept a journal when I was a girl. I started scribbling into it when I was no more than eleven. I wonder if that's still around here somewhere." She surveyed her mess, and my heart sank at the thought of picking through her piles and shelves for a childhood notebook. But the light disappeared with her next words: "Actually, I haven't seen that book in years. I think I left it there. It probably got burnt up in the fire."

My hearing perked up. "What fire?"

"I told you about the fire." When I assured her she had not, she sighed again and relayed the story of the Threatt homestead burning in the 1920s. "Mama was a changed woman after that, all her photos and knickknacks up in flames." She raised her hands, as if mimicking the rising smoke.

"But no one was hurt?"

Her face clouded. "I can't talk about that," she said, and an invisible wall went up, sealing off the topic.

"You know," I started, "if the truth is too painful, you could always just make things up."

She looked puzzled, like she might never have considered writing anything not securely fastened to her own life. "What if I got something wrong about the place?"

The plaintive question made sense. A woman who kept rewriting pages over and over was aiming to get everything "right."

"If you need research, well, I could probably help with that."

Clio pondered that, then said, "I wouldn't mind another cracker."

Chapter 12

November 1983

At our apartment on Fifteenth Street, Barb had become more a visitor than a resident, and our only contact was a series of succinct notes:

"If you see Jesús, tell him the bathroom faucet drips"—an understatement given that it had been full-on running after weeks of ignoring it.

"Help yourself to the rye," which was already growing mold by the time she thought to offer it to me.

"How do you feel about blondes?"—a follow-up to our conversation of weeks back about my lack of dating action.

"Might get a message from a guy named Greg Smart. Give him this number, okay?" My stomach churned at that one, because I recognized Renee and Gerri's shared number. I deduced she was pretty much living with Renee and, more important, that she wanted me to know. And to pass on the information.

I didn't tell Gerri, though, even when she prodded me one night while we were at John's Pizza after a screening of the new feminist sci-fi movie, *Born in Flames*. "You see the Source of All Evil much?"

"Nah. Different hours."

"I just wondered if she was, you know . . ." Gerri didn't need to finish for me to get her drift.

"I honestly don't know what she's doing or even care. And you shouldn't either." Even as I said it, the words sounded callous. Who was I to tell Gerri to get over an eight-year relationship in a few weeks? Especially when I still thought about Hallie, who qualified more as an affair or fling. "Sorry," I muttered.

"No, you're right. I'm better off not knowing." She sighed. "I finally told my mom we broke up."

The statement was a marvel to me. Gerri was so out to her family, she even brought Renee home for holidays. I was a dinosaur still cowering in the closet, pretending I lived the life my family imagined for me. When Hallie was through with me, my mother merely asked why I didn't see my "favorite teacher" anymore.

"I think Mom likes Renee better than me," Gerri went on. "She said, 'I hope you didn't hurt that girl.' Like I was a heartless slob! I mean, she raised me, right? I told her it was Renee who cheated on *me*, and she went all quiet, like she didn't believe me."

In my mind, it was better to have a mother who preferred your girlfriend than a mother who rationalized that you were just too picky to find the right guy. But I said, "Mothers," like I could fathom what she was talking about.

"Thanksgiving'll be tricky," Gerri said.

"I thought you were staying in town."

"Thea got invited to her cousin's in Harlem, and she doesn't know how to say no. Vern has family in New Jersey, and I couldn't cook a turkey if you held a gun to my head. Renee was the cook."

The "misfits" Thanksgiving at Thea's was off the table then, and a stream of sadness washed over me.

"I guess I'll be spending the holiday with a rotisserie chicken."

Gerri eyed me with curiosity. "You could always go home."

At that point, *home* was a baffling word to me. I wanted it to be New York, but the scaffolding still wasn't set up. At the minimum, a sense of home required people who stuck around to buck each other up on holidays.

98

"Too expensive," I offered as a plausible excuse.

Gerri gave her plate a push, but I grabbed another pepperoni slice. In the weeks since her breakup, she'd dropped weight, her round cheeks now almost convex. Even her nose seemed trimmer, her glasses often slipping down it. When I was with her, I ate more to compensate, and all my trousers were snug at the waist.

"You could come home with me," she suggested, peering at me over her glasses.

"Where is home again?"

"Bethel. Western Connecticut."

I'd never been anywhere in New England, and the only Connecticut cities I could conjure up the names of were New Haven and Hartford. "It's not near either of those," she said, describing Bethel as "small-town."

"There's this quaint town square and everything. Old-fashioned ice cream parlor. It's cute, if you like that kind of thing."

I explained that I used to like small towns when I was growing up. As a kid, I roamed the streets of Weaverville freely, my mom rang a bell for me to come home to supper, and everybody admired my dad, who ran a hardware store in Asheville. For lack of a better word, it was bliss—but then puberty set in and there was no hiding the fact that I was different from other girls, especially my three sisters. Then there were fights with my mother about my wardrobe, my haircut, my wanting to go to college, my working at the hardware store after school when I should have been giggling about boys. No one put a name to what I was, but my first weeks in college, I finally found myself, in *Rubyfruit Jungle*, when the character Molly Bolt came right out and called herself a lesbian.

"Your family still doesn't know," Gerri said, confusion plain on her face. "Man, Liv, it's 1983, not 1963. What are you waiting for?"

"North Carolina isn't Connecticut," I said.

"And Bethel isn't San Francisco," she said. "Family's tough everywhere. Still, we do what we got to do."

I mulled that over, aware that she was staring at me, expecting something. "Maybe we should go to your folks' instead. Do some anthropological research. I've never been south of Baltimore. I take that back—once my family went to Williamsburg."

"That's not the South," I said.

I didn't want to go to Weaverville with Gerri; that would only draw more attention to my difference. Not only was I a single girl who shopped in the men's department for herself and had no apparent romantic interests, but I had a friend who was just like me. No one would say anything to my face, but polite suspicions would surface after. ("What's up with Livvie and that Gerri?" and "She's nice enough, but she looks like a man!")

"Maybe we could talk Thea into staying. We could learn to cook."

A stream of Pepsi squirted from Gerri's mouth, and she mopped it up with her napkin.

"It's not that hard to follow a recipe," I pointed out. "I made pimento cheese this week, and it was damn tasty."

"How do you 'make' cheese? You running a dairy on Fifteenth Street?"

Even I had to admit that tossing together cold ingredients for a cheese spread was no doubt a lot easier than pulling off a turkey with all the trimmings, so I relinquished the idea with a sigh.

From the third-floor landing in Clio's building, I heard ragged, dry coughing erupting from Eli's apartment.

The handful of times I'd seen him since the night he turned down dinner, he acted as irritable as an old man whose gout was flaring up. If I asked something as simple as "How've you been?" he laughed with derision: "Well, if your friends were dying left and right, how would *you* be?" He flipped the mood off just as easily as he turned it on, though. Once he took my hand tenderly and asked me to accompany him to a memorial on the weekend, but funerals freaked me out. My excuse about work must have sounded contrived because he didn't ask again.

I didn't know how to deal with Eli's anger, so I handled it like the immature girl I was, knocking on his door less, shrinking away if I heard movement inside his apartment.

But that particular day, I held my ear to the thick wood and put my eye to the peephole in vain hope of seeing in.

"What are you doing?" Clio's voice was usually chirpy when I first arrived—I hadn't done anything to aggravate her yet—but that day I'd annoyed her without even setting foot in her apartment.

"I need to check on Eli," I said. "Can't you hear him coughing?"

"Who is Eli?"

"Your neighbor? Skinny little guy with curly hair?" I pointed at the door, and the coughing ceased.

"The one with the inordinate interest in me and the Provincetown Players," she said.

"I'll just knock and see if he needs anything."

"Well, when you see fit to do your job again, you let me know." Instead of leaving the door open for me, Clio closed it with exasperation.

"Eli, you okay?" I called out. "Eli, it's me, Livvie. You need anything?" I heard groaning from inside and couldn't tell if that was his answer.

"Eli, open up. I could run to the store and get you something."

I waited a long minute and finally heard the click of the deadbolt, accompanied by a hacking cough that was now just inches from my face.

Remington slipped past Eli out into the hallway and coiled himself around my legs. Eli's cotton pajamas, with faded terriers printed on them, sagged off his frame.

"Oh, it's you," Eli said. "Go away, Livvie. I think I've got the flu. You don't want to catch it."

"I could fetch you some cough syrup. It wouldn't be any trouble."

"That won't help." He coughed into his arm.

"You need me to call you in sick?" He taught two watercolor classes at the Art Students League, but I wasn't sure how he supported himself beyond that. The first night we hung out, he said he hadn't scored a set design gig in months.

101

"They hired a sub already." I would have panicked if I lost my job, but his look was more resignation. "You know, I guess Remmie could use some canned food and a bag of litter. It's not an emergency, but maybe you could get it in the next few days, just in case. D'Ag has Friskies on sale. I'll get you some mo—"

"Don't worry about it," I said as I stooped to pet the cat. "We'll get you all set up, Mr. Remmie."

"OK, I owe you. He eats any flavor but beef. Now, seriously, Liv, run for your life." With a wan smile, he coaxed Remington back inside and clicked the door closed.

From Clio's apartment, I continued to hear the coughing. My eyes kept wandering to the door, and Clio picked up on my distraction.

"Miss Bliss, you have not heard a word I said," she snapped. "What am I paying you for anyway?"

"You aren't paying me," I shot right back. My eyes held hers in a defiance I didn't feel. Instead, my stomach was hopping like I'd swallowed Mexican jumping beans.

Shock filled Clio's face, and her lips parted then closed again. "Well," she said after a considerable pause, "I can't remember when someone's used such a tone with me. Certainly not since Flora."

"I'm sorry. I just felt worried about him."

"I didn't know you were friends with that young man. What is his name again?"

"Eli. Eli Pruitt."

In our months together, she'd rarely fished for even innocuous personal information like how many siblings I had or where I attended college. Now her eyes lit with a question.

"Are you . . . interested in him?" She didn't have to add the word *romantically*—it was implied in the tone, almost like one schoolgirl asking another about a crush.

"God, no," I said with a firm shake of my head, then threw in a frown for good measure. I considered leaving it there and letting her intuit the rest, but when I had sassed her it was like I'd already stepped off a ledge in our servant-served relationship. So I added, "Neither of us bats for that team, Miss Hartt."

She seemed to consider that for a moment, then nodded. "Does he have the disease, do you think?"

"I don't know." Since Eli first mentioned Curt, AIDS had played like the background score of our new friendship. We never spoke the acronym out loud, though.

"Well, I pray that's not it," she said. "Now, shall we get on with the work? I've been looking through the stories and trying to pick the best ones."

"Don't you want me to make you some coffee?"

She didn't answer, and so I sat next to her at the desk and tried to focus. Eventually, as she talked, I stopped hearing Eli's cough, either because he'd gotten some relief or because I'd simply become inured to it.

The reconstituted Women's Academy convened at Thea's apartment for the first time on a Thursday evening instead of Sunday afternoon. We made the concession for her roommate, Vern, who worked at a restaurant on Sundays.

At that time, I had no idea where Manhattan Avenue was and I was embarrassed to ask Thea for directions. When I exited the A train at 110th, farther north in the city than I'd ever ventured, I found myself at the tip of Central Park in a neighborhood lined with bodegas. I knew Thea worked at Barnard, so the location made sense. Rents were apparently cheaper, too, and in the break with her ex she'd kept the lease on their rent-stabilized two-bedroom.

The apartment was a palace compared to mine and Barb's. The front door opened onto a long hallway that could have passed for a bowling alley. The walls were lined with framed black-and-white photographs of Manhattan street scenes—Thea's work, I guessed. Even the ones depicting homeless people were hauntingly beautiful. Multiple rooms ran off the hallway (a "classic railroad apartment," Thea observed as she led me down the hall), and at the end was a decent-sized living room with arched windows, where Gerri had been camping out. Although

Vern's room fit only a twin bed, a bureau, a narrow desk, and her bike, Thea's held a full-sized futon with two nightstands, a comfy-looking armchair, a light table, and a dresser. And more photographs—in passing, they looked like female nudes. A separate kitchen was equipped with a round cafe table and chairs.

The salon was reincarnated as a potluck dinner plus literary discussion. "I don't read much myself," Vern said as she eyed the egg rolls I'd brought and the calzones from Gerri, "but I'd like to learn more about what Thea reads." Vern was a head taller than me, and several times wider. She had a young, honest face with flawless skin, and her eyes followed Thea around the room hungrily, like she was just waiting for the word that they could be more than roommates. *Everybody's looking for something,* the Eurythmics sang in my head. Thea treated her more like a kid sister, though, and I felt a pang of empathy for what looked like unrequited love.

"Don't put yourself down like that, girl," Thea said. "You know more about comics than anybody I ever met. Even my little brother!"

Vern cast her eyes down at the compliment. With her man-sized Knicks sweatshirt and close-cropped 'fro, she could easily pass for someone's brother.

"Oh, yeah? What're your favorites?" I asked, even though I knew nothing about comics and was unlikely to appreciate her choices.

"Red Sonja," Vern answered without hesitating. "Spider-Woman. Wonder Woman. You know. All the girl stuff. But I know about the guys, too, if you want to ask me something."

I smiled, not having anything to ask.

"Vern draws comics, too," Thea said, taking the seat next to me. Vern blinked a few times, her long eyelashes sweeping her cheeks. "With a black lesbian superhero. You know anybody who publishes comics?" Thea asked, tapping my leg lightly.

"I don't offhand," I said. "But I'll keep my ears open. What's your hero's name?"

"Jasmine Jeffers," Vern replied. "She's a line cook by day, like me, but at night she turns into Jazz, the superhero." She strung the name *Jazz* out by several syllables and spread her broad hands for emphasis. Her eyes flitted from Thea to me and back, and I wondered if she had caught the tap on my leg.

"Cool name," I commented, right before Gerri steered the conversation diplomatically toward books we wanted to tackle as a group. She'd been crashing at Thea and Vern's for a few weeks, and maybe she'd already heard a lot about Vern's comics. She had asked me recently if I knew about any shares because she was "antsy" about her living situation, but if I'd been sleeping on somebody's couch, my duffle bag stuffed into the corner, I might have been antsy, too.

During our break, I wandered into the kitchen looking for another beer, and Vern followed me. Although she fussed with some empty food containers, she cleared her throat a few times like she wanted to talk.

"I'll definitely ask around at work," I said out of the blue. "About lesbian comics. I work at a literary agency."

"Oh, yeah, that's cool, man," Vern said. "Don't trouble yourself, though." She smiled and reached past me for a can of Coke. "So . . . you and the professor?"

The non-sequitur startled me. I didn't remember telling Thea that Hallie was a professor, and I was surprised to think she might have talked about me to Vern.

"Sorry?"

"Thea. I call her 'the Professor.' Makes her smile." She smiled herself, shyly.

I had never asked Thea what she did at Barnard and stupidly assumed it was not teaching. To me, college teachers were in their thirties or forties, like Hallie, and Thea didn't look more than twenty-five or twenty-six. "I didn't know Thea teaches."

Vern frowned. "For real?"

"We're just friends," I said, although Thea's tap on my leg had stirred something in me. I just wasn't sure what. "So, no, we're not together or anything."

Vern's face lit up, and she nodded repeatedly, like she was letting the words sink in.

"You . . . are you interested in her?" I asked.

Her eyes fell to her chunky work boots, which could have easily demolished my high-tops. "Don't say nothing about it. It'd make her uncomfortable. She could've picked somebody else for a roommate, somebody from school, but we really hit it off one night at Déjà Vu. I made her laugh a lot, and she'd been pretty sad about her girl. So she took a chance on me. I mean, Thea, man—" She shook her head. "You get me?" I said I did, and we fist-bumped to our new, unspoken understanding.

After the salon, Thea escorted me back down the hallway to the door in shy silence. What had the tap on my leg meant? I knew what it signaled the first time I tapped Hallie's leg, then felt hers brush mine in reply.

"This was great, Thea, thanks," I said. "I love your apartment. And these photographs. Did you take them?"

"You like them?" Her humility was unusual among the New Yorkers I'd met, who raced to spout off their accomplishments.

"You could be a professional," I said. She bit her lip, keeping something back, like maybe she'd already sold work or had a gallery show and was too modest to say so. "This one of the homeless guy? Amazing."

"Freddie. He's a Vietnam vet. I don't think he's exactly homeless. He does odd jobs for our super and kind of lives in the basement."

We both cringed. "With the rats?"

"I don't ask. Anyway, he trusts me, so he let me take his picture." After a pause, she added, "That one was in *The Village Voice*."

"Wow, really? I'd love to see more of your work some time." The compliment made her smile.

"Well, thanks for coming and helping to keep the salon alive. It means a lot to me. And I'm glad I got you out of the Village for a change. You know, you and Gerri should get a place uptown. Not that I want her to leave or anything, but . . . I mean you're in a weird situation with Barb. Don't you feel kind of odd?"

"She isn't around much," I said, lowering my voice and glancing back down the hallway. "I think she's pretty much living at Renee's."

106

Thea took in the information. "Well, it could be worse. She could be *your* ex," she said. "Mine kept her stuff here for a month after she told me she was in love with somebody else and was planning to move in with her."

"Ouch." I shook my head in sympathy. "That's rough. You ever see her?"

"We're in touch. I had coffee with her last month." Gerri said lesbians had a tradition of keeping their exes as friends, even when the breakups were less than amicable. She had confessed to feeling guilty at not being up to the challenge, but I didn't blame her. It was something I could have never done with Hallie, even if she'd given me that option.

"Diane's a new client of your boss," Thea continued.

"Oh, yeah? Diane what? In my, um, executive function, I type up all the file labels, so I'm sure I did hers."

Thea favored me with another smile. "Diane Westerly," she said, and my mouth dropped open. "She's going by her initials for the book, though."

"Oh my God," I said. "I just read her manuscript. She's a freaking genius!"

Had a speck of something gotten into her eye? Stupid, I thought. I hadn't considered how my comment, which I meant as praise, might prick Thea's feelings because a "genius" had dumped her.

"Well, at least in her writing," I added quickly. "She was a dumbass to let you go."

That brought the smile back. "I know I should stop seeing her. I must be a masochist or something."

"No, you're a good person," I said. "Way better than me. I can't stomach the thought of seeing Hallie. I'd throw up."

Thea nodded quietly, then opened the door for me. "We should hang out some time," she offered. "Go to a reading or a concert. You're not so bad after all."

On the long subway ride home, I replayed the backhanded compliment several times in my mind and the way Thea's eyes took on that twinkle when she said it.

Chapter 13

Diane Westerly's femme appearance caught me by surprise. She showed up for her meeting wearing a clingy skirt and frilly blouse dressed up with gold chains. Chunky hoop earrings caught on her braids. Her heels made her just a few fingers taller than by gangly five-ten, but she somehow towered over me.

In the reception area of the agency I reached for Diane's hand, wanting to appear confident although I didn't feel it. Her gaudy domed ring bit into my fingers, but I held the handshake as I jumped nervously from sentence to sentence as if they were track hurdles. "I'm Livvie Bliss. Thea's a friend of mine. From the salon? You must know Gerri, too. Thea mentioned she had a friend with this agency and I asked her who. I just loved your book. Minnie is such a great character. Can I get you some coffee?"

Diane's eyelids fluttered with confusion, and she extracted her hand from mine. "No, thanks. Is Bea available?"

"She is! She's expecting you. Right this way."

When I dropped into the seat next to Diane in Bea's office, the author seemed more befuddled, clearly wondering why the coffee girl got to take a meeting with a client.

"I asked Livvie to read your manuscript," Bea explained. "She's been working with Clio Hartt. She had some astute comments."

Diane nodded haltingly, letting it sink in that I occupied a rung somewhere above go-fer but below agent. We both turned our focus to Bea, who proceeded to outline some changes she thought would tighten the plotline. Diane nodded agreeably at each one, but her hands tightened on the arms of her chair as Bea posed my suggestion about deleting the HUD secretary, who didn't seem to serve much purpose.

"That cut isn't an option," Diane said, raising her chin a couple of inches. Although she was talking to me, she didn't glance my way. "You don't understand his purpose."

"I guess I don't," I said, catching Bea's eye. The boss's expression told me to let it go.

"You'll make that decision, of course," Bea concluded. "We're here to give you guidance, not dictate changes."

Bea proceeded with a detailed "plan of attack," as she called it, for finding a publisher, which included an exclusive first look to Sarah Marcus at Random House, Gerri's boss.

"If Sarah doesn't want it, I'll eat it," Bea said. "She's all about timely, and she's all about women writers. And exquisite writing, of course." An image of Bea stuffing paper into her mouth flashed into my mind, and an audible little snort escaped my lips. Diane turned toward me with a snarl in her eyes.

"I'm sorry, that wasn't about your writing," I scrambled to explain. "I loved your novel. I just got this funny picture of Bea eating the manuscript—" That excuse made me sound like a six-year-old giggling over a fart joke, and Bea raised her eyebrows.

"Livvie, why don't you get us some coffee?" she suggested, chopping me back down to the receptionist Diane originally mistook me for.

Banished to the kitchenette, I fumed over my humiliating dismissal, which I'd brought on myself with one stray snort. "Dope," I muttered. "Stupid hick."

Making matters worse, less than an eighth of an inch of coffee remained in the pot, stewing into sludge.

"I mean, you could at least tell me it's almost empty!" I complained to no one as I muscled the pot clean.

I'd been at the task several minutes when I felt someone's presence behind me and turned to see Diane filling the doorway.

"Is this the way to the ladies'?"

"No, it's across the hallway. You need a key." I pointed to the rack of restroom keys on the wall, but both keys labeled WOMEN were missing. Clients were always leaving the keys in there by mistake, and I was always having to call the building manager to retrieve them.

"But it looks like a couple of people are already using it," I continued. With the pot finally scrubbed, I spooned grounds into a filter and switched on the machine. "Sorry you have to wait. Fresh coffee will be right up."

"None for me. As I said before." She fingered one of her chains. "Could you knock on the restroom door?"

"Whoever it is will be out in a minute." I stared at the coffee-maker, willing it to finish its sputtering.

"Look," Diane said after a ticklish pause, "I don't know what Thea told you, but there's two sides to everything."

"I don't know what you mean," I replied. She had moved a few steps closer to me, and her mere proximity felt intimidating. "Thea didn't gossip about you. She just told me your name. Sorry if I gave that impression. The only thing I know about you is that you're an amazing writer." I flashed her a smile, which she returned hesitantly but with a look of relief.

Nan arrived to replace the restroom key and glanced from Diane to me and back again, sensing she'd stepped in something. "You're D. A. Westerly, right? Nan Berger. Your novel does indeed sound amazing, like Livvie said. Can't wait to read it."

The coffee finished brewing with a spurt. I poured a cup for Bea and slid between Nan and Diane to deliver it. In my office, I considered the bizarre scene that had just gone down between me and Diane, and how Bea would likely take me to task for my perceived rudeness to a client. Clearly, my meeting skills needed work. I wondered, too, what Thea had seen in the diva—and more, why I cared.

I caught a glimpse of Diane when she returned from the restroom, scuttling past my open door toward Bea's office. Maybe I was mistaken, but her eyes looked puffy, like she'd had a little cry.

Approaching the gate of Milligan Place for my Friday afternoon with Clio, I flinched at the sight of an ambulance and a patrol car double-parked on Sixth Avenue. An officer held the enclave's gate wide open, while two paramedics hauled a stretcher down the front steps of Clio's building. My heart flapped in my chest.

But the figure under the blanket wasn't Clio. Eli's face had a spectral cast that made me worry he was already dead.

"Eli!" His eyes flickered open.

"Please step back, sir," one of the paramedics addressed me.

"I know this man," I explained as I walked alongside the stretcher. "Eli, it's Livvie. Is there anyone you want me to call? Something I can do for you?"

"Remmie," he said through cracked lips. He swallowed with difficulty. "Super has the key."

"Of course! Don't you worry a minute about him!"

I watched helplessly as they slid him into the ambulance and sped off. The middle-aged super stood in the doorway to Eli and Clio's building, a silver carabiner of keys dangling from his belt. He shook his head.

"Damn shame," he said. "Nice kid. Shitty luck."

"I need to check on Eli's cat. Take care of him till he gets home."

He shook his head again. "Ah, I bet you twenty bucks that boy ain't coming back home." The wager on Eli's survival chilled me, but I nodded so he'd let me into the apartment.

The place was littered with crumpled clothes and empty bottles of cough syrup. The shades were drawn and the room was dark, making it hard to locate the little black cat. He was hiding under the bed, traumatized by his person being taken away.

"Hey, Remmie," I said, coaxing him out with a bag of salmon treats I'd picked up along with the canned food.

When Remington was calmer, I looked around for some way to transport him and his other accoutrements. He'd need bowls, a litter box. On the floor in the apartment's only closet sat a mini-crate that he hissed at, until I sweet-talked him in with the help of more treats. I worried that Clio wouldn't like the extra visitor, but I had promised to return the keys to the super posthaste.

Remington and I knocked at Clio's, my arms full of his supplies, and I heard her grumbling from behind the heavy door. "More disruption!" She looked at me like my arrival was unexpected rather than late. "Oh, I lost track of time," she said. "This building has been like Grand Central Station today! What is all this? Are you moving in with me, Miss Bliss?"

We stepped inside, and I deposited the crate and litter box next to the door. "I hope you don't mind the extra company," I said. "Your neighbor, Eli? The commotion was him being taken to the hospital."

"Well, I know that. I saw the whole thing through the peephole." She squinted at the crate. "Just what do you mean by 'extra company'?"

"His cat," I said. "Remington. He just ate a bunch of treats, so I hope he'll behave while we work. But I'll leave him over here in case he gets noisy."

Clio leaned down to get a peek inside the kennel. Remington was huddled against the side, meowing. "You can let him out," she said.

"But what if—"

"I said, you can let him out," she insisted.

"That would be great," I said. "He doesn't like this crate much. Some mistreatment when he was a kitten."

I'd never seen her interact with anyone but me and the cops, so it was a surprise when I unlatched the kennel gate and Clio bent to offer Remington her fingers for sniffing. He took a few whiffs, then sidled up to her, brushing against her ankles. I was nervous that he might trip her, but she remained steady and unperturbed, even bending over to scratch his tiny head.

"We had cats when I was a girl," she said. "Right up until I came to New York. And Flora had Diamond, but he died before we left for Paris. He was a tuxedo, too, but the white on his chest was so perfectly shaped! This one looks like he didn't button his dinner jacket right." She scooped Remington up to her chest and he didn't resist.

"Did you ever have another cat?"

Her voice caught a little. "Our homeplace cats didn't get out in the fire," she said. The information both answered my question and didn't.

"How many were there?"

"Three," she replied without even having to stop and count. "Taffy, Roscoe, and Beebee. Plus the hound dog, Pepper. I could see one animal getting trapped, but four?" Her steely eyes held mine. "I come from careless people."

I wanted to push her further, ask if that was why she stopped writing about North Carolina. There had been two tomcats described in detail in the Nelle story I'd read. But Clio had moved on from the bad memory, placing Remington gently on her armchair on top of a crocheted afghan. "I could watch him for the young man," she said, more to Remington than to me.

"That would be great. I'm not sure I can have pets at my apartment, and I was wondering where to take him." Thea had crossed my mind, partly because I needed an excuse to call her.

"I see you brought his litter box, but do you have food for him? He's such a little bitty thing, really."

I unpacked the Friskies cans, along with two metal bowls I'd brought from Eli's. Clio set them up in the kitchen, filling one with fresh water, and then disappeared into the bathroom with the litter box.

While we hunkered over Clio's desk, Remington settled in and snoozed. Every so often, I glanced over my shoulder and caught him staring at us, making sure we were still there.

"I've written a new story," Clio announced when I arrived Saturday afternoon. Her face lit with a girlish smile.

My eyes popped open. "You wrote a whole story?"

"Most of one," she said. "Maybe three-fourths. It's like the cat is my muse!"

113

"That's terrific, Miss Hartt! I'm so happy for you."

Remington was nibbling at his lunch in the kitchen, looking as comfortable as if he'd been raised there and not across the hall. The familiar layout of Clio's apartment must have helped him adjust.

"Do you think . . . What was his name again? The young man who's sick?"

"Eli." He'd been at the top of my mind since yesterday, and I intended to try to locate him at St. Vincent's after my visit with Clio.

"Do you think he'd sell me his cat?"

The question both startled and bugged me. Eli might be dying, and all she could think about was keeping his cat.

"I'm going to try to find him at the hospital, but I'm not sure where they took him," I said, tamping down my annoyance. "The cat . . . Well, from the way Eli looked, I don't know if he's ever coming back. Let's just cross that bridge when we come to it."

She nodded. Her face had darkened when I alluded to Eli's possible death.

We moved to the desk and she touched what looked like fresh pages of writing in the schoolgirl handwriting I'd become so familiar with.

"Wow," I said. "Can I read it?"

"Not yet," she said. "As a matter of fact, I don't need you today, really. You go find your friend."

Chapter 14

Turning on my Southern charm didn't get me far at St. Vincent's Hospital. The face of the woman on duty at Patient Information looked pinched, as if she'd been out late the night before and was barely holding it together on Saturday afternoon. She was clearly in no mood for a visitor who claimed to be a "family friend" but struggled with the patient's last name.

"Pruitt. P-R-U-I-T—" I hesitated. "T?"

She scanned the P's. "There's no Eli Pruitt here."

"Are you sure? Admitted this afternoon?" I paused, unsure how much information to give. "He might be an AIDS patient."

Her face softened a little, and she checked the patient roster again. "Nope."

"Maybe I'm spelling his name wrong. Is there another way to spell Pruitt, maybe with just one T . . ." I glanced at her name tag. ". . . Miss Eckhart?"

Her finger ran down the page again. "I'm telling you, there's nothing." She cut me off just as I was about to ask about variants on Eli, like Elijah or Elias. "Nothing even resembling it. Seriously, how close friends can you be if you aren't even sure how to spell his name?"

I slumped against her desk. "Look, we *are* friends, but I haven't known him very long. He asked me to take care of his cat. I don't know how to find him or when he's coming back. I'm worried about him. He looked really bad, and if something happens to him, I don't know what to do about his cat."

"If I were you?" she said, her eyes shooting behind me where a small line had queued up. "I'd stock up on cat food."

"But where else would they take him?" I protested, my voice rising. "He lives on Milligan Place. Wouldn't the ambulance bring him here?"

Miss Eckhart sighed. "Hard to say. Call Downtown Hospital. Or Beth-Israel. Maybe his family uses another hospital. He could be anywhere."

I was just about to protest that he was from Massachusetts, so was unlikely to have a family hospital in New York, when she called "Next, please!" to the person behind me in line.

The sounds of Ferron singing reached me from the landing of my floor, which meant Barb was home. But I heard another voice, too, a slightly higher-pitched one, and I realized as I approached the apartment that Barb was singing along with "Ain't Life a Brook"—one of the most wistful breakup songs ever. I'd played it again and again one evening when I was alone, thinking about Hallie and intent on wallowing.

"For wasn't it fine?" Barb sang as I clicked my key in the lock. She was on the futon couch, her eyes closed, a pint of Wild Turkey open in front of her, and she was holding her Bugs Bunny glass of bourbon so tightly it looked like she wanted to crush it.

"Hey," I said, and her eyes popped open, red and strained.

"Oh, hi," she said, lifting the needle from the record and sniffling away her tears.

"Don't turn it off on my account. I love that song. I almost wore it out one day when I was blue."

"Okay," she said, returning the arm to the record.

The less I knew about her love life, the better, because then I wouldn't have to lie to Gerri. But Barb's sadness spilled right out into the room before I could make it to my own space and close the door.

"Women," she said. "I don't know why I bother."

I nodded, as if in my limited experience I knew anything at all about women.

"I guess you need the eggs."

She tilted her head at me in that way she had, then smiled when she caught the reference to *Annie Hall*.

"Take my advice, Carolina. Never date two women at once. I thought I could handle it, but it's a bitch. Three is a more manageable number—spread yourself thinner."

Her logic made no sense, but I nodded again and inched toward my bedroom door.

"Want a shot?"

I did. The search for Eli had led me to the other two hospitals Miss Eckhart had mentioned, with no luck. He'd been to so many memorials, I wondered if there was anyone left from his circle to visit him—wherever he was.

As we sat together on the futon, Ferron crooned, "But life don't clickety clack down a straight-line track..."

"Ain't that the truth," I said.

"You too?"

I told her about combing downtown Manhattan for Eli, but the story made no impression.

"I never heard you even mention him."

"We were just getting to know each other," I explained. "The whole thing rattles me. AIDS. If that's what he has. I hope not." I examined the liquid in my Foghorn Leghorn glass. "You know anyone who's got it?"

She shook her head, gulped back her shot, and poured another. "I don't hang with the boys. I had two brothers, and that was plenty of men for one lifetime."

I pondered that pronouncement, wondering how you could completely cut off men—unless you lived in a separatist colony.

"It's so sad if he's *sick* sick," I continued. "I mean, he designed the set for *Christopher and Wystan*!"

"Who did?"

"Eli." She looked confused, like she'd already forgotten his name. "My friend."

She sniffed derisively. "Jenny actually spent money to see that. It sounded like the usual gay-boy crap to me. Not a single woman character, just a bunch of pretty boys strutting around the stage. But of course, that's what gets produced."

The topic must have bored her, because she sang along with Ferron for a few lines. Then she switched the subject to elaborate on her pain. "I had two fights in two days—can you believe it? Yesterday with Jill, and today with Renee. Jill said we're done. After four months! No more sharing for her. She wants to be somebody's one and only."

"Sorry," I said.

"Looks like I'll be around here more. You've had the place pretty much to yourself." She swigged her shot. "You know, four months seems to be my record for relationships. What's up with four months?"

I shrugged. "Maybe it's when things start to get real."

"Maybe. Anyway, something about me drives 'em away at that point." Her hand shot out in front of her, mimicking a car zooming off down the road, and her words sounded slurry. "What do you think it is, Carolina?"

"Hey, don't ask me. My record's less than a year, and we were more off than on." Along the way, I'd lost count of how many times Hallie had said, "I can't do this anymore," only to change her mind days later.

Barb refilled our drinks, even though one was plenty for me before dinner. Loosened up, I asked, "So . . . what happened with Renee?"

"Well, that was fucked. She started talking about Thanksgiving and maybe we should go to her folks in fucking Chappaqua, and, well, that whole parent thing is just not me. She kept saying her folks were cool and all, but, I mean, we barely know each other and I'd be there using the same toilet as her kid brother. We had this monster fight about it, and she said she needed space. Space! Already!"

It did seem incredibly fast, no more than a month by my calculation, but then they'd been practically living together. "You know, she was with Gerri for eight years," I noted. "Maybe it was just too fast. Getting together like that."

I expected Barb to balk, but she nodded and kept drinking. "She and Gerri used to see each other's families and shit. She's on a first-name basis with Gerri's mom. I don't get it. Like they're trying to mimic straight couples or something. Girls like that even talk about 'marriage' after a while."

"You mean a commitment ceremony?"

"Yeah, that." Although her tone was laced with disdain, there was something like regret in her eyes, almost like she wished she could be more into the stuff other couples gravitated to.

"Maybe you two are just not a good fit," I offered, already thinking maybe I could run out to a phone booth and call Gerri, give her the promising update.

"Oh, no, we fit. Believe me. I give this needing space thing a week. She'll miss me too much." Her face lit with a lascivious grin that told me more than I wanted to know about their sex life. When Barb resumed singing, I realized her melancholy must be for Jill. "I sold the furniture/put away the photographs . . . But wasn't it fine?"

I picked up enough food to last Remington for a month and a toy mouse stuffed with catnip. On Clio's floor, Eli's door was slightly ajar, and I knocked three times before peeking inside. A young woman who was a carbon copy of Eli, with a halo of curly brown hair and a sizable diamond ring on her left hand, was packing his possessions into boxes. She didn't hear me come in, and when I said, "Excuse me," she let out a high-pitched squeal.

"I am so sorry!" I said. "The door was open, so—"

"Oh, my God! I can't believe I left the door open. Total ditz, right?"

"Nah. A lot of these old buildings have funny locks. Maybe you thought you closed it, and it popped open again."

"That's kind. No, I'm a ditz." She seemed to realize then that there was a stranger standing in her space. "I'm Melissa, Eli's sister. And you're—?"

"Livvie. A friend. He asked me to watch his cat when he went to the hospital."

With that, she exploded in sobs. "Remmie! Oh, thank God! I couldn't find him! I thought he got out somehow. I'm so—" She broke off abruptly and sank onto the floor next to the box she was packing, leaving me to fill in the missing emotion.

"Is Eli moving out?" I asked slowly.

"He's going to live with me for a while," she explained. "He's pretty fragile, and there's nobody else to take care of him. I'll just try to keep him comfortable for a while, like he did for Curt."

The words "for a while" and "like he did for Curt" suggested such finality, they hit me like a swift jab. "I'm so sorry," I said, but the sentiment rang pathetically hollow. "What can I do to help?"

"I don't even know what to do myself. I was supposed to get married in January and move in with my fiancé. I can't do that now." She motioned toward the boxes. "Then there's all Eli's stuff. There's no room for it at my place. Most of it was Curt's, and his family wrote him off when he got sick. Would Goodwill take it, you think?"

As she rambled, I picked up some flat boxes and assembled them for her. She told me her apartment was on the Upper East Side, close to where Eli and Curt had lived. It turned out Eli was at Lenox Hill Hospital, which explained why I couldn't find him.

"You know," I said, "if you don't have room for Remmie, I'd be happy to keep him for Eli."

Her face glowed like I'd given her the best present ever. "Would you, really? He's a cute cat, but I'm allergic. Plus, the fur wouldn't be good for Eli. Thank you, thank you, Libby."

I didn't bother to correct her.

When I saw Melissa again at the end of the week, Eli's place was nearly empty. Her fiancé had taken charge and gotten Goodwill to haul his furniture and kitchen items away. "I can't thank you enough for Remington," she said. "I really thought I was going to have to live in misery with a cat!"

"Um, what are you doing about the apartment?" I tried to sound casual, but she was a New Yorker, too, and would probably guess my ulterior motive.

"Subletting," she said. "Eli doesn't want to let go of a rent-stabilized place."

"I know someone who'd love to sublet," I said. "She's super responsible. I can vouch for her. What's the rent?" Gerri was actively looking, but had run into the same problems I had a few months back—rising rents, ridiculously small shares, too many New Yorkers willing to grease someone's palm to go to the head of the line of potential renters.

"I'll talk to Joe. Eli's got no income now, so we'll have to consider that." That was another problem Gerri had encountered—lease-holders who subsidized their income by subletting at several times the actual rent.

It turned out Melissa and Joe weren't greedy, although the six hundred they were asking was probably a markup. It sounded exorbitant to me, since my share at Barb's was just under two hundred. But Gerri said it was doable if she watched her restaurant and bar budget and didn't buy any new jeans, sneakers, or albums . . . ever.

Thea, Vern, and I helped her move in right before Thanksgiving. Vern did most of the furniture lifting with ease, and Thea took the stairs nimbly, but I puffed and panted up the three flights with Gerri's seemingly endless boxes of books.

The convenience of having a friend move in right across the hall from Clio appealed to me. I looked forward to being able to knock on Gerri's door and hang out whenever I finished up my Clio responsibilities for the day.

"You could have kept this place for yourself," Thea said while the two of us took a soda break. "Anybody would have understood that. It's really cute."

"Ah, Gerri needs it more than me," I replied. "I may not like Barb that much, but my living situation is okay."

The truth was, I still carried the guilt of not being upfront with Gerri about Barb and Renee; I'd succumbed to the peculiar indifference of New York. The new apartment served as reparations for something neither Gerri nor Thea knew I'd done.

"You're a good friend," Thea said, squeezing my forearm and letting her hand rest there for a moment.

The word "friend" felt like a segue into the subject of Diane. "You know, speaking of friends, I met Diane. Your Diane."

"She's not my Diane." She polished off her Coke quickly. "At the office?"

"Yeah, she came in to meet with Bea, and I got to sit in for a while." I swigged at my own soda. "She's kind of a diva."

Thea laughed out loud. "*Kind* of?"

"She actually wanted me to find the bathroom key for her and be her attendant."

Her face scrunched up.

"When she heard I knew you, she kept asking me what you told me about the breakup, like she was the focus of everyone's gossip. You hadn't told me much, so it felt weird." I bit my lip, wondering how much to divulge, like my suspicion that Diane had cried in the restroom. "She's pretty and all, and a good writer, but honestly? You deserve better, Thea." I rarely said her name out loud, and I liked the way it rolled off my tongue.

Thea cast her eyes down in a bashful way. Where the conversation would have gone after that was anyone's guess, but we didn't get to find out. Vern arrived, sweating like a dock worker as she lugged in Gerri's new futon mattress all by herself.

"You two ever plan to work?" she asked, dropping the mattress in the middle of all the boxes. Vern gave me a look that said she didn't believe for a minute there wasn't something going on between me and "the Professor."

"We're on it," Thea said, heading back down to the U-Haul for another box.

Chapter 15

With Thanksgiving creeping up, I faced a hard decision: Was twenty-three old enough to spend a holiday away from my family? If I decided it was, would I regret it on the day, when I had nowhere to go? On the one hand, I hated missing my mother's dinner, the expectant, hungry looks at the table as we passed bowls of cornbread stuffing and candied yams. On the other, I dreaded having to dodge everyone's questions and feeling the yawning loneliness of keeping secrets.

In the end, New York won out, a choice that brought sniffles from my mother and crisp coolness from Sue.

"Oh, that's just *sad*," my sister said. "Like you're some kind of derelict with no home." How could I tell her that home wasn't really a comfort?

A quiet day on my own awaited me. Barb had caved and agreed to dinner in Chappaqua after she and Renee reconciled (within a week, as she predicted), so once again I had the apartment to myself. My plan was to pick up a rotisserie chicken on Wednesday, then enjoy a holiday of sleeping late, wandering over to the Macy's parade, reading *On Strike Against God* for the next salon, and bringing a plate of food to Clio.

But at the last minute before Ramona cut out early on Wednesday, she poked her head into my office, surprising me with a friendly question: "Hey, Liv, what are you doing tomorrow?"

I outlined my agenda, which made her fall back into her snooty mode. "Nobody who lives in Manhattan *ever* goes to the parade," she said. "Just like nobody who lives here goes to Times Square for New Year's. It's all tourists and BATS."

"Brats?" I said, picturing gangs of small children.

"Bridge and Tunnel Set," she said, sighing at my naiveté. "New Jersey-ites, Long Islanders."

"My sister is pissed at me for not coming home, so I thought I'd send her pictures of the floats. She loves the Macy's parade."

"So just go to West Seventy-Ninth tonight. They inflate the balloons up there."

"Wow, thanks." A behind-the-scenes look seemed like something that would really tickle Sue.

Ramona dropped a card onto my desk. "And . . . if you're interested." It was an open-house invitation, the kind you might buy at Hallmark, with a cascade of colorful fall leaves down the side. I hadn't known till then that she lived in a prime block of Gramercy, just across the park from where I'd roomed at the Parkside.

"Swanky neighborhood," I commented, thinking that a high rent plus a closet crammed with clothes explained her perpetual lack of money.

"I adore it! I've been there a few months. I was in this hovel on Twenty-Fifth Street for three ghastly years. Almost in the East River. Then one of Bea's clients relocated to London and agreed to sublet to me. I couldn't believe it!"

"Lucky."

"Anyway, come. If you want." The hesitation in her voice touched me. "It isn't a *meal* meal. There'll be turkey, of course, but then everybody's signed up to bring a side dish or dessert. Nan and Therese are in, and even Bea said she might show up. I thought you could make that pimento dip. It would be a novelty for all the Northerners."

After she mentioned the pimento cheese and the other agents and Bea, I figured my attendance wasn't optional, but part of me was relieved to be included. Ramona's party might counter whatever loneliness set in on my first holiday away, so I flashed her a smile and said, "I'd love to."

I was going to be uptown anyway, I told myself. I puffed up my courage and phoned Thea to ask if she wanted to watch the balloon inflation with me. "You could give me photography pointers," I added, trying to sound spur-of-the-moment, even though I'd planned what to say on my walk home from work. "I'm taking pictures for my sister."

My invitation was met with silence, and I waited on the line several long seconds before I tacked on a cowardly, "You could bring Vern." The idea of Vern tagging along reminded me of all the times my mother would only let Sue go on dates with "questionable" boys (meaning anybody whose folks she didn't know from church or anyone who was a senior when Sue was a sophomore) if she brought her kid sister along.

"So, is this a friend thing then? Because at first it sounded like a date," Thea said, and my heart picked up a few beats.

"Um, do you *want* it to be a date?" Dumb, dumb, dumb.

"I don't know." I heard a sharp intake of breath, then a slow release, and my face felt hot while I waited for rejection.

"Okay," I said—another dumb response.

"I mean, I don't know what to make of you. After that first night at Ariel's, I thought I should stay the hell away from you, that you are major trouble. But then later I thought maybe I rushed to judgment. Maybe you're just naive and don't know when someone's interested in you. My gut instinct about you might have been right, and you aren't just another clueless white chick."

"Gee, Thea," I said. "Who knew you were such a sweet-talker?"

Laughter rippled from her end of the line. "I'll meet you in front of the Natural History Museum at eight," she said.

"With Vern?" I asked after a pause in which I had weighed whether to push my luck.

"No . . . without."

125

Thea's Nikon occupied its own camera bag, putting my Kodak Instamatic in its place.

"I wasn't trying to one-up you, I swear," she said when she saw me looking from her camera to mine with an open mouth, then shoving mine back into my messenger bag.

"My camera may never recover from the shame."

"You said you wanted photos for your sister, and this takes great night photos. I just thought—"

"Hey, no problem. I'm grateful. Shoot away."

Central Park West was a sea of families, and though it was hard to imagine, Thea said the actual parade route was much more jammed. "I made the mistake of going my first year here," she said. "I didn't think I'd make it out alive."

As she snapped photos of Spiderman and Kermit, I pried into her life as discreetly as I could. "So do you teach photography? I don't think I ever asked. Oh, look, could you make sure you get Snoopy?" Snoopy was flat on his belly on the avenue, with Woodstock propped on his back.

"Some Black Studies, some Women's Studies," she said. "I fit art and literature in whenever I can. I'm just finishing up a Women and Creativity class. We studied Berenice Abbott's New York photos."

"Cool." My comment sounded flat and junior-high. I knew from experience I had to try harder to keep up with a professor. "I just can't believe you teach at Barnard."

She lowered her camera and gave me a quizzical look. "Why?" she asked.

"You're so young," I said quickly. "Or you look young. To me. That's all I meant. How old are you anyway?"

"Twenty-eight," she said, returning to shooting. "I started college a year early and went straight through to grad school. My adviser got me this teaching job while I finish my dissertation. But I'm looking for something permanent. Tenure track."

Grad school. Dissertation. Tenure track. Even though she was only five years older, I felt young and out of my league. When I first knew her, I'd imagined Thea was just like me—a struggling

126

young lesbian trying to make her way in New York. Now I felt embarrassed by my assumptions.

Still, I'd been out of my league before.

"How old are you?" she asked.

"Twenty-three." Not much older than her students, with a dumb-ass camera to boot.

"Bea Winston must really trust you," she said, looking me directly in the eyes. "To have you work with Clio Hartt, I mean."

"Oh, I don't know. It helped that I look a little like Flora Haynes."

"I'm sure that's not all of it," Thea said. "Don't sell yourself short. I do it, too, all the time, and most of the women I know. A liability of being female." She snapped rapid-fire shots of me until I held my hands in front of my face for her to stop.

"I take horrible pictures!" I objected. "You'll see. My eyes will be closed in every single one, or I'll look like I just ate a pickle."

She tucked the camera back into its bag. "I think we got enough, don't you? My fingers are cold. Let's grab some coffee and warm up."

We slid into a booth at a nearby diner, where she stripped off her scarf and hat and unbuttoned her peacoat but left it on. A ribbed cherry-red turtleneck peeked out. Every time I saw her, she was wearing primary colors like red or royal blue that made her stand out, while most New Yorkers seemed to prefer black and gray. My own wardrobe was an unimaginative mix of neutrals that helped me blend into the landscape.

"You cold?" I asked, to say something.

"Yeah. Which isn't too unusual when it's thirty degrees, right?" Her tone was teasing, a little flirtatious. "How can you dress like that and stay warm? You're like a teenage boy or something."

"It's warmer than it looks," I said, flipping my Carhartt jacket open so she could see the Sherpa lining. "I didn't need more than this at home."

"Well, you're coming up on a New York winter, so I'd get you some gloves. A hat at least."

"It'd muss my hair," I joked, running a hand over my freshly

127

cropped cut, which was poker straight and stood up without any gel or foam.

"You lose half of your body heat through your head," Thea said with professorial authority.

She ordered coffee, like a grown-up, and I had hot chocolate with tiny marshmallows. Thea smiled at my choice, and I stared, amazed, as she added three sugars to her mug.

"You take a little coffee with your sugar?"

"I have my vices." The emphasis on "vices" made her seem mysterious. And sexy. She kept stirring, way more than she needed to, and I wondered briefly if she was as nervous as I was. "You're one to talk about sugar," she added, nodding toward my cup.

As we exchanged quips, awareness that there was no Gerri or Vern to act as a buffer, that we were alone on a quasi-date, hit me. We'd exhausted the trite subjects of cold weather and beverage choices, so I lunged forward.

"Tell me . . . your dissertation. That sounds daunting. Like writing a book."

"Said the woman who works for a literary agent." It was another quip, but she looked a little relieved that the topic had turned to a more thoughtful one.

"Sure, I like to read them," I said. "I want to help writers shape them. I don't think I could ever write one." I sipped at my hot chocolate, taking extra care not to get foam on my lip. "What's it about? Your dissertation. Or is that a stupid question?"

"There you go undercutting yourself again. It's not a stupid question at all, Livvie." My name sounded softer than usual. "It's good you asked. I need to be talking about the damn thing so I'll keep plugging along and finish by May. It's about black women writers of the Harlem Renaissance, specifically Nella Larsen, Dorothy West, and Angelina Weld Grimke."

Even though I'd been an English major, I had never heard of any of the women she named and was embarrassed to admit it.

The gap between us widened: She'd gone to Cornell and Columbia, while I'd attended a state college in the sticks.

"You might not have heard of them," Thea added, and my chest swelled with gratitude. "So many women writers have been forgotten. Like your Clio, for one. I'm surprised you even read her in college. You got a good education." I could feel my face warming with the compliment.

"I had this professor," I said, and Hallie's face popped unbidden into my head at the word *had*. I squeezed my eyes shut to dismiss the image.

"She must have been something. You look like you're about to cry."

"No, I—" I stopped myself from lying. I liked Thea, and wanted to know her better, and denying Hallie didn't seem a good way to start. "Yeah, she was something. She was my lover. For a while. But I'm not about to cry."

The waitress refilled Thea's mug, and she stirred the sugar in slowly before speaking again.

"She the April Fifteenth one?" Thea asked, and I was amazed that she remembered my exact breakup day. "The married woman who broke your heart when she went back to her husband."

"That's her."

Thea nodded with a stiff smile. She started to button up her coat, and I panicked. "So you do have a 'type,' just like you told me," she said, her words as tight as the look on her face. "For a minute, I thought you actually saw me. But you've been lining up your next professor."

"No, Thea, that's not it," I protested. I reached across the table, taking her hand away from her buttons, and she didn't stop me. "Don't rush to judgment, remember? I do like super-smart women. The professor part—well, who's smarter than a college teacher anyway, tell me that."

We held hands for a long minute, until the waitress came with another refill. Thea freed her hand to wave away the offer.

"I can be a hothead," she said.

"Fiery women keep you on your toes."

We said good-bye out on the sidewalk. I wanted to be asked back to her apartment, which was closer than mine, but I just stood with my hands in my pockets, biting my bottom lip. Thea stepped up to acknowledge the awkwardness. "I don't do that kind of thing," she said.

I suspected she meant go home with someone on the first date, but I shrugged like I didn't have a clue.

"I have to know you better," she continued. "I've been burned, too, and I can't tell what you want."

"You're not so transparent yourself," I said. "First, you tell me, basically, to buzz off. Later, you put your hand on my knee, you touch my arm, you say, 'You're not as bad as I thought.' Not the clearest signals, Professor."

Her coy smile said she remembered everything I was talking about.

"I guess not. Is this clearer?" She pulled my face gently down to hers and we kissed right there on Seventy-Ninth Street, a soft, open-mouth kiss.

With Hallie, the first kiss had been firecrackers exploding in my body. Now, right in the open with Thea, our first kiss made me lightheaded, like the city around us was dissolving. Our tongues continued their exploration until a sharp cackle broke the spell: "Oh look, Jack, faggot ladies!" We pulled apart just in time to see a couple of punks with Brit accents pointing our way. They sauntered up the avenue without looking back.

"I can't believe it!" I said. "In Manhattan!"

Thea shrugged off the incident. "You haven't been harassed yet? It's the price of being out. Gerri has zingers she shoots back at them, but I can't come up with them fast enough."

I was still a little dizzy and off-kilter from the kiss. "You want to . . . meet up . . . tomorrow?"

"I'd love to, but I can't," Thea said. "I have a lot going on."

"All day?"

"Pretty much." She glanced off toward the subway. I didn't push her, and she didn't ask me what was on my plate for the day. One chaste date and a kiss didn't transform us into a couple— or me into a girlfriend with rights.

"Well, Happy Thanksgiving! I'll call you. Soon," she said giddily, leaving me to head down the station steps on legs like overcooked noodles.

Chapter 16

It would have been a near-perfect evening, one for the lesbian storybooks, if the answering machine hadn't been flashing urgent-looking blinks as I walked in the apartment door. The first four were hang-ups, the fifth was an audible sigh that sounded like Clio, and then the sixth got down to business: "Miss Bliss, where *are* you? It is quite late to be out, going on ten o'clock, and I require your time. Please call me."

My watch read 10:48, and I decided it was too late to call her back. Plus, she didn't sound like she was in pain or emotional distress, so I opted to postpone the callback until the morning. But a few minutes after eleven, the phone squawked again, and I raced from the bathroom to get it before the machine picked up.

"You are out of breath, Miss Bliss."

"I ran to the phone because I didn't want to miss your call again."

"Where were you?"

She rarely asked me personal questions—in this case, both personal and intrusive—so I was taken aback. "A friend and I went to see the Macy's balloons being blown up," I said. "For tomorrow's parade? It's very cool. You might enjoy it." I knew it was a stupid thing to say the minute it came out of my mouth, almost like I'd forgotten I wasn't talking to Gerri or another friend. Clio never went anywhere, she didn't use the word *cool*, and she had never expressed any interest in holidays or cultural traditions.

"I have never been to Macy's nor had any desire to do so. In fact, I have made it a lifelong practice never to patronize any store larger than the general store in Hendersonville."

The long and eventful day had caught up with me, and I yawned as quietly as I could. "What can I do for you, Miss Hartt?"

"I thought you might stop by tonight, but it is too late for that now. I started calling you at seven-thirty, to no avail." She paused. "It is too late, don't you think?"

I didn't relish going out again, especially if she hadn't fallen or hurt herself in any way. "It is. Do you need something? I can bring it by tomorrow, although I don't know what stores will be open."

"I don't require anything but your presence," Clio said, her tone as crisp as one of my laundered oxford shirts. She sounded more awake than I was, and I wondered how late she tended to stay up if she napped on and off all day long. I heard a soft purring through the line and pictured her holding Remington on her lap.

We set our meeting for ten o'clock, which was much earlier than I would have liked. I had imagined lounging in bed late, replaying the details of the evening with Thea. And I wasn't sure if Bea would pay me for working on Thanksgiving, so my holiday duty might end up being a freebie. Still, it was Clio, and I did what she wanted.

The sun threw a golden puddle onto Clio's desk, where a pen lay poised on top of a sheet of paper. I was fifteen minutes late, and I hoped she'd been so occupied with writing that she hadn't noticed. It had been an effort to drag myself out of bed, and I hadn't even bothered to shower.

"You look a little unkempt, Miss Bliss."

Sleepy, I found myself short on snappy retorts. I let the sound of Remington lapping milk from his bowl in the kitchen fill up the silence.

"Cat's got your tongue, too, I see."

"It *is* Thanksgiving, Miss Hartt. My day off?"

"Artists don't get a day off," she said. "Holidays are just like any other day to us. And a day without artistic output . . . why, it's a lost day, really. Flora and I even worked on our birthdays."

I was surprised by the reference to Flora's rigorous work ethic, remembering Gerri's almost poetic assessment that Flora Haynes "drank, fucked, and snorted too much . . . and produced too little." One night at her apartment, Gerri had pulled out a copy of Flora's play *Portrait of a Madwoman*, which a feminist press had published in the mid-'70s. "It's a weird play," she told me. "Creepy. You wonder how anyone ever managed to produce it." She wouldn't elaborate, and her mysterious "review" made me take a pass on borrowing it. Now I wondered how Flora the artist had had time to carouse, and where the rest of her output had gone.

"You look like you don't believe me," Clio said.

"No, no, I've heard many writers write every day," I said. "It's admirable. I was just surprised by . . . Did Miss Haynes ever write anything besides *Portrait of a Madwoman*?"

Her fists flew out in front of her like she wanted to strike me, but I was not within reach. Even Remington sensed her rage and slinked away behind the armchair. "Of course, she did! Flora Haynes was a genius. Her plays are masterpieces. There will never be her like again. So much talent . . . gone! If I had only—" But she bit off the end of her regret.

"I'm sorry," I said. "I didn't mean to offend you. I asked because a friend told me about that one play."

"She had several produced before that one—that's how we met at Provincetown Players," she said, her hands lowering to her sides. "I fancied being a playwright, but I didn't have the talent for it. Flora's plays were complex, exquisite flowers." Clio's face softened. "The theater world didn't understand her, really, and that took a toll. She could have tried another form—" Again, Clio cut her thought short. In the throes of maudlin reminiscence, she picked up Flora's photo and stroked the frame, like she was comforting a loved one in pain.

"I didn't know. I'm sorry."

Clio replaced the photo and flashed me a quizzical look. "I don't know why you're sorry," she snapped. "You didn't know her. She died in 1958. Were you even born then?"

"No, but I mean I'm sorry because she was such a talent," I said as a quick save. "I'm sorry she was misunderstood. Maybe someone will stage a revival of her work someday."

Clio frowned like that was the most unlikely thing she'd ever heard and returned to her desk. "Well, I didn't ask you here to talk about Flora," she said, and relief washed over me. "I have finished my story."

"That's wonderful!" I imagined reporting the news at Ramona's party later in the day. But then worry set in: "You don't mean the 'Madame Louise' story, do you?"

"No, I mean the story that fellow's cat inspired." Remington must have sensed he was being praised, because he crept out of the shadows, purring.

"Well, he's your cat now if you still want him. Eli can't take care of him anymore."

"Yes, yes, yes," she said with impatience. "Anyway, I considered what you said—" she would never give me, or maybe anyone else, credit for advice, "—and wrote a North Carolina story."

"Wow, that is spectacular."

Lines of disapproval creased her forehead again, and she busied herself gathering up pages, presumably of the story. "It is not literally 'spectacular,'" she said, causing me to make a mental note to look up the literal meaning when I got home and could consult my pocket Webster's. Clio was certainly in a cantankerous mood—"tetchy," as the old folks said back home— and I wondered how she could tolerate my presence at all. I expected to be dismissed at any moment.

"I just meant . . . well, I'd love to read it whenever you like." I stopped myself from mentioning that I might see Bea later in the day. "What's it called?"

"The working title is 'Before the Fire,'" she replied, handing me what looked like at least thirty pages. "You will read it here, as I do not have another copy."

I plopped down in the stiff-backed chair I usually occupied there and read.

The delicately mysterious story roped me in with its first line: *The officer's question scratched like sandpaper: "And what happened just before the fire?" he said again.*

I finished with a sharp intake of breath, loving the seeming effortlessness of it, its clear affection for the animals who did not survive.

"This is just beautiful, Miss Hartt," I said. She had been staring at me from her place in the armchair, Remington in her lap—probably throughout the thirty or so minutes of my reading. As much as she downplayed my importance as a reader and adviser, she was clearly waiting for my assessment and maybe just a tad uncertain that it would be approval. I felt a pinch of sympathy for the great artist who spoke a confident game but underneath doubted her own talent.

"I fell in love with Pickles and Henny," I continued. "They're such full, complete characters, more than many human characters I've read. It's crushing when they pass."

She sighed, and I worried for a second that my praise was somehow wrong, my emphasis on the animals too intense, and that she'd chastise me for not understanding her writing. But she simply said, "Thank you"—something I wasn't sure she'd ever said to me before. "It's not finished," she went on.

Baffled, I looked back through the pages. "It feels complete to me, Miss Hartt. I mean, the ending is so—"

"I can't see it," she interrupted.

As I'd read, I easily pictured each detail of what I assumed was the Threatt homeplace. "Really? The setting's so vivid," I said. "Right on down to the cast-iron cornbread pan on the stove. Is it based on your family's home?"

"It is, but I can no longer see it. My head just doesn't work the same, and everything's fuzzy." Her voice cracked. "And until I can see it, I won't have communicated what I want to, and this won't be finished."

She blew her nose into a balled-up handkerchief she pulled from her sweater sleeve.

"Are there any pictures?" I asked.

Clio shook her head with impatience, but then a dim light went on in her eyes. "Rufe might have some, though. He still lives down there."

She'd never mentioned anyone in her family by name, and given her advanced age I was surprised anyone besides her still survived.

"Who's Rufe?" I asked.

"My little brother. Well, he's going on eighty now, so he's not so little."

"And you're still in touch?"

She scowled. "Well, of course, I am! Aren't you in touch with your kin?"

"You just never talk about them," I observed. "You've talked about Hendersonville, and the homeplace, but I don't remember anything about siblings."

"There were eight of us, ten if you count the stillborns, but Rufe and I are the only ones left," she said. "I've got nieces and nephews, but there were so many so fast, I don't recall their names."

"Wow, eight kids. Your mama must have been busy." The size of her family felt very old-timey; my grandparents had also hailed from families of eight-plus offspring.

"I didn't care much for the six sisters, but Rufe was such a smart little fella. Kind of my pet when I was a teenager. I haven't heard from him in a while."

"Maybe you could call him about pictures?"

"Yes, I'll do that. I can wish him a Happy Thanksgiving." Before I left, I helped her locate her address book, and there, sure enough, under the T's was an entry for Rufus Threatt. It struck me as funny that she had written out her own brother's last name, as if she might forget it.

I heard the click of her phone's rotary dial as I stepped into the hallway.

Ramona's address on Gramercy Park East was a classy building I'd passed many times when I roomed at the Parkside—a turreted edifice that Sergeant Sal had explained was the oldest apartment building in the city. "Jimmy Cagney lived there in the sixties," Sal had said with pride, as if she owned the building herself. "You'd always see him walking his little dogs in the park. Nicest man ever!"

With its stained-glass panels, the front door alone was enough to intimidate, but then the mosaic tiled floor and grand fireplace in the lobby made me feel like I'd stepped into an Edith Wharton novel. When the doorman asked which apartment I was visiting, I lost my voice for a moment and held out my invitation to him shyly. "Ramona Costa," I managed to say, and he steered me toward the elevator, an ancient Otis cage that took its sweet time as it wheezed its way to the third floor. I marveled that someone not much older than I could live in such opulent style.

There were only two apartments on Ramona's floor, and I veered toward the one with a coatrack situated in the hallway. The door was slightly ajar and led to a foyer with an elaborate herringbone-patterned wood floor. Handsome people were laughing and socializing, cocktails in hand, very Gatsby-esque; a few gave me curious looks as I edged past them. I was willing to bet I was the only guest who'd arrived in jeans and a Carhartt jacket, bearing a box of Triscuits and a Tupperware container of pimento cheese.

"Livvie!" Ramona called out from the galley kitchen. She was wearing a tight black dress and comically high heels, but she maneuvered in them as easily as I did in my high-top Chucks.

"I didn't know this was a dressy party," I said. "Sorry."

"You live in Chelsea, right?" I wasn't sure if that was good or bad in her eyes, or how the question followed from my observation, so I simply handed her the crackers and pimento cheese.

"Oh, you brought it! You have to try this cheese," Ramona said to another skinny, heel-clad woman in the kitchen, who bore a striking resemblance to her. "Livvie's from the South, and this is some kind of delicacy down there."

"I'm Raquel," the second woman said. "Ramona's sister."

"Oh yes, my sister *Raquel*." Ramona rolled her eyes.

"I told you, casting directors call back Raquel more than Rachel." Two actresses in the same family? I wondered if that had any impact on Ramona giving up on acting.

"Well, could either Raquel or Rachel point Livvie in the direction of the food? I'll put this heavenly cheese on a plate and bring it out. Right after I sample a little."

Raquel led me to the living room and, after a quick motion toward the buffet table, left me to my own devices. My entire apartment on Fifteenth Street would have fit into Ramona's spacious living room, which had two window seats facing out onto Gramercy Park. Cross-legged as a Buddha in the grandest of the two seats and flanked by partygoers was my boss. Bea caught my eye and raised an eyebrow in acknowledgment, which seemed like an invitation to join her.

As I approached Bea's social semicircle, I realized the woman talking to her, whose back had been facing the crowded room, was Diane Westerly. Now that Thea and I had ventured into the murky area of friends who kiss, I felt both more awkward around Diane and more protective of Thea.

"Happy Thanksgiving, Bea," I said before greeting Diane. "It looks like the gang's all here."

"Livvie, isn't it?" Diane asked in a way that suggested she knew my name perfectly well.

"I just had to see Ramona's apartment," Bea said, as if she needed to explain why she was there. "This building! Absolutely gorgeous. The elevator alone should have landmark status. Jemima invited me to a party here a few years back, but I couldn't make it." I guessed Jemima was the client who'd moved to London and bestowed the place on Ramona. There was a Jemima Somebody whose file folder I recalled seeing. If I stuck around Bea's agency long enough, maybe I could score a fabulous sublet, too.

Diane and Bea exchanged comments about the parquet floors and the stunning view of the park.

"The rent must be through the roof, though," I commented, to add to the conversation. Bea looked like rent was a distasteful subject, a transaction that simply happened, and then proceeded to steer the subject toward a short history of Gramercy Park: "the only private park in Manhattan, like some sort of Victorian lady," she said.

"Have you ever been inside?" Diane asked.

"Yes, it's lovely. Wonderfully calming," Bea said.

As a resident of the Parkside, I'd had access to a park key for three months. But because I'd never actually used the key—someone else always seemed to have it when I had free time—I kept the fact to myself. I remembered telling my sister about the key, and Sue had exclaimed, "Who locks a freakin' park?"

I was about to change tacks and ask Bea where she lived, when our circle was interrupted. "There you are, Dee! This place is so big, I—"

My heart pulsed like a jackhammer at the voice.

"Hey, Thea," I said weakly. Her face looked like someone had pinched in both cheeks.

"What are *you* doing here?" she asked. After the previous evening, I didn't think she meant it to come out so rudely, but it did.

"I work with Ramona. The hostess?" I said, all the while thinking, *What are* you *doing here?*

"This is a work party?" Thea said, turning a scornful look to Diane. "You just said it was someone you knew and it was in a great building and did I want to come and see it."

With a cough, Bea rose from her perch at the window; the drama of a client's life was more than she was interested in. "If you will excuse me, I need to be somewhere else," she said.

"I'll walk you out, Bea," I offered. "I have some good news about Clio."

Thea grabbed at my sleeve. "Are you coming back?"

"No," I said, holding a smile that hurt my jaw as I glanced from her to Diane. "I have a lot going on."

Thea winced at the blow of hearing me repeat her own words from the night before. Before she could respond, I turned away, following Bea for a quick good-bye to Ramona and then out into the hall, where the cooler air hit me with a welcome blast. My report about Clio's new story grabbed Bea's attention, and our conversation as the elevator clanked its way down to the street kept my mind off the gash in my heart.

In my hurry to escape the hurt of seeing Thea with Diane, I hadn't eaten anything at Ramona's, not even a cracker with cheese. By the time I scuttled back to the West Side, my stomach was moaning in protest. I hadn't bothered getting a rotisserie chicken as originally planned, because I thought I'd be eating at the party, so I stopped at my favorite Korean grocery for a turkey sandwich.

"How come no turkey dinner for you?" Mr. Park, the owner, was staffing the deli counter by himself, the wife and teenaged kids who usually worked with him noticeably absent. In addition to stocking high-quality cold cuts, Mr. Park's customer recognition and service skills were superlative, and he had started building my turkey with Havarti on a baguette before I even got the words out of my mouth. "You like turkey."

"I do like turkey," I said. Usually, I found it effortless to make small talk with Mr. Park, an affable guy with the look of a nerdy NYU professor, but that day my mind was elsewhere.

He cocked an eyebrow, maybe sensing a bigger story. But instead of explaining, I turned the conversation to him. "How come you're open today, Mr. Park?"

"Closing at six." That spoke for itself, since the place was always open until late. "My wife home cooking."

"Nice," I said. I'd never thought about the Parks having a home where they went after serving everyone else, but I suddenly imagined him making the trek home on the train—to Queens?—every night.

"I am lucky man." He was just adding the final flourishes to

141

my sandwich when he asked if I wanted cranberry dressing, either on the side or right on top of the turkey. "Taste really good." He nodded toward a hand-printed sign that said cranberry sauce could be added to any turkey sandwich through Saturday for an extra fifty cents.

He waited for my response as I shifted from foot to foot, trying to decide. I loved cranberry sauce, but in my vulnerable, slightly disoriented state the addition of it to my order seemed like the biggest choice I'd ever faced.

"Hey, no charge today for good customer." He wrapped up my sandwich and gave me the sauce on the side. The small kindness almost moved me to tears, but I sniffed them back and thanked him.

I considered going right home, maybe donning my pajamas at the ridiculously early hour of six o'clock and losing myself in some sappy made-for-TV holiday movie. But I kept seeing Thea's face in my mind—first her beatific expression when we pulled apart from our kiss, and then the drawn, worried look when she spotted me at Ramona's.

At that moment, I felt as isolated as if I'd landed in New York days, not months, before. I wanted nothing more than to spill my woes to a friend. Gerri wasn't home, but I found myself heading to Milligan Place anyway—and knocking at Clio's door for the second time that day.

"I saw you already today, didn't I?" Clio said in a worried voice, like maybe she'd dropped a day or two from the calendar.

I considered lying and saying I just wanted to make sure she was OK, but my drop-in was wholly about me. "I had a really bad day," I said, "and I needed to see someone."

Clio clicked her tongue as she let me in. "You need to cultivate some younger friends, Miss Bliss." Her voice shifted to a softer, less judgmental tone. "But I suppose most young people are away with their loved ones. There's just us old curmudgeons. And our cats."

She looked strangely disheveled, with her hair sticking out in wisps, and her gray sweater buttoned wrong. Remmie's food bowl was empty, and he was positioned in front of it as if willing the Friskies to appear.

"Have you two eaten?" I asked. "I have a killer turkey sandwich that I'd be happy to share. There's cranberry sauce and a pickle, too. And I'll open a can for Remington."

"I had a fried egg," she replied, but her glance toward Remington in the kitchen suggested uncertainty about the statement. "I'm not . . . I don't think he ate." My grandmother had lapses like that, too, and couldn't be trusted to eat every day unless someone stopped in to remind her.

A vague smokiness rose from the kitchen nook. Clio's cast-iron frying pan was pushed to the side of one of the burners, which still emitted a low blue flame. I rushed to turn it off but didn't chide her about it. "Well, you might like a bite of the sandwich anyway," I said. "Mr. Park knows his way around a turkey sandwich."

After fixing a bowl for Remington, I cut the sandwich into quarters and portioned them and the cranberry sauce between two small plates. I placed hers on the stack of books next to her chair and pulled up a wooden chair for myself. When she ate a quarter of the sandwich in just a few appreciative bites, I wondered how long ago she'd turned on that burner and fried the egg.

"Well, this is simply delicious," she said. "But you must finish it. I'm quite full."

I didn't argue, and inhaled my own portion and the rest of hers without speaking. The speed was more about my melancholy than about hunger. The day Hallie dumped me for good, I'd eaten a large sausage pizza on my own, then topped it off with a pint of chocolate ice cream.

"And what could have possibly made someone so young have such a bad day?" she asked, wiping her mouth on the paper napkin I'd given her. The question surprised me. I assumed she would have forgotten the statement about my day in the fifteen or so minutes that had passed.

"Love," I said after a dramatic sigh, as if Thea and I already enjoyed a romantic relationship.

Clio crinkled her nose in distaste. "Well, I'll be no help to you there," she said. "Love confounded me, really."

Gerri, the Clio expert, had never mentioned anyone but Flora, so I assumed that was who she meant. "Miss Haynes?" I asked after a pause.

"The most baffling woman who ever lived," she said. "She could be a loving creature for one week or maybe even one year, but in the end you couldn't count on it. There were others."

"For you?"

"No!" she said, but then took her time and explained. "Of course, there were others before and after. But not while we were together, even though I could have had plenty of lovers, women and men. I was good-looking in my day, Miss Bliss. Man Ray called me 'a fine specimen of a woman.'"

My silence was the wrong response, and she clicked her tongue at me again. "The illustrious photographer?" Clio lifted herself slowly from her chair and pulled down a heavy volume on a bookshelf. She dropped it in my lap so I could note the cover, *Photographs by Man Ray,* then flipped it open to a bookmarked page. The photo of her was exquisite, a seated portrait in a rakish fedora and silk blouse seductively open to the third button, a strand of pearls circling her neck. The caption read "Clio Hartt, Paris, 1929."

"I could have had him if I wanted," she said.

"Wow," I said, more to the photo than to the idea that she might have slept with a famous photographer—and a man, no less. I rifled through the pages of photos—James Joyce, Gertrude Stein, Pablo Picasso, and Flora Haynes herself, in a tie and a haircut so short she would have fit right into my own circle of friends. Transfixed, I held Flora's dark eyes for a minute before I said, "So, he asked you to sleep with him?"

"Not in so many words," Clio said. "But you come to understand these things." She paused then added, almost as an afterthought, "Besides, he'd already had Flora, and there's nothing a man likes as much as a matched set."

The words were iced with bitterness, and I offered the volume back to her. "I'm sorry. I know something about betrayal."

"Yes," Clio said, her eyes fastened on mine, "I expect you do." She refused the book and told me to keep it. "I've seen it more times than I care to. Besides, it might be worth something someday, and I don't have much else of value to give you."

She was still standing, and I wasn't sure if I'd been dismissed. I was loath to return to my empty apartment, so I asked if she'd connected with her brother.

"I spoke to his wife," she said, the lines in her face deepening. "It seems I'll soon be the only Threatt left."

"I am so sorry to hear that. What happened?"

"Cancer. He's in a home for people with terminal diseases."

"Hospice?"

"Yes, that's it. I talked to him not six months ago, and he was fine, really." Her voice cracked. "He's the baby of the family. It should be me."

"Don't say that," I protested. "You're still in tip-top shape."

She smiled at me sideways, the subtle flirt in her popping out. "You do flatter me, Miss Bliss."

We stood facing each other for a moment in silence, and because I couldn't think of anything else to say at such a poignant moment, I gathered up my coat to leave. I was embarrassed to have intruded on her grief just because a woman I'd kissed was not who I hoped she was. Still, Clio and I had shared that fine sandwich. For a few minutes at least, my visit had perked her up.

"Do you need me tomorrow?" I asked at the door. "Or should I come by on Saturday instead?" The questions seemed to overwhelm her, and I said I'd call the next day to check on her.

I was at the end of the hallway, getting ready to descend the steps, when I heard her call out to me. "Miss Bliss! Oh, Miss Bliss!" The tone was urgent, almost like the first phone call I'd received, when she had fancied she was in imminent danger.

Sprinting back to her door, I expected her to say she was having heart palpitations or something worse, and I steeled myself to leap into action. But when I reached her, her eyes were sparkling with their intense blueness.

"I have the most wonderful idea! We will go together!"

"Go . . . together?" I said. "Where, Miss Hartt?"

"Why, home, of course."

My family was expecting me to visit in a month for Christmas—I'd promised as much when I sidestepped Thanksgiving—but I'd made no airline reservations and the thought of skipping a second holiday had briefly crossed my mind.

Now Clio wanted me to accompany her so she could see her brother one last time. His wife said she wasn't sure how many pages were left on his calendar, but the doctors had estimated a few months at most. Christmas would be the perfect time, Clio said.

Considering how new I was to my job, I told her I doubted Bea would be amenable to my taking more than just the twenty-fourth and twenty-fifth off. "So many new clients." "Manuscripts up the wazoo." The excuses rolled off my tongue like prayers from a preacher. In fact, I'd heard from Gerri that the publishing industry pretty much shut down in December, especially the closer it got to the end of the month, so Bea likely wouldn't fuss about a few additional days.

"I will call Bea myself," Clio said. "We'll take the train. A sleeper compartment for each of us. I do so love trains."

The thought of a long train ride with Clio gave me considerable pause, but she expressed a strong aversion to planes. When pressed, it turned out she had never flown and saw no reason to start at her advanced age.

"How did you get back and forth to Paris?" I asked—a naive question I realized when Clio clicked her tongue.

"Young people. Only interested in newfangled things, really." As if she knew any young people but me, and as if the Wright

Brothers had launched their flying machine just last month. "Flora and I sailed on the *Majestic*, of course. Why would we rattle around in a little tin can when a floating hotel was available?"

I walked home in the dark, pondering a trip back. Having to assist Clio could offer me an out from some of the most heterosexually focused family festivities, those times when the Blisses would gather to coo over the youngsters being adorable, and when the grilling from aunts and sisters and cousins would commence: "Any fellas up there in New York, Livvie?" Like the only thing stopping me from marrying was that I was picky and North Carolina men didn't meet my high standards. Focusing on Clio would also keep me occupied so I wasn't even tempted to look up Hallie, whose phone number I still knew by heart.

Hallie! Thea had bounced her right out of my mind, but now she was back, along with my deep shame at how I'd behaved after our final fight. I'd said vicious things, but so had she. I'd never admitted to anyone that I'd phone-stalked her, calling her office nearly every day, sometimes several times in a row, hanging up as she answered. "I know it's you, Liv!" she screamed into the line one day.

And Thea! I wondered briefly if she'd been thinking about me, if she'd called, maybe left a message while I was at Clio's. As I turned the corner onto Fifteenth Street, I got my answer: Even from down the block, I recognized the petite frame sitting on the stoop next to mine. My heart picked up a beat, but my tone stayed icy.

"If you're looking for me, you've got the wrong building."

Her mouth flopped open as she watched me sprint up the steps of my building.

"I was only here one time," she explained, then added quickly, "when Barb hosted the salon. How was I supposed to remember? These buildings are twins." Frustration thickened her voice.

It was true: With their heavy stone facades carved with gargoyles, the turn of the century apartment buildings were mirror images of each other, separated by a narrow airshaft. When I'd first moved in, I had occasionally made the same mistake as Thea, but only when it was dark and I was drunk. Still, I didn't give Thea the satisfaction of affirming her confusion.

"So what are you doing here, Thea?"

"I tried to go after you, but you disappeared. And then I tried calling from a phone booth, and when I finally found one that worked I got the machine. Ate up all my dimes. So I called my cousin and begged off supper and walked over here, and I've been sitting on this fool stoop for who knows how long. Where were you?"

"Why?" I snapped. "What's it to you?"

"Stop being a child," she snapped right back. "You ran off and didn't even let me explain."

"What's to explain? You're still seeing your ex. That's your prerogative. End of story."

"I am not seeing my ex," she said, exasperated. "I was helping her out. She invited me to this party a week ago, and I had nothing going on but my cousin's so I agreed. She said she didn't want to go alone. And you and me . . . we weren't happening. I had no idea her agency was throwing the thing."

"Not the agency," I corrected. "Ramona. One of the agents."

"Don't be nitpicky."

"I mean, when the agency throws a party—"

"I get it, Livvie." She turned away, her arms crossed tightly over her chest, her tone as crisp as a schoolteacher's.

"And why didn't her girlfriend go with her?" I said.

"I'm not sure." Thea's eyes drifted down to her feet as if she was fiddling with the truth. "They might be having problems. Or something."

"Or something." I flashed a smug smile, which she caught. "You must think I'm a real hick."

"Why?"

"Hallie was always telling me her husband didn't understand her, and that they were 'having problems.' It's how she'd reel me in after she'd thrown me back. And if you want to be reeled . . . well, then." I shrugged. "I spent months being reeled back in."

She pulled the collar of her peacoat up around her ears and stuffed her hands into her pockets. "It's freezing. Can I come in?"

"I'm not sure what there is to talk about," I said. "I don't have any claims on you. We flirted. We kissed once. If you're secretly hoping to get back together with Diane, it's none of my business. Just don't expect me to watch it." Hurt flapped in my chest as I tried to stay calm and steady. I didn't know if Thea could hear the crack in my voice as I finished my statement.

"Livvie. Please, just let me come in."

And there was my name again, but this time it was as supple as a flannel shirt. I finished my ascent to the front door and nodded toward her to follow me in.

"Five minutes," I said. But in the foyer, I seized her hand and led her up to the fourth-floor landing where we kissed for the second time. She pressed me up against the wall and slipped a skillful hand between my legs.

"Wait," I said in a husky voice. "Inside."

"Here?"

"No. I mean. Let's go inside," I managed to say.

At the apartment door, I cursed the sticky lock that was acting up again. "Holy crap, Jesús!"

"Is that some guy you know," Thea said, laughing, "or you practicing praying in Spanish?"

On my third try, she slid the keys out of my hand, pulled the doorknob firmly toward her, and turned the key in the lock like a pro. "Little trick I picked up," she said. "Works every time." Thea had other tricks that worked equally well, and I learned a few of them that night.

Chapter 17

"Well, it's about time," Gerri said.

We had laid claim to our favorite booth in Mi Chinita, toward the rear of the skinny diner.

"You mean you knew?"

"That Thea was interested in you? I lived with her for a month, remember?" Gerri munched her eggroll, then pointed the bitten end at me for emphasis. "Now you, I wasn't so sure about. Thea kept asking me to get a read on you, but you've got this hard shell when it comes to matters of the heart."

That explained why questions and comments about Thea had peppered my conversations with Gerri, like "Isn't Thea smart?" and "Thea's looking for someone to go to the Dykes Against Racism benefit."

"I mean, Thea thought she was just going to have to jump your bones to get you to understand."

"And that she did," I said, blushing at the memory of her mouth traveling the length of my body.

"Stop right there. I'm horny as hell, and I just can't take it anymore." Gerri mopped up a pool of duck sauce with her eggroll. She professed to not liking sweets, but always ordered extra of the sticky condiment. "So, where'd you leave it? Are you two together now or what?"

"We didn't talk about it." Which was kind of true—we hadn't discussed "us" outright as we lingered all day Friday in my loft bed, only getting up to use the bathroom or order food. On Saturday, Thea suggested a couple's shower—my first ever, and an experience that left me, literally, cold. After bagels I asked her to stick around one more night, but her boundary wall went up. "Let's not rush this," she said, with a light peck on the mouth.

"Well, I for one hope you are," Gerri said, forking up some of my fried rice. She was eating more than usual, and her face looked a bit fuller. "Together, I mean. I will personally help unload the U-Haul."

We talked about her Thanksgiving, how she'd gotten all the expected questions about her split with Renee, which she parried like a pro. She told me a vividly funny story about her younger brothers rolling around on the floor after dinner, moaning with the ache of bloated bellies. "Little pigs," she concluded with a snort.

But it felt like she had another story to tell. She alternated between looking at me furtively and then averting her eyes.

"What?" I asked finally.

"*What* what?"

"You look like there's something else you want to say."

She exhaled deeply, like she was deflating. "Yeah, now that you mention it, this thing *did* happen. Late that night. When I was watching TV. You're not gonna believe it. Renee called."

I put my fork down and listened. "What did she want?"

"To talk," Gerri said, a bashful smile forming at the corners of her mouth. "About us."

I had it from Barb's own mouth that she'd gone to Westchester with Renee, but I'd kept it from Gerri, trying to spare her. Now I couldn't hold it in.

"You know she was with Barb, right?" I said, as evenly and slowly as I could. "That Barb went with her to Chappaqua?"

Gerri's face clouded. "I think you're wrong about that, Liv. In fact, I'm sure of it."

"Look, you knew things about Thea because you lived with her, right? Well, I know things about Barb for the same reason. I didn't tell you because I knew it would hurt you."

"You don't know this," she insisted. "I know Renee, and I'm telling you Barb was not there." Her tone was almost pleading, like she could insist her way into making me believe it, too.

I held up my hands in truce. "Whatever you say."

"No, it's not 'whatever I say.' It's what fucking happened." The imploring tone shifted to a fierceness Gerri had never directed at me before. Her muscles strained as she leaned in toward me, waiting for my acquiescence.

"Okay, okay. I must have gotten it wrong."

Her shoulders and neck relaxed then, but the space between us widened. I was debating whether to leave when Gerri hopped to her feet, waving to someone who had just come through the front door.

I felt Renee's hand on my shoulder before I heard her distinctive purr. "You two," she said. "With all the restaurants in this city, this dive is still your favorite."

Bea called out to me as I passed her office hauling a shopping bag full of coffee, sugar, and half-and-half for the kitchenette. "Can I drop these off first?" I asked.

"This won't take a minute," she said. But then she motioned me into a chair, which suggested a longer conversation, and I plopped the grocery bag onto the floor.

"This trip to North Carolina," she began. "Will it help Clio write?"

"Is that what she told you?"

"No, she told me it was to see her dying brother. But she's asked me to give you a week off from work to accompany her, and I don't see what the connection is. And who takes a train all the way to North Carolina anyway when a plane gets you there in a couple of hours?"

"She's never been on a plane."

Bea's lips twisted into a frown. "New experiences help you flex the writing muscles."

I nodded, worrying that she would expect me to convey that to one of the foremost Modernist writers.

"What I need to know, Livvie . . . in your opinion, will the trip help her write?"

I shrugged. "She says she doesn't really remember North Carolina. That she can't see it. Plus, it's been decades, and a lot has changed."

Bea removed her glasses and tapped them against her desk blotter. It clearly wasn't the definitive answer she was looking for.

"This has gotten out of hand," she said.

"This—?"

"I never intended for you to be her full-time assistant! I would have had to hire two of you so there'd be someone running the office. And I haven't even seen a single story from her, not one in what—three months? I need to know these demands for your time are going to amount to something. I care about Clio, but she could easily hire one of those nurse-type helper-ish . . . people." Bea, who was so adept with words, was surprisingly undone by the word for an attendant. She put her glasses back on and gave me a hard stare through them. "Can you get me the story she just wrote? That might help me see the value of all this."

"She won't let it out of the apartment."

"What if she spills something on it? Or loses it? I can just see that happening! Christ!" Her extreme reaction didn't add up; it was like something was simmering in her, just below the surface.

"I think any request to see it might be better coming from you," I said. "And so would the part about us taking a plane because it flexes the muscles." I was careful to phrase my suggestion lightly, aware that I was telling my boss what her own job was. So I was flummoxed when Bea's eyes watered over, like I'd hurt her feelings.

"Oh, I'm sorry, Bea. I should never—"

She waved me off brusquely, cutting off my apology. "Never mind."

Later, Ramona entered the kitchenette looking like she'd just gotten a pink slip. "Steer clear of Bea today," she warned.

"Now you tell me."

153

Ramona's voice fell to a hush as she glanced toward the door. "Husband number three," she said, making a slicing motion across her throat. "Kind of a soap opera plot line, if you ask me. He's been cheating with his paralegal for months. Got her pregnant. Bea just found out. About the pregnant part. She'd been trying to overlook the cheating part."

"Poor Bea."

"Whatever you do, don't act like you feel sorry for her. She'll pull herself together and be back in form in no time. Bea Winston is the queen of bouncing back."

"Seriously?" Thea asked. "We just get something going and you're taking a trip?" Her tone was teasing, but with an undercurrent of something else.

We were lounging in my loft bed after some especially athletic sex that involved contortions I didn't know I could do and the magical "69" I'd never tried. To spare Vern's feelings, we hadn't "done it" at her place yet; and since Barb was working the graveyard shift, my place had become our love nest.

"It's not like a vacation or anything. It's just babysitting." My fingers traced her breast in lazy swirls. "Think how much you'll miss me."

"Are you going to see . . . anyone you know?" After only a week, we weren't a couple and mentioning Hallie directly would have sounded way too possessive—just like I hadn't asked about Diane since Thanksgiving.

"Family, I guess," I said, just as cagey. "Clio's brother's at a home in Asheville, so it seems like we'll be there more than in Hendersonville."

I didn't intend to seek Hallie out, but there was always the outside chance we'd find ourselves on the same street or in the same restaurant at the same time of day. I had fantasized about that casual sort of tripping over her, just so I could see the look on Hallie's face when I let it drop that I was "seeing someone." Sometimes, I let the fantasy progress even further as I imagined her calling me at my parents' house to say she had made a mistake and wanted me back.

Thea sat up abruptly and hugged her knees like she was guarding her body. "Well, I have a trip of my own coming up in January. I just found out this week."

"Oh, yeah? Where?" She had mentioned going home to Charleston for Christmas, and I assumed that's what she meant.

"Western New York." She rested her chin on her knees, her face turned away from me so I couldn't read it.

"You going to a college reunion or something?"

"I got an on-campus interview," she said. "For an assistant professor job at Hamilton College."

The lingo of academic job searches eluded me. I understood that Thea was looking for a permanent teaching position because she was finishing her dissertation and her teaching contract at Barnard expired in May. In my ignorance, though, I didn't realize her job search would begin a full six months in advance, or that she would cast such a wide net.

"That's great," I said, but emotion thickened my voice. With that voice, I could have passed for Kathleen Turner. Taking a trip with Clio for a week was one thing, but Thea moving out of the city was another. "How far away is that, anyhow?"

"About three hours. Well, more like five on the bus."

"Five hours!"

"Yeah. I'll be gone two, three days."

"Wow."

"I just found out. This week."

"Yeah, you said that."

She slipped back under the covers and rolled on top of me. Her frame was slight, but Thea had extraordinary power in her arms and legs that she told me came from running track in high school. She was still a runner, and her favorite route involved laps around the reservoir in Central Park.

"These jobs are super competitive," Thea added. "I probably won't get it."

I seized her words as if I were falling off a cliff and she'd tossed

155

me a rope. Still, I suspected Thea was either being modest or downplaying her chances in case she didn't get the job.

"Did you apply for other jobs, too, maybe something, you know, closer?"

"Well, there's one in Philly, so that's just a quick train ride," she said, kissing the freckles on my chest lightly. "I love Philly, don't you?"

"Never been," I said, her butterfly kisses annoying me rather than turning me on. "You apply anywhere here?"

"I would love to, but there isn't anything for me to apply for except at Bronx Community College." Her nose wrinkled in distaste as if she'd mentioned a janitor's job. With her educational pedigree, a position at a two-year college was not going to suit.

"You can't re-up at Barnard?"

"Livvie, this is how it works in academia." Her voice was steady and slow, but with an edge of pique. "You go where the jobs are. And that could be Wisconsin."

"Wisconsin!"

"Hypothetically," she said, quickly. "I didn't apply for anything in Wisconsin."

"Phew."

"D.C., Baltimore, Philly, Atlanta . . . and Boston." She scanned my face. "We weren't together in September. You barely noticed me. I didn't know this was going to happen."

I hugged her to me and closed my eyes, blinking back my disappointment. It didn't matter that we were virtual strangers; I'd already flashed forward in my imagination, with mental pictures of us holding hands on Valentine's Day, marching on Fifth Avenue for Gay Pride, taking day trips to Coney Island or Montauk. I could even see myself moving into the apartment uptown. My attitude toward her job search was selfish, but I couldn't help secretly hoping the positions either didn't work out or that Thea recognized the folly of leaving me and turned them all down.

"Maybe I could come with you?" I suggested, although I knew it sounded needy and grasping and way too fast. "Make it more fun."

"There won't be time for fun," she said, slipping herself out of the hug and pulling on her turtleneck, which she had peeled off the night before and tossed to the side of the mattress. She tried to smooth it out now, but the wrinkles had settled in. "It's all meetings and dinners, and I'll be anxious about my job talk. Don't make this harder, Livvie. It's hard enough trying to land a teaching job without—" She broke off, and I wondered if she had almost added "without thinking about your feelings."

"—projecting into the future," was what she actually said. "You know, when I was applying to grad school, I was in a pretty new relationship with Diane and I only considered schools in New York because she'd moved here to be a writer. This time, I want to think about what would be best for me, not someone else."

I nodded in acknowledgment, but couldn't help picking at the topic like a scab. "So . . . if you get one of these jobs, when would you, um, leave?"

"Livvie, stop." Thea made for the ladder but hesitated in mid-descent. "Let's just take things as they come, OK?" Without another peep, I followed Thea down the ladder and started a pot of coffee while she brushed her teeth.

Every night Thea and I had been at my apartment, I had wondered what Barb's reaction would be if she came home and found us together. Thea had fretted about the possibility, like she was almost scared to face Barb. That morning we got the opportunity to find out, when my roommate stumbled inside the door after wrestling with the lock.

"That door's gonna kill me," she muttered. When she caught me staring at her in my open-mouthed way, she looked around with suspicion. "Wait a minute . . . you finally score, Carolina? Is it the blonde I gave your number to?"

Thea emerged from the bathroom rubbing lotion into her hands. "You need more Jergens," she said, then stopped short when she saw Barb. "Oh. Hi."

"Well, well," Barb said, her eyes pivoting from me to Thea. "The lotion's mine. But please, help yourself."

157

"I'll buy more and bring it next time," Thea said, the words "next time" hovering in the thick silence that fell like a curtain.

"Coffee?" I said finally to neither of them.

Thea grabbed her peacoat from the chair where she'd dropped it the night before and buttoned herself into it for the trip outside. "I'll get some at home," she said. "Got to go grade." I craved a kiss good-bye, especially given the queasy-making conversation we'd had that morning, but all I got was a wave as she headed out the door mouthing, "Call you later."

Barb helped herself to a mug of coffee, shaking her head. "You hold your cards close to the vest, Carolina."

"It's new." I shrugged it off. I didn't feel like sharing whatever Thea and I had with Barb, whose favorite game was musical beds.

"I never saw it coming. I was so wrapped up in Renee. Which is off again, if you must know. Thanksgiving was a fucking nightmare."

The need to know wasn't burning in my chest, and I let the statement drop. The triangle of Barb, Gerri, and Renee had become dizzying and too reminiscent of me, Hallie, and her husband.

"So you're a thing?" Barb asked, a smirk on her face. "You and the ice queen?"

The insult poked me in the ribs, but I didn't flinch. This was the Barb Gerri and Thea had warned me about, but who had treated me like her pet until now. I wondered how badly Renee had hurt her, that she lashed out at the closest person in her path, the roommate relishing a new affair.

"Rude, Barb. Really rude."

"Hey, sorry." Her apology was as flimsy as an old T-shirt. "Who am I to judge? Whatever bakes your potato." She reached for an orange from the bowl of them I'd bought especially for Thea. They were heavy, juicy globes, and Thea had eaten one the night before with sexy gusto.

On instinct, I grabbed the fruit from Barb's hand and returned it to the bowl. She looked like a hungry puppy whose kibble I had snatched away. "I bought those for Thea," I said. "They weren't cheap, so please don't eat them."

"Wow, you are a piece of work," she said. "After all the food I've given you."

"Why am I not remembering all this alleged food?" I asked. "Oh, yeah, there was some moldy bread once and a handful of Doritos. I'm pretty sure I paid for everything else."

Barb snatched the orange back, and before I could stop her started peeling it. "This is still my apartment," she said. "If you don't like it, you should just move in with your girlfriend. Come to think of it, why don't we call this whole roommate thing off? I could use some space." She bit down on an orange section like a dare, and the juice squirted out onto her sweater.

"Are you serious?"

"Yeah. I'm going to be around a lot more, and there isn't room for three of us here."

I thought of fighting for my right to stay, but with Barb so hostile I didn't want to. With a shaky hand, I poured myself a mug of coffee and took it back to my room. I kicked the door shut behind me, just firmly enough to make a statement. I suddenly wished I'd kept Eli's apartment for myself.

That was how I ended up back in Gramercy Park, but this time in fancier digs. Ramona wasn't in the market for a roommate, but when I mentioned at work that I needed a new share and asked her to keep me in mind if she heard of anything, she showed an unexpected empathy.

"Did you . . . break up with someone?" she asked, her voice low and husky. "Oh, God! Your ex has the lease! That's how I ended up in that rat trap on Twenty-Fifth Street." Her eyes widened as she relived the traumatic experience.

"Not quite that bad. I thought my share was long-term, but it turns out it's not."

"The things you find out too late," Ramona said. The mysterious nature of my homelessness held her attention. "Well, you can stay with me for a while if you don't have any place else. I mean, till you find something. I've got a spare bedroom in the back. It comes with a bed and a dresser and even has its own little bathroom. I don't want you out on the street or in some SRO." She bit her bottom lip as if already reconsidering her offer. "You don't have a lot of stuff, do you?"

I laughed, relieved to have an escape from Barb's place. "I travel light."

"No animals? I'm allergic to everything." When I shook my head emphatically, she continued, "It should be fine then. Till you find something." It was the second time she'd added that stipulation in the space of about thirty seconds, so I said I understood the offer was temporary and appreciated the generosity. But I secretly hoped that if I proved myself a thoughtful and respectful roommate, she might extend my time. A plan was already germinating in my mind, to keep stick-skinny Ramona happy and satiated with down-home food, like my mama's buttermilk biscuit and cornbread recipes.

When it came time to leave Barb's for good, I didn't bother Gerri. We'd had one stilted phone conversation since she had exploded at me in Mi Chinita. After leaving Clio's one evening, I had knocked on her door to see if she was up for pizza at John's. As a peace offering, I was prepared to treat and let her order her favorite pie—mushrooms and sausage with extra mozzarella, not my favorite because I had to dig down to pick off the mushrooms I hated.

At her apartment door, though, Gerri whispered that Renee was staying over, so I backed away and stammered something about catching up with her later.

The loss of closeness with Gerri was a dull but persistent ache.

"She'll come around," Thea assured me. "She has such a history with Renee, and love makes people crazy."

"It hasn't made us crazy."

Thea looked puzzled and let the comment fizzle.

160

On moving day, Thea and Vern helped me load boxes into a Ford pickup that belonged to Thea's cousin. Malcolm insisted on coming along and driving his own baby, even though Thea assured him I knew how to handle a stick shift. He didn't seem to be interested in lifting anything, though, and appointed himself as our watchdog: "Nobody's gonna steal shit with me sitting right here," he said.

We were in and out of Fifteenth Street in under an hour; that's how little I owned and how fast we moved. Malcolm said we were so quick he hadn't even finished the Bud I bought him. Thea was especially nimble, sometimes taking the steps two at a time.

As we shuttled back and forth, Barb stood guard in the living room in front of her stereo and record collection. Thea couldn't resist a dig: "Believe it or not, Barb, these black girls don't want to steal your shit." That made Barb color a deep red and retreat to her room, slamming the door and leaving us to finish in peace.

On the street, Vern headed back uptown to go to work while Thea and I cozied up together in Malcolm's passenger seat all innocent, like we were just the best of friends. "Good thing you gals're skinny," he observed as we jerked our way across Manhattan. With the help of the creaky elevator in my new building, the other side of the move proved much easier and even faster, but at the end Thea and I collapsed in a heap on Ramona's living room rug.

"I'm parched," she said, jumping up and heading for the box we'd deposited in the kitchen. She returned a minute later with the Foghorn Leghorn jelly glass from Barb's prized collection. "Hey, isn't this—?"

Caught, I flashed Thea a sheepish grin. "That glass deserved a Southern home," I said.

161

Huddled in a placid valley, Crab Creek, North Carolina remains an intensely rural area, with the local catfish pond among its biggest draws. Surrounded by the impressive peaks of Jeter, Evans, Pinnacle, and Ann mountains, the area also attracts hikers and outdoors enthusiasts.

"My daddy used to talk about going climbing with his big sister from when he was just a little fella," recalls Rufus Threatt Jr., the son of Clio's youngest brother. One of eight Threatts still on the area's property rolls, Rufus and his two sons run a small apple orchard and molasses-making business.

"Daddy said Aunt Birdie was the most fearless of 'em all, not like a girl at all," Rufus continues. "I don't recall her much, but Daddy always talked about her, said she was something."

—from *Dismantling Clio Hartt: Her Life and Work*,
by Ingrid Coppersmith

Chapter 18

Western North Carolina
December 1983

There was no direct train service to the North Carolina mountains, a fact that Clio at first refused to accept. "Not to Hendersonville, but to Asheville surely," she insisted.

When Clio first left North Carolina in the twenties, Asheville was a popular destination for the well-heeled, but it had not been that in a long time. In my teen years, most of the downtown businesses fled to the new Asheville Mall, leaving the city proper with a saggy, forlorn air. My daddy had opened a hardware store on Lexington Avenue after World War II with a low-interest government loan, but he had to shutter the place thirty years later and scramble to eke out a living as a handyman. Our family had never been well-to-do, and if I hadn't gotten a scholarship and worked in the college cafeteria, we could never have afforded even the in-state tuition at UNC Asheville.

I told Clio I could get her as far as Charlotte by train, but then we'd have to hop a Greyhound bus for the additional hundred-odd miles. I knew that bus ride. I'd gone to Charlotte with my sister Brenda in high school, and with the sticky seats, dirty windows, and sloshing noises coming from the bathroom, it had been a nasty experience, not to be repeated. Especially not with Clio.

"Then we'll drive," she said.

But I was still a couple of years under the legal age for car rentals, and Clio had never acquired a driver's license.

"How is that even possible?" I asked.

"Young women did not drive in my day, Miss Bliss," Clio reminded me. "And no one needed to have a car here or in Paris."

Bea kept a Volvo station wagon so she could visit her house in the Catskills on the weekends. The wagon was at least twenty years old and rode that way. She'd taken me and Ramona on a clickety-clacking ride to Leonia, New Jersey, one evening for a client's book party. Ramona teased her about the car, calling it her "granny-mobile," and wondered why someone as important as Bea Winston didn't buy a newer model. "Because this one still runs," Bea said.

When I mentioned my predicament in booking the trip, Bea stared at me with a bored look while she finished chewing something—probably a Hershey's Kiss from the bowl she kept on her desk.

"Clio cannot use my car," she said, like a parent accustomed to her teenager's requests.

"Oh, I just wondered if you had any other—"

"You'd probably break down before you hit Maryland anyway," Bea said. "It's got almost two hundred thousand miles on it. I told you before, you're flying."

"But I don't think you told Clio," I said, so low it was almost under my breath. Bea sighed and punched some buttons into her phone.

"Hello, dear, it's Beatrice," she said. She listened for a few seconds. "Yes, well, we can talk about that later, but first I'm calling to say you've got to give up this idea of trains and cars to North Carolina as it's simply too unwieldy. You must fly and stop worrying Livvie about it." Bea stared at me as she continued to listen. "I understand. There are pills for that, dear. We'll have your doctor call in a prescription to Bigelow's. Yes. Yes, yes, all right. I can do that for you. Yes. You too, dear."

Bea replaced the receiver and drew an American Express gold card from her top desk drawer. "Book the flight," she said, handing it across the desk slowly, as if entrusting me with a family heirloom.

Clio's doctor prescribed a calming dose of Valium, and she willingly accepted the offer of a wheelchair to get her onto the plane ahead of the other passengers. When we were in our seats, her fingers wrapped themselves around my right wrist in a death grip.

She barely spoke throughout the flight, and without use of both of my hands it was difficult to do anything but sit quietly and drink my complimentary Coke with my left hand. Once, Clio wailed "My ears!" and I fished awkwardly in my pocket for a Chiclet for her to chew on. Another time, she cast a furtive glance out the window and muttered something about the wispy clouds that sounded poetic, but forced. Finally, when we hit the tarmac a bit too forcefully, she let out a cry of "Oh, my! Oh, my!" When it was time to disembark, she was still gripping my wrist.

"We're here, safe and sound," I said in as reassuring a voice as I could, slowly prying her fingers away. "My sister is meeting us at the gate, so it's ground transportation from here on out."

Clio smiled. "I had no idea you were such a seasoned flyer," she said. "What do they call it—a jet-setter?"

"I am hardly that, Miss Hartt," I said, my face flushing. "But I'm flattered that you think so." I'd hidden my inexperience from her, but in truth my traveling had been limited to that bus trip to Charlotte, a few weekends in Emerald Isle with a college friend whose family had a cottage there, and an overnighter to Boone with Hallie to visit a fellow professor at App State. Those were the only stamps in my nonexistent passport—until the one-way flight that had transported me from Asheville to New York.

I spotted Sue waving both arms over her head. She had no children in tow, though I had expected at least one; there was always at least one. What I also didn't expect was her rounded belly, a sign that a fourth was on the way.

"You left something out of our conversations," I said, hugging her. "When did this happen?"

"You keeping track of when Jimmy and me screw?" she asked with a smirk. Her voice was loud enough to elicit stares from strangers.

"You know what I mean, Sue," I whispered.

"I'm due in April," she said, the grin disappearing. It wasn't clear if congratulations were in order or if she was just making the most of an unwanted situation.

"Well, here comes Miss Hartt, so please keep it clean. I'm working."

Slumped in her wheelchair, Clio looked the worse for wear. The buttons on her coat were fastened hastily and incorrectly, and her cloche hat, a remnant from the thirties, was askew. Maybe the tilt would have been rakish on a younger woman, but on Clio it just looked like she'd fallen asleep in it. To straighten it for her would have been presumptuous, so I gave her a signal with both my hands and she quickly righted it herself.

"Miss Hartt, this is my sister, Sue Welch. Sue, this is Miss Clio Hartt."

"You are so kind to rescue us, Mrs. Welch," Clio said. "Have you ever flown? My Lord, I'm not a drinking woman anymore, but I wouldn't mind a brandy right about now."

Clio's charm brought a spark to Sue's eyes. "Let's see what we can do about that. There's a lounge—"

"Miss Hartt doesn't want to go to a bar, Sue. And this nice attendant needs to get his wheelchair back, don't you?"

Sue was only five months gone, but already had to squeeze behind the steering wheel. She had never been a dainty girl to begin with. As tall and slim as I was, she was short and plump, almost as if we'd come from different parents. Our daddy liked to quip, "Side by side, y'all look like the number 10!"

"You sure you can still drive with that belly?" I asked, as I helped Clio into the passenger seat of the Fiesta. The car, which Jimmy had bought when their oldest, Pokey, was born, had become a stretch for three kids, and the fourth would have no place to go but the roof.

"Just get in," Sue said.

We drove without speaking for a few miles, which was odd for the Blisses, especially Sue, and I wondered if she was feeling intimidated by having a "famous author" in her car, sitting right beside her, no less. My family could get touchy about things like that. When I was in college and spouting something about Virginia Woolf's "A Room of One's Own" at the supper table, my father and mother had exchanged a knowing look. "You keep doing all that reading and pretty soon there won't be nothing to talk to you about," my daddy had said.

Sue finally broke the silence, announcing she had booked Clio "deluxe accommodations" at the Dry Ridge Cottages, a cluster of cabins that had been on Weaverville Road since the 1940s. The place had seen better days, and I was surprised by the choice.

"You checked out the cabin?" I asked from the back seat. "I mean, to make sure the place is clean."

"Daddy has known Mr. Bell for forty years," Sue snapped—which I knew meant she hadn't bothered to inspect it in advance. "And Mrs. Bell does all the cleaning herself." That was precisely what I was worried about. Mrs. Bell was somewhere between my parents and Clio in age, and the last time I'd seen her she had had a hump starting on her upper back.

"Well, if it there's any problem, we'll just—"

"What is it with you?" Sue interrupted, glaring at me in the rearview mirror. "Is this some New York thing? Because I don't remember you being such a little bitch—" She clapped a hand to her mouth. "Oh, I am so sorry, Miss Hartt, I've got no manners at all."

"Don't apologize on my account," Clio said, a smile forming at the corner of her lips. "I had a dear friend with a mouth like a sailor." After a pause, Clio added, out of nowhere, "You must be the oldest sibling, Mrs. Welch."

"How'd you know?"

"Miss Bliss told me her big sister would be picking us up, and that term is usually reserved for the oldest. I was the oldest on my sibling ladder, too, and I took to my baby brother but to none of the others. Would you say that's true for you, too?"

I met Sue's eyes in the mirror again.

"I would say it probably is," Sue admitted. I stuck my tongue out at her and she laughed.

It *was* true for us, no matter how much we might fuss at each other and despite the gap of seven years. Brenda was closest to Sue in age, but they barely saw each other, even though they lived within a five-minute drive; and Gaynelle was only sixteen months my senior but we hadn't spoken since the last family holiday. In my juvenile way, I still resented Nelle pulling rank on me to dictate the decorations in our shared bedroom, plastering the walls with posters of teen heartthrobs. Every night, David Cassidy had smiled creepily at me from the wall facing my bed.

At Dry Ridge, the Bells had put holiday touches on all the cabins: a pine cone wreath on each door, a string of red and green lights along the porch railings. Cabin no. 7, the "deluxe" cottage, was not the embarrassment I expected. Tucked into a stand of bare willow oaks, it sported a fresh coat of yellow paint and a front porch with two white rocking chairs. One of the porch floorboards was wobbly, but it was December and hardly the weather for sitting outdoors. Inside, the bedroom, kitchenette, and bathroom were respectably clean and tidy. In fact, the place was larger than Clio's apartment, and she clapped her hands together when she saw it. "Oh, this will do very nicely," she said. "I will be comfortable here, I'm sure. Thank you, Mrs. Welch."

Clio's face was lined with fatigue, and she muttered something about wanting to test the bed, so I left her with my parents' phone number and the assurance that I would be back for her in a couple of hours so we could get some supper. But she declined the offer, and even though it was only late afternoon, said she was ready to turn in for the night. "Now you pick me up bright and early," she instructed. We'd been back less than an hour, and I could already hear the echo of a twang in her voice. "I will need to see my brother first thing."

"Tell me again," my mother said as she passed the collards, "why you can't stay longer." Although I would be under her roof for four days, Mama focused on the fact that it wasn't two weeks or more.

I gave the answer that popped into my head first, even though it wasn't exactly true. "Work, Mama," I said, helping myself to the greens and wondering if I could learn to make them—if, in fact, you could even buy collards in Manhattan. And what about ham hocks?

"It's Christmas, Livvie," my father said, as if the artificial white tree with flashing red lights in the living room didn't give it away. "How much work you got at Christmas?"

"Seems like work's all you ever talk about," my mother added. "Aren't you having any fun?"

"I have lots of fun," I said but I left it at that. She didn't really want to know what I was doing for entertainment.

"You ride the subway much?" Daddy asked through a mouthful of chicken.

I laughed at the non sequitur, until his face told me it was a serious question. I wondered if he was poking around to assess the danger in my life, or if he didn't know what else to ask a daughter whose life had become so foreign to him.

"Not so much, Daddy. I walk most places. There's so much to see. Walking in New York is definitely fun." I told him about some of the sights, like the Thanksgiving Day balloons being blown up and the lights on the Christmas tree in Rockefeller Center. "New York is beautiful this time of year. I wish y'all could come and see it."

My parents exchanged glances that suggested a trip to New York was one they would never make. Mama shifted to talking about Sue's pregnancy, Nelle's advancement to assistant manager of housewares at Belk's, and Brenda's husband, who was on unemployment again.

"That boy can't hold a job," she said.

"Well, they ain't living with us this time," Daddy said.

When they ran out of daughters and sons-in-law to talk about, Mama expounded on casual acquaintances, like a neighbor I'd barely spoken to since high school ("She was the most beautiful bride!") and the new assistant choirmaster at our church who had acted tipsy at rehearsal last week. As I often did at home, I fell into a silent funk, the meaningless small talk like being with strangers instead of family.

While I was helping her with the dishes, my mother poked at a sore spot for me. "I saw that teacher of yours in town," she said. "But now her name's gone right out my head."

Something caught in my throat and I coughed. "Which teacher is that?"

"Oh, you know. The chubby one who was always inviting you over. With the handsome husband that runs the sports store, looks like Tom Cruise?"

My ears flamed. "You mean Hallie Shepherd."

"That's it."

"I'd hardly call her 'chubby.'"

"Well, she's not skinny, that's for sure. Or maybe she's pregnant."

"That ship has sailed," I said, trying to hide my discomfort. "She's over forty now. Besides, she never wanted kids."

"Well, what a thing to tell her student! And what kind of woman doesn't want kids?"

"And her husband's name may be Tom, but he's no Cruise." My tone might have been too clipped because Mama gave me a curious look before proceeding with her story.

"Anyway," she continued, "we went to the library to get Pokey some new books—that girl sure loves to read—"

Sue's daughter was a kid after my own heart; she had started to call herself Pete and to ask her family members to address her that way.

"—and your teacher, that Mrs. Shepherd, came right up to me at the counter. I'm not sure I would've known her but she said she remembered me from your graduation, isn't that something? I told her you went to New York, and she told me to tell you hey."

"Oh," I said, because I couldn't think of anything else.

"Isn't that something?"

"Small world," I said, wiping the last supper dish. My ribs pinched, like my heart was pushing at them too hard. "Mama, you mind if I make a long-distance call?"

"You just got here. Who d'you need to call so soon?"

"My roommate," I lied. "I forgot to tell her something important she needs to know before she leaves for Christmas."

There was that curious look again, the one that said she didn't buy what I was selling. "Well, don't be on too long," she instructed. "I haven't paid the bill yet for that last time you called here collect."

My parents had two phones, one in the kitchen and another in their bedroom. I opted for the latter, even though it wasn't optimal, because Daddy had turned on *Family Feud* and I figured they would be engrossed for a half-hour. I just needed to make a connection.

Thea wasn't home, and I wondered if she had decided to leave early for the holiday. In case she was still around, I left a guarded message on her machine: "Hey, just needed to hear a friendly voice. It's really kind of special being home, but maybe you're already finding that out. Hope you have a good Christmas."

I stopped myself from adding, "Love you," knowing Thea wouldn't know what to do with the words.

Chapter 19

My mother had a pineapple upside-down cake recipe that she baked almost every weekend when I was growing up and brought to the elderly, especially those in hospitals and nursing homes. Sometimes we were related to the people, and sometimes they were strangers to me, church members she felt obliged as a Christian lady to visit. When Gaynelle and I were about nine and ten, Mama started dragging us along in the car, ostensibly to mind the cake but more likely to teach us that this was what folks did for their elders.

Because of this training, the facility where Clio's brother was living out his final days was one I'd been to at least a dozen times. Back then, it was called Mountain Something Nursing Home, but now it was Margaret House. A plaque near the front door indicated the name honored a pioneering nurse in the field of hospice care.

Despite the name change, the low-slung brick building looked the same from the outside, and the interior seemed to have escaped refurbishing, too. Although the carpeting bore none of the stains that had fascinated me and Nelle back in the day (dropped food? bodily fluids?), the tables and chairs were still motel blond, and the paintings that had captivated me were right where I remembered them. Every wall bore an almost identical woodland scene, complete with soft-eyed deer and wily red foxes posing in front of a stream or waterfall. What made the paintings so special to me as a kid was that each had a lamp at the top of the frame that threw light onto the water and made it appear to ripple—an optical illusion, but a memorable one. Now the bulbs were either turned off or burnt out.

Clio gave the surroundings a once-over as we proceeded slowly through the lobby to the visitors' desk. "I thought Rufe was doing better than this," she said under her breath. "He owned a printing company at one time." But she admitted she couldn't remember if he still owned it.

The attendant on duty pointed us to a wing extending from the right side of the lobby, where I located the nameplate "R. Threatt." I stood aside for Clio to enter, which she did only after squeezing her eyes shut and then opening them again.

Rufe looked better than I expected. For one, he wasn't lying down or in a flimsy hospital gown but was sitting up in a rocking chair, completely dressed, his thinning white hair neatly combed. The only embarrassing thing was a smear of something yellow on his brown sweater, maybe a breakfast egg.

Clio walked right up to him and patted his head in a way that seemed like habit, even though she had not seen him in decades. "Rufie," she said in a small voice, summoning up a girl from long ago. It wasn't clear to me if Rufe recognized her at first, but then his blue eyes, which matched hers perfectly, welled up.

"Sister," he said, his voice as small as hers. Witnessing the tenderness of the moment reminded me of all the times I had crawled up beside Sue on the couch just to feel her next to me.

I brought Clio a chair and offered to wait in the lobby. I'd come prepared: I had a copy of Audre Lorde's *Zami*, which I'd borrowed from Thea, tucked into my bag for killing time. But Clio told me I should go away, busy myself, and come back for her at two o'clock.

I hadn't planned on Clio freeing me like that, and wasn't sure what to do with a luxurious four hours—with my daddy's car, no less. The last thing I wanted was to go back home. I could drive to campus to see if anything had changed, but the place would be deserted in the days leading up to Christmas, making the trip pointless. I considered driving past Hallie's street. If she or Tom spotted me, though, I'd be caught shame-faced, without a plan. It wasn't a main thoroughfare, but a side street in the Montford neighborhood that you had to go out of your way to get to.

I quickly shook myself out of that idea and drove in a more sensible direction. Because I'd overslept and skipped breakfast to be on time for Clio, I opted to read my book over coffee and eggs at the Mediterranean, a diner in town.

The waitress was a girl I'd gone to high school with. She'd sat in front of me in a few classes, so her last name had to be something alphabetically close to mine. "Livvie Bliss!" she said, like we were lifelong pals. If she hadn't been wearing a name tag, I would have labored to excavate her name. "Hey, Peg!" I said, as friendly as could be. A memory of her shiny blond hair rippling down her back popped into my mind.

"Where've you been, girl? I haven't seen you here in ages."

"Oh, I moved out of town," I said, thinking that admitting I now lived in New York might sound uppity.

"Don't tell me! You're in Charlotte, right?"

"How'd you guess?"

Her face lit with pride. "You always said you were going to get the hell out. I figured you for a city girl." I had no recollection of ever telling Peg my future plans, but from a young age I'd dreamed of adventure and excitement beyond the confines of our little mountain town.

"I'll never forget. You wrote the funniest thing in my yearbook," Peg said. I braced myself; I'd been such a dork in high school. "You said, 'We'll always have Paris.' Nobody wrote stuff like that. Most people just said 'Friends forever' or 'Don't change' or something dumb. You sure were different."

My youthful affectations made me flush to the roots of my hair. Did I write that in everyone's yearbook or just Peg's?

"'Different' is sure a nice way to put it," I said. "And what are you up to now?"

She chuckled at the question. "Well, right now, I'm taking your order." I tugged at one of my very hot ears as I recited an unusually large order of fried eggs, crispy bacon, home fries, and two biscuits. With jam.

"Good appetite," she said, turning to the kitchen.

I'd gotten a few pages into *Zami* when Peg returned with my order and a coffee refill. "Still a reader," she commented as she poured.

"Always."

"How do you say that title?"

"Zah-mee," I pronounced—something I only knew because Thea had said it for me first.

"Sounds, maybe, African?"

She was a nice girl, but now I really wanted her to go away so I could enjoy my breakfast. "It is," I replied, hoping my curt response would end the conversation.

"What's it about?"

I sighed. "I just started it. I don't know," I lied. Thea had told me it was a memoir about growing up in Harlem and coming out as a lesbian in the fifties. "It's so vivid, I felt like I was right there in the old bars!" she'd said. But I wasn't going to admit that to Peg, even though the truth would probably send her scurrying away for good. "I'll let you know." The snippiness in that last comment was uncalled for and sounded more like Barb than me.

"Well, I'll leave you to it then," Peg said, her own face reddening as she stepped away from the table.

My rudeness to Peg distracted me so that I kept reading the same line over and over, as if it were in a language I vaguely understood but whose vocabulary I hadn't mastered: "She taught me that women who want without needing are expensive and sometimes wasteful, but women who need without wanting are dangerous—they suck you in and pretend not to notice." On the edge of grasping the first clause, I'd realized that the twist in the second clause had left me stymied.

And that was only the introduction.

I slapped the book closed and finished my breakfast staring out the window. Peg came back once to refill my cup and to rip my check off her pad. When she slid it onto the table, she put something else down, too—a flyer on mint-green copy paper.

"I don't know how long you're around," she said in a casual way that suggested she was trying too hard. "You asked what I've been doing. Long story short—textiles."

Her words didn't register at first. I'd placed her in a little box that said, "Waitress: Not worth my time." The flyer advertised a group mixed-media show at an art gallery I'd never heard of. Artists had been filtering into Asheville over the past decade, taking advantage of a depressed real estate market to create a nascent art scene. Peg Bailey was apparently part of it; her name topped the list of about seven artists.

"This is very cool," I remarked. "What kind of textiles?"

"Mostly fabric collages," she said. I tried to meet her eyes, but she kept them down on the flyer. "Some quilting. That kind of thing. You're probably busy with your family and all—"

"No, I'm definitely going to try to fit this in," I said. "Maybe Christmas Eve. I'm here till the twenty-sixth."

"I know it's a little show," Peg said with a shrug of her left shoulder, "but I'm psyched. This—" she nodded toward the rest of the diner, "—just pays the bills."

"I used to wait tables," I said. "I hear you." She finally caught my eye and smiled. Relief that she hadn't dismissed me as a pretentious loser flooded through me.

My eyes had been bigger than my stomach, as my mother would have said. I left a lot on my plate and took one of the biscuits I'd ordered to go. I reckoned that Clio might like a taste of home after spending the morning with Rufe.

Clio had dozed off in a wingback chair in the Margaret House lobby. Although I tried saying her name, what roused her were several gentle nudges of her shoulder.

"Oh," she said. She removed a handkerchief from her bag and wiped a bit of drool from the corner of her mouth. "How long have I been asleep?"

"I just got here." I checked my watch, which read 1:50. "I'm a little early. How was your visit?"

"We can go now," she said, waving off the hand I'd extended to help her from the chair. As we passed the reception desk, she called out to the attendant. "Thank you again for the sweet tea."

How long had she been sitting in the lobby?

"I brought you a biscuit," I said when we were back in my daddy's car. "Thought that might hit the spot." I located the tinfoil wrapper in my bag, but she declined it.

"So did something happen back there at the home?"

"Not to speak of."

"Well, when I left you, you were petting your brother, but when I came back—"

"We talked a bit and then he slept the rest of the time while they piped in Mozart or Bach or some other music he would have hated." Clio smoothed the folds of her skirt. "It was a waste to come all this way to watch him sleep."

"Was he lucid?"

"I don't know if I believe anything he said." She paused for a long minute, considering the passing landscape. "Where are we going?"

"I thought you might like to rest back at your cabin. Later . . . well, my mama invited you to supper, if you like. She's making chicken stew."

Clio didn't seem to register the invitation. "I've been resting for hours. Do you know how to get us to Hendersonville? I need to see something."

The more precise instructions I was waiting for weren't forthcoming, so I just headed for the road I'd always taken to Hendersonville and drove. After a few minutes of silence, I flipped on a local radio station that was playing back-to-back Christmas carols from singers like Amy Grant and Charley Pride.

"Rufe would have liked this," Clio commented, her focus still on the scenery. "This would have been the music to play."

As we approached downtown Hendersonville, Clio leaned forward slightly in her seat like a restless child. Main Street had gone from straight to serpentine only a decade earlier, and I knew she must be unprepared for the change in her hometown's appearance.

"Where are we?"

"Hendersonville."

"It can't be." But then I pointed out landmarks like the old train station and the county courthouse, and she slumped backward. "I don't understand why they did this."

"I think it's pretty," I offered. "Artistic."

"Sickening, if you ask me," she said, "making people weave back and forth like that."

The change in the road threw off her sense of direction, and we made a couple of wrong turns before she directed me onto Kanuga Road.

"We're heading out of town," I said. "Are you sure?"

"The homeplace was in Crab Creek," Clio replied. She'd never told me that, but I couldn't fault her for fudging the location. After all, I always said I was from Asheville.

As a kid, I'd been through Crab Creek many times on the way to the state forest or with my daddy to buy bushels of apples in the fall. Clio hunched forward again, gripping the dashboard. I couldn't tell if she was excited or confounded.

"Here!" she screamed out. "Turn here!" We made a couple of additional right turns that finally led onto a dirt road. A weathered wooden sign read "Threatt Way." The region had experienced a dusting of snow in recent days, and the tires on my daddy's Nova didn't spit back as much dust as they might have in a dry season. He wouldn't complain about how dirty I'd gotten his baby.

We snaked along at ten miles an hour, and I joked that Clio didn't find her own road "sickening." Whatever she was feeling, she didn't say, spending the entire trip with one hand on the dash and the other clutching her armrest.

Our route took us past several rickety cabins sprouting satellite dishes in the yards. Each cabin also had a tractor in front and roaming animals, pigs and skinny hounds. On one porch, a man looked like he'd stepped out of *The Beverly Hillbillies* or *Green Acres*. I was a small-town girl whose family had kept a few chickens, and this was more country than even I was accustomed to.

Finally, we rounded a bend and came upon a pond with daubs of dirty snow ringing the edges. "Stop!" Clio commanded, her eyes traveling up the slope opposite the pond to a frame house. The siding could have been aluminum, but the building was in the style of a nineteenth-century farmhouse. Behind it were rows of neatly planted trees—an apple orchard, looked like.

"That's it. That's the Threatt homestead." It was like a photographic image of the setting Clio had written about in her story "Before the Fire."

"I thought you said it burned down," I said, as I watched her wrestle with the car door handle.

"It did," she said, right before she alighted and took off up the path to the house like a woman forty years younger.

I followed her to the front porch, where she stopped to survey the landscape with a contented sigh. From that vantage point, the wobbly-looking cabins we'd passed were hidden in trees, and all you could see were the pond where I'd parked the car, barren fields, and a ring of snow-dipped mountains in the distance, looking like marshmallow sundaes. "That's Jeter Mountain, just over yonder, and Evans, and that big one's Pinnacle," she said, calling them out with delight. "We hiked there as kids."

"I've been there, I think," I said, a shadowy picture of a picnic with extended family forming in my memory. "So is that an apple orchard in back? We used to come out here to buy apples."

"Threatts have been growing apples since before I was born. Made molasses, too." She motioned toward the fields below us. "That was all cane. Looked like corn in the summer, and then in the fall the plants got yellow and red stripes and you knew it was time to cut. Daddy and the boys used machetes, and then they crushed the sap out of the stalks in a mill that was—" a hand waved vaguely to her left, "—over there, somewhere. It's gone now. Then there was all the boiling and the jarring. Went on day and night."

"Did you help?"

"That was men's work," she said.

"Well, I bet the molasses was good." Nostalgia welled in me for the molasses we'd bought at farm stands when I was little, bringing it home to slather on my mother's biscuits.

That snapped Clio out of her reverie. "Can't bear the taste of it to this day." She turned back to the front door and rapped on it loudly.

An elderly woman with a bosom like a shelf and more salt than pepper in her hair kept the screen door closed between us. Her eyes scanned both of us quickly but settled on me. "Yes?"

"Ivy?" Clio said. "It's me, Birdie."

The woman's mouth flapped open. "Birdie!" she said. "Is it really you? Come in, come in!"

It was strange to hear Clio called by her given name; she never spoke about the decision to abandon her identity. I followed her into the house, throwing a shy smile toward Ivy.

"This your . . . well, it can't be a grandson, can it?"

"This is Miss Livvie Bliss," Clio corrected. "Don't let her clothes fool you. Her folks live over in Weaverville, and she was kind enough to escort me here so I could see Rufe one last time. This is my sister-in-law, Mrs. Ivy Threatt."

"Oh, oh, Miss Bliss," Ivy said, coloring at her mistake.

Before long, I was settled in a chair with some Swiss Miss in a chipped Santa Claus mug, but I still had no idea how it was that we were in a house that had supposedly burned to the ground—and with the family pets in it. The grisly story had stayed with me since Clio first related it.

The sisters-in-law swapped notes on Rufe's condition like I wasn't in the room, so I entertained myself watching Ivy's dog sleep by the fireplace. She was a sweet senior with the face of a lab and a long, low body like a hound. Her mostly white legs and face were painted with butterscotch freckles. Every few minutes, her eyes would pop open to assess me then close dreamily again. I tried to pinpoint how many breeds had contributed to her lineage, but then I overheard the women's talk switch to the house.

"—and I had to see the place for myself," Clio said.

Ivy motioned us to take a quick tour of the downstairs, with Clio marveling that the rooms were laid out just as she remembered them. I poked my head into a compact space equipped with an old white iron bed and a brightly colored star quilt. "We had three beds in here!" Clio said. "Six of us crammed like peaches in a jar." Trying to imagine it made my shared bedroom with Gaynelle seem luxurious.

"So Rufe built this back up himself?" Clio said when we retook our seats in the main room. "He told me that at the home, but I thought he was delirious from the drugs they give him."

"It took him years, mind," Ivy said with pride. "He started before I even met him, whenever he could save up a few dollars for wood and nails. Some buddies from the Balfour mill pitched in to help, and then Rufe Junior learned carpentry right on this spot. We moved here in forty-eight. The siding came later."

"Like the phoenix," Clio mused. The reference was a hazy memory to me from a mythology book I'd read in school, but Ivy was the one to chime in: "What's that about Phoenix? Isn't that out west somewheres?"

"It's a bird in Greek mythology," Clio said with a self-satisfied smile that suggested she knew Ivy would be baffled. "A sun bird that dies in a burst of flames, then rises again from its own ashes. This homestead is like that—rising from the ashes of its own ruin. Not better, really, just different."

Ivy's body tensed visibly. "This house *rose* because of my Rufe's sweat! Nobody cared a speck but him. Y'all just left the bones of it on this hill, rotting."

Clio straightened in her seat, too. "Well, he should have told me when I came for Mama," she said with pique. "I couldn't bear to see it in ruins or think about all the animals, so I didn't even bother to come by. It was my house, too! Seeing him build it back up would have meant something."

"Birdie Threatt," Ivy said, her eyes flashing, "the last time anybody saw you was at that funeral. That's gotta be forty years ago, and you was here for about a minute. That was the only time I ever saw the mysterious Birdie, wasn't sure you even existed. Lord, you wouldn't recognize your own nieces and nephews if they passed you on one of them New York City streets!" The way she drew in a breath with a pained expression, like it hurt, made me wonder about her own health. "And you sit here telling me what your brother *should* have done? That this house was *yours*? You never cared about your own kin, let alone some old farmhouse!"

The raised voices made the dog sit up, her head swiveling from Ivy to Clio, just like mine.

"It's like Mama Threatt used to say about you—that girl thinks the sun comes up just to hear her crow!"

"Well," Clio said, lifting herself up by the arms of the wooden rocker she was in, "I think it's time to go."

"Oh, sit down," Ivy said. "You got my knickers in a knot is all. If you knew me, you'd know I have a short fuse."

"We have taken too much of your time," Clio insisted. "Miss Bliss—"

I bent over to pet the dog, who leaned in to get the most from the head scratch.

"See?" Ivy said, nodding toward the dog, "Even Flecks wants you to stay."

"I've been up since eight, and I am fatigued. Miss Bliss will take me back to my cabin now."

"Cabin? When your old room is just sitting here?"

Clio hastened toward the door without replying.

"Thank you for the hot chocolate, Mrs. Threatt," I said. "It was nice to meet you."

"You bring her back for Christmas," Ivy instructed when Clio was already out on the porch.

"We are not staying in town for Christmas!" Clio called back over her shoulder.

"We aren't?" I asked, as I slipped down the hill after her.

"I have seen my brother and I have seen the homeplace," Clio said. "Why would we stay?"

At the car, I glanced back up the hill, where Ivy was poised in the doorframe, waving.

"What about Mrs. Threatt?" I asked, nodding toward the

house as I held the passenger door for Clio. She harrumphed and settled in without waving back, so I lifted my arm and gave Ivy a proper good-bye wave.

Clio's question about why we would stay was rhetorical, but when we had crunched along Threatt Way and reached the paved Crab Creek Road, I answered it just the same.

"Because it's Christmas," I said, as if it was the most obvious thing in the world.

"What?"

"We would stay because it's Christmas, and you spend Christmas with your folks. And *my* folks are expecting me. I'm not sure what my mother would do if I took off back to New York now." She was facing the window, and I wasn't sure if she was listening. "Besides, I don't see as we could change our flight that easily. There would be a penalty, and I'd need Bea's charge card to do it." I wasn't sure that last part was true, but it sounded authoritative coming out of my mouth, and Clio had already mistaken me for a jet-setter.

She crossed her arms over her chest, like she was cold, and I cranked up the heat a notch. "This place gets to me," she said. I sensed her eyes boring into me, but I kept mine on the road. "No one appreciated my ambitions. I didn't want to marry, so I was odd. I would have been just an old maid, really, relegated to teaching girls their ABC's at that fancy academy in Hendersonville, I forget the name. That school would have been my coffin. You heard Ivy. All these years gone by and still, 'It can't be a grandson, can it?' Like children were the most fulfillment a woman could have."

It was the first I'd heard of a teaching job in Hendersonville, but I had read only a few chapters of the thick biography of Clio that Gerri had lent me. Clio turned her head and focused elsewhere, and my hands relaxed on the wheel. After the fierce emotion of her last words, I was surprised by what came next.

"I don't suppose you'd want to drive me all the way back to Crab Creek on Christmas Day and then pick me up, too."

"I'd be happy to drive you, Miss Hartt! I would welcome a

break from my nieces and nephews playing, and from all the adults teasing me about New York."

Her eyes turned toward me again. "They don't understand you any more than my family did me."

"No Bliss has ever left," I said. "Well, my Aunt Sass tried. She went to New York, too, for a couple of years, but she got tricked into coming back."

"And you've been pressured to come back, too."

"Not in so many words." I paused to gather up my thoughts. "They get in a lot of digs. They think I'm questioning their way of life."

"Aren't you?" Clio asked. It was the most she'd ever asked me about my North Carolina exodus, and I found it both uncomfortable and strangely comforting at the same time, to be a fellow ex-pat of Clio Hartt. "My leaving questioned the narrow box my family, this culture, put me in."

"I take it no one in your family read your work."

"Rufe read some stories in the *Saturday Evening Post*. He wrote to me in Paris saying he liked them. He was still young. I'm not sure he'd married Ivy yet. Later I signed a copy of *The Dismantled* and sent it to him, but he never even told me he got it." I wondered if Ivy still had that valuable edition.

"If we're staying, I will need to call Ivy about Christmas," she said, rummaging through her purse. "I have her number in here somewhere."

"Oh, you would be very welcome at my folks', if you'd rather," I offered. Selfishly, I wanted her there as a distraction and a buffer. "They're curious about you."

Clio chortled. "That is the biggest lie I've heard in quite a while, young lady, and I've heard a few in my day. No, I will go to the homeplace since Ivy invited me."

"Then we'll call as soon as we get back. You're making the right choice, Miss Hartt. About staying."

"I don't know as I have much of a choice, Miss Bliss."

Chapter 20

My whole life, Aunt Sass and Uncle Emmett lived about a quarter-mile from my folks. When I was young and my mother kept the books at Daddy's hardware store, I'd head to Aunt Sass's after school to do my homework. They had four boys to match our girls, and I grew up playing with Cash, who was a year younger.

Sass had yearned for a daughter, "for company," she said. Her past was appealingly mysterious to me, what with those months in New York, so I latched on and became the next best thing to her own. She spotted my independent streak from an early age, and as I grew up I confessed dreams to her, like wanting to work with books somehow and live in another place. Years before she gave me money to help fund my move to New York, she was whispering subversive wisdom to me like, "You don't need to get married to be happy, Livvie. A husband's just another kid who can't take care of himself." Not that Uncle Em wasn't a sweet guy, but he couldn't have made his own supper if his life depended on it.

I didn't want to miss the chance to drop in on her after I deposited a weary Clio at her cabin. I'd written my aunt regularly since moving away, especially after I got my job and started working with Clio—I saw it as reporting to her on her investment—but she was not much of a correspondent and there'd been no letters from her in return. That didn't mean she hadn't missed me. The bear hug she gave me at her front door forced all the breath out of my lungs: She was my height, and almost twice my weight.

"Oh, honey, it is so good to see you!" she said between squeezes. "Let me look at you! What's this jacket you got on? Looks like something your daddy'd wear to go out in his truck." As much as she appreciated my independence, she had never really approved of my chosen attire.

Uncle Em, a plumber, was out on an emergency job. "Somebody's poop broke their toilet again," was how Sass said he'd put it, and we had a chuckle over that. We sat in her yellow kitchen at the built-in maple breakfast nook that had been there since I could remember, and she offered me coffee and a cigarette. "Thought you might have taken it up in the big city," she said, when I refused the Newport. "That's where I got started. Everybody did it." She smoked when my uncle wasn't around to scold her, and I noticed that her smoker's cough was hoarser than when I last saw her.

She was eager for news of my life, and she lobbed questions at me that felt good to answer, like I was actually being seen by someone in my family. What did my job entail? ("You like all that filing? I was never much for it.") How was my apartment? ("You moved again? I can't keep up!") You got some nice friends? ("Sounds like you found every girl in the city who likes to read.") How was it working for a famous author? ("She related to the Threatts over in Bat Cave?")

And then: What was my favorite part of living in New York?

That one tripped me up, and I cast my eyes down into my coffee mug while I mulled my options. Without a doubt, my favorite part was being openly gay, not just with my friends or roommate, but at work, too. I hadn't come to Sass's house to out myself, but I'd always been honest with her. When I looked up again, she was staring at me with an expectant look.

"I never knew Livvie Bliss to search for words," she said, after a long drag on her cigarette.

I drew in a breath. "What I like best about New York is that I can be open about myself all the time," I said, as preamble. "With everybody." I paused, and she held my eyes through the cloud of smoke that hovered between us in the nook.

"I'm—"The admission wouldn't surface, and I shifted uncomfortably on the wooden bench as I struggled to pry it loose. "I'm gay, Aunt Sass," I said in a rush. And then I burst into tears, the weight of telling the first person in my family lifting off me.

She extinguished her smoke and reached over to pat my hand. "Oh, honey, I figured that. I never heard you talk about a boy, not in all these years. Your sisters? They just couldn't stop with all the Jimmy this and Ray that." She motioned toward my flannel wool shirt, which I'd bought in the young men's department at Macy's. "And those clothes of yours—"

I laughed, wiping my tears with my sleeve, but her face remained serious. Just because she knew didn't mean she was happy about it.

"It's a hard road you've chosen," she said. "And I can see by those tears you know that's true."

"Oh, no, Aunt Sass!" I said. "I'm not unhappy. My life doesn't feel any harder than the next person's. I'm just crying because I'm so relieved! It's like I've been bottled up. Imagine you got a Coke, and you shake it and crack it open and it all comes spraying out."

"Well, your secret's safe," she said, sitting back in the nook in a way that felt distancing. I worried briefly that I had ruined everything between us in a momentary surge of truth, all those years of sharing my thoughts and hopes at this very table. Sass zippered her lips. "Your mama won't hear it from me."

I swallowed hard and offered a weak smile. Deep down, I had hoped Mama *would* hear it from her, but after I was safely back in New York.

I really needed to talk to another lesbian. With Thea unavailable, my best prospect appeared to be phoning Gerri.

Renee was Jewish, and they were in the city for the holiday, so Gerri had agreed to watch Remmie while we were away. But my reception when I first rapped on her door and asked for the favor had been chilly. "Renee's not big on cats," Gerri said. "And I'd be scared to have him around Alice."

"Remington could stay at Clio's, and Renee and Alice will never even see him. I'll give you my key to check on him. He's an easy cat and cute, too. Please? Forget that you're hating me right now. You'd be doing a favor for a literary legend!"

The prospect of snooping around Clio's apartment had won Gerri over. And after accepting the cat-sitting duties, my friend had made a peace offering that loosened something inside me, like when you finally get a stubborn screw to turn. "I could never hate you, Livvie," she had said, before asking if we could make a date after New Year's to "process" our friendship.

Now I had the perfect excuse to call her—to check on Remington and make sure he had adjusted to his sitter. And if I happened to add that I'd just come out to my aunt, well, Gerri might offer some needed words of support from years of experience.

Calling from my parents' house was out of the question, so I collected a bunch of change and headed to Cowboy Jack's, a local dive bar. The place was empty for a Friday night, with only a few sad drunks at the bar as Merle Haggard crooned, "If we make it through December we'll be fine." I knew the bartender—I'd drowned my sorrows there quite a few times after the split with Hallie—and waved to him as I made my way to the phone in the back, on the wall between the men's and women's rooms. "Please be there," I whispered as I dialed Gerri's number in Milligan Place.

Gerri sounded breathless, like she was either hurrying in or out when the phone rang.

"I just left Clio's," she explained.

"Lucky for me! I called to find out how Remington's doing." After a pause, I added, "Clio was wondering. I told her he'd be fine, but you know."

"Sure. Well, he's a good little guy. We're becoming great pals. He's eating and shitting and everything he's supposed to do." Her jocular tone lifted me up, like we'd never been estranged. "And he loves that catnip mouse. It's kind of obscene."

We chatted about her and Renee's plans for Christmas. They had tickets for *Silkwood*: "I hear Cher plays a dyke! Isn't that wild? We're bringing Kleenex for the ending."

The Kleenex comment provided an artful segue into the topic I needed to get off my chest. "Speaking of crying, you'll never guess what I did today."

"Ate collards?" she said.

"That's an everyday occurrence at the Blisses', and nobody cries about it," I said.

"Eating collards every day seems pretty sad to me."

"Think bigger. More . . . unexpected."

"Beats me."

A pause for effect. "Drumroll, please! I came out to my aunt. First person in my family to know."

Gerri exploded. "You did not! That is great, Livvie! I'm so proud of you. This calls for a celebration!" Then my words sank in. "Wait, who did the crying?"

The details of my talk with Aunt Sass spilled out of me, down to the emotional moment of reveal. My pocket of change got lighter with each minute, but I was hesitant to hang up. The hardest thing about being home was that, although the place was familiar, I didn't fit anymore.

"Who's next? Your parents? Will you do both at once? I prefer the group method myself."

"Oh, it's not the right time. I'm not ready for them."

"There's no right time, Livvie." She paused, and the sound of her lighting a cigarette traveled through the line. "But you've got kind of a good setup right now if you think about it. Wait till Christmas Day. Drop the bombshell, say, right after dinner. Everybody has a good cry or maybe a scream, and then the next morning you get on a plane and fly away. You seriously limit the length of the dramatics and knock them all off in one fell swoop."

A cartoon image of the words "I'm gay" toppling one family member after another like a bowling ball striking pins crossed my mind. In reality, I couldn't fathom telling my family as a group and watching nieces and nephews hurriedly transported to other rooms. Plus, it was hard to get a word in edgewise once all the Blisses were together. Still, I said, "Yeah, well, maybe," just to shut down the conversation.

"Try it, you'll like it!" Gerri said in a fake New York accent, mimicking the guy from the old Alka Seltzer commercials.

Her pushiness began to grate on me, like she couldn't understand the hugeness of coming out to my aunt and wanted more. I pivoted into bringing the call to a close. "Anyway, thanks for listening. I really needed a lesbian ear!"

"My lesbian ears are all yours."

I laughed, but for a few minutes after hanging up, I stood motionless at the phone, my hand sweaty from clutching the receiver. A call that had started off supportive ended by leaving me tense, almost as if I'd talked to one of my sisters instead of a friend. But I wasn't sure if I was more upset because Gerri didn't understand me, or because I lacked the courage to jump in and take her suggestion.

The bartender had popped open a Bud for me. "Looks like you could use some holiday cheer," he said.

On Christmas Eve, Daddy relinquished his old Nova to me once again. The station wagon served mostly for church on Sundays, grocery shopping, and my mother's Christian-duty visits, so the mileage was stuck at around sixty thousand. A used black Ford pickup he'd bought for his handyman job was his preferred transport because he could stash all his supplies in a truck box in the bed and be ready to slap up drywall at a moment's notice.

"You're helping me out, taking the old girl for a spin," he said as he dropped the keys into my open palm that morning. Daddy was being generous, too, because Sue had called and invited me over to help her wrap presents for the kids after I'd fulfilled my duties with Clio. "You have a good time with your sister," he added.

In fact, I was scheming to postpone going to Sue's and to wander over to Peg Bailey's art show, which was open for a few hours that afternoon in downtown Asheville. I didn't mention the art show to Daddy—not because he would care where I went, but because I knew the gallery's existence would pinch him like a tight waistband. He dismissed the artists and bohemian retailers in downtown Asheville as "squatters" or "damn hippies."

With a care package of food from my mother—homemade cornbread, a three-bean salad, and leftover chicken stew—my first stop was Clio's cabin. Clio seemed tempted by the cornbread but then said she'd had a funny taste in her mouth all day and would put it in the refrigerator for later.

"You up for another visit to your brother?"

"I don't believe so," she said. "I was trying to work, but I started getting this tingle in my fingers."

Open on a round table in the corner of her room was a cloth-bound notebook—the one she'd requested and I'd located for her at a stationery store in the Village. Her vintage Sheaffer fountain pen rested across its pages. Although I'd helped her pack for the trip, she must have tossed her writing materials into the bag when I wasn't looking.

"Miss Hartt! Is that a new story?"

"Can't say yet."

"Well, it's good news, whatever it is. But what about your tingly feeling? Do you want to see a doctor?"

"Lord, no! What a lot of fuss, really. I was just gripping the pen too tight."

"I will leave you to it then. Get some rest, and I hope your taste buds get back to normal real soon. My mama's cornbread is a thing of beauty." We set a time for me to pick her up for Crab Creek the following day, and then I headed to town with Peg's flyer folded into my coat pocket.

The 51 Gallery (named for its street number) was nearly empty when I showed up; even Peg wasn't around. A young white guy with dreads was in charge and jumped up to greet me. He was one of the artists, he informed me as he showed off his oversized metal sculptures fashioned out of rusty machine parts. When I asked about Peg, he pointed to some pieces mounted on a wall that were no more than twelve inches square, some even smaller. There were six or seven in all, fabric and paper collages that celebrated women's history. While each of the guy's metal works was priced at four or five hundred dollars or more, Peg was asking only thirty apiece for hers. "She needs to go bigger," the guy said with a dismissive air.

"Is she coming in today?" I asked, after I'd made the tour of the show and decided my favorites were Peg's work and photos of dilapidated barns shot by another female artist.

"Nah, she was in yesterday," he said. "She's home with her old lady." My face must have registered confusion because he added, laughing, "Her girlfriend, man. You dig?"

Walking out of the gallery, I marveled at how little I knew about my own hometown. Peg, a girl I'd sat behind in high school, was apparently living as a lesbian—with a girlfriend!— and making delicate, woman-centered art in the place I'd fancied such a backwater. What would have happened to me if I'd stayed?

That question made me take a detour past Hallie and Tom's bungalow. Their house was forsaken-looking, with no outdoor Christmas lights and no sign of movement inside. I wondered if they had gone to Tom's parents in West Virginia for the holiday, or if they were just out for the day. But then I noticed a funny thing—a child's tricycle in the side yard. With the motor idling, I puzzled over the trike, thinking it must be a neighbor's, when a rap on my car window made me lurch forward and bash my chest against the steering wheel. It was a neighbor I recognized from all the times I'd been to visit Hallie, a guy who lived across the street with his wife and kids.

"Livvie, right?" he asked through the rolled-down window. He was carrying a bag full of wrapped Christmas presents.

"Hi, Mike," I said, proud I'd unearthed his name.

"You know they moved, right?"

My mouth fell open. "No, I've been gone—"

"Yeah, they sold the place in the fall, right after they split up. Tom said neither one of them could bear to stay."

"No, I guess not," I muttered, my mind replaying the words "split up."

"Real shame," Mike went on. "Nice couple."

"Do you know where they went?" I asked. "I mean where Hallie went? I knew her better than Tom . . . because of school. But I knew him too, of course." My words were tripping all over themselves in my attempt to stay cool.

"No idea. Tom got an apartment, I think over in West Asheville, but he didn't say anything about her. Some bad stuff went down. Cheating type stuff. Her, not him." Mike stamped his feet from the cold. "Gotta get inside now. Santa's big night!" He extended his paunchy stomach and I worried he was about to deliver a "Ho, ho, ho!" But he spared me and simply said, "Merry Christmas!"

Because I knew that Hallie and Tom wouldn't be driving up at any minute and that Mike didn't have contact with them, I took a few additional minutes to stare at the house. My thoughts traveled to the bedroom and the dive I'd taken out the window the last time Hallie and I were together. It was late afternoon and we'd fallen asleep, forgetting to set the alarm so I could leave well before Tom got home. Hallie practically pushed me out of bed when she heard Tom's keys in the front door. Only half-dressed, I'd pitched myself out the window like a burglar, and crushed a hydrangea. I hunched out of sight, waiting to dash away until I heard Tom and Hallie screaming at each other. Hallie had driven me to her house, so I had to hitch a ride back to Weaverville.

After a few days, I had called her from Cowboy Jack's, begging her to see me, but she told me she couldn't. "Not in that way. I'll always have fond memories of you, Livvie, but I love Tom."

"You said you loved me!" I protested. "In your office that time, and then at the motel—"

"Well, I did. At that moment. That's something people say."

195

Her voice had dripped with annoyance, like I was a student protesting my grade, and that was what had made me fire back. "Well, here's something else they say! I hate you! And I could fix you good, Hallie! What if I told Tom you've been sleeping with your student? What about that, Professor?"

She had sighed, knowing as well as I that I'd never follow through on such a threat, that spilling our secret would hurt me as much as her. "Please, Livvie, don't be like this. We had something special for a while, didn't we? Let's leave it at that."

As I drove from Hallie's old house to Sue's, the memory made my eyes fill. Luckily, my sister either didn't notice I'd been crying or was so frazzled by the duties of being a parent on Christmas Eve that she ignored it.

Chapter 21

The next day, I rapped at Clio's cabin door, but she didn't answer. Where would she be on Christmas morning? My cheerful raps turned to urgent bangs as I called out her name. I moved to the window, but the shades were drawn, so I tried tapping on the glass. Still no response. A man in the neighboring cabin saw my distress and fetched Mr. Bell to unlock the door.

"Doesn't seem good," Mr. Bell said as he fussed with a ring of keys before finding the correct one.

Clio was sitting in the armchair, not moving. Her azure eyes registered terror.

"Miss Hartt! It's Miss Bliss. Can you hear me?" I crouched in front of her, searching for signs of recognition. When she opened her mouth to answer, she couldn't form words.

"Bet it's a stroke." The man from the next cabin over made the pronouncement from the doorway where he and a few other motel guests had gathered. "Happened just like that to my Pawpaw. Sat in his own piss for half a day."

"Be quiet, this isn't like that," I snapped. "Miss Hartt, we're going to get you to a doctor. Do you understand?"

She nodded. At least she could hear me, even if she couldn't answer.

"Call 9-1-1, would you?" I asked Mr. Bell. But he was elderly himself and navigated with a cane, so I jogged back to the main cabin.

By the time the EMT van arrived, Clio was talking again. "This is too much fuss," were her first words, but I reminded her that moments earlier she'd been unable to talk at all. One paramedic knelt beside her, examining her eyes and quizzing her on her name and mine, while the other brought in a gurney ready for her transport.

"I am sorry to take you away from your families on Christmas Day," Clio said with complete clarity, making me wonder if she really did need to go to the ER.

I had called my parents, too, to tell them what happened and that it appeared I'd be spending Christmas in the ER. "But what about your supper?" Mama said with a tinge of annoyance in her voice, as if Clio's episode was something I'd planned.

"Save me a plate, would you?" I said, as upbeat as I could. "Make sure I get some of your amazing stuffing."

Her tone softened, and she told me to be careful on the roads.

The hospital had a bare-bones holiday staff, which meant Clio waited a couple of hours to see a doctor. She did get her own ER cubicle, though, and a cheerful nurse in an elf's hat checked all her vital signs.

"What is that?" Clio said, pointing an agitated finger at the nurse's name tag.

"Why, that's my name, honey," she said, shooting a glance at me. "Though folks just call me Lou." The tag read "Louise German, R.N." in white letters on a black background.

I followed Lou back to her station and asked what she thought had happened—a stroke? We were supposed to travel the next day. Would that even be possible?

"Let's wait and see what the doctor says, hon." She flashed a smile that seemed rehearsed.

Back in the holding room, Clio remained shaken. "Do not let that woman near me!"

"The nurse?" I glanced toward the nurses' station; Lou seemed to be one of only two on duty. "I think that'll be hard, Miss Hartt."

"There must be someone else." Clio held my hand in an unyielding grip, like on the plane.

"Well, we'll see," I said. The problem dissolved soon enough when the ER staff left us on our own with nothing to occupy our time, not even a TV. Christmas Muzak seeped through the PA system, and I soon found myself humming along to, "Frosty the Snowman."

After we'd been sitting for fifteen or twenty minutes, Clio announced, "You go to the hospital and they find something horrible you didn't know you had and then you die."

"Nah," I said. "Hospitals fix you right up."

"Well, all I know is that's how it happened for Flora."

I struggled to remember if I'd ever known what Flora had died of. Alcohol? Drugs? Gerri would have access to that fact.

"May of 1958. By June she was dead." Clio's grip tightened. "She called me the day she went in. She was coughing up blood. They ran lots of tests. Doctor said her lungs were full of tumors. She died on her sixtieth birthday."

"Oh, Miss Hartt," I said, squeezing her hand. "I am so sorry you went through that. And that Miss Haynes had to suffer."

Clio corrected me. "Flora didn't suffer. She left on her own terms."

I wasn't sure I took her meaning, but I hesitated to pry. Something else to ask Gerri about—the possibility that Flora had committed suicide.

An orderly took Clio away for a brain scan, and brought her back after an hour. During that time, I rummaged through her purse for the scrap of paper with Ivy's phone number on it and called to tell her what had happened. "Well, I just can't come on Christmas Day!" the frantic Ivy kept repeating, even though I reassured her I had the situation in hand, and the call was just a courtesy.

While my wait dragged on, I did something my mama would have smacked me for: I went on a full-blown hunt through Clio's handbag, which I'd been left to guard. It was a weathered brown leather satchel with a hefty gold clasp, resembling an overnight case more than a purse.

Making sure Lou the nurse was out of my line of vision, I snapped it open and checked all the pockets and folds for their secrets. The contents were mostly old-lady stuff: a lace-trimmed hankie; a comb with numerous teeth missing and strands of gray hair caught in it; a compact with a cracked cake of face powder and a black-spotted mirror; the worn leather change purse she always carried; an accordion-style credit card holder. Instead of plastic, though, it protected photographs—a tattered picture of her and Flora, young, on the cobblestone streets of what must have been Paris, and a blurry shot of Clio, Flora, and the bottom half of an unidentified woman at the foot of the Eiffel Tower; the woman's torso had been sliced out of the frame. From the clear sleeves of the holder, I dislodged a yellowed newspaper clipping, so fragile-looking I feared it would disintegrate upon unfolding. I handled it as gingerly as I could, as it turned out to be Flora's obituary.

GUILFORD, Conn.—Flora Haynes, a playwright whose work won acclaim in the 1920s, died at home in Guilford, Conn., on June 5, her sixtieth birthday.

The playwright, who lived in a carriage house on the grounds of the estate of Mrs. Louise Durand, also maintained an apartment on West 10th Street in Manhattan. She had been in failing health for several years, according to Mrs. Durand, a personal friend. The cause of death was cancer.

Miss Haynes was born in Tarrytown, N.Y., in 1898, to Broderick and Leticia Haynes. Her father was a physician and prominent patron of the arts. In 1920, Miss Haynes studied at the Art Students League, and late that year married her life drawing instructor, George Littlejohn. The marriage was annulled the following year.

Miss Haynes's literary work includes three full-length plays, three one-acts, and a libretto. She first emerged in literary circles in 1920, when her play, *To Call It Suicide*, premiered to acclaim at the Provincetown Players. Critics marveled at the youth and sex of the author, who was just twenty-two. In addition to her credit as playwright, Miss Haynes played the minor role of Thelma.

She told the *New York Herald* that she preferred acting to writing because it allowed her to "live the lives of other people, who are so much more interesting than I." Over the next several years, she appeared in small parts in plays by Eugene O'Neill, Susan Glaspell, and Djuna Barnes. She also designed sets for the troupe.

The Players produced her second play, *Nothing Happened*, in 1923, again to positive reviews. Shortly after the play closed, the Provincetown Players formally disbanded.

Her connected one-act plays, grouped together under the title *Portrait of a Madwoman*, were produced by the Cherry Lane Theater in 1927 to mostly unfavorable reviews. *The New York Times* wrote, "Although her career started with enormous promise, Flora Haynes's new work is as dense as mud. In its unrelentingly bleak portrayal of one woman's life and descent into madness over three decades, it succeeds in being little more than a feminist screed." In an interview after the trilogy's opening, Miss Haynes derided critics as "sad little men who have never created anything."

The following year, Miss Haynes left for Paris, where for the next ten years she resided on the Left Bank, sharing an apartment with a fellow writer, Miss Clio Hartt, author of *The Dismantled*. Miss Haynes was a well-known member of the expatriate artists' community on the Left Bank, taking part in several literary salons. Her plays were translated into French and performed by "Union des femmes," a theater company she co-founded to produce plays by women.

After returning to New York City in 1938, Miss Haynes attempted to interest producers in an absurdist play she wrote while living abroad. Based on an obscure incident in French history, the play was "too avant-garde, too ahead of its time," Miss Hartt said, and it has never been produced. A libretto Miss Haynes wrote in 1940 was likewise never produced.

In 1943, Miss Haynes won brief recognition for her work as a visual artist, when her original set designs for Provincetown Players were exhibited at Peggy Guggenheim's Manhattan gallery. Of the exhibit, Mrs. Durand commented, "It showed the startling breadth of her genius. There was nothing Flora couldn't do."

Miss Haynes was preceded in death by her parents. She is survived by her brother, Theodore Haynes, two nieces, and one nephew.

The information in Flora's obituary tantalized me. She'd been married, but only briefly. Clio was almost an afterthought in the article, "a fellow writer"—but then, that was how they appeared to the outside world. And there was the mention of Louise Durand—possibly the Louise so reviled by Clio. I reread the obituary a couple of times. But when I heard the squeaky wheels of Clio's gurney rolling back into the ER, I quickly tucked the clipping into its sleeve and snapped her bag closed, ashamed for invading her privacy.

Fatigue clouded Clio's eyes. Concerned, I asked what they'd done to her, but she just waved me off with annoyance, as if I were to blame. She fell asleep for a while, and I read an old copy of *People* I'd found in the waiting area.

After another hour or more, a middle-aged doctor whose face wore the burdens of his job arrived in her cubicle. Maybe a patient had died, or maybe he was simply bummed to draw the Christmas Day straw. He managed a faint smile and a "How are you doing today, young lady?" to Clio.

"I am hardly a young lady," Clio said.

I stepped out of the cubicle so the doctor could examine her. The jovial Lou offered me a slice of gingerbread some grateful relative had just dropped off at the nurses' station, which I accepted eagerly to quiet my grumbling stomach. The cake was drier than it looked and could have benefited from a glass of milk, but I ate it just the same.

"You had a scare like this with your granny before?"

"Oh, we aren't related," I said. "I kind of work for her."

"You mean like an attendant?"

"More like a companion. She's a writer."

"Really? She write anything I heard of?"

"*The Dismantled*," I replied, looking distractedly toward the drawn curtain of Clio's cubicle.

"The who?"

I repeated the name, suspecting she wouldn't recognize it, and she shook her head like it was the strangest title she'd ever heard.

"It's pretty famous," I pointed out.

"If you say so, hon."

My cake was long gone, the crumbs licked clean from my fingers, by the time the doctor emerged. He waved me to the cubicle.

"She asked for you," he said, making notes on a clipboard.

"You tell her what you said to me," Clio told him. "You have my permission. I don't have any kin to speak of."

"The good news is that the scan showed there was no stroke," he pronounced.

"That's great!"

"Tell her the rest of it," Clio instructed.

"The results suggest to me that Miss Hartt had a transient ischemic attack."

203

"A transient . . . what?"

"—ischemic attack. A ministroke. There's no significant brain damage, as with a stroke, but the danger is that she could keep experiencing them. She may have even had a few already that we don't know about, but she says she doesn't remember any other time she couldn't speak or felt numb."

"And if they keep happening?"

"A succession can lead to an actual stroke, which is often incapacitating, or to a gradual loss of cognitive function. Losing vocabulary, repeating herself, not knowing how to tell time, neglecting medications or meals, eventually needing help with toileting and basic functions. But then, Miss Hartt is—" he glanced at her chart, "—almost eighty-eight, so she's likely experiencing some of these symptoms anyway."

I thought of the little signs I'd noticed, like her forgetting if she'd fed the cat and leaving the stove burner on. Writing the same page over and over in slightly different ways. But then, she'd completed a story that was first rate, in my humble view, and she'd been working on something new just the day before. She might have years left with all her faculties.

The doctor said she could travel as long as she wasn't experiencing any symptoms, and that he would give her a prescription for a blood thinner to help keep blood flowing to her brain.

"My blood is already too thin!" Clio complained, when I told her what the prescription was for. "I am cold all the time."

Clio put up a fuss, but there was no question in my mind of leaving her alone for the night, not after that scare. Short of my sleeping upright in a chair in her cabin, the only choice was to check her out of the Dry Ridge and go to my parents'. By the time we got there, my sisters and their families had left, Daddy was watching a rerun on TV, and my mother was washing a mess of dishes in the kitchen by herself.

"I'll help you with that, Mama," I said. "Just let me show Miss Hartt where everything is."

"You got to have food," Mama insisted, although Clio had shaken her head at the first offer. "I won't take *no* for an answer!"

And indeed, my mother didn't, setting us up at the kitchen table with two plates of turkey breast, cornbread stuffing, biscuits, and candied yams.

"I don't know how I could possibly eat all this," Clio said, looking alarmed.

"Miss Hartt doesn't eat much, Mama," I said.

"Well, I'm not surprised! What is there to eat in that city anyway? When I ask Liv about food, she's always talking about Chinese this and Cuban that. What kind of food is that? You must be starved for down-home cooking."

My mother had hit an important truth, judging by the way Clio approached her meal, with measured bites that grew into confident forkfuls. Although she didn't finish her plate, Clio ate generous amounts of everything, more than I would have thought possible.

My mother didn't join us at the table, instead calling out pleasantries over her shoulder from the sink as we ate. Much of her small talk made me cringe with embarrassment ("So Livvie says you're a famous writer?"), but Clio replied with the old-school politeness I'd seen her summon up many times. I kept waiting for her to tire of it, but she didn't seem to. The meal revived her, and she even agreed to tea and a piece of chess pie. "Just a sliver, mind," she instructed.

I waved off the dessert, but "I'll have a sliver with you," Mama said with a girlish giggle. "Don't tell anyone, but I had one earlier." Her weight had crept up each year since her fiftieth birthday, and in profile now I noticed her second chin.

"This was about the finest meal I've ever had, Mrs. Bliss," Clio said, and Mama beamed. This would be a story for her church friends, for sure—a famous author from New York City, albeit one she'd never heard of, had come to supper and complimented her meal to the heavens. "And she lived in Paris once!" I could hear Mama bragging.

Clio's energy finally flagged as Mama trotted out stories about her grandkids opening their toys. Even I could only tolerate so many anecdotes about Pokey and Fletcher and the littlest ones, and Clio's eyes took on a glassy sheen as Mama droned on. Finally, I reminded Mama of the trying day we'd had. My mother sputtered out her apologies for "yammering on" and helped Clio settle in to Sue and Bren's old bedroom.

Although Clio brushed me away, she didn't seem to mind Mama helping her into her nightgown, pulling the covers up over her, and turning out the light. "I will remember your kindness for a long time," Clio said in a reverent voice.

"Sleep tight!" my mother called out as she pulled the door closed.

I grinned at my mother from across the hall, where I was waiting to hit my own bed to give *Zami* another try.

"What?" she asked, as if she'd never seen me smile.

"Thank you, Mama. That was real sweet of you."

"Just bein' folks," she said.

For our trip back the following morning, my mother had prepared a hearty breakfast of eggs, Jimmy Dean sausage, and cornbread. Clio looked rested and ate heartily again. It was likely just my imagination, but her cheeks seemed to fill out in two meals' time. My mother was delighted with the positive reception of her food. "I may just have to send you some care packages from home, Miss Hartt."

On the drive to the airport, Sue's eyes avoided mine in the rearview mirror, and I could tell she was disappointed with me, even though my excuse for missing dinner was airtight. We'd had very little time to talk sister-to-sister, except for those few hours on Christmas Eve.

"Miss Hartt, I am just so happy you're feeling better," Sue gushed, trotting out the charm.

"I'm afraid I kept your sister from her family," Clio said.

"Don't you worry," Sue replied. "We'll get her back here for Easter."

After we'd settled Clio into her wheelchair for boarding, Sue tugged at my coat sleeve. "I mean it about Easter," she whispered in an urgent tone. "I'm due April 20, and it would mean a lot to have my baby sister home in case there are any, you know, complications."

I thought of Aunt Sass, and how she'd been lured home from New York in 1950 by news of my mother's miscarriage. But this was the 1980s, and Sue had popped out three healthy babies over the past eight years without a problem. It had never occurred to me until that moment, when I saw a hint of fear in her eyes, that Sue was still not at ease with childbirth.

"You'll be fine," I assured her, patting her hand. The Blisses weren't the most openly demonstrative folks, and although my next words felt unnatural, I said them anyway: "You are one of the strongest women I know"—which made her face soften. We hugged as best we could over her rounded belly.

On the return flight, Clio didn't reach for my hand, even during takeoff. I tried to make chitchat, and she offered that she had liked my family, especially my mother, but her tone was crisp and she didn't meet my eyes.

And then, when we must have been over Pennsylvania, she popped the latch on her handbag.

"I was looking for Ivy's phone number last night," she said, "and imagine my surprise when I realized my bag had been looted."

A sip of Coke went down the wrong way, and I choked on it. Clio reached behind me and gave me a hard thump on the back. I didn't see how it was possible that she'd noticed, as I'd been so careful to replace the clipping of Flora's obituary where I found it and to slip the holder back into its pocket.

"My, what a fuss," she remarked about my coughing fit. "Now my bag . . . it wasn't ever out of your sight in the hospital, was it?"

"No, ma'am." I took a smaller sip of Coke to steady myself. "Is something . . . missing?"

"No, it isn't that," she replied. "I have nothing to steal, really. The things I have mean something to me, but not to anyone else."

I waited, not wanting to push her too far in the direction of identifying me as the culprit.

"I had a newspaper clipping," she said slowly. "It was put back in the wrong place."

"I am so sorry, Miss Hartt," I confessed, hanging my head a little. "I was looking for your sister-in-law's number, to let her know how you were doing, and I just sort of stumbled onto your photo holder. And then I saw the obituary, and I just couldn't—"

"Resist prying into my personal belongings?"

"In my defense, it was printed in a newspaper—"

"Then you should have gone to the library to read it!" she said. A deep, sorrowful sound spilled out of her, almost like she was keening. "You might have torn it, and then what would I do? What would I do, Miss Bliss? Tell me that! I have some photos, a few mementos, and that scrap—"

The flight attendant stopped at our row, appearing out of nowhere with a tray of drinks. "Are you all right, ma'am?" she said, leaning in toward Clio. "Would you like some water?"

She shook her head. "No, nothing. I am sorry for your trouble," she said, waving her off impatiently.

I knew she still loved the long-gone Flora, but until this moment, I hadn't understood how deep the river of her feelings flowed. There were so many questions I wanted to ask, but in her current state she was unlikely to give up the answers. Flora felt like her private possession, something she kept as close as the worn obituary.

Her bag closed with a solid snap. "I told you things in the hospital. If you had asked . . . but now I feel . . . invaded, really. It will be hard for me to trust you again, Miss Bliss."

Her compatriots in the Paris generation remembered Clio not just for her intellect and wit, but for her startling beauty, especially her chiseled nose and china blue eyes. "Those eyes saw into your soul," Natalie Barney recalled in 1970.

A distinctive taste in clothes accented Clio's features and statuesque height. She rarely went out on the streets of the Latin Quarter without a hat, high-heeled boots, and a sweeping cape, the overall effect rendering her even more imposing.

"She cut a handsome figure," Barney said. "She might have had anyone, man or woman, but she was Flora's."

—from *Dismantling Clio Hartt: Her Life and Work*,
by Ingrid Coppersmith

Chapter 22

New York City
January 1984

When we got back, Clio was pleasant with me, often even warm, but then soon after New Year's she threw a grenade between us.

"I want to go back to our old schedule, Miss Bliss," she said.

"Which schedule was that?" She'd added days to my weekly visits over the months, so now I was sometimes stopping in six days out of seven.

"I don't see the need for you to be here so much. Certainly not on weekends. A young woman like yourself doesn't need to be fussing over me. You have a life of your own to live."

Her consideration would have been touching if it were sincere. Instead, I assumed the change was about what I'd privately come to think of as "the handbag incident." I hadn't confessed my crime to anyone, not even Thea.

"I don't see it as fussing, Miss Hartt," I insisted. "Besides, Bea's approved it and wants me to be here."

"I will call Beatrice then and tell her it isn't necessary." She sighed, deep and full of bother.

My stomach lurched at the thought of Clio disclosing my transgression. "Oh, I can tell her. Don't trouble yourself. I'll tell her today." I knew what Bea's first question would be, though, so I asked it myself: "But what about your book? We've been making such good progress. You have a pretty tight table of contents for the older pieces, and then there are the new ones."

Her second sigh had even more air to it. "I don't know as I want to continue with that book," she said. "Or any book, really."

It had occupied so much of our time, and she'd enthused about it every time I saw her. She had finished one story and made headway with another. I couldn't believe she'd just give up, and I said so.

"You're feeling a little blue. Our trip was hard. The ER, and seeing your brother like that—"

"—was devastating!" she finished for me. "My little brother, reduced to that." She tucked a few errant strands of hair back into her bun. "But no, that isn't it. I don't have the desire for it anymore. I don't see the point."

My mouth popped open, but I closed it. A writer who was down was one thing; a writer who no longer wanted to write was another.

"I can pare back to three days a week. How about that?" I said at last. "No pressure on you or the book. And we can assess after a few weeks."

"We might get by with one or two days. Afternoons. For an hour, maybe." She hunkered down into her armchair as if she didn't intend to leave. Since we'd been back, I'd noticed that the papers on her desk hadn't moved, and the notebook she'd taken with her to Asheville was nowhere in sight.

"Miss Hartt, I know I upset you," I said. "I truly did not mean to. I would hate to see you give up on your book because of something I did."

She let out a sharp cackle that cut like a piece of paper, a shallow slice you barely notice until it hurts like the devil.

"Miss Bliss, you have a grand idea of your powers. This has nothing to do with you."

"Oh," I said, both relieved and mortified.

"You know very little about me." Disappointment darkened her face. For a moment, I wondered if she'd looked at Flora this same way. "Someday I may tell you more. Things that will clear up everything."

"Ma'am?"

"For the record. Because you know they'll be snooping around my papers after I'm dead."

I snorted without meaning to at the word *snooping*. I imagined Thea and other academics with magnifying glasses and Sherlock Holmes hats.

"I'm glad I amuse you."

"I'm sorry. It's just . . . Well, you're famous, Miss Hartt. Scholars will want to write about you. It's their *job*."

She raised an eyebrow. "A silly job, if you ask me." But then she favored me with a smile. "Like writing novels."

"Or buying groceries for novelists," I added.

The joke pleased her and deepened her smile. I thought she might have forgiven me for trespassing in her bag.

"Go now," she said. "Enjoy whomever it is you're with. You *are* with someone, aren't you?"

Thea's face came to mind. "I am."

She sighed again, but this time it was slow and measured.

"Her name is Thea."

Clio's eyelids flickered like hummingbird wings, as she worked to take in the information I'd offered.

"The godly one," she said. By the time I understood she was referring not to Thea the woman but to *Thea* the name, she put her head back and closed her eyes and looked for all the world like she'd fallen asleep.

Thea and I had been "enjoying" each other pretty much nonstop since my return. That included my first-ever romantic, adult New Year's Eve. Ramona was out of town so we had the grand Gramercy apartment to ourselves. Thea cooked coq au vin, a dish I'd never heard of until she presented it on Ramona's grandmother's china.

"Where did you learn to cook like this?" I asked as the tender chicken fell off the bone and into my mouth. It was an innocent question, and one I hadn't intended to embarrass her with, but

Thea's light skin flushed rosy when she admitted it was Diane's recipe.

"But I have always wanted to make it for someone special," she added.

After dinner, we strolled to Cinema Village and a D. H. Lawrence film festival, a double bill of *Women in Love* and *Lady Chatterley's Lover*. Even though the movies were aimed at heterosexuals, they got us heated up just the same, and we raced back in the early morning hours of 1984 to a chilled bottle of Freixenet and a marathon of lovemaking.

Within days, reality intruded: Thea's on-campus interview at Hamilton College. In an atlas kept at the agency for reference, I looked up the little town of Clinton and let the inches between it and New York City sink in. Hamilton's history went back almost two hundred years, and I knew Thea was beyond excited about the prospect of teaching there.

"I'd be their second dedicated Black Studies professor!" she said. "I could help shape the program."

"Are there many black students in western New York?"—a fair question, I thought, but Thea's response sounded ticked off.

"Well, no, not now. But having a strong program with courses about women writers would give them an edge in recruitment." She divulged this on the A train as we made our way uptown to her apartment. Thea had avoided telling Vern about our relationship and had asked me to casually show up with her and spend the night so we could "out" ourselves without a lot of fuss.

We were pressed close together on the subway seat, our thighs and shoulders touching, and I noticed the middle-aged white woman across the aisle from us had a twisted look of revulsion on her face—because we were lesbians or because we were different races? If I'd brought Thea's attention to it, she would have done something provocative like sticking out her tongue or grimacing right back. So I forced my eyes away from our fellow passenger and toward Thea's slender fingers entwined with my own.

Vern was drawing her comic strip, which had started running

regularly in the local feminist newspaper, and my appearance with Thea that evening was barely a blip on her radar screen. She called "hey" over her shoulder and later even declined Thea's offer to share our takeout pasta. It wasn't until the following morning when I emerged from Thea's bedroom and faced Vern in the kitchen that the new turn in our relationship sank in.

"Hey," she said, pouring coffee into a Snoopy mug.

"Hey, Vern," I replied. "I didn't get a chance to tell you last night, but I've been loving your strip. I can't wait to pick up *WomaNews* and see what Jazz gets up to this month!"

The compliment floated in the chilly air between us as she slurped her coffee. I reached past her to pour some into a Cornell mug for myself.

"Maybe an editor will see it and want a whole book," I added. She'd already thanked me several times for asking around and helping her make the connection to the paper, and I wasn't fishing for another thank you. I just honestly didn't know what to say. I kept stealing glances at the hallway, hoping Thea was out of the bathroom and on her way to the kitchen.

"Yeah," Vern said. "Believe it or not, somebody from *Ms.* called and asked me to do a cartoon for their June issue."

"Wow, that's terrific, Vern! What of?"

"Dunno." It wasn't clear if she really didn't know or just wasn't interested in talking to me about it. I heard the whine of pipes, which suggested Thea had just turned off the water and would be finishing her grooming.

But before Thea could come to my rescue, Vern faced me, her eyes registering hurt. "So, you lied to me, huh?"

"You mean about Thea? No, no. It's a new thing, I swear. It kind of caught us both by surprise."

"I trusted you, man. I thought we were friends."

"Oh, we are, Vern! I'm sorry Thea and I didn't tell you. But like I said, this thing . . . it's new. We would have told you last night, but you were drawing and all."

She nodded, like some part of my apology and explanation had finally penetrated her consciousness.

"The last thing either of us wanted to do is hurt you."

She opened the refrigerator and brought out a carton of half-and-half, which she sniffed first, then passed to me. "You take it light, right?"

"I do. Thanks." The cream barely affected the coffee, made with Café Bustelo. "And thanks for understanding."

"I got a new lady myself," she said after a pause. "I figured I couldn't wait around for the Professor forever. A girl's got needs."

"That's great!" My response was a bit too enthusiastic, so I toned it down. "Where'd you meet?"

"Déjà Vu," she said. I had been to the bar once with Thea, right before my trip South. "Name's Pauline."

"I'm so happy for you, Vern."

"Well, we ain't done the deed yet," she admitted. "We kissed and all, and she lets me hold her close when we dance, but that's it. Pauline lives with her mama in Bushwick, and I didn't know if Thea would want me bringing her home. But now I know about you—"

"Bringing who home?" Thea asked. Her clothes were dressy-casual, the kind of thing she taught in—tailored gray pants, a plum-colored turtleneck, strands of silver chains, and a serious-looking watch, not the Minnie Mouse one she usually wore. A member of the faculty would be picking her up at the bus station, she said, and she needed to look "professorial."

"Vern's got a girl," I said with a wink.

Thea punched Vern on the arm. "You keeping secrets from me?"

"You should talk," Vern muttered.

"Livvie told you?"

"I got eyes, man," Vern said. "And ears."

I flushed to my roots. In bed, Thea had pressed a hand over my mouth to stifle my guttural noises.

Out of gallantry, I offered to carry Thea's suitcase to the subway, but she insisted on taking charge of it. Standing in the crowded car, our hands brushing on the pole, we didn't talk all the way to Forty-Second Street, but traded shy smiles. As our train approached the station, Thea took my face in both her hands and kissed me full on the lips. I was nervous about a PDA in such a crowded place, but the other commuters either didn't notice or pretended not to.

"Don't spend your time worrying," she instructed me, although she must have known that would be impossible. "I've got to get the job first."

I wished her good luck, trying to make my tone upbeat and convincing, but as she stepped onto the platform my heart did a backflip in my chest. The feeling took my breath away, the impending loss of something I barely had.

"Would you be interested in starting up the salon again?" Gerri asked over burgers and mugs of beer in a wooden booth at Chumley's. The historic speakeasy was a reliable hangout when it was too early for Ariel's or we weren't in a dancing mood.

When I didn't answer immediately, Gerri continued, "I mean, at our old apartment."

"You're . . . moving back in?"

"Not yet, but soon," she said. "We talked about it, but I think we could use a little more space."

"Who would be in it this time around?" I munched on a fry, dodging Barb's name.

"You, me, Renee, Thea, Vern," Gerri said. "Jill said she's interested."

"Jill!"

"Well, she ditched You-Know-Who, so that shows she's got sense. She told me Jenny's back from L.A. and they're trying to make it work. So maybe Jenny, too."

The spinning of relationships in my immediate circle made me dizzy. Tracking who was on and who was off would soon require a scorekeeper.

"I have to admit I'm worried," I blurted out.

"About Jill?"

"About trying to restart the old group. Honestly, I don't know if I can take any more drama with y'all."

217

Gerri's mouth twitched, and I wished I could retract my words. We'd been getting along, and I didn't want to slip back into the sticky mire we'd found ourselves in before Christmas.

"I didn't mean 'y'all' as in you and Renee," I added quickly.

She held her burger with both hands, poised for a bite, but then she put it back on the plate. "Well, you barely know Jill, and you never met Jenny," she said. "So-o-o, process of elimination."

"Look, it's none of my business. I think I'm worried that we'll all split up again. And it could be drama from my end with Thea, you know."

"Already? I thought you two were good."

"No, no, we're fine. But . . . did you know she's looking for a job outside New York?"

"Well, sure. I proofread her applications. Her CV was a mother!"

"And you didn't tell me?" I knew I wasn't anywhere close to the moral high ground, having kept information about Barb from Gerri over the months.

"That I proofread?"

"That she was applying."

"Why would I?" she said. "You guys were just friends. If Thea wanted you to know something, she would have told you herself." She paused. "Right?"

It was a strong point, and I stepped back from my indignation.

"She really needs a job, Liv. And she's got three strikes against her—black, woman, dyke. I hope you're being supportive and not moping around about it."

"I'm the picture of support. I . . . Look, we just got started, and the end's already in sight."

"Hey, if you two really have something going, distance won't take that away. Look at Jill and Jenny."

"I don't even know Jenny, remember?"

"Don't get technical on me. It's just an example." She drained her mug and signaled our waitress for another round.

"Or here's a thought," Gerri went on. "You're a small-town girl—maybe she gets the job and you go with her. Hell, *I* might

218

even go with her! There are some awesome small publishing companies in that neck of the woods. We could start our own!"

The idea of having a future with Thea and Gerri made me feel feathery. "That would not be a bad way to live," I said, and we toasted with two fresh mugs of beer.

My mood of hopefulness lingered until Melissa Pruitt got in touch. Eli had been living at his sister's since before Thanksgiving. During that time, he and I had had a single terse phone call in which he'd groused about how Melissa had deprived him of the only thing he loved, his cat. Assuring him Remington was safe and well cared for pushed him to rumbling sobs that I listened to helplessly for several long moments.

When there was a break in his crying, I said, "Oh, Eli, I feel terrible. I'd bring Remmie to see you if I could, but the fur would be bad for you."

"How would you know?" he hissed and hung up. And that had been our only contact in weeks.

Now Melissa's voice was frayed. "Joe and I really need an evening alone," she explained. "But for that to happen, Eli needs a babysitter." There was an audible gasp through the line. "Oh, God, that sounds horrible. I'm sorry, I'm sorry! Listen, I need someone to visit Eli and give me a break, that's all. Most of his friends are sick themselves or gone. I won't ask you to take a weekend night, that's not fair, but could you possibly come every Wednesday?"

I gulped. "I'm not sure I can commit to every week. There might be work stuff. Could we take it week by week?"

She said, "Yes, thank you," in a polite but clipped way that suggested prior attempts to book a regularly scheduled visitor had also failed.

Melissa's building was a glass-and-steel structure that towered over Third Avenue with upper-class swagger. The two white doormen on duty used formal-speak with the guests and residents who passed their polished mahogany desk. But then when the lobby emptied and I was the only person standing at the shiny elevator bank, I overheard them jaw with each other in New York accents as thick as calzones.

The elevator car had mirrors on three sides, and I spent considerable time smoothing down my cowlick on the way up to the fourteenth floor. When the car came to a noiseless halt and the doors slid open, I heard Melissa call out, "Hold it!" from the hallway.

"He's so excited!" she said as she rushed in, her breathless voice suggesting she was pretty keyed-up, too. "You're so sweet to help us out." Before I could ask for instructions, like whether Eli had eaten dinner, she'd stabbed the "Down" button, and I had to hop off or ride down to the lobby again.

Melissa had left the apartment door ajar. Eli greeted me from a plush sofa with a half-smile and a rippling wave of his fingers. He lay reclining in a light blue flannel robe printed with dancing black cats, the creases from being packed in a box still visible.

"Birthday present," he muttered when I complimented him on the robe. I was about to ask when his birthday was when he continued, "She actually thinks this makes up for Remmie! I should spite her and not wear it, but it's warm and she keeps this place so damn cold."

"Well, you look cute in it," I said, even though he didn't. His eyes were ringed with bluish-black circles, and the robe did little to disguise his gaunt frame. He'd shed more weight since the day he'd been whisked away to the hospital, and now looked as small as a prepubescent boy.

"I look like shit," he countered. "Admit it. Go on."

"I'm not playing this game, Eli," I said, sitting down next to him, careful not to brush his extended legs and feet. Melissa had warned me that "just about everything hurts" and that he randomly moaned, "Ow, ow, ow" as he padded through the apartment.

"You're no fun," he said. "You're as big a bore as Melissa and everybody else." He sighed and inched a rainbow-socked foot closer to me. "Margo at the Art Students League actually called

220

today to ask how I am! 'How are you feeling, Eli?'" He mimicked a sickeningly sweet voice in a falsetto register that I doubted belonged to anyone he knew. "How does she think I am?"

Without turning my wrist, I glanced down slowly at my watch: Two hours to go. But Eli caught the eye movement anyway.

"You don't have to stay till nine," he said. "I don't need a babysitter. I've got takeout menus and a remote control. My life is complete." Despite his petulant tone, his feet were now nudging closer to my thigh.

"Eli, I get it," I said. My instincts hovered between wanting to give him more space on the sofa and letting him put his feet right in my lap. "You're mad at me."

"Why would I be mad at you?"

"I haven't been around."

"Do you think I noticed? I've been kind of busy, Livvie."

I stopped myself from asking "Doing what?" How did I know what he'd been up to? When I didn't take the bait, he offered, "I actually did a sketch the other day."

"Wow, that's great!" It was maybe too enthusiastic, maybe too quick; his feet retreated a few inches back toward his butt. "I'd love to see it."

He made a *pfft* noise out of the corner of his mouth. "It's nothing. Just a dumb still life of a rotting banana on the counter. Melissa threw it out the next day."

"Your sketch?" I asked in horror.

He smiled and stretched his feet toward me again. "She's not *that* evil. I meant the banana."

The talk of food, even rotten fruit, made my stomach groan.

"Hey, have you eaten?" I asked. "I'm kind of starving. Want to order some Thai?"

Steeled for a rude dismissal of the eating idea, I was surprised when Eli answered, "Oh, Livvie, I'd love that! That would make me feel so normal." He slid his left foot onto my thigh. "My feet are so achy these days. Would you rub them?"

"I will. But only after we eat," I said.

We ordered more than even two healthy people could possibly eat—several colors of curry, Pad See Ew, Pad Thai, spring rolls. As I was finishing the order, Eli called out, "Oh, and chicken satay, please, please, please!" and I added that to the list.

"You'll have Thai food for a week," I said as I unpacked all the cartons. I took generous servings of everything, and Eli helped himself to a spoonful of this and that, half of a spring roll. As we ate, Eli expressed interest in my job and my love life and finally wound the conversation around to Clio.

"I should have told you sooner. Clio's the one taking care of Remington."

His face glowed, like he was a movie star bathed in beauty lighting. "Clio has Remmie? Oh, God, Liv. That's just . . . I mean, that's too great."

"And she just loves him, Eli. You should see them together. It's like he's right at home."

That was one step too far. Eli's bony chest sagged, and he put down his fork. "So he doesn't miss me."

"Oh, I'm sure he does!" I said. "But you want him not to be sad, right? And he isn't sad, Eli."

He nodded and picked at his food. "Maybe you could take a picture and send it? Or even, I don't know, maybe bring it by? I have some shots of him when I first got him, but nothing recent."

After dinner, I massaged his feet and he purred like Remmie. "I'm such a drag on everyone," he said with a sigh. "I've become a bitch."

"You do have this sort of dark, brooding thing going on," I said, choosing the words carefully. He raised an eyebrow, and I continued quickly, "But so did Heathcliff."

That made him laugh. "Yeah, I'm such a romantic figure."

He fell asleep with his feet on me, knobby weights that bit into my thighs and made them go numb. Ignoring the discomfort, I put my head back on the sofa cushion and dozed off myself, until I woke to Melissa's nudging.

We had a smattering of regular Wednesdays after that, and Eli's brooding returned sometimes, but all in all he successfully curtailed the time his darker personality spent on stage. One Wednesday I couldn't make our appointment, and the next he went back to the hospital for another stay.

And then one week, Eli, too—like Curt and all their friends—was gone. His was the first AIDS memorial I ever attended, and it wasn't the last.

Chapter 23

Even though I'd assured Clio I would inform Bea about the revised schedule, I didn't do it. Every time I tried, the words simply wouldn't come. I worked on numerous variations in my head: Clio doesn't think she needs as much help anymore. Clio needs a looser schedule right now. Clio feels more confident about being alone. Even the dreaded Clio isn't working on her book anymore. No matter how I phrased it, the options sounded like I'd failed at my job. So I remained mum, and hoped Bea didn't take heed of my increased presence in the office.

Unfortunately, Therese noticed, and she blurted it out during a staff meeting in Bea's office. "Shouldn't you be at Clio's?"

Ramona chimed in, "Yeah, I thought I'd have to take notes."

Nan joked, "Who are you again?" which brought a ripple of laughter from the other agents.

Bea didn't even crack a smile. She simply looked up from her stack of contracts, waiting for my reply to Therese's question.

"Clio is feeling more self-sufficient these days," I said, measuring each word. "She doesn't need me as much, so I guess all y'all will be seeing more of me!" My tone was light, and although everyone else took my explanation at face value, it didn't fool Bea.

Bea adjusted her glasses, the better to glare at me. "Clio's had a stroke. She is not self-sufficient."

"It wasn't a *stroke* stroke," I said.

"Don't split hairs. The woman isn't well. How is she supposed to work on her story collection without help? It seems unlikely to me that she'll make any progress if you aren't there."

"Well, I'll still be there." I paused as her eyes drilled into me. "Just not as much."

Bea frowned and launched into the staff meeting, but as she drew the agenda to a close and we all rose to return to our respective desks, she said, "Livvie, a few words." And then, as the agents filed out, "Close the door, please."

I'd never been behind a closed door with Bea, and I knew it wasn't good. It had been on Ramona's list of tips on my first day: "Try not to do anything that makes Bea say, 'Close the door, please.'"

"Sit," she said. I waited while she made some notes on a legal pad, presumably about the meeting. Then she leaned back in her chair, her lips set in a stern line.

"You know why you got this job, don't you?"

I nodded.

"You remember how light your resume was when I took you on. Some internship or another."

I nodded again.

"Now, just because I've questioned your extra hours—or you going to North Carolina for a whole week on my dime—that doesn't mean I want you to let up on your hours with Clio. You understand that?"

Another helpless nod.

"Good. I hoped I hadn't given you the wrong impression. You're doing valuable work with Clio, even if you may feel at times like a glorified babysitter. And there will be rewards if it all works out as we hope."

"Thanks," I said, for want of something better. I shifted in my chair and fingered the worn edge of the notebook I'd brought to the meeting.

"So are you going to tell me what this cut in hours is about?"

I laid it out as best I could, careful to omit the part about my looking through Clio's handbag. The picture I painted was

225

mostly accurate—Clio becoming more pensive and quiet after our trip. Her brother in a worse way than she'd imagined. The spat with Ivy, and the upset of the ministroke. Memories of Flora that haunted and troubled her. I stretched the truth and said she'd shared Flora's obituary with me, and that it made her more morose than I'd ever seen her.

The mention of Flora's name made Bea wince. "It's my fault," she said. "I thought you resembling Flora might help Clio, but maybe somehow, unconsciously, it's made it more painful. Though I honestly do not understand how you can pine for someone who's been dead twenty-odd years."

"It's not about how I look," I added quickly. "It was about being in the hospital. It brought back memories of Flora suffering from cancer—"

A confused look clouded Bea's face. "Flora killed herself," she said. "At least, the Montrose biography strongly hints she did." I'd had an inkling of that from what Clio had said, but I hadn't known for sure.

"Here's what you'll do," Bea went on. "It sounds like Clio is going through a patch of moody reminiscence about Flora. She'll get over it, she's done it before, and I want you there when she does. You can trim your schedule a little, miss a day here and there. She probably won't notice."

I was waiting for further instructions, which weren't forthcoming. "Anything else?" Bea asked, as if I'd initiated the closed-door meeting.

I hesitated, then blurted out the question I'd been pondering for a while. "Do you know who Louise was?"

Bea's interest was piqued. "Louise Durand?"

"Clio gets perturbed by the name Louise for some reason, and there was a nurse at the hospital named Louise who set her off." I left out the part about the editor named Louise and the "Madame Louise" story Clio had written.

"She was Clio's benefactor," Bea said. "I met her a few times when I was young, not through Clio but in another context. She died a few years back, had to have been a hundred."

Having a benefactor would explain why Clio might have more money stashed away than I originally imagined.

"Her husband made a fortune in railroads, but then he died and Louise made a career of spending it," Bea went on. "Somewhere along the way, she cut Clio off. Abruptly. Even Montrose doesn't say why, and it was well before my time."

I let the information sink in.

"Livvie, are you trying to tell me Clio stopped writing again? Is that why she doesn't need you as much?"

Cornered, I had to admit that Clio was abandoning her idea of a collection.

"But I want you to know I didn't do anything to cause it," I said in a voice that sounded pathetic, even to me.

"No one said you did," Bea snapped. "Although you were so sure that trip of yours would help her progress, not hinder it."

I didn't recall being that certain, but it seemed futile to disagree. "I was wrong," I said.

Bea grunted something under her breath and dismissed me by saying she had to make phone calls. Her tone made me suspect that my months-long streak as the golden girl of the office had officially come to an end.

To understand Clio better, I knew I needed to finish reading *Clio Hartt: A Life* by Sylvia Montrose—the book Gerri had lent me. There had been an earlier biography of Clio written by a man, Gerri explained, but it studied her only in juxtaposition to her male counterparts, and Montrose had employed a feminist lens. Still, Gerri faulted Montrose for shying away from using the "L" word for Clio, despite her relationships with women.

My three boxes of books stood in a sturdy tower in my bedroom, unopened. I hadn't seen the point of unpacking everything at Ramona's because it was unclear how long she'd let me stay.

When I removed every book from the boxes and spread them across the bed and floor, the Montrose volume wasn't there. I searched the assortment twice. I remembered it as an expensive-looking hardcover that would be hard to miss among my mostly paperback collection. Gerri had pointed out with pride that it was even signed by the author, whose reading she had attended at Brentano's.

Panic didn't set in until after the second pass through all the books. There were only three hardcovers, all Norton anthologies from my college days.

Thea had helped me pack everything before my moving day, so I called to ask if she remembered seeing the Montrose biography.

"I didn't know you owned that," she said. "I would have liked to read it."

"It's Gerri's, and it's missing."

"I know we double-checked the bookshelves in your room before we left. Did you give it back to Gerri at some point?"

"No, I always intended to finish reading it."

"Well, you could buy her another one."

"It was signed." I sighed, worried that only one option remained. "You think Barb took it?"

"I wouldn't put anything past Barb."

On an afternoon after I'd brought Clio some cat food for Remington and coffee and bread for herself, I wandered over to Fifteenth Street at the time I knew Barb would be getting ready to leave for work. Luckily, the intercom, like the door lock, never worked well—it was mostly static—so she buzzed me in without knowing who it was.

She stood with arms crossed outside the apartment door.

"Carolina. I never thought I'd see you here again. What'd you do, forget where you live?"

"It seems like I left something behind when I moved."

"What was that, your pride or your common sense?"

"Ha ha," I said. "Look, did you . . . do you by any chance have my biography of Clio? The one by Montrose?" I stopped short of hurling the accusatory, "Did you take . . ." at her.

"Let's see," she said, her hand to her chin in mock considera-tion. "I'm not sure. Do you by any chance have my Foghorn Leghorn glass?"

I'd expected the question, so I had the glass tucked into my messenger bag. I withdrew it and held it out to her.

"That book is worth way more than this," I said, as if cost alone could justify my nicking one of her prized possessions.

She snatched it from me. "I can't believe you actually stole from me," she said. "I was good to you, Carolina."

Barb went into the apartment and left the door open for me to follow her.

"Well, you stole from me, too. Where's the book?"

"For the record, I didn't steal from you," she said, emerging from her bedroom with the Montrose volume and a second book, too, a paperback with a green cover. "I saw it on your shelf and just wanted to take a look, but I guess I forgot to put it back."

"What were you doing in my room when I wasn't home?"

"Oh, please. Like you never went into my room?"

I had, but I hadn't taken anything, which seemed less reprehensible.

"So let's drop all the indignation and call it even, okay?" she suggested. "We both got our property back."

"Thanks," I said, accepting the book.

She startled me by shoving the paperback at me, too—*But Some of Us Are Brave: Black Women's Studies*.

"What's this for?"

"Your girlfriend. If she still is your girlfriend."

Total confusion set in. "You bought Thea a book?"

"N-o-o," Barb said with fake patience. "She gave it to me. I don't want it anymore."

My eyes darted back and forth from Barb to the book.

"Hasn't she given you any Black Studies books yet? She made it kind of a mission with me. I would have thought you'd have a whole shelf by now." She smirked. "Oh, wait, you didn't know I came before you? Well, we weren't together long enough to qualify as 'girlfriends.' I sure don't count *her*."

Thea always acted like the very sight of Barb turned her stomach, but I'd never considered that was because they'd dated before we met and the affair came to a bad end.

Careful not to look at her and betray my alarm, I slipped the two books into my bag, and the weight of them made me list to one side.

"Have a nice life, Carolina," Barb said as I headed for the stairs, desperate to be out in the cool air. "You and me probably would have been okay if Gerri and Thea hadn't flipped you." A curious choice of words, I thought, like I was a double agent.

I waved over my shoulder, figuring there was a chance I might run into her again at Ariel's or someplace else in the small sphere that was Lesbian New York. But in fact, I never saw her again.

When I appeared, uninvited, at Thea's apartment door, she was dressed in baggy sweats and an oversized Cornell hoodie she had lent me the night I slept over; in fact, it was the only thing of hers that fit me. Tortoise-shell glasses made her look like the nerdy professor she aspired to be. I knew she wore contacts—our first night together, we had to trek to a deli for solution so she could spend the night—but we'd been together such a short time, I'd barely seen her in glasses.

"Livvie, I'm prepping for class," she said, without any movement to let me in. "Eight o'clock comes early."

I had planned for this all the way uptown and was not prepared to back down. Reaching into my bag, I fished out the book.

"Barb asked me to return this to you."

"What is it?" she asked.

After I had left Barb's, I'd opened the front cover and read the inscription: *In Sisterhood (and more!) – xoxo Thea 5/83.* It was the "xoxo" that had made my blood start pumping and set my feet on the path to the A train. Thea had never had a single good thing to say about Barb, but as recently as seven months ago she'd given her a book with an "xoxo" inscription.

I flipped the cover open for her now.

"Oh," she said, taking it without looking at me. "I forgot all about this. Well, thanks. You can't have too many copies of *But*

Some of Us Are Brave." She stood aside so I could enter, and then continued down the hallway to the living room. Vern's room was empty so I was free to make a scene.

"That's all you're going to say?"

"I gave that to her before I met you, before you even lived in New York," Thea said.

"But in all the times you were bad-mouthing Barb, you never thought to tell me you two had gone out?"

"It was hardly 'going out,'" she said, making air quotes. She flopped onto the couch and tossed the book onto the coffee table, where it landed next to texts she was reading for class. "It was a few weeks. Maybe a month."

"And that means what? You had dinner? Went to movies? Slept with her?"

Thea bit her bottom lip. "All of the above. At first, she acted like she was into me, but pretty soon she told me I was too *vanilla*. Can you believe it? The only chocolate girl she probably ever dated!"

I just stared at her.

"You think I'm crazy, but Barb's smart and you know she can be charming when she wants to be. She was flattering about my job and the PhD thing, and I fell for it. At first I even liked that she tried to run the salon. I thought we could have a casual thing, something to dull the pain of Diane. I probably could have even overlooked the kinky stuff she was into. Hey, I was at the Barnard conference, she wasn't. I know about that shit." I didn't know what "the Barnard conference" referred to, but she was on a roll and not to be interrupted. "But I was too *vanilla*." This time the word had even more sting to it as if Thea still smarted from the rebuke.

I thought she'd finished, but she rambled on, not even bothering to look at me—almost like I wasn't there. "She couldn't even let me down smooth. No, that would have been too uncool. She had her reputation to preserve. I saw her more clearly after that and we started taking swipes at each other."

When she finally looked at me again, her face displayed a

231

weird blend of emotions—maybe embarrassment at having withheld the truth, but also annoyance that she had to defend herself. "Everything with Barb got worse and worse, and when you first came to the salon, I wasn't even sure I was going to stay."

A big, sad bubble welled up in my chest as I realized I'd been a casual thing for Thea, too. That would explain why she didn't tell me about her job search, why she kept urging me to keep things light. I was another step in her ascent away from Diane.

"I should go," I said.

"Livvie, don't be like this."

Don't be like this. Her words vibrated in my ears; Hallie had said the same thing.

Maybe I should have known we would fizzle out like this, like the lyrics of that old song Aunt Sass liked: "our love affair was too hot not to cool down." Maybe the incident with Diane on Thanksgiving should have been a clue. Or maybe I should have spent more time puzzling over why someone like Thea was interested in me in the first place.

She made a few attempts to get me to stay and talk it out, but everything she said sounded halfhearted in my ears. On the other side of her apartment door, I listened for the click of the dead bolt before heading to the nearest pay phone.

Gerri was working late, and I caught her before she left the office. "I'm meeting Renee," she said. "Can you tell me in thirty seconds? Or better yet, can it wait?"

I raced to summarize. "It might be over with Thea," I said because that was the quickest way to the problem.

"Oh, man, look, meet me at Renee's," she said. "I'll be there by six-thirty."

"But Renee—"

"She's good in somebody else's crisis. I'm really sorry, Liv."

I stopped at a bodega for a Bud, which I swigged from a paper bag like a derelict. On the C train, a rider or two glanced at me like they couldn't believe I was openly defying the law. When a transit cop strolled through our car, I tucked the bag behind me on the seat. A guy across the aisle nodded at me as the cop passed as if to say he would have done the same thing himself.

There was a doorman on duty at Renee's building whom I hadn't seen before. His name tag read "Miguel," and his uniform was identical to Jorge's, but he didn't bother with the bellhop-style cap and his tie was loose. In fact, he seemed looser in general, like it had been a long shift and he couldn't wait to get back to his real life.

"I don't think Renee's expecting me," I said, as he buzzed her apartment. "But Gerri told me to come. She's on her way."

"She ain't here yet," Miguel said. "But I believe you." I looked a little more respectable because I'd swallowed the last of the Bud on the sidewalk, pitched the bottle, and tossed a Tic Tac into my mouth.

"Livvie Bliss. Nice name," he said into the phone, with a faint smile in my direction. "She says Miss Gerri invited her. Okay. Sure." He listened, then laughed. "Sí. Tuve un mal día." He listened again, then said something I didn't catch, and finally mumbled, "Gracias" and replaced the receiver. "You can go up." I'd had a year of Spanish in high school, which amounted to just enough words to figure out he'd had a bad day. It wasn't necessary or expected, but I tipped him a couple of bucks—first because he'd said he believed me, but mostly because he got my name right on the first try.

Renee was opening the door as I stepped off the elevator. "What, no cookies?" she asked with a flirtatious tip of her chin. "I'm not sure I can let you in without cookies."

"No cookies, sorry."

"Then you owe me."

Renee had staged the apartment for romance, and I instantly regretted coming. She lit tapers and pillar candles in different locations, and set two wineglasses out on the coffee table alongside a bottle of red with a French label.

"Oh my God, I'm the third wheel," I said. "I'm so sorry."

She shrugged. "If Gerri told you to come, it must be important." She opened the wine while I slumped in a chair and tossed down my bag. My coat stayed on so I wouldn't look like I expected too much of their time.

"Here," she said, handing me a glass. "You look like shit, by the way."

Which made me smile through my misery. I took the wine gratefully, and it was smoother than anything I'd ever been able to afford.

"I never knew wine wasn't supposed to taste like vinegar," I said, to keep it light.

Renee poured a glass for herself, too, and took a seat across from me. "So . . . what happened? Or you want to wait for Gerri?" She was a lot nicer than I remembered, but then I'd met her when the whole drama with Barb was first going down. Maybe this was the Renee that Gerri loved and had been with for years. Maybe the other Renee was just an aberration, someone who went wild briefly and then returned to sanity. The wine soothed and warmed me, and once I started, my words tumbled like a rock slide. In the chronology, I had just finished telling Renee about handing Thea the book when I heard a soft knock at the door. They were together again, but Gerri still didn't walk in using her own key.

"Uno momento," Renee said, jumping up to answer the door. I cast my eyes down to give them privacy but heard a distinct smack of lips as Gerri entered. Alice came running from wherever she'd been sleeping and scraped at Gerri's legs until she picked her up.

Gerri carried her little dog to me and set her gently in my lap. "Let Miss Alice comfort you. She's really good at that." As if on cue, Alice licked my nose and then circled three times before arranging herself in a comfortable curl across my thighs.

If Gerri reacted at the mention of Barb's name, it wasn't noticeable. Renee's eyes fell to her glass, but Gerri held my gaze with admirable stoicism. The affair with Barb had hurt them both, and the wound had barely scabbed over. What I felt about Thea was nothing in comparison—disappointment more than grief—and my angst seemed almost juvenile.

Gerri sipped her wine, and reserved comment until I finished. "That's tough, Liv," she said with a sympathetic nod. "All I can tell you is there are peaks and valleys in relationships. You get through them and move on, learn to trust each other again." She and Renee, sitting so close together on the couch, were indeed a testament to "moving on." But Gerri was seeing my situation with Thea through the wrong lens.

"There's more to it," I said. "It's not like you guys. You have this history. I mean, ever since Thea told me about her job interview and that she was only applying to schools out of town, I had this weird feeling she doesn't want to be as invested in me as I could be in her. In a funny way, even though she was the one who pursued me, it's like I'm more into her than vice versa."

"Talk more about what worries you," Renee chimed in, the therapist-in-training trying to push me toward a breakthrough. "That Thea will move away?"

My hands rested along Alice's warm sides, and the comforting in and out of her breathing made it easier to talk. What also helped was reading compassion and concern on both their faces, not just idle interest that might fuel future gossip.

"I'm worried I'm just repeating what I did with Hallie. I found someone who was into me, sexually at least, but then when it came right down to it, I was second fiddle. With Hallie, her husband was number one, and with Thea, it's her career. I want—"

Renee leaned forward a little, which brought her closer to Gerri, and I noticed their thighs brush together in a casual way that didn't elicit a reaction from either of them. It just was.

"I want what y'all have. I want to play first fiddle for somebody. I just don't know how to get that."

"You might have to leave New York, my friend," Gerri said, with a wry smile. "This city chews up relationships and spits them out. Renee and I were just talking about that the other day, that maybe we need to jump ship."

"Seriously?" I didn't think I could stand it if Gerri moved. And was it fair to blame New York when people everywhere carried emotional baggage?

"It's just hypothetical for now," Renee added quickly.

They invited me to stay for dinner, but as much as I wanted to, the tapers were burning down fast, and they had a romantic evening to embark on.

"You don't mind if I keep this a little longer?" Gerri waited with me at the elevator, and I lifted the flap of my bag to reveal the Montrose biography.

"That? Oh, you can have it," Gerri said. "I read it twice. Pass it on when you're done."

"But it's signed!"

"Well, it's not like a signed copy of *The Dismantled*, is it? If you could ever get me one of those—" she winked, "—I'd be forever in your debt."

I wished I'd known Gerri didn't care about the Montrose book before I stormed over to Barb's and then uptown to Thea's, but of course, I didn't say that. In a strange way, realizing the book was missing had spared me from getting in too deep with Thea, in whose biography I'd never have an index entry.

Chapter 24

Thea and I didn't "break up," which would have been like a fractured bone. Without ever discussing it, we took the "drifting apart" route—a sprain you could still hobble around with.

Our relationship shifted the very night I got home from delivering the book to her and talking to Renee and Gerri. On the phone table in the hallway, Ramona left two messages, both from Thea. *This girl needs to LIGHTEN UP,* Ramona had scrawled at the bottom of the second message.

I didn't call Thea back, but wandered into the living room where Ramona was watching *Dallas*. Since moving in, I'd discovered that nighttime soaps were her guilty pleasure and that she didn't want Bea to know about it. Since I'd never watched *Dallas* or any of her other favorites, Ramona relished filling me in on the characters and the twisted plot.

"Okay, Sue Ellen is unhappily married to J. R. because he's a serial philanderer. Total prick, right? So she's having this tawdry affair with Peter, a hottie college student who's about half her age. You missed the best part—somebody just mistook her for Peter's mother and she's flipping out!" The plot line cut a little too close to home; once, a motel clerk had mistaken me for Hallie's daughter.

Through a wicked grin, Ramona took a sip of her Diet Coke, her beverage of choice; the refrigerator shelves were crammed with the white and red cans. "Seriously, Livvie, you've never seen this?"

My sisters and mother all watched *Dallas*, so I knew who J. R. Ewing was in the way you pick up bits of popular culture without really understanding them. But I didn't admit that to Ramona because I enjoyed our new camaraderie even if it amounted to bonding over junk TV. At home, Ramona was casual and laid-back, her face clean-scrubbed, her hair pulled back with a rubber band. She had a pink terrycloth bathrobe that enveloped her and slippers that were fuzzy green frogs. ("My baby sister gave them to me, okay?" she explained the first time my eyes traveled to her feet.) Although Ramona dated several times a week, no guy got more than one chance. "Snore," she'd say about each one. Her heart had been broken, and badly, by a guy she only called "Mr. Creep," so I understood her reticence about men.

At the commercial break, Ramona asked me about the messages from Thea. "Is she stalking you, or what?"

"We had a fight," I said, a little uncomfortable. I was out at work, but I never talked about my love life. All the women at the agency were straight, and it almost felt like bad manners to talk about my dating experiences with them. "Hey, you want some popcorn?" I asked, to change the subject. A Presto popper was the only piece of kitchen equipment I owned, a present from my parents on my twenty-first birthday. "For your hope chest!" my mother had said.

Something about feeding Ramona gave me enormous pleasure. I felt sisterly toward her, even though the women in my family were hearty eaters not the least bit shy about first or second helpings. In contrast, Ramona never thought to eat until I suggested it.

She agreed to the popcorn and we shared a big bowl of it, dressed with Parmesan cheese. ("What is on this? It's the most delicious thing I've ever eaten!" High praise for someone who'd been to every chichi restaurant south of Houston Street, although I wasn't convinced she ever ate on any of her dates.) While we gobbled it down in lieu of dinner, the phone rang again, and I could just make out Thea's voice leaving another plaintive message. By that time, J. R. was suggesting that he and

Sue Ellen have another baby, and the drama was just too good to interrupt.

Later, I pulled the phone into my room—Ramona had outfitted it with an extra-long cord that reached from one end of the apartment to the other.

"I'm sorry," Thea said immediately. "I should have told you about Barb."

"It would have explained a lot."

"I acted like a bitch tonight."

"Maybe we've been taking this too fast," I said. "You know, us."

She sighed heavily. "You're breaking up with me."

"Maybe we should slow things down. I mean, you're busy with your job search and all."

"Oh, is that what this is really about?"

"What?"

"You're mad at me for looking for a job somewhere else. Even though I explained to you—" Her tone was stern, professor-ish, and I cut her off.

"Of course, I'm not mad about that. You think I'm an infant?" A pause in which she didn't reply. "When do you find out about Hamilton?"

"Soon." Another long pause. "I didn't get a chance to tell you, I got two more on-campus interviews."

I nodded, even though I knew she couldn't see me.

"Livvie?"

"Yeah, I heard you. That's great, Thea. I'm really happy for you. We'll have to celebrate. Soon."

"Soon?"

"How about Saturday?"

We'd been seeing each other four or five nights out of the week, and now I was proposing we skip four nights in a row. The change wasn't lost on Thea.

"I leave Sunday afternoon for Boston, so I'll probably be packing and shit on Saturday," she said. "Plus, I need some new shoes."

"Okay, why don't you call me when you get back?"

"Sure." She stretched the syllable into three or four.

"Well, break a leg, or whatever it is they say."

"That's theater talk," she said.

The call made me queasy, and I regretted making it. I couldn't sleep, but didn't want to bother Ramona with the TV or music, so I stayed up most of the night reading Clio's biography.

Reading a book about someone you know and see regularly is deeply intimate, like having a hidden camera that films them while you're apart. Surprises abounded, like the fact that in 1921, when she first met Flora, Clio was living (in sin, presumably) with a male artist named Laurence Tolliver. Their meeting ended both Flora's marriage and Clio's live-in relationship with Tolliver. She and Tolliver remained on friendly terms, though, and he cropped up on several pages of her life story, even helping her get her apartment in Milligan Place.

The biographical parts of Montrose's book were overshadowed by what I found to be dry literary criticism, and I skimmed it as I plowed through the pages. According to the author's introduction, Clio had refused to be interviewed for the book, so Montrose was forced to rely on files and manuscripts Clio released to the New York Public Library in the 1970s. Montrose filled in the details of her subject's private life by interviewing Tolliver, Louise Durand, and the Paris lesbians who were still alive, such as Janet Flanner and Berenice Abbott.

I knew Clio hated biographies, which she called "voyeurism," and memoirs, which she deemed "nothing but narcissism."

"My work was meant to stand on its own," she maintained.

But the Paris expatriates she had lived among had written memoirs. "Natalie, Janet, all of them!" she complained. "I begged my friends not to include anything about me, but Janet said, 'My dear, how could I write about those years and not include you?'"

The picture that emerged of Clio's life was a patchwork of facts. Flora left first for Paris, and Clio followed a few months later. They rented a two-room flat on the Left Bank, and drank a lot of wine and smoked a lot of cigarettes in famous places like Café Flore with famous people like Flanner and her "companion" (as Montrose called her), Solita Solano. But their lives weren't just about drinking and frolicking with friends—they wrote, too, including the stories I'd tracked down in American magazines. Flanner described Clio as "writing every day, feverishly almost, filling up notebooks with her delicately woven stories. She put so many other writers to shame."

On the streets of Paris, Clio cut a dashing figure in velvet capes of different, striking colors—wine, jade, plum. Her wit was biting, and everyone wanted her at their dinner parties and salons. "To be taken down a notch by Clio Hartt was considered a badge of honor," Louise Durand said. Louise met Clio and Flora at Gertrude Stein's, and gifted each of them with a generous monthly stipend.

Although other expats, like Gertrude Stein and Natalie Barney, stayed on in France during World War II, Clio and Flora set sail for New York after Kristallnacht—the wave of pogroms that swept across Nazi Germany. Flora's mother had been Jewish, and it seemed safest to flee Europe while they could.

The details of Clio's life back in New York became sketchier. She and Flora lived together on West 10th Street, but by 1941 Clio was ensconced in Milligan Place. She enjoyed a modest but comfortable existence and for a few years even had another "companion," a painter named Moira McGough.

But then Louise abruptly announced that she could no longer support both Clio and Flora, and chose Flora. The break caused a rift between Clio and Flora, too, and they didn't speak for almost fifteen years.

"Flora was a remarkable talent who needed me more," Louise told Montrose, as justification for her decision to cut Clio off. "She was a true genius."

Yet history hadn't borne out Flora's exceptionalism. In fact, Montrose concluded that Flora was better remembered for the celebrities she'd had affairs or relationships with, not for her own creative endeavors. And there were many entanglements—not just with Clio (and presumably Louise), but women and men alike, from Berenice Abbott to Edna St. Vincent Millay to Ezra Pound and Man Ray.

A few years after the split with Louise, Clio's writing output dried up, Moira was out of the picture, and she became a near-recluse. After Bea Winston signed on as her agent in the 1960s, Clio no longer had any reason to leave her apartment.

She did have a phone call with Flora not long before she died. Clio had referenced it with me in the Asheville hospital, when Flora called to tell her she was coughing up blood and submitting to tests.

Before that, though, Flora had written to Clio from Connecticut, where she was living part-time with Louise, and Clio sent the letter back to her unopened. Louise apparently let Montrose read the letter and use the two photographs Flora had tucked into the envelope.

"Darling," the letter read, "I can't bear to have these with me anymore. It's as if they mock me. I'm in a bad way, Birdie—nothing to do with drink or powder, haven't done anything like that in 8 years, you must believe me. I want you to take care of this sweet memory for me. That weekend in Deauville! My hair's gone grey, has yours too? You will always look like this to me—so delicious & true! Please call me, just once, & I can tell you something I must not keep from you. Yours, Florrie."

Darling . . . Birdie . . . Yours, Florrie.

I read the words several times and stared at the two photos, which Montrose included side by side in her book. One was of Flora in a revealing bathing costume—more like underwear than a bathing suit—posed on an empty beach, her pert nipples poking against a sleeveless tank. With her lascivious grin and sexy bob ruffled by the ocean breeze, she looked like someone New York lesbians might trample each other to enjoy even one night with.

The other photo was of Clio, barefoot on what seemed to be the same beach, in rolled-up pants and a gauzy shirt and smiling so radiantly I had to check the caption to make sure it was really her. All the photos I'd seen of her as a young writer showed her as more regal—beautiful, for sure, but rigidly posed. Here she was unfettered and simply stunning: "Clio Hartt, Deauville Beach, June 1929."

"I can't say I ever understood their connection," Montrose quoted Louise as saying. "They were a tortured pair." You could almost hear a heavy sigh lifting off the page.

Within the next few paragraphs, Louise's words intimated that Flora had committed suicide rather than suffer through the cancer that had taken over her body. "She decided not to go on," she said. "I was powerless to stop her. No one could have." Any more exact explanation of her death was missing. Louise scattered her ashes off Long Island Sound.

That morning, before work, I dashed to D'Agostino to buy baking supplies. When I checked on Clio later that day, I wanted to offer her something special. I had been impressed with Clio's hearty appetite for my mother's cooking and had copied Mama's recipe for buttermilk biscuits before leaving for the airport.

What stood out most for me in the Montrose biography was how Flora had addressed Clio as "Birdie." I always assumed Clio had rejected all vestiges of her past self when she moved to New York and then Paris. "I named myself Clio," she told me on our trip south, "because I read that it meant 'to celebrate.' And I was celebrating my liberation." She abandoned the name Threatt, because people mistook it for "threat," which sounded too ominous. She said she preferred the openness of Hartt and had almost spelled it "Harte," like the short story writer. But at the last minute, when she was sending off a story to a publisher using her new moniker, she added the extra *T* as a hat tip to her birth name.

Still, even at the height of her luminous career, even though she'd been photographed by Man Ray in all her self-confident beauty, even though she was one of only a few people allowed to call James Joyce "Jim," Clio had been plain old Birdie to Flora, the woman she never got out of her mind.

I left the flour and baking powder in a bag in the kitchen with a note for Ramona saying, "Please don't move this!" and stuffed the butter and buttermilk behind a stack of Diet Cokes in the refrigerator. Ramona rarely went into the kitchen except for a can of pop, so I doubted she'd even notice it.

After work, I got to baking. On her way out to an author signing, Ramona wondered what I was doing with flour all over my face and hands. "It's in your hair, too," she said. "Looks like you're prematurely white." When I told her what I was up to, she asked, "If you have any extra, save one for me?"

The biscuits were still warm when Clio buzzed me in. At her apartment door, I brushed a spot of flour off the leg of my jeans.

"Miss Bliss, whatever is it?" Instead of being dressed in her usual sweater and skirt, she wore a men's flannel bathrobe so old the cotton seemed almost see-through and so large it swept the floorboards. A thick wool scarf obscured her neck, and a gold stocking cap covered crown to ears. Her hair hung loose on her shoulders, with a charming natural wave to it. The ensemble gave her the appearance of a Dickens character.

"I am so sorry to bother you, Miss Hartt!" I said. "I just thought I'd check on you."

"At this time of night?"

I showed her my wristwatch. "It's just after six."

"My. Well, it does get dark early this time of year. Come in."

The room was colder than usual and darker, with the only light coming from the lamp next to her armchair. Remington had tucked himself onto a pillow next to the lamp. I recognized it as the one Clio placed behind her back when she sat at her desk, and I made a mental note to get the cat a proper bed.

Clio switched on the overhead light, then blinked several times from the brightness.

"Oh, don't turn it on for me," I said. "I won't stay long. I wanted to bring you these." I held out the bag of biscuits with pride.

A smile turned up Clio's lips as she glanced inside. "Did you make them yourself, Miss Bliss?"

"From my mama's recipe." They looked fluffy, but I realized with a spurt of panic that I hadn't bothered to test them. "I hope they're okay."

"I am sure they will be delicious. But I'm afraid we have nothing to put on them."

"I thought of that, too," I said, drawing a jar of apricot jam out of my bag. It wasn't homemade but it was French, which seemed like the next best thing—the mingling of home with memories of Paris.

I hadn't eaten anything since lunch, so I made a biscuit for each of us, slathered in jam. Even Remington looked up like he might be interested, but I gave him a tuna-flavored treat instead.

"What is the occasion, Miss Bliss?" Clio asked after her first appreciative bite. "Are you still trying to make up for invading my privacy?" We hadn't spoken of my offense in weeks, but her tone was light. I'd been coming around less, as she requested, and I wondered if she might possibly have missed my company.

"I just thought you'd like a taste of home," I said. "You liked my mama's cooking so much."

"I did indeed," Clio said. "It brought to mind the good things about home and pushed the bad things right out."

The room was so cold my breath was visible, and I left my jacket on as we ate. I brought a blanket from the daybed and draped it around Clio's shoulders as she nibbled at half of the biscuit.

"Why is it so cold in here, Miss Hartt? Isn't heat included in your rent?"

"It's the radiator, I'm sure," she said. "It's been sputtering a lot. The superintendent should bleed it. Terrible word for it, really. Like he has to apply leeches!"

"I could call him."

"He has not been answering his phone."

"Let me run down and knock on his door then."

"Oh, let's enjoy our little meal first," she said. "The quilt warmed me right up. Help yourself to another biscuit, Miss Bliss."

Chilled, the biscuits weren't quite as tasty as they'd been just minutes earlier, but I ate another anyway as I watched her dawdle over her second half.

"Except for my mama's food, I've never seen you eat much," I remarked mid-bite. "How about in Paris? Did you like French cooking?"

"Well, the pastries were, of course, divine," she said. "But we didn't have trust funds, like Natalie and Gertrude, so it was a modest lifestyle and we lived mostly on bread, cheese, wine— inexpensive fare. You know." Although I imagined the bills added up if they drank as much wine as Montrose implied.

"I've never been to Paris," I admitted. "Or anywhere in Europe. I would love to go."

"Do go while you're young and you can get by on very little. Live there if you can."

"I don't know what I'd do!" I said. "You wrote for magazines to earn a living. What did Fl—Miss Haynes do?"

Her laugh had a tinge of bitterness to it. "What didn't Flora do?" she said. "She wrote, of course, but she didn't like journalism or short stories, and that was where the money was. So she had to get money here and there." Clio pointed at herself on the word *here*.

"You supported her?"

"Among others. People were always giving Flora money. She had multiple patrons. She was quite good-looking, you know." I wasn't sure what her looks had to do with patronage, but I could guess. Clio made her lover sound like a prostitute, and maybe that was how she thought of her. Her tone suggested her anger still simmered below the surface, even after all these years.

Clio pointed toward the framed sepia of Flora standing on a cobblestone street in Paris looking like she owned the place.

"She was a looker," I commented. "That's a handsome photo. But the one on the Deauville beach—hoo-wee!" It slipped out before I realized what I'd said.

Clio had been slumped comfortably in her chair, but the mention of the beach photo made her bolt upright. Her voice hit a shrill pitch that roused Remington out of his sleep, and he stared at us with annoyance.

"The Deauville beach? Where did you see that one? No one has seen that!"

Had she never been curious enough to glance through her own biography, even if only to look at the pictures? If someone ever wrote about me for posterity, I would check every detail.

"Those photos are mine! Flora said she didn't want them, and I—" She was practically spitting.

"They're in Sylvia Montrose's biography of you."

Her face drained of color. "But . . . Flora was almost . . . she . . . Those photos weren't meant to be seen by anyone but us. They were private." She sagged back into her chair again, defeated. I thought about Louise Durand handing the photos over to Montrose, a sort of "fuck you" to Clio and Flora both—for what, it wasn't clear. Maybe the answer lay in Louise's brittle comment in the biography, that she never understood the connection between Clio and Flora: "They were a tortured pair," she had said.

"I'm sorry," I said. "I guess these things just get out somehow when you're famous."

"Do you have that book?" she demanded.

"Yes, I have it at home."

"In Asheville." The corners of her mouth sagged.

"No, here. Over in Gramercy. I could bring it next time. I would have brought it before if—"

"Bring it tomorrow," she said, forgetting our loosened schedule. And then, also forgetting that she sometimes didn't get up until noon: "In the morning."

The next day, I dropped in at the office first, in case Bea had left any tasks on my desk that had to be handled immediately. She hadn't, but only because she was still drawing up the list of things for me to do while she went for a few days to her house in the Catskills. It was unlike her to take an evening off, let alone several weekdays, but Ramona said Bea was trying to patch things up with Unfaithful Husband, whose name, amazingly, was Dick. Apparently, the pregnant paralegal had dumped Dick and returned to her former boyfriend "who seems to be the father after all," Ramona explained.

"Therese is in charge while I'm gone," Bea said, ripping the list off her legal pad. "But you can always call me in an emergency. There's no machine, so keep trying."

"Don't worry about a thing," I assured her. "You just enjoy yourself."

"Well, I will hardly do that." The look on her face suggested the "patching up" was more a chore than a pleasant getaway. "I hate the country. Dick's the one who wanted the place. Why anyone needs to escape the city is beyond me." Her tone softened. "But he has promised to cook for me, which is lucky since there isn't a decent restaurant in fifty miles. And he's made himself a gorgeous gourmet kitchen."

When she handed me the list, I assumed it was time to go, but she asked me to sit down instead.

"Clio called me early this morning. At home."

Expecting a rebuke for something, I headed it off: "I know, she wants me to stop in. I'll be walking over there just as soon as we wrap things up here."

Clio didn't seem to have mentioned anything about the Montrose biography to Bea, though. What they did discuss surprised me.

"She said she's ready to part with her manuscript," Bea continued. "You must have been wrong about her losing motivation. Anyway, it seems to have just two brand-new stories and a third no one's ever read, but then you can't have everything."

Manuscript? *Three* stories? It was all news to me.

"She's gotten it into her head that she's going to die soon. Do you know why she'd think that?"

"Not unless she's had another ministroke. But I was just with her yesterday and she didn't mention feeling bad." *Biscuits.* They were not the best food to bring to someone at risk for a stroke. I wondered if she'd eaten more after I left.

"She even asked me to call her lawyer. You know, I'm not sure he's still alive. He was older than Clio. She said she tore the room apart last night looking for her will and couldn't find it. Now she wants to draw up a new one and make sure everything's in order. And she's very anxious to get the manuscript into my hands."

The overnight change in Clio puzzled me, and I wondered if my visit—and possibly the Montrose biography—had anything to do with it.

"I'm driving up to Ulster this morning, so I'll need you to call the lawyer. It's at the top of the list."

I glanced down and saw that, indeed, calling Mort Barber at Barber, Barber, Barber & Barber was point number one. The firm's name made me snicker—why couldn't they have settled on just one Barber?

"He's a lovely man . . . or was. If he's dead or retired or something, talk to his daughter, Miriam. She's a partner in the firm." Her name and number were second on the list.

"Get whatever Clio wants to give you and bring it here right away! Do not pass 'Go,' do not collect two hundred dollars!"

That was point number three. In parentheses was a notation to make five photocopies of whatever Clio handed me. That would tie up the photocopier for longer than any of the agents would like, but I understood why Bea didn't want to entrust the manuscript to a copy shop.

"And then start reading it."

"Me?" She hadn't bestowed any reading duties on me since Diane Westerly's manuscript.

"Yes, you. I won't be able to look at it until next week, and no one here has been working with Clio. So you're it. Type up a report, like you did with Diane's."

Grabbing my bag with the Montrose biography in it, I scurried to Clio's. Since she'd already spoken to Bea that morning, I didn't bother to call and remind her I was coming. Yet, at the apartment door, she looked as dumbfounded as when I'd surprised her the day before.

"You asked me to come by," I reminded her gently.

"Oh, yes," she said, but her tone sounded unconvincing. I wondered if she was having a brain blip, like the doctor in Asheville said she might, and I debated whether I should even mention the Montrose book.

Then her memory kicked in. "Did you bring it? The horrid book about me and Flora?"

"It's actually about you and your work," I pointed out, slipping the volume from my bag. "Although there's a bit about Miss Haynes."

"And how long has this been out there?"

"Ma'am?"

"When was it published?" She grabbed it from me and made for her reading chair, pushing Remington gently to the side so she could ease in next to him. He stretched out long against her leg.

"A few years ago. '78, maybe? It'll be on the copyright page."

"I think I remember," she said, cracking open the spine. "Beatrice said someone wanted to interview me, here, in my home! I said absolutely not!"

I smiled at the contrariness of it. As much as Clio wanted to be revered for her work, she staunchly resisted cooperating with scholars who might bring the desired attention to it—and help sell more copies of *The Dismantled*.

She flipped through the pages with fury. I knew what she was looking for. The book had a dozen or so photos scattered throughout, many of them the museum-worthy studio portraits that had become iconic. When she arrived at the side-by-side pictures of her and Flora at Deauville Beach, a little moan escaped her lips.

The text of Flora's last letter to her was on the facing page, and I watched as she read it, moving her magnifying glass the length of the page as her finger traced every word.

"Miss Hartt—"

She stopped me with an upraised hand while she finished reading, her breath now a series of tiny gasps.

"Oh," she said, setting down her magnifier.

"The book was very well reviewed," I said, not sure why I felt the need to come to its defense. "It was probably why the critical edition of *The Dismantled* has done so well in colleges."

"I sent the envelope back to her," she said, not looking at me, maybe not even hearing me. "I didn't bother to open it. I saw the return address—at that woman's!—and I felt sickened, like the unpleasantness between us had just happened. And I could feel it was heavier than a letter, that it had something inside. Miss Bliss, I am a monster."

"Please don't be so hard on yourself! You spoke to Miss Haynes before she died."

"Only because she called me." Her voice caught on the final word. "Only because when I picked up the phone she said, 'Darling, it seems I'm dying.' Not even the vilest of monsters would hang up on that."

I didn't know how to respond, so I remained quiet.

"If I'd opened the letter, these photos would be here in this apartment, and the letter would be mine. Flora's torture wouldn't be in black and white for all the world to read about. Our most intimate moment wouldn't be on display! Deauville . . . We were in love! That's for us, not for anyone else."

Her sobs sounded like they might strangle her, but as suddenly as she'd begun to cry, she stopped and blew her nose on her handkerchief. My eyes followed her as she got up and moved to the walk-in closet, disappearing inside. She emerged a few minutes later with a vintage travel bag, the kind ladies carried their hats in decades back. And I knew that Clio had been famous for wearing hats—turbans, cloches, derbies, fedoras; they were in the portraits of her. She snapped the bag open and I could see that there were no hats inside. Instead, she drew out an envelope of photographs.

"Those photos were mine!" she said, rifling through the images, which from what I could see by craning my neck were all of Flora or of the two of them together. "I meant to burn them. I did burn a few that were especially . . . intimate. Flora must have sneaked

251

some when I left Tenth Street. And Louise—" she snarled the name of her nemesis, "—she gave them to this woman, this Montrose person, this despicable lesbian looking for gossip."

"Montrose's bio says she's married and has two sons," I said, a bit haughty. The condescension toward lesbians wore down my patience.

"You're very naïve if you think lesbians don't marry men," she said.

I shrugged, but I was suddenly thinking of Hallie, who claimed she didn't identify as gay or lesbian. "I'm just me," she had insisted when I cornered her.

"Where are the photos now?" Clio said. "Where is my letter?"

"The caption says the photos are 'Courtesy Louise Durand.' Bea said she died a few years ago, so whoever handled her estate must have them."

"Nineteen-seventy-nine," Clio said, and I half-expected her to recite the exact date, too. "Good riddance! The woman was trouble." She sighed heavily and continued, "Someone is always ruining something for someone else"—the kind of vague, grumpy statement a child might make when she hasn't gotten her way.

Clio shifted in her seat, and the hat carrier fell with a thunk. I could see then that it was almost empty, except for two items that spilled onto the floor: a pearl necklace with a broken clasp and an antique stuffed monkey with a frayed satin ribbon tied around its neck. The toy's stuffing poked through various seams, and its tail hung by a few threads.

"Is this one of your childhood toys?" I asked, reaching to replace the monkey.

"Don't touch that!" she snapped at me without answering the question. "It's very old and very delicate."

"I was just—it looks like something the cat would go after," I said. Remington was, in fact, inching toward it. Clio grabbed the toy, ignoring that it was "very delicate," and tossed it back into the hat carrier, where it landed face down. Then she picked up the pearls and rolled them over in her hand before extending them toward me.

"You may have these," she said. Since I didn't look like a woman with the wardrobe for pearls, I was startled. "You could get the clasp fixed. I'm not sure the pearls themselves have much value, but Flora gave them to me and I wore them in the Man Ray portrait, so maybe you can sell them for their provenance."

"Oh, Miss Hartt, I would never sell them!"

"Then give them to your lady," she said.

"We aren't . . . I'm not sure she's my . . ."

Clio became impatient. "Oh, I don't care what you do with them!"

"Are you sure you don't want to keep them?"

"I'm going to die soon." Her tone was without a trace of self-pity.

"Don't say that!"

"Miss Bliss," she said, "I'm not being morbid, just factual." She reached over and forced the necklace into my hand. "If you prefer, we can do an exchange—a tit for tat."

I thought she was going to ask to keep the Montrose book, but I was wrong.

"If you would, I would like to hear you call me 'Birdie.'"

"Miss Hartt—" My throat tightened: Was I was going to have to say her name on the spot? There were a million reasons the request was difficult for me, and she hit on several of them.

"I know, I am your employer of sorts, and your mama taught you never to address an older woman by her Christian name. But I would like to hear it just the same. Not now, but on some day when I might not expect it." Her eyes filmed over, and I couldn't help but think about the letter from Flora calling her "Birdie."

"But don't wait too long," she added hastily.

"It's still a struggle for me to call Miss Winston 'Bea,'" I said. "But she insists."

"Well, you have gotten past that, so you will get past this, too. I insist. And for your effort, you go home with the pearls of Clio Hartt." She had tucked the envelope of photos beside her, where Remington had been, and I watched anxiously as she shifted again in the chair and the packet slipped beneath her.

253

"Your photos—" I said, pointing.

Her eyes followed my hand, and she retrieved the envelope.

"Don't you think you've seen enough of me and Flora?" she growled, waving the envelope. "I should burn these."

Someday a literary scholar would be looking for photos of Clio Hartt and come up empty-handed, except for the posed portraits and a handful of snaps that had survived in the collections of her friends and colleagues.

"Come to think of it, I should burn other things," she said. "The library will have what's important." She stood up with difficulty and ambled to the fireplace. The mantle was narrow and white, jutting out only a few inches from the wall, and there was a small iron grate in the opening. But the grate was free of ashes and, in all the months I'd been visiting her, I'd never seen a log in it, fresh or burnt. From the beginning, I'd assumed—as was the case in other old apartments, including Barb's and Ramona's—that the flue was sealed off and the fireplace had reverted to quaint decoration.

"Oh, no!" I objected. "You'd burn things in there? That doesn't seem safe, Miss Hartt."

"Nonsense, I've done it before. In fact, it's been so cold lately, I thought of making a fire just to keep warm, but I don't have any wood. Maybe you could bring me some. Come look." She gestured up the chimney, where I spotted a patchwork quilt blackened with soot. Cold air seeped through where it didn't fit tightly.

"No wonder it's so cold in here," I said. "That should be boarded up properly. I'll get the super to—"

"Absolutely not! Then I would have to burn my papers in the sink and that would be such a mess."

I tried to remain hopeful that she didn't mean to burn anything significant. "Um, by papers, what do you mean—old phone bills and things like that?"

"Why on earth would I burn a phone bill? I've hardly spoken to anyone but you and Miss Winston in years. No, I mean a few letters. A manuscript or two that might confuse people."

I went from stunned to horrified at the speed of light. My mind raced to Bea, who would salivate over Clio Hartt manuscripts, no matter what state they were in.

"That is so wrong, Miss Hartt! Please, you just can't. Your safety—"

She clicked her tongue dismissively.

"And, and posterity!" I said, switching tracks. "Anything you wrote is valuable to the literary world. You're *the* great Modernist writer. You said so yourself."

"I did not. I was simply repeating what Tom Eliot said." For the first time since I'd met her, she blushed a bright pink.

"So where are these manuscripts? Are they under your desk? In the closet?" With a frantic three-sixty twirl, I did a visual sweep of the apartment.

Clio placed her hand on her chin as if she were studying a poem or essay she couldn't quite figure out. "Let's sit down, Miss Bliss," she said, "and calm ourselves. I can see you're getting worked up over nothing."

"It's hardly nothing!"

"Well, since you feel so strongly about posterity, there's something I'd like to tell you. A secret. But you must promise to hear me out—to listen and not judge."

It was an hour, maybe a little more, before I left Milligan Place. Under my arm were two manuscripts in a brown paper bag, each fastened separately with twine.

My throat scratched, but I didn't dare stop at Mr. Park's for a Coke or—what I needed more—a beer. I went straight to the office, set the parcel down in the middle of my desk, and stared at it.

Chapter 25

She had instructed me just to listen, but I proved an unwilling recipient of her secret. I blurted out, "I thought you didn't trust me anymore."

Clio nodded in a halting way, as if she only partially recalled her own words. "You're used to keeping secrets."

How did she know that? I had never told her about Hallie, never mentioned that my parents and sisters didn't know I was gay. I'd also never confided the deep relief I'd experienced when I unburdened myself to Aunt Sass.

Although I wasn't one to defy my elders, I couldn't keep myself from protesting. "I'd rather not know yours. It's too much, Miss Hartt. Wouldn't Miss Winston be a better choice?"

She shot me a frown. "Miss Winston wouldn't suit. And I should share this before I die."

"I wish you'd stop talking like that. It's so morbid."

"It would be morbid for you to imagine your death," she snapped, "but not for someone my age."

A picture of Eli formed in my mind, but I didn't say anything.

"Miss Bliss," she said in a gentler tone, "telling Miss Winston would be a mistake. She might rush into something. I need someone who can take a longer view, really. That's you."

A longer view. Her words tumbled out smoothly. I didn't understand them, but they sounded in my young ears like high praise.

"Where do you hope to be in thirty years?" she asked.

In thirty years, I'd be my mother's age. Instead of raising kids, though, I wanted to be sitting behind an editor's desk in a prestigious press, my days booked with clients and agents. Or maybe I'd have my own publishing house that fostered women writers and writers of color who'd been ignored. Nothing lightweight, but work that really mattered. It would be my legacy, my—

"You are ambitious, Miss Bliss," Clio said with a sly smile that made me realize I'd been rambling. "You think big." I don't think she meant her next words to undercut my dream, but they did. "Thirty years ago, I thought I'd be back in Paris by now, but that never happened. Well, let's get on with it, shall we?"

I found myself helping her pull a slim storage box, the kind you might keep out-of-season clothes in, from under her daybed. I got down on all fours and reached back with the fireplace poker to grab onto it. Dust bunnies scuttled out, and Clio suffered a brief coughing fit that required a glass of water.

The box bore a thick coating of dust I attempted to clean off with several paper towels. With each swipe, the towels came back charcoal gray.

"How long has it been since you looked at this?"

"I moved here in 1941."

The dust had begun to settle when my parents were teenagers who had not even met.

Stacked in the box were five yellowed manuscripts, each tied with twine, each bearing a different title page. The titles were nondescript, forgettable—except for one that read, "All This." Clio had been writing a story or novella by that name when I first knew her, then changed it to "The Less We Know."

"Bring them all out," she said.

As I withdrew them one by one, the title page of a manuscript near the bottom read clearly, disturbingly, "The Dismantled: A Novel by Clio Hartt and Flora Haynes." My eyes darted to Clio's, but she simply stared at the stack of paper in my hands.

"You wrote it together?"

She reached for the manuscript that bore both their names and sat down on the bed with it in her lap.

"This was the beginning of our end," she said.

She had written, she said, four successive drafts of "a very bad novel."

"Perhaps the worst novel ever written," Clio said. "It read like the sentimental stories I'd published so successfully in magazines. The ones they practically threw money at me to write."

"I love those stories! They're so well-plotted and so evocative. You underestimate them, Miss Hartt."

Clio half-smiled, as if thinking, "What very bad taste you have!" But what she said was: "There's nothing wrong with them technically. They just aren't art, really." She sighed. "The very bad novel was all about a poor Carolina girl who gets involved with a sophisticated artist and her life is changed forever. It had substance but no style. It challenged nothing and no one. It would have gotten published, to be sure, but you would never have read it in college. It wouldn't even be a footnote in someone's thesis."

She ran a hand over the title page.

"Flora had written those wondrous plays, so daring and fresh. She saw me struggling, running out of money, getting more and more frustrated and close to giving up on the thing. She secured Louise's patronage so I wouldn't have to keep writing the magazine stories, and I could just focus on the book. That money was a godsend, though what Flora had to do to get it—"

Clio's mouth twisted into a grimace, and she didn't elaborate. With nothing specific to go on, my mind pictured sexual contortions, acrobatics, silk scarves, handcuffs, the wax on Barb's breasts—

The sound of Clio gulping water interrupted my thoughts. I hoped for a moment that the story had come to an end, that Flora's role in the novel was maybe simply pimping herself to Louise—and others?—to get an influx of cash for Clio.

"Then Flora offered to look at the thing. It had swelled to a bloated size, and I was despondent. 'A quick edit,' she said. I jumped at the chance. She was working with a theater group, and she was in peak form, writing such sharp dialogue. Her taste was impeccable."

A headache started just between my eyes. The throb of it made me close my lids briefly while she continued her story.

"She ended up infusing my very bad novel with life. Wrote new scenes, like that luminous ending Hemingway raved about in his review. She even dreamt up its title. Literally—it came to her as she slept. But when I insisted on putting both our names on the thing, she just laughed. 'You're the novelist, darling,' she said. 'I helped a little.' I dedicated it to her, which was something at least." I recalled the vagueness of the dedication: "To F—for love, for life." Hallie had told me it referred to Flora, or else I wouldn't have known.

Clio coughed, rough and rasping, like part of her lungs might come up through her throat. When I refilled her water, she drank down the full amount and then drew the story to its close.

"She was so thrilled when the reviews poured in and critics compared me to Joyce! Not a shred of jealousy in her. There wasn't a lot of money from the book, but there was literary acclaim, which we both thought was better. Especially since we had stipends from Louise. And after a while, I forgot which words I'd written and which she'd written. It was like we were one artist."

I opened my eyes to find her staring at me with a questioning look on her face, gauging my response. "It was all so innocent, really. We were a team, so completely in harmony. And if we'd stayed together, it would have been fine. But after we came back to New York, Louise demanded more and more of Flora's time, and Flora just gave it. There was so much drinking—and other things. Flora would wink and say, 'I have to go powder my nose,' and everyone would laugh at the joke she'd become."

When Clio couldn't abide it anymore, when she had found herself drinking away her own career and needed to take back control, she moved to Milligan Place for breathing room. In the depths of her addiction, Flora called it a betrayal and threatened to tell their secret, claim her place in the novel's birth. Her own playwriting was suffering from the debauchery of her lifestyle, and she couldn't get anything produced in New York or elsewhere.

"She did manage to tell my editor, one night at the White Horse Tavern, but he brushed it off. He laughed about it when he told me and called her pathetic. I felt sorry for everything that had happened between us and decided to make peace. But then I heard from Louise that she was cutting me off, and I knew it was Flora's doing. It was over."

She was gripping the manuscript to her chest.

"It was wrong to take full credit. The best bits were likely hers."

"You don't know that," I said. "You said you forgot who wrote what."

"Anyone could check it," she said. "It wouldn't be hard. There will be crossings-out everywhere, new pages added, pages deleted. Flora had a distinctive hand, more like printing than handwriting. She used blue ink. It wouldn't take a scientist to decipher who wrote what." The manuscript shifted on her lap, as if sliding toward me.

My stomach dropped, and I must have lost color in my face because she added quickly, "Then again, I could just burn the thing."

"Miss Hartt, that's like—" I couldn't think of anything to compare it to, but it felt like a form of murder. "I can't let you do that. It needs to be preserved."

"Then take it with you, Miss Bliss. Get it out of here. If you don't, I'll be forced to destroy it. The thought of my dying in this room, and you know I will someday, with strangers finding it, and having no explanation—" Her voice had cracked on the word "strangers."

She had roped me in good. The room felt even colder now that I had become her accomplice.

In her kitchen, I located a brown paper bag from Gristedes and put the damning manuscript at the bottom of it. On top, Clio placed a second manuscript with the title, "Before the Fire: The Collected Stories of Clio Hartt" on the front page. This was the work she had told Bea about and promised to submit for publication. At the door, she patted the side of the bag as if it was a cherished pet.

"Don't lose it," she instructed. I couldn't help but notice the singular, but I wasn't sure what she meant—the bag itself, or one of the manuscripts in particular.

"Please don't burn anything while I'm gone," I said.

Chapter 26

February 1984

With the news of her first book in almost fifty years, Clio was set to ascend to the literary heights once again. It didn't matter that only three of the sixteen stories were, in fact, new—she was a rock star, the Michael Jackson of the publishing world. Luckily, "Madame Louise" was not among the included stories. The sharp resemblance of its plot to that of her masterpiece would have caused critics to bare their fangs. Also absent was "The Less We Know," the piece she had been writing and rewriting the first pages of since I'd known her, giving it different titles, never feeling it was quite "there." She had never let me read it.

What she did include were the two North Carolina-themed stories. "Before the Fire," the lovely novella she finished before our trip and named the volume after, was first. "An Old Woman's Bed," the piece she had conceived in her Dry Ridge motel room—and set in a very similar cabin—was second. She had obviously completed it at some point without announcing it to me. It was a delicate story of looking back on a long life with both wisdom and regret.

The third new story, called "Monkey," revolved around a stuffed monkey—not unlike the one that had tumbled out of her luggage. The toy was at first the cherished "child" of two women who lived together (coded lovers, it seemed), and later became the focus of a vicious argument that ended their relationship. The monkey in the story, in fact, came to a violent end, wrenched apart by its arms.

Now that I knew the story of Clio and Flora and *The Dismantled*, I wondered if "Monkey" was an extended metaphor for what had transpired between them. Clio couldn't set the record straight, but maybe she had devised a code she hoped a literary scholar would someday unravel. My theory seemed like a stretch, and of course I couldn't share it.

Bea speculated that Clio might have held onto the story for years, never feeling it was quite polished enough, or that maybe a magazine had rejected it long ago, and she'd filed it away out of annoyance or frustration. Knowing Clio, Bea's theories seemed plausible.

Within days of offering the collection, Bea had sold the manuscript and had me deliver the contract to Clio for signing. The apartment felt cozier than it had in weeks, and at first I thought the super had finally bled the radiators. Then I noticed a pile of ashes in the fireplace.

"Miss Hartt," I said, alarmed, "what were you burning?"

"Just a few little things. Nothing to trouble yourself about."

"But we talked about—"

"I said, do not trouble yourself," she repeated.

We huddled together at her desk so that she could sign the three copies of the contract.

"And Miss Winston thinks this is all in order?" she asked with her trusty Sheaffer pen in hand.

"She does." I smiled at the memory of how Bea had described it, and I thought the phrasing would tickle Clio. "She said, and I quote, 'This contract is as tight as a virgin on her wedding night.'"

Clio let out a little snort. "Are there any virgins on their wedding nights anymore?"

Putting her signature to paper proved a hard task, and my heart ached as I watched her. At first, she hesitated, as if she'd forgotten how to sign her own name, and I leaned into her, hoping my closeness could impart some oomph. Then she began, her pen scratching across the page as she formed each letter deliberately and awkwardly. The end result looked like a bad forgery, something accomplished on a light table by a novice, but I had witnessed it and knew it was genuine.

Then she had to do it again and again. At the end, she leaned back in her chair, spent.

"And you're done!" I said proudly.

"That was not half as bad as my new will," she remarked. I had made the call to her lawyer's office and arranged the meeting, not with Mort Barber or his daughter Miriam (who had both passed), but with Mort's grandson, the third generation of Barber lawyers. I hadn't been present for the will signing, but now I knew it had happened.

"I feel so much better," she said. "I think I'll have a nap. Would you just escort me to the bed?"

She'd always been so adamant about not needing assistance with daily routines, I felt worried. If signing a few papers could strip so much energy from her, she must be feeling very weak. I worried that she'd suffered more ministrokes while she was alone. Her repeated assertion over the past few weeks that she wouldn't live much longer seemed less far-fetched.

I offered my arm, and we made it slowly to the daybed where I pulled back the quilt and helped ease her down.

"Could you . . ." she said, pointing to her shoes, and I slipped them off and raised first one stockinged leg, then the other, onto the bed.

"I don't know why I'm so tired," she said. She occasionally took sleeping pills, because her rest was far from satisfying, and I wondered if she'd slipped up and taken more than one.

"There, that's nice," she said, patting my hand.

"You rest now, Birdie," I said, keeping my other promise to her. She smiled and closed her eyes.

A few days after Clio signed the contract was Valentine's Day, and I had a date with Thea for Indian dinner on Sixth Street— an evening we'd planned before I'd found out about her affair with Barb. Thea had a favorite restaurant, both for the dishes and the romantic tone set by twinkling white string lights. In all my months in New York I had never been brave enough to try Indian food, thinking it too spicy for my taste; but for the first Valentine's Day I'd ever had a lover to celebrate with, I agreed to step outside my comfort zone.

"Do you still want to?" Thea had asked on the phone the day before, giving me an easy out. But I had a present for her, and I acted enthusiastic even though it felt like the evening could be a small disaster.

Since our fight, Thea had made two additional trips for job interviews. We'd had no sleep-over dates, just a couple of nights of talking and drinking and trying to be casual, plus a few slap-dash make-out sessions where we either missed each other's mouths or accidentally clacked our teeth together. We acted like a married couple who'd tried counseling with no luck. I didn't know what would happen on Valentine's Day, but I changed my sheets just in case we gave it one last go.

The Indian menu undid me: I didn't know Tandoori from Vindaloo, so Thea chose. She ordered vegetable curry and chicken tikka masala and instructed the waiter to tone down the spice with a coy smile in my direction. She probably meant it as thoughtful, but it felt strangely condescending, as if they shared a joke about me.

"I have something to tell you that I want to get out of the way," she said when the waiter had disappeared. I cracked open the bottles of Singha we'd brought along to the BYOB venue, and we tapped our bottles before she spoke.

"Happy Valentine's Day," I said.

She took a gulp, then blurted out her news. "Livvie, I got two job offers."

"Wow," I said. "Which schools?"

"Spelman and Wellesley."

"Wow. Congratulations." I touched my bottle to hers a second time, the clinking sound reverberating in my ears.

"I'm disappointed about Hamilton. I thought I aced that. But my choices aren't shabby." Both were prestigious colleges, but Spelman was historically black, which carried a special appeal for her. "It's an established department, though, so I'm not sure how much room there is to grow."

For most of our dinner, I listened to her voicing first her enthusiasm and then her concerns about each school. Sometimes it seemed as if Spelman was winning, but other times she leaned toward Wellesley. Never once did she acknowledge that the biggest drawback, from the standpoint of our wobbly relationship, was distance—Spelman was in Atlanta, and Wellesley just outside of Boston.

"Of course, with Atlanta I'd be closer to home . . ."

I had heaped food onto my plate, but I ended up picking at it. Not because Indian cuisine disappointed me; the aromas alone were enough to make a novice like me get high. But I kept picturing Thea's cousin Malcolm loading her possessions onto his truck.

"You sure are quiet," she had observed over after-dinner chai. "I know you aren't happy about my news."

I forced a smile. "I am," I insisted.

"Liv," she said, her stern tone piercing my bullshit. "This isn't about you. Or us. It's about something really big for me. I don't think you get it. Well, you couldn't. You're not in academia, and you aren't black."

Her emphasis on what I *wasn't* stung, but I didn't react. I was determined to act grown-up and supportive, even if my inner adolescent was screaming, *It's just not fair!*

"I get it," I replied, then joked at my own expense. "I'm not that much of a stupid white girl."

She backtracked. "I'm sorry. Nobody thinks you are. Hey, would I go out with stupid?"

"You know, I can get it and be happy for you and sad for myself—for us—at the same time. I'm sorry I let the sad part show."

266

What might be our last evening as a couple was in danger of dissolving into an exchange of apologies. So I reached into my jacket breast pocket and pulled out a tissue-paper wrapped package that I inched across the table toward her.

"Oh, Liv!" she said with what sounded like genuine delight.

"It was supposed to be a Valentine's present, but now it's kind of a congratulations present, too."

She leaned down and brought a package out of her bag. I could tell from the rectangular shape that it was a book, and I was relieved it looked too thin to be *But Some of Us Are Brave*.

"You first," I said.

She ripped the paper and gasped at the pearl necklace nestled in the folds. A jeweler near the agency had fixed the clasp beautifully.

"You can't afford this!" She fingered the strand warily, and I worried for a moment that she might refuse it. Hallie had returned every present I'd bought her, and when she ended our affair, she actually gave me back all the notes and cards I'd ever written to her.

"It's Clio's," I explained. "It's the necklace she's wearing in the Man Ray photo. That really famous portrait?"

Thea shook her head and pushed it across the table. "Oh my God, no! You can't give this to me! You have to keep it."

"Do I look like I'll ever wear pearls? It'll sit in the back of a drawer for the rest of my life." I slid it toward her again. "It'll look great on you. You can wear it when you're an academic star and get your author photo taken."

Thea lifted both eyebrows, like she was poised to tell me to take my quietly snide comment and shove it. But she held whatever she was thinking and reached back into her bag to produce a penny, which she pushed firmly into my outstretched palm.

"For my thoughts?"

"I have to pay you something," she said. "Getting pearls as a gift is bad luck."

"Since when?"

"Since forever," Thea replied, fastening them around her neck. "Your mama or grandma never warned you?"

"Pearls weren't exactly something they could afford." It came out a little snippier than I intended, and I softened my tone. "Clio said Flora gave her the necklace. I wonder if she knew about the superstition."

"Well, Clio's literary reputation sure didn't suffer any bad luck."

The secret behind *The Dismantled* almost bubbled up out of me. The necklace rested elegantly against Thea's black sweater, and a compliment seemed like a good way to shift my thoughts. "Looks like it was made for you."

She smiled and raised a hand to the necklace. "I'll wear it always."

Thea had wrapped her present for me in a thin-striped paper that looked like something left over from Father's Day. She reached a hand across the table to stop me from opening it. "Let me take it back and get you something better."

Inside the paper were two slim volumes of poetry: *The Black Unicorn* by Audre Lorde and *A Wild Patience Has Taken Me This Far* by Adrienne Rich. My lack of appreciation for poetry was something we'd debated more than once, and Thea had only half-mockingly threatened to "force" me to appreciate it. "How can you be an editor if you don't read everything?" she'd said.

"These are great." I tamped down my disappointment. "I will finally be more educated about poetry."

I flipped open the covers, but she hadn't written in either one, and relief coursed through me.

"I couldn't think of anything that didn't sound trite," she explained.

"No problem. Really." I tucked them back into the paper.

The waiter brought our check, which we split down the middle, and it was time to go. Other couples were waiting for our table. But for a final long minute, we stole shy glances at each other, like we were on our first date and neither of us was brave enough to take it to the next level.

"So," I said.

Thea stood up and put on her coat. "You want to go somewhere else?" she ventured. Even though we both knew our affair was careening to an end, I did very much want to hold her again, to experience something of what we had the first night we spent together. I was about to ask her back to my place, when she added, "Ariel's?"

And that's where we were headed when everything shattered.

It was a mild evening and we decided to walk. At first, I regretted the choice. Awkward silences stretched between us as we snaked our way to Astor Place and then across Eighth Street, dodging in and out of the other pedestrians and glancing into shop and café windows. Then, when someone jostled her as we waited to cross Fifth Avenue, Thea suddenly looped her arm through mine like a promise. The gesture sent a ripple of excitement straight down my legs, and I think I squeezed her hand and whispered something sexy as we continued on our path to Sixth.

The exact details are lost to me, though. Because in that long block, even as we nudged closer to each other, siren squeals pierced the night and fire trucks and ambulances roared up Sixth. We sped to the avenue, where several blocks up I could see the emergency vehicles jolting to a stop.

I tasted vegetable curry all over again. Somehow, I disengaged from Thea's arm and began sprinting.

She was a runner, though, and was next to me in a flash. "Livvie, stop!" This time, she took my arm with force, and I'm pretty sure she was screaming my name when I yanked away from her again and tore across Sixth.

A crowd had formed on the sidewalk in front of the Milligan Place gate. I recognized the white-haired guy from the second floor, now shivering in his flannel pajamas while a medic wrapped him in a blanket. The middle-aged woman in 1B whom I sometimes ran into at the mailboxes clutched her overweight pug and repeated, "dear God, dear God" like a mantra. And propped against the gate with a wild look on her face was Gerri, holding—improbably—a bouquet of long-stemmed red roses.

269

My feet stopped moving, though, and I couldn't wend my way to her. I watched, like I was watching a movie, as Thea appeared from behind me and rushed to hug Gerri, crushing the roses between them. I watched Gerri's frantic gesticulations and her tearful explosion against Thea's chest. I watched Thea's eyes travel toward the courtyard. I watched her turn back to the crowd, scanning. When she caught my eye, my legs failed me completely. I staggered from the fray and sank down heavily on the sidewalk.

I'm not sure how long I sat there before a medic tugged at my jacket sleeve and asked if I needed assistance. "She's okay," I heard someone else say—a familiar voice that turned out to be Gerri's. "She wasn't inside the building." She knelt next to me on the cold ground, still holding the roses. They were so red I couldn't look at them.

My head was squeezed and dense as if I had a hangover. A trail of disjointed words reached my ears: *Alarm. Courtyard. Axe. Chainsaws. Clio. Smoke.* I watched Gerri's lips, trying to understand how the words all fit together. She reached over and took my hand, a tender gesture that had never before passed between us.

Then Thea was towering over us, saying, "They brought her out!" and sourness filled my mouth again. I swallowed back the bile and stopped myself from vomiting onto my pants, onto Gerri's roses, onto Thea's cute black boots.

I peeled myself up from the sidewalk and attempted to push my way through to the ambulance, but a wall of blue interceded. Just over one cop's shoulder, I could make out the gray halo of Clio's hair on the stretcher. "I know her!" I explained to the cop, who looked unimpressed. "Please! That's Clio Hartt!" When he continued to ignore me, I called out directly, "Miss Hartt! Miss Hartt! Miss Hartt"—like if I screamed her name enough, she would hear me and wake up.

"Stop, honey, stop." Thea enfolded me in her arms. Her peacoat was thrown open and Clio's pearls pressed against my collarbone. "I don't think she can hear you."

The words lurched out of me like hiccups. "It's my . . . fault! I told . . . her . . . not to . . ."

"Not to what?" Thea's hand reached up and massaged the back of my neck. Mesmerized, I leaned in to the sweet, insistent pressure and stopped trying to explain.

While Thea worked at calming me down, we lost track of Gerri. By the time we saw her again, two ambulances had sped off, one carrying Clio, one another resident. The swarm of bystanders thinned out. Gerri made her way directly to us, and I saw she had abandoned the roses and was cradling something else.

"A fireman rescued him from the fire escape," she said, stroking his head. "He was terrified, poor thing."

"How did he get there?" Thea asked.

"Clio must have put him out the window."

I knew that window, with so many coats of paint that it opened no more than six inches—not enough for a human to escape, and not enough to dispel the smoke that was filling the apartment and hallway. But enough to push an undersized cat through.

I badly wanted to keep Remington, but Ramona had been firm about her no-animals policy. Instead, Gerri brought him with her to Renee's, where he and Alice unexpectedly took to each other and became siblings.

Chapter 27

After the Fire

By the time I spotted her on the stretcher, Clio was already gone. She was the only casualty of the fire. A neighbor who was rushed to the ER survived.

Clio's part of the building sustained the most damage, partly from the fire but also from the rescue efforts. Water ruined tenants' belongings, and the firemen carved holes in the roof with chainsaws to release the smoke.

All this hastened Gerri's move back to Sheridan Square—but it was something she and Renee both wanted anyway. She had picked up roses for her one true love on the way home from work and had stopped at Milligan Place just to change her clothes for their special date night. But when she arrived at the gate, the fire alarm was blaring, and tenants were already spilling out of the building.

After the fire, Thea had wanted to see me home, but I stoically refused. In the morning, following a night of tortured sleep, I had tried to get out of bed but was so dizzy I was unable to stand. Bea instructed me to stay home, and Ramona brought me chicken soup every evening after work for the rest of the week as if I had a cold or the flu. Thea accompanied me to the doctor, but he couldn't find anything wrong and sent me home with some sort of prescription I didn't fill.

By the weekend, the papers reported that the Milligan Place fire had originated in an apartment down the hall from Clio and Gerri. A space heater that an older tenant, Mr. Alfred Rossi, 79, was using to warm up his chilly apartment had malfunctioned, creating a spark that sent his curtains up in flames. In his escape, Rossi had panicked and left his apartment door wide open, which allowed the blaze to engulf the third floor in short order. Clio had suffered a stroke before the firemen could reach her, and some combination of that and smoke inhalation had killed her. Her terrible end haunted me—the fact that she had gotten Remmie out but couldn't save herself. Or did she give up trying and resign herself to her fate? After all, she'd been anticipating her own death for weeks.

There was no memorial service for Clio. Her friends from the Paris generation had preceded her in death, except Berenice Abbott. The great photographer told *The New York Times* that she hadn't seen Clio since the '40s, although they talked on the telephone twice a year. "No more, no less," Abbott said, outlining a routine that seemed to me quintessentially Clio.

In lieu of a physical gathering, Bea wrote a stunning "appreciation" of Clio that appeared in *The New Yorker* just as the city's crabapple trees were starting to bud. The essay didn't gloss over Clio's faults, but showed her in high relief, her strengths and flaws perfectly chiseled. Unknown to me, Bea had maintained a journal of their conversations over the years, to keep Clio's turns of phrase fresh in her mind. The essay was full of both love and frustration. "I have never known a more maddening person," she wrote, "or one so hauntingly brilliant."

Per the instructions in her will, found in a strongbox in her apartment, Clio's remains were shipped back to the mountains. But instead of being buried in the Crab Creek Baptist church-yard with her parents and siblings and cousins, Clio rested by herself in Hendersonville, in the historic Oakdale Cemetery, as if in recognition that she was both part of and separate from the Threatt clan. Not far from her grave, but facing in the opposite direction, was the stone angel Thomas Wolfe's father had carved that lent its name to the novelist's first novel, *Look Homeward, Angel.*

"She can't possibly have requested that," Bea complained, when we heard about her grave's placement. "She didn't like Wolfe. Poor soul will probably be cringing for all eternity."

When I went home for Easter to meet Sue's new baby boy, I visited the grave. Clio's adopted name graced the marble tombstone, with "Neé Birdie Threatt" in smaller block letters toward the bottom, followed by a quote from a man she'd been on a first-name basis with: "The end is where we start from. – T. S. Eliot." It sounded appropriately poetic, but it left me puzzling over what message she wanted visitors to take away.

Random House rushed Clio's story collection into production, and by early June it was a handsome volume on bookstore shelves. The publisher held a launch party, and Bea enlisted Joanne Woodward and Jeff Daniels to read from the stories.

I spent the spring and summer falling in and out of depression. Ramona gave me the name of a therapist her shrink recommended, but I never used the referral. Clio's death left a yawning hole in my routine. I no longer needed to be at her apartment at a set time. I didn't have to swing by Bigelow's to fill her prescriptions, or stop at Jefferson Market to pick up whatever sparse order she'd called in. My weekends were entirely my own.

And then Thea chose Spelman and Atlanta.

The last time I saw her, Thea handed me Clio's pearls in the same wrapping paper I'd used for her Valentine's Day present.

"Those are yours," I objected. "You paid me good money, remember?"

"You need to keep them, Livvie," she said, pressing the lumpy package into my hands. I had to admit, it felt right to have them back, even though I doubted they would ever grace my neck.

The break with Thea intensified my malaise, and Ramona agreed to let me stay on as her roommate. Our unspoken agreement was that I would continue to feed her whenever the spirit moved me to be in the kitchen. "I'm used to you," she told me, in what passed as affection.

My spare hours at work quickly filled up. Bea assigned me to reading manuscripts from the slush pile. It was a welcome distraction, and it proved important in my editorial education by helping me hone my critiquing skills. Still, it was probably fall before I stopped expecting a message from Clio on my answering machine: "Miss Bliss, I need you!" or "Miss Bliss, I simply cannot find my pen!"

It took a while, too, before I could get "back in the saddle," as Gerri put it. My social life consisted entirely of work-related events—book parties, readings, lunches that Bea let me tag along on. Nights when Ramona and I both wound up at home, we watched TV at opposite ends of the couch in our PJ's and slippers, like an old married couple.

One evening, though, Ramona turned to me with a mouthful of cracker and pimento cheese and said, "We need to start dating, Liv." I might have spat out my Diet Coke if she hadn't added quickly, "I mean, look at us. We're pathetic. You haven't been to that bar you like in ages, and I've turned down so many dates, pretty soon I won't get any invitations." We made a pact: she would ask out the cute marketing guy she'd met at a book party, and I would venture back to Ariel's.

As I got out again, my thoughts turned surprisingly more to Hallie than Thea. One evening, I pulled out the slender stack of cards I'd given Hallie over the months we'd slept together, which she had returned to me at the end and which were held together with a rubber band. At different times in our relationship, I'd slipped them under her office door, dropped them into her briefcase when her back was turned. Cards with roses and glitter, bites of love a besotted girl would find heart-poundingly romantic.

"But they're yours," I had protested.

"I can't have them in my office anymore, Livvie. I don't even trust putting them in the garbage. They're yours, not mine. Burn them, hide them in a drawer, I don't care." What I had wanted her to say was: "Read them, treasure them, remember me." What a big mistake I'd been for her. She'd risked everything carrying on with a student—and a female one at that.

Clio had felt her photos from Deauville Beach were too personal and painful to even take up space in the world. In what seemed like a fitting end, they were destroyed by the firemen's hoses. Now, I found I couldn't stand even the idea of my cards to Hallie. If I didn't get rid of them, they could come back to mock me, reminding me I'd handed over my heart to someone who didn't want it. And that I had done it again with Thea.

On a night when Ramona was out with the marketing guy, the bits of flimsy cardboard went up in flames in our kitchen sink. I swept away every ash and aired out the apartment so Ramona wouldn't sniff even a trace of smoke. Later, however, she did ask me about a dusting of purple glitter on the kitchen counter, but I just shrugged it off and she forgot about it.

My ceremony felt cathartic, like using a smudge stick. And in the moment when the first card, with a riot of yellow daisies on the front, caught fire, I thought I understood Clio better than I ever had.

The first responders had found two metal strongboxes in Clio's ravaged apartment. The larger one, a compact safe squirreled away in the back of her only closet, held a miscellany of papers, including a thick manila folder labeled "Ephemera." The file contained letters and postcards from contemporaries like Janet Flanner and Natalie Barney, correspondence from editors, contracts with magazines, and other business-related material that would prove a treasure trove to literary scholars. Also inside the strongbox was her will, which stipulated that the new archival material be catalogued with the rest of her papers at the New York Public Library but be closed to the public for thirty years. No reason given.

The second metal box held only a lumpy, oversized envelope addressed to *Miss Bliss* in Clio's unsteady hand. In it were her fountain pen, a letter, and the unfinished story I'd watched her struggle with for months, still titled, "The Less We Know." Her will referenced the envelope—"Miss Bliss will know what to do"—and my stomach lurched when the lawyer read that part of the codicil to me. At not quite twenty-four, I now had not one, but two literary secrets to protect.

I kept the story to myself, but I used Clio's Sheaffer proudly at work. "Bequeathed to her by *the* Clio Hartt," Bea liked to brag to clients when they admired its rich, marbled green color. "It's the one she wrote *The Dismantled* with." Clio had never specified that, so I didn't know if Bea had fabricated the story for effect. I *did* know Clio treasured it, though, and preferred the fountain pen to the typewriter Bea had given her when they signed their agency contract. I had always suspected the pen was from Flora, but I never asked. Having Clio's pen in hand, so smooth and solid, let me pretend she'd merely lent it to me and that I'd be seeing her soon to return it.

In the privacy of my bedroom, I read Clio's letter—a succinct half-page written with the pen before she locked it away in the strongbox. The very sight of her shaky penmanship made my eyes well up.

After, I moved on to the story, which I perused three or four times, stopping to reread lines and paragraphs like they were breadcrumbs dropped expressly for me. And then I returned it to its envelope, taped it up, and added it to the brown paper bag holding *The Dismantled*.

January 18, 1984

My dear Miss Bliss,

   *I can almost hear you chiding me for writing something
you will only read when I am lying in Oakdale Cemetery:
"Don't be maudlin, Miss Hartt!" Perhaps you will understand
better when you are closer to my age, that I can see the end
coming like it is the cat slinking out of the kitchen for his nap.
I don't think you will be disappointed there is no money for
you—what I have left will help my brother's wife get by in
the homeplace. But I <u>am</u> leaving you something. I am too tired
now to be writing or signing anything and am putting my
pen away so that can be yours. Like the pearls, the old thing
isn't worth much, but it holds value for me just the same.*

   *As for the story . . . it remains unfinished, it never quite
came together, although the bulk of it is there. It should <u>never</u>
see print. I have burned the earlier versions of it, which I
know you will not approve of. I do trust you on this, Miss
Bliss. I trust you too to know what it means and where it fits.
You are sharper than I was at your age, and you know I have
no taste for memoir.*

   Please do not squander a moment of your luminous future.

With gratitude from your friend—
Clio Hartt

The Longer View

October 2017

The day Ingrid Coppersmith contacted me, I had gone home early complaining about a headache. Hunched in the unfinished attic, which didn't quite accommodate my height, I found the liquor store carton labeled "NYC," the one I sidestepped every December when I retrieved the Christmas decorations. Lacy cobwebs connected it to the eaves, and a film of dust coated the top.

As I unpacked it, I took silent inventory. Clio's story and novel manuscripts rested under layers of the documentary detritus of my fifteen years in Manhattan. Playbills from shows like *The Normal Heart* and *Angels in America*. Faded snapshots of annual Pride parades, Gerri and Renee popping out of them in T-shirts bearing slogans like "Silence = Death" and "Read My Lips." Yellowed copies of *WomaNews*, where Vern first published her comic strip. The Audre Lorde and Adrienne Rich books Thea gave me, skimmed but never devoured. The program from Eli's memorial service, complete with Auden poems. A framed photo Ramona had taken of me and Bea, the day I left the agency to become an assistant editor at NYU Press. Bea was half-scowling, but my face glowed. My first boss's voice came back to me: "I spent three years training you just to lose you to a *university* press?"

The box of memories had moved with me from apartment to

apartment, relationship to relationship, until it ended up here, in the Craftsman-style house my wife and I bought together when we moved to the Finger Lakes region and I became a senior editor at Cornell University Press.

I lifted out the old Gristedes bag that held Clio's secret. Inside, the envelope Clio entrusted to me in her will was still secured with tape that had yellowed and curled with age. My fingers slipped under the flap and pried it open easily. Although I hadn't read it since the day Clio's lawyer presented me with the envelope, "The Less We Know" was as fresh in my memory as if no time had passed, as if my psyche had stored it away for this moment.

Clio had never finished the melodramatic story, and the language and plotting were rougher and less cohesive than the other stories she had written before her death. This was the piece she'd started over and over again, amassing first pages until they mounded into a small stack that I had mistaken for a novella. She had burned all those early efforts with their different names, reducing the pile to a fourteen-page remnant about two sisters— the older, a brilliant sculptor wasted by alcohol and drugs; the younger, a workman-like portrait painter struggling to disengage from her sister's excesses. Serena, the older of the two, turns the care of her illegitimate daughter over to Odette, who is married and therefore seen as more stable. But years later, when she learns she's dying, Serena regrets the decision.

At the top of page fourteen, at what felt like the climax moment of the story, the work simply dropped away mid-scene. The final paragraphs, written with the Sheaffer pen I still owned, read like something out of a nighttime soap opera, but they had scorched my memory just the same.

So many ugly words passed between them that day, they blurred in Odette's mind. "You stole my daughter, my flesh," were among the words her sister spat at her. Serena's pores oozed with the stench of alcohol, and Odette shrank back from her.

"I stole nothing! You asked me to raise her. You don't even remember." Serena had plotted it out all those years ago, how Odette and Thomas

would give her girl a better life, and she'd begged her sister to see it her way and comply. "I didn't want to, Serena. You insisted! You said I could give her stability, and I respected your wishes. Now you come back, all these years later—for what?"

"I'm here to claim her."

Odette's heart skipped. Claim? she thought. Who had the better claim—the sister who birthed her, or the one who raised her up from an infant? Each saw their claim as equally strong, their ties to the girl equally unbreakable.

"Maggie needs us both," Odette began, to crack open the part of Serena that might still hear reason. "Just please let me be the one to tell her."

And that was it.

I had tucked something else into the envelope, too. The only interview Clio had done between 1936, when *The Dismantled* was published, and her death in 1984 had appeared in the *New York Review of Books* on the thirtieth anniversary of her great novel. She was obviously enamored of "thirty years"—maybe it carried a roundness or fullness for her, or maybe it held some other significance. After her death, I had retrieved a microfiche of the *NYRB* piece at the library.

NYRB: Many of your fellow writers penned memoirs and autobiographies about their expatriate time in Paris. You've no doubt read the most recent ones, Hemingway's *A Moveable Feast* and Janet Flanner's *Paris Journal*.

CH: Actually, no, I haven't. No offense to Hem, poor man, or to Janet. I was fond of them both, really. But I don't need to relive those days. They're up here *(taps temple)*.

NYRB: Then, you won't be publishing a memoir?

CH: Why would I? I have said everything I wanted to say about my life in my fiction.

The Dismantled was still bound with the original twine. I had scissors in front of me to cut it, but it took a glass of Syrah before

283

I could manage the snip. This was the moment Clio had trusted me with, the "longer view" that had seemed so vague when I was twenty-three.

After a lifetime of editing, I knew what I was looking at—pages slashed through and rewritten, chapters removed, sections shuffled. Flora's blue ink had faded to an azure color and contrasted sharply with Clio's preferred black. I marveled at the audacity of editing with pen; the rare page bore no marks at all. Clio had not exaggerated Flora's role in the novel's birth.

I poured myself another glass.

On the second pass, I realized that Flora had also peppered the margins with comments like: *Birdie, this took my breath away!* and *I love this! Please don't change it!* and *Genius!* She'd maintained the integrity of Clio's story, but she'd infused it with her own flourishes and style.

"Who had the better claim," Clio had written, *"the sister who birthed her, or the one who raised her up from an infant? Each saw their claim as equally strong, their ties to the girl equally unbreakable."*

Were the changes greater than what, say, Maxwell Perkins did for Thomas Wolfe or Gordon Lish for Raymond Carver? In the thirty years of my own career, had I never sliced and diced someone's work? I could think of several authors indebted to me for honing their manuscripts into top-notch books in just this way; one had been short-listed for the National Book Award. Flora had a talent for editing, even if her writing went unappreciated.

"Maggie needs us both," Clio had concluded.

Her secret weighed on me like a box of books, but I couldn't follow Clio's wishes until I gave three people a heads-up.

My wife, Mel, a professor at Ithaca College, stared at me with her mouth agape. "That's what was in that ratty old box?" she said. "Jesus Christ! And to think I wanted to throw it out when we moved here. I was tempted, you know. Where did you squirrel it away?"

"The attic, of course."

Mel smiled. She hadn't been in the unfinished attic in all the years we'd lived there. Now the historian asked gingerly, "Do you think . . . Could I have a look?"

The second person I told was Ramona. She'd headed the Bea Winston Agency since Bea's retirement, when she also assumed responsibility as Clio's literary executor. Not that there was much execution involved anymore. *The Dismantled* had slipped from university syllabi, as it had in the 1960s, before Bea helped revive it. "It's too slow for readers nowadays," Ramona explained once. "All those winding paragraphs don't work with the 140-character crowd." And Clio's posthumous volume of short stories, which I'd helped bring into existence, had long been out of print.

Through the phone line I could sense Ramona's shudder of excitement. She had soaked up so much of Bea's personality over the years that I sometimes joked about her being Mini-Me. "Oh, my God, Livvie, this is *fabulous*," she said. "Thank you, thank you, thank you! This is going to break the literary world wide open." I didn't bother to correct her impression that my revelation was somehow for *her*. Ramona and I had shared the Gramercy Park apartment for four years, until she married the marketing guy, and I still harbored affection for her, talking to her more often than I did two of my sisters.

And then there was Gerri. She and Renee had moved to western New York a few years before I did, and Gerri had accomplished her dream—founding an independent publishing house called Aurora Books, which had become a leader in literary fiction and nonfiction.

"Can you do dinner this week?" I asked as casually as I could.

"Renee's booked solid for weeks. I hardly see her myself. How about the end of the month?"

"I meant just you and me," I said, and my oldest friend let several long seconds slip by. We always met as a foursome, either at their house or ours. "There's something I want to tell you."

"You okay, Liv?"

"I need some help."

She breathed in sharply. "Is it Mel?"

"No, no. It's a work thing."

The next evening, I met Gerri at the Moosewood Restaurant in Ithaca—her favorite place. She and Renee had become vegetarians after they left the city; I tried in solidarity, but it didn't stick.

"You scared the shit out of me on the phone," Gerri said when we had our soups and salads. "First thought, cancer. Second, divorce."

It wasn't as paranoid as it sounded: Gerri herself had pulled through breast cancer, and Renee's parents had stunned everyone by divorcing after fifty years of marriage.

"This isn't anything you could ever imagine," I said. I laid out everything as she picked at her salad and ignored her squash soup. A thin skin formed on top as it cooled in the bowl.

Gerri waited until I finished to speak. "You didn't . . . Did you bring it with you by any chance?"

Of course I had. "Holy shit," Gerri said as I removed it from the trunk of my Subaru. We sat in the car with the lights on while she leafed reverently through the manuscript, nervous about cracking the brittle pages. "Wow, she really did carve it up. We're talking literary bombshell. Or at least a scholarly one." Her next words made heat rise to my cheeks. "And you're sure this is what Clio wanted?"

There's a specific way that a family member—like, say, an older sibling—can work their way under your skin to your vulnerable spot, and Gerri was nothing if not my sister-of-choice. We had annoyed the hell out of each other so many times over the years and had even stopped talking for brief periods. Now, I hated her for homing in on my self-doubt: *Am I doing the right thing?*

I snatched Clio and Flora's work from her hands. "So, you're basically saying you don't trust me."

She stared at the manuscript in my lap like it was some strange species she didn't recognize. If she knew how to rile me, she also knew how to win me back. "You're the best editor I know, Liv." She flashed an exaggerated, confident smile. "After me, that is."

286

After several meetings with Ingrid Coppersmith, we settled on this: I would permit her access to my own recollections and to Clio's literary showstopper, but only if Aurora Books could publish the new biography. At first Gerri protested what she viewed as nepotism, but she eventually gave in when I suggested that the press's proceeds could fund a residency for a woman writer at Cornell. She agreed, then, that keeping Clio close seemed like the safest route.

When the biography appeared in the front window at my local bookstore, the cover stopped me cold on the sidewalk. I'd seen it on the Aurora website, of course, but the printed volume carried so much more weight. There were Clio's penetrating eyes, their azure translated to smoky gray in the black-and-white photograph, the dashing novelist sitting for her portrait in the Paris studio of Man Ray wearing the pearls I still kept in a drawer—*Dismantling Clio Hartt: Her Life and Work,* by Ingrid Coppersmith. I found myself buying a copy, even though Gerri planned to deliver copies to me herself.

"You see the review in the *Times?*" the blue-haired bookstore clerk asked. "The author's here for a signing next week, which should be freaking lit."

I winced at the idea of a bookstore event related to Clio being "lit."

Sinking into a comfy armchair, I flipped through the pages. There was my name in the acknowledgments, but after all my years in book publishing, I'd grown accustomed to that. Ingrid's thank-you was more effusive, though: "It's no exaggeration to say that without Livvie Bliss, this would be a very different book—not much of a book at all. She is a hero and a visionary."

The block of references in the index to "Bliss, Livvie" startled me. I ran my finger down the list, but didn't turn to those pages. Instead, I hunted for the story's climax.

In advance of publication, both Ingrid and Gerri had offered to tell me the book's assessment of Flora's edits, but I said I could wait. I had only asked to see the direct quotes Ingrid attributed to me. Now as I skimmed the chapters, relief surged through me. She had done a bang-up job on Clio's short stories, and her measured treatment of *The Dismantled* set the scholarly record straight without repudiating Clio's talent or playing psychoanalyst to her relationship with Flora. My words popped off the page at me: "She told me they were a team. 'It was all so innocent,' is what she said. If they'd stayed a couple, Flora's role might not have been an issue."

There would be endless articles about the revelation, reviews attracting readers with misleading, almost lurid headlines like the one in *The New York Times*: "The Dismembered—Clio Hartt, Flora Haynes, and the History of a Hoax." I couldn't control what happened after I told Clio's secret, and that had to be all right.

Recently, Ingrid returned Clio's manuscript to me so that it could join the Clio Hartt archive. My plan is to transport it to New York City myself. But right now, it rests on a shelf in my office in the royal blue manuscript box I special-ordered for it. The sight of it every day comforts me. "For me, Miss Bliss?" I hear my friend say. "What a divine color!"

Acknowledgments

As a young lesbian in New York City in the early 1980s, I was amazed to learn that legendary writer Djuna Barnes was still alive and living in Greenwich Village—a part of the city I knew intimately. I would pass Patchin Place, her little corner of the Village, on my way to Djuna Books, a women's bookstore on West 10th Street—named in her honor, although not with her approval. Many years later, while I was doing research for an LGBT history project, I read a memoir of Barnes in her declining years, and the fact that she belittled lesbianism—even though the great love of her life was a woman named Thelma Wood—stuck with me. In these bits and pieces of information, Clio Hartt had her genesis. While Clio isn't Djuna by any stretch, she shares some of the famous writer's experience and personality.

For help with this novel, I have many people to thank. The book was made possible in part by a Regional Artist Project Grant from the Arts and Science Council of Mecklenburg County and the North Carolina Arts Council. The grant allowed me to spend a week in June 2017 at Tinker Mountain Writers Workshop in the beautiful Blue Ridge Mountains of Virginia, where I workshopped the first two chapters.

Many thanks to my cohort there, especially Corey Stewart Hassman and Amy Hill, for insightful comments and edits; and to our workshop leader, Fred Leebron, for his wisdom and generosity.

My longtime writing buddies, Selene dePackh and Lucy Turner, read the manuscript in its entirety twice, and offered savvy suggestions about both content and format. They generously read the parts about Livvie in the present an additional two times and gave comments that helped me zero in on plot issues. Thanks also to Debra Efird, who read an early draft; her comments helped steer me toward a better understanding of some of the characters.

As always, my spouse, Katie Hogan, deserves huge thanks—not just for putting up with me when I fussed and fretted and cried out, "I can't finish this thing!" but also for reading multiple drafts and offering detailed comments about language, plot, and characters.

The women of the Lesbian Herstory Archives in Brooklyn, New York, get a shout-out for pointing me toward online copies of the defunct feminist newspaper, *WomaNews*; thanks especially to Rebecca Arciprete and Marguerite Campbell. Rereading that newspaper—where I was a volunteer and then staff member for four years in the 1980s—brought back the New York City of my young womanhood in vivid detail. Most of the places I mention as Livvie's hangouts are actual spots I frequented as a young woman; many are gone, and some readers may remember their physical layouts differently than I do.

For my understanding of the Paris lesbians and their world, I'm indebted to the following books: *Paris Was a Woman: Portraits from the Left Bank* by Andrea Weiss; *Women of the Left Bank* by Shari Benstock; *Djuna: The Life and Work of Djuna Barnes* by Phillip Herring; *Sylvia Beach and the Lost Generation* by Noel

Riley Fitch; *Wild Heart: Natalie Barney and the Decadence of Literary Paris* by Suzanne Rodriguez; and *Genet: A Biography of Janet Flanner* by Brenda Wineapple. Hank O'Neal's memoir, *"Life Is Painful, Nasty and Short . . . In My Case, It Has Only Been Painful and Nasty": Djuna Barnes, 1978-1981,* gave me a glimpse into the final years of that great writer's life.

And finally, thanks to the women of Bywater Books—in the short term, for bringing this novel to life, but over the long haul, for their amazing dedication to lesbian-themed literature.

About the Author

Paula Martinac is the author of a book of short stories and five novels, including *The Ada Decades* (Bywater Books, 2017), a finalist for the 2018 Ferro-Grumley Award for LGBTQ Fiction; a 2017 Foreword Indie Award for LGBT Fiction; and a Golden Crown Literary Society Goldie Award for Historical Fiction. Her debut novel, *Out of Time,* won the Lambda Literary Award for Lesbian Fiction (1990; e-book 2012) and was a finalist for the American Library Association's Gay and Lesbian Book Award. Her short stories have appeared in *Raleigh Review, Main Street Rag, Minerva Rising, Bloom, A&E,* and many others. She has also published three nonfiction books on LGBT themes, including *The Queerest Places: A Guide to Gay and Lesbian Historic Sites,* and authored plays that have been produced in Pittsburgh, New York, Washington, D.C., and elsewhere. Her full-length screenplay, *Foreign Affairs,* about the love affair between journalist Dorothy Thompson and novelist Christa Winsloe, finished second in the 2003 POWER UP screenwriting contest. She is a lecturer in the undergraduate creative writing program at the University of North Carolina at Charlotte and a writing coach with Charlotte Center for the Literary Arts.

Read more at www.paulamartinac.com.

At Bywater Books we love good books about lesbians just like you do, and we're committed to bringing the best of contemporary lesbian writing to our avid readers. Our editorial team is dedicated to finding and developing outstanding writers who create books you won't want to put down.

We sponsor the Bywater Prize for Fiction to help with this quest. Each prizewinner receives $1,000 and publication of their novel. We have already discovered amazing writers like Jill Malone, Sally Bellerose, and Hilary Sloin through the Bywater Prize. Which exciting new writer will we find next?

For more information about Bywater Books and the annual Bywater Prize for Fiction, please visit our website.

www.bywaterbooks.com